1

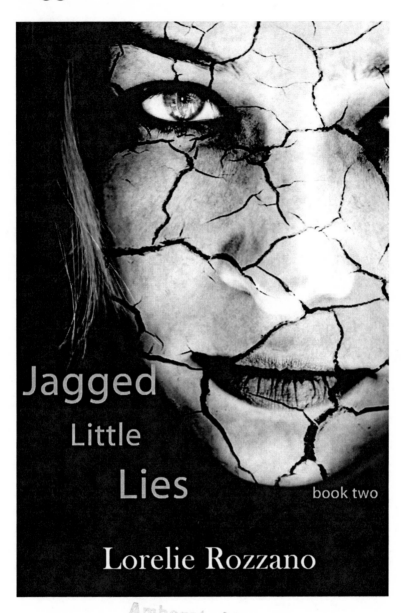

Jagged
Little
Lies

book two

Lorelie Rozzano

Disclaimer: This book may contain explicit sexual content, graphic, adult language, and situations that some readers may find objectionable which might include: male/male sexual practices, multiple partner sexual practices, strong BDSM themes and elements, erotic elements and fetish play. This e-book is for sale to adults ONLY, as defined by the laws of the country in which you made your purchase. Please do not try any new sexual practice, especially those that might be found in our BDSM/Fetish titles without the guidance of an experience practitioner. Neither Rebel Ink Press LLC nor its authors will be responsible for any loss, harm, injury or death resulting from use of the information contained in any of its titles.

Publisher's Note: This is a work of fiction. All characters, places, businesses, and incidents are from the author's imagination. Any resemblance to actual places, people, or events is purely coincidental. Any trademarks mentioned herein are not authorized by the trademark owners and do not in any way mean the work is sponsored by or associated with the trademark owners. Any trademarks used are specifically in a descriptive capacity. Final edits rest with the author of this work. We give them a bit of space. They are Rebels after all...

A Word from Rebel: Thank you for purchasing this title. We support authors and ask you to remember that the only money most authors make from writing comes from book sales. If you like this work, please check for upcoming titles from this author via the link on our website and spread the word. If you see "free shares" offered or cut-rate sales on pirate sites, please report the offending entry to editor@rebelinkpress.com. Thank you for not pirating our titles. Pirates suck!

10 9 8 7 6 5 4 3 2

ISBN: 978-1-940315-39-3

Cover Art by Steelyard Graphics
Second Edition
©2014, Lorelie Rozzano
Exclusive publishing Rights granted to Rebel Ink Press, LLC by permission of the author

Jagged Little Lies

LORELIE ROZZANO

Acknowledgements

Addiction is the only disease that tells you, you don't have it. The nature of this illness is progressive and terminal. However, there is good news. Addiction is very treatable, and like any other illness, the sooner it's treated, the more successful the outcome. One in ten is affected and the number is growing. It is my hope that someone reading these books will recognize their behaviour and seek the help they so desperately need and deserve.

Without my friend's encouragement, enthusiasm, and support, I'm not sure Jagged Little Edges or Jagged Little Lies, would have come to pass. A special thanks to Lisa S, Lisa O, Bonnie B, Karen S, Dale B, Denyse E, Michelle S, Kayla P, John M and Kimberly P.

Thank you to Edgewood for giving me the tools to get my life back.

To all my co-workers--thank you for your everlasting patience, throughout this process.

Thank you to Mel for his helpful editing hints. Thank you to Ryan for his technical support.

Thank you to the marketing ladies for your kind words and wise suggestions.

To my husband--your love and support mean the world to me.

To my family--together we've walked a long and windy road, our path strewn with obstacles every step of the way. Although we have travelled different roads, and at times were lost, we have finally, found our way home.

Jagged Little Edges
Jagged Little Lies
Years of pent up anguish
And un-heard cries
Searching for *something*
To fill this endless hole
A sucking wound so vast,
A broken little soul
I'll smile and pretend
And go crazy in the end
I'll tell you I'm fine
And try not to whine
I'm keeper of the secrets
I've lost track of the lies
My heart is still beating,
I'm surprised it's still alive
Can somebody help me?
It's dark, and I am lost
Pretension is exhausting
I'm tiring of the cost
Jagged Little Edges
Jagged Little Lies
Years of pent up anguish
And unheard cries.

Jagged Little Lies

Oh, what a tangled web we weave when first we practice to deceive." - Sir Walter Scott

Jagged Little Lies

Susan's life was beyond broken, it was ruined. There was nothing left but the hollowed out empty spot she used to call her family. Dick, her husband, left and her beloved son Declan was in jail. All she'd ever wanted in life was to have a happy family. What happened to them? Her days were spent consumed in misery, wondering. Restless in spirit, bitter and resentful, the ache was unbearable. Her only relief came in the form of a tiny tablet.

Miranda met the love of her life. Declan. He was gorgeous, sweet, and charming. His smile lit up the room and stole her heart. He was the best thing to ever happen to her. Trouble was - he was also the worst. Without him she was halved; with him, she might end up in jail. On the verge of bankruptcy and being fired, Miranda wonders if she'll ever be able to tell the truth again.

Declan stared up at the ceiling thinking. He needed more dope and soon. The prison bars closed with a final clang. The sound reverberated through his jaw and down his back. It echoed down the miles of endless hallways. His bowels quivered, and nausea churned. Yup, he was going to need something fast. He counted the hours trying to calculate how long before he'd be writhing on the floor. Six, at the most, but he could already feel it begin.

Lyndsey never believed in fairy tales and pinched herself. She couldn't have dreamed this big. Her life in recovery was more than one she'd ever dared to hope for. When you've been on the edge of death, and live to tell about it, life was sweet. No longer hopeless, or living in despair, Lyndsey makes it her life's purpose to help others. But would they listen?

Chapter 1

The prison bars closed with a final clang. The sound reverberated through his jaw and down his back and echoed down the miles of endless hallways. The shouts and taunts began immediately. "Come here bitch." "Yo boy, you be my bitch now." "Hey pretty boy." "Come say hello to my little friend."

The catcalls were endless. The tones varied, but all were male. Declan shivered. *How the hell had it come to this?* Bars rattled next to his and he jumped. He couldn't see them, their cells were lined side by side down the long hallway, but he'd caught a glimpse. Men of all shapes and colors stared at him. They'd been strangely silent as the guard marched beside him. Their only form of communication hand signals. His knees were still knocking from their easily discerned gestures.

The bars rattled again, this time accompanied by a low moan. The moan intensified and was joined by wet, kissing sounds. Disgust rose in his throat. Sweat was beginning to gather on his forehead and under his arms. It wouldn't be long now. He shivered again. The noise he heard outside his cell was nothing compared to what he'd soon face.

Declan counted the hours trying to calculate how long it would be, before he'd be writhing on the floor. Six hours, at the most. But he could already feel it begin. His legs ached, as if the bone marrow were being leached from their very core. He was getting cold, clammy-cold and reached for the stiff prickly blanket folded at the end of his cot. Wrapping himself up the best he could, Declan huddled against the cement wall. The bed underneath him was every bit as hard as the wall he huddled next to. He used his breath to warm his hands, blowing warmth against his aching digits, hoping to lessen the stiffening. The blanket irritated his skin and prickled his forearms, closing his eyes he thought back.

He'd been so fucking stupid and awake for days. With a thick wad of cash, he was king. Christ he'd been invincible. Or so he thought. He'd just scored a shitload of the little pills he'd come to love. The tubular little soldiers rattled in his pockets, promising nothing but sheer bliss. Strangers' names were on the labels of the pilfered bottles before they were carefully torn off and shredded. The image brought Miranda's face to mind and he winced. He'd been such an asshole and she hadn't deserved it. Her only crime was in loving him. He wondered if she'd been fired. He could see her, the ghost of her image haunting him. The look in her eyes as she sat in the courtroom staring up at him. She was never one to hide her emotions. Shock, disbelief, and confusion surfaced on her beautiful face. These first emotions quickly wore off however, leaving behind a portrait of pain and hurt. It was the last two that'd caused his Adams apple to bob.

Declan wished she would have screamed and hurled insults, or slapped him like he deserved. He would have welcomed it. Thanked her even. But she hadn't done any of those things. Instead she'd just looked at him. Her eyes wet with tears, her lips trembling. He was left with her ghost. A ghost with the most wounded eyes he'd ever seen.

A voice interrupted his thoughts. "Hey! Pretty boy! Watcha doing in there? You want some company?" Ribald laughter filled the hallway. It wasn't a comforting sound.

A different voice joined the first. "Hey pretty boy why so quiet? Cat got your tongue? Wish I did!" More laughter followed with beating of the bars.

The noise seemed to close in on him. The room closed in on him. Declan closed his eyes hoping to will his headache to a more tolerable throb. It didn't work. He opened them again. *It was definitely starting.* Looking around the room he wondered if there was anything he could find. He was pretty sure he'd need something. A weapon of some kind in which he could use, either to protect his life, or to end it.

14

Jagged Little Lies

Bleary eyed, he scanned the room looking for odd shapes or protrusions. He needed something sharp or pointy. The room held the cot he was sitting on, a sink, toilet and shelf. High up on the wall was a window. A tiny portal of freedom so small you'd need to squint just to be able to see out of it, *if* you happened to be over seven feet tall.

The noise level outside his cell grew, as men called to each other and the guards. "Hey I'm hungry! Let me outta here!"

Prison bars rattled up and down the hallway. The stark reality of being locked up to much to handle. The incarcerated, their minds bored, their behaviours wild. Declan tuned them out as he closed his eyes and thought about Miranda. What was she doing right now? Who she was with? God he could still smell her. She had an exotic fragrance. Clean, like fresh air, with just a hint of citrus and something sexier. He'd never smelt anything like it before. It was addictive. He'd only needed one whiff. Declan frowned thinking, sure if she could bottle her scent the boys would be lining up, all eager for purchase. Not wanting to go there he pushed the thought aside. Christ they had laughed. In the beginning, it was all they ever did. He was high as a kite just being around her. Her smile floored him. She'd been so good, so trusting. Fuck!

He wondered if his mom knew yet. Maybe they'd let him use the phone soon and he could call her. She was always bailing him out of something. She was a good mom, but she was so damned gullible. She'd believe anything he told her and he'd told her some doozies! It was hard to respect someone like that. She tried too hard. As if to make it up to him, like somehow it were her fault he'd been given up for adoption. Christ you'd think it'd be the other way around. He knew he owed her better than he'd given her. But she made it so easy. He didn't like the way she kept rolling over. Still, he was fully prepared to take advantage of her. *Again.*

If only he hadn't gone there. It had been hilarious at the time. He'd always gotten away with everything he did. If by chance he ever did get caught, well there was always mom - mom to the rescue. It'd be almost funny, if it weren't so fucked up. Consequences were something that happened to other people. Not him, not ever.

Years ago, when they'd still been a family, they use to fly kites. He knew he'd been spoiled, protected even. As if ordinary rules just didn't apply to him. And in a way, they didn't. His mother always smothered him with love. It grew tiring, and it felt so clingy, so *needy*. After a while his skin crawled with it.

Then there was his dad. His adoptive dad, that is. He'd been a good dad. He really tried. But his mother overrode any attempt to discipline Declan. As a little boy, he'd seen the tired look on his father's face, after his exhaustive efforts in trying to get his mother to stop spoiling him. The joy he used to see when his father looked at him changed, fading, to be replaced with a look of caution and wariness, and finally, resentment.

Declan ran a shaky hand through his hair and shook his head. His brain slogged inside his skull pounding in rhythm to the beating of the bars. His stomach cramped. His bowels churned. He used the blanket to swipe the moisture from his face.

"Pretty boy... oh pretty boy, I can smeellll you!" The high falsetto screech reached inside his cage, adding to the pounding in his head.

Dear God how long must he be here? The judge said two years, but it didn't mean much. Christ, he didn't think he'd make it through tonight.

With the blanket pulled up to his chin, he hoped to ward off the sound of the freak in the next cell. His stomach rolled. Nausea churned. His legs throbbed. His bowels twisted. His head pounded. He was so fucking cold.

Jagged Little Lies

Chick, chick, chick, echoed inside the cold walls, as his teeth chattered, sending knife-like pains shooting throughout his jaw.

Huh. It looked like he was wrong after all. It wasn't going to be six hours.

Withdrawal was already starting.

LORELIE ROZZANO

Chapter 2

Lyndsey looked up from her desk. The shrill ringing of the phone pierced the paperwork fog she'd been under. Christ not again! The darn thing hadn't stopped ringing all day. Opening the drawer, she ignored the ringing hoping it would go to voicemail. Her fingers automatically searched for the bottle of Tylenol. She stopped just short of reaching them. *Do I really need this?* Withdrawing her hand from the open drawer she propped it on her desk. She eyed her fingernails, which were too long under the chipped polish. Her head pounded in unison to the shrill ring. Seriously, would the damn thing never stop ringing? And what was wrong with her voicemail?

Tired and cranky, she snatched up the phone barking out a rather sharp "Hello." The phone hung limply in her hand, its weight more than she cared to bear at the moment.

"Hello?" Lyndsey tried again, this time with less bark.

A sniffle greeted her from the other end of the phone. Lyndsey pressed the receiver tightly against her ear trying to hear. Muffled sobs followed the sniffle and then a very faint "Hello..." The voice trailed off into tears and then silence.

She didn't have time for this right now. Her fingernails drummed impatiently on the desktop. Hoping her irritation didn't change the tone of her voice, she took a deep breath. The headache was worse and she felt bitchy. She tried again. "Can I help you?"

"I ahh..." The voice trailed off overcome by a fresh wave of sobs.

"Yes?" She voiced, the pain of the tears on the other end finally reaching her heart. The bitchiness dissolved, the edginess in her tone softening. Lyndsey waited.

No longer noticing the weight of the receiver Lyndsey listened as the crying on the other end thickened with hiccups, muffled by pain and hurt. It wouldn't be long now.

"Are you still there?" The soft voice questioned, after the short pause, in a hesitant tremble.

"I am. How can I help you?" She was all ears now. Gone were the headache and the bitchiness, even the room disappeared. There was only one thing she was intent upon now. Lyndsey gave the voice on the other end everything she had, as she listened with complete concentration.

"My ahh... the woman paused clearing her throat. My son, he, is, in jaaiillll." She wailed. "He aahhh... Oh! How can I get him out?" Her words broke, her breath turning rapid like a dog panting, as she choked on a new batch of tears.

Concerned the woman on the other end of the phone would pass out from lack of oxygen, Lyndsey spoke. "I want you to breathe. Right now, with me. Let me hear it. Inhale in through your nose and out through your mouth." Lyndsey encouraged the distraught woman, no longer embarrassed by the act of breathing on the phone with a complete stranger.

They drew breaths, vital air binding them together far more than words ever could. The woman's breathing quieted and then slowed. She sighed, a large gust of pent up air caught at the bottom of her diaphragm. Lyndsey sighed too. *Ok she was ready.*

"Why don't you tell me about it?" She encouraged.

Slowly, hesitantly, the woman's voice grew stronger as she told Lyndsey the story of her son. It was a story Lyndsey had heard many times before. But it was new to this mother. She sat listening quietly, encouraging the woman on the other end of the phone when her pain became too great to breathe, just breathe.

The woman's words quickened and her tone grew sharp, blaming the judicial system for being "grossly negligent and unfair" toward her son. Her anger spurred on a whole litany of cruelties her "poor son" needed to bear. Lyndsey interjected quickly, trying to help the woman see what was happening.

"What do you think your son's part in all of this might be?" She asked the distraught woman.

With a brittle laugh, the woman's tone of voice turned vicious. "How dare you ask me that? I just told you! None of this is his fault! Don't you understand English?"

Lyndsey waited a beat and then said. "Look, I'm just trying to help you. This is why you called?"

"How is this helpful? What are your credentials?" The woman snarled.

"Do you really want to talk about my credentials, or do you want help." *Jesus this was tiresome and her headache was back.*

"Well obviously I called to get help. I think my son has abandonment issues, the poor thing." The woman was crying again.

"Look, we're not going to be able to solve this over the phone. What is it you need from me?" Lyndsey questioned, rubbing her temple.

Why I... I thought that would be obvious! I want help for my son!" The lady stuttered, seemingly offended by the stupidity of the woman she was speaking with.

At last! Lyndsey thought. "OK, well I think I can help you then."

"You do?" Her question was suspicious, "How?"

"I want you to attend the family program." Lyndsey offered.

"What? What for? What's a family program?" the woman asked.

Lyndsey sighed, mouthing an unseen prayer. *Please Lord. Help me to be patient, loving and kind.* "The family program is a place where individuals can go to get help with difficult family situations. It will *help* you."

"But I don't need help. Aren't you listening to me?" The woman whined.

Lyndsey threw out the hook. "It will help your son too."

"Oh?" This caught her attention. "How will it help?"

"By taking care of yourself, you will help your son. Just like the pilot in the airplane says to put on your mask *before* placing it on your child. It's the same thing. If you come at this with panic, you're going to make rash decisions, which won't be in the best interest of your son."

The woman conceded with, "You have a point there."

Lyndsey reminded her, "Just a few minutes ago you couldn't breathe. I suspect you're not sleeping very well either."

"How did you know?" she snapped, once again angry.

Jesus Christ it was like riding a roller coaster. Her fingers played with the drawers clasp pulling it open. The bottle of Tylenol peered out at her. It wasn't like it was a big deal. It wasn't even a *real* pill anyways, feeling frustrated she closed the drawer. *No quick fixes Linds, wait it out.*

"I *said* how did you know that?" The woman's shrill voice demanded, startling Lyndsey from her thoughts.

OK back door approach. She changed tactics, softening her tone and gathering every last ounce of empathy as she began. "I know, because when I'm worried sick and can't turn my thinking off, that's what happens to me. In the wee hours of the morning, when everyone else is sleeping, I lay wide awake thinking of worst case scenarios. I feel like the loneliest person on the planet and it feels like my world is crashing down around me."

"Really?" the woman asked. "That happens to you, too?"

"Yes it does, sometimes." Lyndsey answered truthfully.

"Oh, do you have children?"

Lyndsey winced. Her heart cringed and for a moment she stumbled. It always happened. Every time the topic was raised, children, or more specifically, her son. It never felt right saying she didn't have any kids, but she certainly wasn't going to get into the truth of her situation with people she'd just met either. After an uncomfortable pause she replied, "No, no I don't."

"I'm not sure you can understand then."

Yes, yes I can. More than you know. "I may not have a son in jail, but I know what it feels like to be scared or worried and sick to your stomach with guilt," Lyndsey assured her.

"Well..." The woman trailed off clearly not convinced.

"I also know if you don't do something different, you could be heading for a nervous breakdown."

"Well..." the woman paused, thinking for a moment before she spoke. "My doctor has given me sleeping pills and Ativan to help me with the stress."

"You know those are highly addictive medications you are taking. Did you tell your doctor what's happening in your life?" Lyndsey questioned.

"Of course I did not tell the doctor my son is in jail. I mean, what business is it of hers? I don't want her to think less of him. She is *his* doctor too, you know," the woman's tone rose. Lyndsey had managed to piss her off, again.

God grant me the serenity. A silent prayer and then Lyndsey responded. "This is part of the problem you see. Everything is so secretive. When you don't disclose the truth, or minimize the nature of it and yet expect a solution for an undisclosed truth, well, we have a real big problem. We call that problem addiction, or family disease."

"Look you're confusing me. I'm tired. Just tell me what I need to do," the woman complied.

To accept the things I cannot change. "Well first, I would start by attending the family program. You'll get the tools you need to help not only your son, but yourself. I would also recommend you attend start attending Al-Anon meetings, for family members who are going through the same thing you are."

"Fine, she snapped. How do we start? I don't have all day you know!" The woman said bordering on hostile again.

To change the things I can. Lyndsey doodled on a pad of paper before replying, *"Well, we could start with your name."*

Bitterness was a daunting foe. The poor woman must have bathed in it, hanging up the phone Lyndsey recorded her phone time. Forty three minutes. It felt like a lifetime. She rubbed her aching head, turning to the mountain of paperwork still on her desk. Hoping to get a minute free from the phone, she attempted to begin her long overdue report. The pen was out of ink. Tossing it in the garbage and choosing another, the phone rang.

Shit! She blinked, staring at the phone. *Ring, Ring, Ring,*

How can you ignore it knowing someone was probably in crisis on the other end?

Jesus she did not want to pick it up!

A brief emotional tug of war ensued, *and the wisdom to know the difference.* Should she pick it up, or let it go to voicemail? With a sharp eye on her forever pile of paperwork, she made the choice.

Lyndsey answered. "Hello."

"Help me. Please! I need help."

Sitting up straighter in her chair she listened.

Once again, she was all ears.

Chapter 3

Susan slammed the receiver into its cradle. The nerve of that woman! What the in the hell was wrong with everybody? Seriously, she was just sick to death of the looks and attitude she got when mentioning her son and his troubles. Why these people didn't know him. There was no one in the world who knew Declan as well as she did.

Not able to sit still, she'd called the lawyers office earlier. They wouldn't give her any information due to client confidentiality. For Christ sakes, she was his mother! But it didn't make any difference. She hadn't made it past the secretary.

Really! She still couldn't believe it. Her son in jail, he sure as hell didn't belong there, and she needed to get him out *quickly*. It made her sick just thinking about the danger he must be in. Why the hell hadn't he called? Maybe he didn't want to upset her. That must be it. But still... her thoughts trailed off as a fresh wave of grief hit, almost paralyzing her with its force. Damn Dick. She really wished he'd been more involved. Maybe if he were, none of this would be happening.

Hot and sour anger boiled within her belly, turning her grief to rage, as she sat thinking about Dick. Maybe she should try calling him again. The problem was Dick was now screening her calls, the little coward. Jesus, why couldn't it all be like it used to? They'd been happy. Hadn't they? In those days Dick was away a lot on business, and when he returned home they'd have such fun.

She always thought he could try harder as a dad though. They'd gone to such lengths to adopt a child. Susan remembered the years of trying before their son came along. Her arms literally ached at the absence of child within their fold. Dick had been good to her during that time. After each business trip he'd

25

come home, bringing her little gifts from souvenir shops of whatever city he happened to be in. He'd tease her by saying she could call him anytime, anywhere, and he'd be right home. For awhile making love was fun. But then as each month ended in yet another bleed, the fun wore off. Having a thermometer dictate their sex life grew tiresome. It became a chore and eventually they couldn't do it anymore.

A smile twisted her lips as she remembered the day they brought their son home. She'd been over the moon. He hadn't been quite as happy, but she'd put it down to nerves. Susan insisted their son sleep with them. She couldn't bear to put him down. Dick was always trying to convince her she was going to ruin the boy. Ha! As if love could ruin anyone.

Their first really big blow up came about a month after bringing Declan home. They'd been up all night. The baby was fussy and Dick wanted her to put him down, insisting it was OK to let him cry. To her it was obvious their son was distraught and in pain, but Dick wrote it off as a minor ailment.

That night an invisible line was drawn in the sand. On one side her and the baby, on the other side, Dick. It grew worse over time and she was forever trying to make up the incompetence of the father. Grinding her teeth in frustration Susan went in search of her tray.

Sorting through the rolls of tape and sewing kits, odd pens and bits of paper she spied the tray at the far end of the drawer. It was a clear mold of her teeth and fit snugly over them. She'd forgotten to put them back in the case that came with them. Little bits of unknown material clung to the plastic teeth. Her hand halted, stopping midway, as she noticed the drawings beside them.

The tray all but forgotten, Susan pulled the dog-eared papers from the drawer, sitting at the kitchen table she reviewed each one. They were more precious to her than the Mona Lisa. Declan loved drawing and coloring; his pictures were expressive and filled with color. He'd been so happy. The memories brought on a fresh wave of pain. Huddled in her chair, feeling the sobs rising in her chest, Susan cradled the pictures, pressing them tightly to her breast as if somehow, she could transfer the essence of Declan to her arms.

Aware of what she was holding, she cried cautiously, careful none of her tears smeared her papered treasures. Each picture conjured up a new memory. She held each scrap of paper, reviewing better days for all of them. The picture of the rainbow she held a little longer than the rest. Eyes closed she could almost hear him.

Look mommy, look what I did!

Oh honey that's beautiful!

Do you like it mommy? Do you?

Of course darling! I love, love, love it!

Declan giggled. He giggled a lot in those days. She had too. The only one not giggling was Dick. She thought maybe it was because he was tired, or stressed out, or dare she say it, even a little jealous of her relationship with their son.

Exhausted she pushed the artwork to the side and rested her head on the table. It wasn't very comfortable, but with the sudden heaviness it was difficult to keep holding up. *God she was tired!* She couldn't remember ever feeling this tired. Even with the medicated sleep she was now getting, it didn't seem to help. Everything seemed to drag on her these days. As if her worries had added on extra pounds.

Her finger stroked the rainbow as she wondered if Declan was scared. The idea of him scared and alone, in his jail cell, pierced her heart. The thought of what might happen to him in there stopped her breath. A fresh wave of panic spread throughout her. Her body trembled with it. Her heart seemed to beat erratically and her breathing came in short gasps.

Susan's eyes flickered across the room and stopped. She managed to get up and walk the four steps needed to the kitchen counter, where she'd left her purse. With her hands trembling violently, it took her a few tries before she was able to open the clasp. On the verge of hysteria, opening the bottle of pills seemed to take forever. Eyes screwed shut in concentration she gave a furious twist. The childproof lid came off the bottle with a *pop*. Pills spilled over the countertop. One landed near her hand and she picked it up putting it under her tongue. Not trusting her legs to take her back to the table she stood there, waiting.

Hurry, hurry, please work. She didn't like the reliance she had on the pills. But she didn't know what she'd do without them. With her arms resting on the countertop she lowered her head, staring at the swirls of cream and chocolate patterns in the granite. She remembered when they picked this slab of granite out. Years ago, it seemed like such an agonizing decision. They were remodeling the house and she'd been out of her mind with the mess and ever growing costs. They'd argued endlessly too, every little swab of material, or paint chip, creating another difference of opinion.

Dick had changed by then. He looked at her differently. She could see the hostility on his face. They no longer touched. Each of them to hurt or angry at the other one, as they co- existed under the same roof. The nights were worst. Side by side, and yet a million miles apart, as they lie stiffly in their marital bed. It would have been far less lonely lying alone.

The fist gripping her heart unclenched. Her tense, knotted muscles, loosened as the little pill worked its magic. Her breaths became deeper, her windpipe relaxed.

As she lowered herself onto the plush leather sofa, she settled into her old familiar indent. Far too many nights spent in front of the TV trying to doze. She needed the noise for comfort and she would lie there, listening to other families laugh and bicker. Susan shivered, cold to the bone, pulling the blanket from the top of the couch she covered herself, snuggling momentarily in the soft fleece.

Jagged Little Lies

Did her son have a blanket? Was he cold or scared? Was he hungry or hurt? Please God be his blanket. Cloak him in safety and keep him warm. Was there really was a God?

Heavy, thickened eyelids lowered, closing off the last bit of light. Her breathing evened out, slow and shallow. Her mind let free its tortuous images. Sleep found her shortly after her last conscious thought.

Oh my poor, poor son.

Chapter 4

Stop it! Miranda shook her head trying to clear away Declan's image and forced herself to concentrate on counting the pills correctly. She was very aware how easy it would be to make a mistake as she numbered off the pills before putting them in their proper bottles. Next she checked and rechecked the label and count a final time before placing the cap on. *OK, one down and a million to go.*

John was out at the front counter using his friendly voice, a voice only the customers heard. "You almost ready Mandy? We got a line up out here and we don't want to keep these good folks waiting."

Mimicking his tone she replied, "I'll be right out." With three little white bags in her hand, she waltzed out.

Mr. Reed stood at the counter. He was grey and stooped, his arthritic knobs holding tightly to the walker. "You got my medicine, Mandy?" he questioned her.

"Hello Mr. Reed, she replied. It's Miranda, and yes, I've got your medication."

John scooped the bags from her hand, his smile firmly in place. "All right Mandy. I'll take it from here." With shooing motions, he indicated she was to go into the back room, where she belonged.

The limelight belonged to John. He seemed to like it. He also liked that Miranda did most of the work, while he soaked up the glory. John was a pharmacist from a time back when the good old boys made all the rules, and the women catered to them. The times had changed, but John hadn't. If she wanted this job, which she did, she needed to bite her tongue.

In the back room, again she could hear Mr. Reed. "Thanks again John. I don't know what I'd do without you."

"Why it's no problem Mr. Reed. That's what I'm here for." Miranda recognized the warmth in his tone, the one that said I know you adore me and so do I. John reminded Mr. Reed to be careful with his medication, as he read from the label Miranda had just printed.

Mr. Reed's parting words rang in her ears. "John, I don't know how you keep all that information in your head. You're a goddam genius!" He chuckled, his laughter followed by the clink and shuffle of his walker as he slowly made his way from the counter.

Ha! If only they knew! John seldom did anything these days, other than play on his computer. She did it all and John's pharmaceutical license carried them. It wasn't supposed to be this way. She was only a technician and not licensed to be doing the job she was, but she was doing it anyways. Not that she minded really.

"Mandy, I'm out of quarters." John hollered at her.

Yeah, yeah, "I'll be right there," she hollered back. The numbers on the lock slid easily into place as she opened the safe and pulled out a new roll of quarters. John kept his money and narcotics in the safe. Roll in hand; she remembered the first time Declan saw the safe. John was out for lunch. Declan was in the habit of stopping by whenever he was gone. She'd been showing off, trying to impress Declan with her vast pharmaceutical knowledge, as she described to him, at length, the medication she was working on. He was attentive, listening to her as if they were the most important words he ever heard. And of course now she knew why.

"Mandy!" John hollered again, the friendly tone wearing just a little.

Yes Master. Once again pushing Declan from her thoughts she marched back out front. Mrs. Johnstone was waiting next in line. Right next to her was her young granddaughter Cindy.

32

Jagged Little Lies

"Hello Mrs. Johnstone, how are you today?" She greeted, handing John the roll of quarters.

John, turning his head away from Mrs. Johnstone, gave her one of his condescending looks as if to say, *what are you doing giving these to me!* Message received, she retrieved the quarters from John and cracked open their paper casing using the cash register drawer. Not missing a beat, she bent down to look at the little girl standing next to her grandmother. "How are you today Cindy?"

"I'm okay, thanks Miranda." Said the most courageous little girl she ever met. Cindy had leukemia and the toll was visible. She never complained and always had a shy smile to offer those around her.

"That's great sweetie. I think this will help to brighten your day!" Miranda offered, pulling a large lollipop from a display shelf on the counter. She cast a sideways glance at John defying him to say anything, and when he didn't, she unwrapped the colorful treat and handed it to Cindy. Cindy smiled, thanking her with her huge, pain filled, eyes. Her smile was heartbreaking.

John, tiring of the interaction, motioned for her to get back to work. She gave Cindy a high five before entering the back room once again. The gaping door to the safe stood open and she pushed it closed without locking it. Back on her stool, she thought about Cindy. The little girl's eyes carried within untold depths of sorrow and suffering. Miranda could relate. Only unlike Cindy, she was responsible for her suffering.

Jesus, what was she thinking? She wasn't, that was the problem. She'd simply met Declan and lost her mind. She remembered the first time she'd seen him. She was a mess. She'd been out running and was climbing the last gruelling hill. Sweat dripped down her forehead into her eyes, stinging. With a sweaty arm she cleared her vision, chanting under her breath *I hate running, I hate running.* And she did, she'd never gotten the runners high she heard some of her friends describe. All she ever got was sweaty, and she despised every minute of it.

Head down and caught up in her own misery, she hadn't noticed him standing next to the tree. Arms pumping she'd knocked them both down. He landed on top of her knocking the wind out of her. Literally. He stole her breath and her heart that very instant. His killer smile pulled something from her midsection she'd never felt pulled before.

He got up first and helped her to stand. She couldn't stop staring at him. Self conscious and uncomfortable, she looked like a drowned rat. But he didn't seem at all fazed by her appearance. As if being run down by a miserable runner were an everyday occurrence, he asked her name. This beautiful man spoke to her with such ease. His face animated, his eyes blazing, and his words charming, he seemed very comfortable in his own skin. She hadn't known it then, but he was high. High as the kite he was trying to untangle from the tree branches.

With a wink he climbed the tree. Miranda watched open-mouthed, while he chattered away climbing higher into the branches. This man seemed to have no fear of heights, as he laughed his way up the tree. She should have known then, something wasn't right. If she looked at it now, it was easy to see. His pupils were pinned, his talk incessant. His laughter bordered on the edge of hysteria.

The judge gave him two years. She wished she could tell him to rot in there. But she couldn't. The truth was she wasn't even sure she could stay away from him. He'd gotten to her. She needed him. Just like the junkie needing their next fix, she craved him. And the cravings were only getting worse.

Now there was a constant ache on the inside, spreading to parts of her only he could slake.

Her body throbbed. Her heart ached. Her head fought with the rest of her.

And still, she couldn't shake him.

34

Chapter 5

An endless sea of mind-numbing pain, a vast universe of never ending misery, he was dying. At least he thought he was.

Declan lay in a pool of vomit. His legs were melting and he was pretty sure he'd shit himself. His bowels twisted, the cramping so intense little beads of sweat popped up on his forehead. He lost his mind. "Aaagghh" escaped his cracked and ragged lips. The noise outside his cell faded for the moment, as pain consumed his entire world.

He tried calling for help earlier. He called to the guards just out of sight. He called for a nurse or a doctor, and finally, just for help. They ignored him. His was just one more voice among many. Things were getting worse by the minute and it wasn't even close to how bad it would get. It was going to get *bad*. Really bad. He'd never gone all the way through it before, but he heard of others who had. Withdrawal from opiates scared him more than anything else. As a matter of fact, it terrified him. There was nothing he could do about it either.

Another cramp hit, this one worse than the one before it. He groaned in agony, sure his intestines had ruptured. Wave after wave of hot intense pain radiated throughout his lower abdomen. He wondered if he would lose his mind. A window of hearing seemed to open up as he lay on the floor listening to the beating of the bars. *Rat tat tat. Rat tat tat,* played on the bars, an endless jungle tune from primates in heat.

"Pretty boy. Oh, purittee boy! We know your there! Don't be shy, pretty boy. We're not!" Ribald laughter greeted falsetto's words.

"Quit your racket!" An impatient guard evil eyed the cells trying to determine who the noisy culprits were. The guard shuffled up and down the hallways, his baton playing a cruel song on the bars it passed.

The hallway quieted becoming strangely silent, like a big eye watching, just biding its time. The men behind the bars were silent, waiting until the coast was clear, waiting for just the right opportunity, waiting to pounce.

Declan lie waiting too, waiting for it to end, waiting to die. For an instant, he wondered if this is what women went through in childbirth. Then he thought about her. What he wouldn't give to have her arms wrapped around him right now. On second thought maybe not, he was wreck. He was glad she would never see him like this. His teeth chattered uncontrollably. Jesus, he wished he had one little pill. Just one and he could make this whole damn thing go away.

His back arched, seizing for an instant. The scream caught in his throat and his windpipe swallowed it. His legs stiffened, his knees ached. His shoulders throbbed. *Dear God please let this be over soon.*

Dinner was pushed through the opening in his bars. He didn't see it. Nor did he know the brief lull happening around him was because of this. Men guilty of various crimes sat on their beds while devouring their meals. The odd complaint landed on uncaring ears.

"This tastes like shit!"

"Oh yeah? Well, it tastes better than your girlfriend!" Voices no longer silent grew louder, as they competed with each other, upping the sarcastic ante.

The odor coming from his cell carried down the hallway causing a new ruckus. "What's that smell? Who did that? I'm coming to kick your ass!" The inmates gagged at the sudden smell of offal and vomit floating into their living quarters.

The door to his cell opened. A flashlight pierced the gloom. A mountain of a man stood above him. The man gagged too, apparently suffering from a weak stomach. With one gloved finger he poked Declan, trying to ascertain if this human wreck of a person he touched still lived. He did.

36

Jagged Little Lies

Beyond speech he was, the help had come far too late. The man poked him again. "I need you to get up!" he shouted in the tiny cell.

The words ricocheted around his swollen brain. The gloved giant shook him. Still not getting any response, he forced Declan into a sitting position. Declan rolled back into the fetal position, but not before spewing more vomit. This time he managed to share the gore.

The guard retreated quickly, afraid he was going to add to the mess. The cell doors banged closed. The guard's footsteps faded just as quickly as he did.

Declan floated in a sea of pain.

The beating of the bars started up again, with wolf calls, whistles, taunts and jeers. "Oh pretty boy. That better not be you. Don't be packing your shit now! That be my job; you hear? You better watch out pretty boy! I can still smell you!"

Laughter cloaked in insanity played up and down the hallways. But it didn't matter. It all landed on deaf ears anyhow. Besides, there was really nothing at all pretty about the boy left writhing on the floor.

Chapter 6

Lyndsey sighed as she closed her office door and locked it with the key she wore around her neck. The building bustled with the ever-present motion of bodies. People of every sex, race, shape, and age habituated this building. Some of them glowed with renewed hope and purpose. Others were still broken from hopelessness and addiction and some remained somewhere in between.

Strangely she never got tired of them. They taught her a lot about herself and she was still learning. It wasn't her job to fix people, and it would be pretty arrogant to think she could. But still, she knew she tried, and sometimes it cost her.

Six steps away from the front door she heard it, "This is bullshit! They expect us to eat this crap! I didn't pay all that money to come here and eat this garbage!"

Lyndsey stopped. She knew the young man who complained to his crony. He wore gangster clothing and puffed out his chest. Anger had changed his facial expressions and he looked *high*. His behaviour was way over the top. It would be so easy to walk away. She could be home on time for a change, and eating dinner with Drake. All she had to do was close her eyes and pretend she hadn't seen it.

Shit, she couldn't do it. She'd been programmed to do the next right thing. It was just too bad the next right thing was standing here in front of her, with his little chest expanding by the second. She turned away from the door closing the gap between them. Jason, still high from his anger, never realized she was standing beside him and his comments were getting more bizarre by the minute.

"This place is just a money grab," Jason said, waving a thick finger circled by a large gold ring. "I expect steak and lobster every night for the dough I'm shelling out," he snarled.

Tyrone, who had seen her coming, elbowed his buddy trying to warn him. Jason never even noticed. Lyndsey interrupted before Jason could begin again. "Did you say *your* money," she questioned him.

"Yeah, well close enough," he retorted his tone argumentative, his face hostile. Jason stared hard at her, hoping to intimidate. Apparently it worked for him in the past. It didn't now.

"Not even close," she replied, forever trying to reveal the truth. She knew whose money it was and so did Jason, at least when he was sane.

Of course insanity was part of the problem. It was easy to see that for the moment, his addiction was running the show. He stood toe to toe with her and ready to fight. His anger was every bit as mood-altering as the crack he was smoking before getting here. In front of her was a very delusional young man. There was no sense in taking him on, at least not like he wanted. A power struggle never worked. All it did was enable addiction. He had baited the hook. It was her job not to bite. Instead she changed tactics. "Jason what were you eating before you got here?"

"Huh?" He asked, clearly thrown by her question.

"Food? What kind of food were you eating, say in the last week or so, before getting here?" Lyndsey repeated the question, being careful to keep her tone friendly and neutral.

Jason's face clouded in confusion, his anger momentarily left behind as he thought. "I wasn't eating. And then, well maybe a little. I don't know, maybe a hot dog at Seven-Eleven or a bag of chips. Eating wasn't exactly my number one priority, now was it?" he concluded, the anger creeping back in.

"What's for dinner tonight?" she asked.

His chest almost touching hers he said, "Pork tenderloin with roasted potatoes, asparagus, salad and soup. Cheesecake for dessert," he responded smugly. Glad he knew something she didn't.

Jagged Little Lies

It wasn't unusual the folks here knew the menu, or that they could recite it to you word for word. Now learning the words for step one, well that was a different story.

"Tonight's menu, is this like the food you were eating before coming here?" Lyndsey asked innocently enough.

Jason looked surprised before smirking, "Hey Tyrone what do you think man? Was I eating pork tenderloin?" They both smirked, once again in charge and safe in their grandiosity.

"Well was it?" she asked again.

Jason looked incredulous and then replied, "Hell no! I wasn't eating no pork tenderloin, that's for sure. I spent my money on crack. I was lucky if I got the leftovers of somebody's Chinese food!" He rolled his eyes at Tyrone, his meaning clear. *She sure ain't from our world.*

"That must have been rough."

"It wasn't that bad," he replied, a sneer pulling down his bottom lip.

"So you mean to say, you'd rather be out on the streets eating someone's leftovers, than the pork tenderloin they're serving here tonight?"

"I didn't say that!" he roared.

"You just said it wasn't that bad." Lyndsey reminded him.

"I didn't mean it like that! I would much rather be eating pork tenderloin. Are you kidding me? Who wouldn't?" His mouth was open, his face twitched.

"Do you like pork tenderloin?" she asked her tone soft.

Jason stood on the balls of his feet. He swayed just a little, trying to figure out the airhead who was talking to him. "Yeah, I like pork tenderloin," he admitted.

"So it's ok if it's not steak and lobster?"

The gangster deflated to be replaced by a confused looking little boy. The aggression which was running the show ran away. Looking confused by its abrupt departure, Jason nodded his head. "Yeah. I suppose," he agreed.

"Well that's good. Enjoy your meal." She smiled as she left them to find their way to the dining hall. Glancing back she saw they looked different now, less puffy and more human. The truth would do that to you.

Exiting the building, Lyndsey used her fob. It was like an old friend, opening the door to the job to the job she loved in the morning, and closing it in the evening when she went home. The light turned from green to red. Lyndsey closed the door behind her, pulling on the outside door just to make sure. It didn't budge. The doors were locked, but only from people who wanted in. You could leave anytime you wanted. Well... Sort of.

Lyndsey's steps retraced the familiar long driveway. It was those first halting steps on this very driveway that had set her free. Tears blurred in her eyes as she choked up, her heart swelling with gratitude and joy. Freedom was the best rush she'd ever experienced. Her pace quickened in anticipation. She couldn't wait to see Drake.

Her shiny black SUV waited in the parking lot. Lyndsey grinned pressing the button on another fob inside her purse. The door unlocked with a soft *click*. Once settled into the leather seat she switched on the button to heat them. She wasn't cold, not in the least. She just turned it on because she could. It was new, a feature she'd never had before.

Her recovery had brought more than she'd ever hoped for. Never, in her wildest dreams, would she have believed her life could be the way it was now. Home was their haven. Each pay day she'd scrimp and save to buy something to make their home just a little homier. Over the years it added up. Now they had all the material things like a new car, a home, nice clothes, even a little money in the bank. They weren't living paycheck to paycheck anymore. They both worked hard, harder than they ever did before. It was awesome, building their life together, and having a life.

Jagged Little Lies

Thank you. Thank you. It was just a little prayer, but she thought it daily. The SUV handled like a dream. She loved the way it felt under her. It cornered nicely and she felt safe in it. The leather smelled of luxury, making it an intoxicating ride.

It was a far cry from the car she used to drive, the one that had a constant flat tire. It was weird how she attached to it. She really didn't want to let her old car go. It represented so much *more* than a rusty body and flat tires. It had come close to being her casket. She'd finally given it to a newcomer in recovery, a woman who was just starting out. The woman, whose name was Linda, was single and supporting a couple of kids. Lyndsey would see her at meetings and then drive by her at the bus stop, with her kids beside her. She'd heard Linda describe how she would bus her kids to daycare and then herself to work. Then reverse the trip at the end of her workday. It was a huge load *with* a car. Lyndsey couldn't imagine it without. One day she introduced herself. She shook Linda's hand and offered to give her the car, then they had both cried.

Grinning at the image of the old car, she remembered when Drake fixed the tire for her. It was soon after she completed treatment. They hadn't been able to afford a new tire, but he'd been able to patch it, at least temporarily. She really loved that car. It was a part of her past, one in which she prayed daily to no longer be a part of. It was also part of her present. At least she got to see her old car at meetings. The pleasure she got from giving still surprised her.

Things had always been important to her. It was difficult for her to let anything go. Plain objects, or stuff, that she developed a bond with. Her counselor explained it to her, describing it as an emotional attachment. Her home evoked this response in her every time she got near to it. Home was her safe zone.

They had spent countless hours fixing the place up, from remodeling, to landscaping, and then putting on a new roof and exterior. When they first bought the house it hadn't been much more than a rundown shack, but it had good bones. Thankfully, Drake was handy. He'd been able to see potential where she couldn't. To her it looked like a lot of work, but she'd been amazed by what a coat of paint could do.

The garage remote was on her visor. It was still a thrill pushing the button. Lyndsey watched as the garage door began its descent. A smile tugged the corner of her mouth and before long she was laughing. It was hard to explain how watching a garage door close, with you safely inside, could bring about such a heady feeling. Gratitude came to mind as she brushed past the boat and motorcycle occupying the next stall. They had so many toys and not enough time to enjoy them. It had become their mantra. One they both laughed about, overjoyed to have such a dilemma in their life.

Where had the time gone? She still couldn't believe it. More than a dozen years had passed since she'd first gotten sober and left treatment. She never forgot. Not ever. With the garage behind her Lyndsey spotted the plaque. *HOME SWEET HOME* beckoned.

Opening the door she hollered "Honey I'm home!" It was corny, but then so were they, these days, and loving every minute of it.

"Hey babe," hollered back, in Drakes sweet, low sexy tones.

Her dog, Meelee, wandered into the kitchen to greet her. She didn't move as quickly as she once did and her hearing wasn't nearly as good, but she was still a notorious mooch.

Lyndsey bent down to give her a pat and a rub behind her ears. Scooping a doggie treat off the counter, she said to Drake, "How was your day?"

"Not bad he replied, and yours?"

Lyndsey frowned.

"Can you give me a minute?" he asked, meeting her eyes. He looked tired. Weary. She wasn't the only one with a stressful job.

Jagged Little Lies

Concern replaced the frown. "Sure." She said leading him to the couch.

Drake lay with his head in her lap. She ran her fingers through his hair, caressing his scalp. He sighed, the tension in his body lessening. She massaged his head and he groaned. She loved the way he felt and marvelled his physical body was capable of so much. As yet, there was nothing he couldn't repair.

"You okay?" she asked after a little while.

"Yeah, I guess. I lost another guy today."

Damn, she knew what that meant. He was short-staffed again and needed to do the work of two men to make up for it. She felt the ridged muscle under his lean arms. "I'll come and work for you." She teased.

"Ah, no thanks. I'm not that hard up." He teased back and they had already tried that in the beginning when she had first gotten sober. She was nowhere near as strong as Drake and it hadn't worked.

They quieted, Meelee trying to nestle between them. Lyndsey divided her attention, her hand absently patting them both as she looked around the living room. Her eyes landed on the frame. The color had faded, the picture curled inside the glass. But she could still make it out and the message moved her. Git wel son.

Once she realized her best thinking was killing her, she'd climbed on board with a vengeance. Lyndsey had given rehab her all and then some. It was the hardest thing she'd ever done and one of the most important. The other significant event, the possible artist of the faded drawing she now sat staring at.

The little ache kicked in, her missing piece. She knew she'd done the right thing, the loving thing. But it was still there. Her beautiful son, whom she might never get to meet, Lyndsey wondered how he was doing, hoping he was in university by now. She prayed his young life had been everything, hers wasn't.

45

The genetic component worried her. Her eyes closed and she was comforted by Drake's breath. It was slow, deep and steady and she thought about her son some more.

She'd do anything to spare him horror of going down the same road she did.

Chapter 7

Susan's head was heavy as she raised it off the sofa. The bright room swam drunkenly in front of her. The effort was just too much for her and she lowered it back down, resting once more on the soft leather below. An image of her son behind bars surfaced and her pulse kicked up a notch. Willing away the fuzziness an idea began to take shape. Declan would need a lawyer, a competent lawyer. One who could overturn the trumped up farce of a charge. The real problem of course was she'd have to call her, the little bitch who caused all this.

The girl was a mistake and she'd known it right from the beginning. Declan brought her home for dinner and he hadn't been able to take his eyes off of her. She shuddered at the memory. He did everything for her too. He got her a plate and filled it, then fed her forkfuls of meat while doting on her. It was like she didn't exist anymore. She'd come close to screaming that night.

Of course, the little princess ate it up, all the attention and adoration, as if it were no more than her due. She hadn't even offered to do the dishes. Declan insisted on doing it all. He'd left the two of them in the living room to *get to know each other better,* while he cleaned up. Christ that was awkward! Just looking at the pretty little thing made her skin crawl.

It had been awful. The girl was lost without Declan's constant attentiveness. She didn't say much leaving most of the conversation up to her. They'd spoken about the weather and god only knows what else. Her son eventually returned from the kitchen, wrapping his newly wrinkled hands around his little princess and planting a big wet kiss on her forehead. To her he simply acknowledged, "Thanks mom, good dinner."

Susan shrugged. There was no other way around it. Not that she could see. She'd have to phone her and play nice. Willing

47

her woozy body up off the sofa, she staggered to the bathroom. Christ she was shaky. When was the last time she'd eaten anything? Or showered for that matter? She vowed to do better today. She would shower and eat, but first coffee.

She fumbled the K-cup into its pod and pushed the button. She barely registered the rich aroma of fresh coffee, as the steaming contents filled her cup. *It was all her fault.* She knew it. If he hadn't met her none of this would be happening. Oh sure, he'd gotten into trouble before meeting her. But nothing alarming. Nothing like this.

The coffee was strong and bitter and she winced, adding milk to it she tried it again. Halfway down she gagged. *Oh shit,* retrieving the milk carton from the fridge, she poured it down the sink. As she rinsed the carton with cold water she wondered if she was suffering from an early onslaught of Alzheimer's disease. Thickened milk circled the drain, leaving behind white chunky curdles.

She made a fresh cup of coffee and drank it black. Her brow creased. She seemed to be forgetting everything these days. When was the last time she'd bought groceries, or paid bills, or gone anywhere? It was like she was being consumed. Something had stolen her daily life and everything else that mattered. Well, everything that is, except Declan.

With no other way around it, she'd just have to suck it up and call. Susan picked up the phone, remembering her commitment to attend some kind of group. Not that she wanted to, but her doctor had insisted when she'd gone in to see her for a refill of pills. She was afraid if she argued, she wouldn't get them. So she'd smiled and nodded in agreement and then went home and made the call. Now she'd have to go to. She was almost out of pills again and needed more. The doctor was sure to ask if she'd gone and why her pills were disappearing so fast. She figured she could probably BS her about the pills. She wasn't so sure about the group thing though.

Jagged Little Lies

Susan sucked in a lungful of air as the phone began to ring. Her heart beat erratically and accelerated with each ring. She wondered if she was having a heart attack.

Hello, you have reached the voice mail of Miranda. I'm sorry I missed your call. Please leave a message after the beep.

Oh, shit! Now what? Susan placed the receiver back in its cradle, grateful to be rid of it. She hated talking on the phone, but wished she'd left a message. Christ why hadn't she? Now she'd have to phone again. Her finger hovered over the button. All she had to do was press a number. Her heart hammered wildly. She stood frozen, not able to make herself do it.

Maybe she should take another pill. Just one, to help with the incredible pressure she was under. No she'd promised herself. No more pills, at least not in the daytime. They clouded her thinking and she couldn't get anything done. She sat down to a dry piece of toast. It stuck in her throat.

There was a time when she'd loved cooking breakfast. It was so much fun cooking for her two hungry men. In those days, Declan was always hungry. He could never get enough food and always wanted more. For her there wasn't anything she liked better than to see him happy. She loved to accommodate his needs. His favorite breakfast was pancakes and sausages. She'd decorate the pancakes with whip cream and smiling faces. They'd laugh, even Dick, while waiting with an open mouth for their 'shot' of whip cream. Sometimes she'd purposely miss and they'd have a whipped cream battle while sitting at the kitchen table.

A tear trailed down her cheek. Susan brushed it away while finishing the toast. Absently, she licked the dry crumbs from her fingers. The toast helped a little, to ease the burning pain ever present in her stomach these days. Yes, they had been her world, those two. The reason she got out of bed each morning. When Dick left, her world shifted and she'd clung to Declan even tighter.

Declan's newly gaunt face flashed before her. She wondered if he missed her, or even thought of her at all. They hadn't seen much of each other lately. But she would change that. Once she got him out of jail it would be different. Maybe they would go away for awhile, just the two of them, like it used to be. She might even put the house on the market. She'd been rattling around in it for way to long and she would need the money. God only knew what it was going to cost trying to get him out. She just hoped she had enough. Dick had left her in pretty good shape, but it had dwindled over the years. Declan was always, so well... needy. Not in a bad way of course, it was just he never seemed to get a break.

She'd first noticed it when he was little. It seemed there was always one teacher or another picking on him. She'd get the phone calls and reports. The teachers said he wasn't being cooperative, or he wouldn't focus on the task at hand. She would argue, insisting they weren't approaching it right. She knew her son and how to handle him. They just didn't handle him correctly. One teacher was even rude when she mentioned this. Secretly, she understood why Declan was so bored in class. She found their lessons ridiculous too. For some reason, they just never seemed to get how special her son was.

More out of habit than necessity, she rinsed the plate and put it in the empty dishwasher.

OK Susan you need to get it together. You can do this. Determined, she headed for the shower preparing for the day to come. She had the stupid group thing to attend and she needed to call Miranda back and find a lawyer.

The heated marble tiles on her luxurious bathroom floor were warm below her feet. She no longer even noticed them, running the water in the steam shower as she stripped off her clothes. Her reflection stopped her. Susan stood gaping at the image in the mirror. *When had she gotten so old?* Her recent weight loss was not an attractive look. Her skin sagged in places it never used to. Her face look tired and she had grey roots. Long grey roots. Her lips were mere pencil lines and she noticed the new creases etching the corners of her eyes.

The mirror she stared into clouded with steam, erasing her image, and the spell was broken. She showered in the stall big enough for six. For one, it was just another reminder of times long gone. In her large walk in closet, she pulled on the first pair of jeans she could find. They hung loosely and she covered them up with a thick cotton sweater, followed by a vest. Maybe no one would notice with the extra layers.

With her hair pulled up she pinned it, trying as best she could to hide the grey roots. More confident now, she vowed to make the call. Susan picked up the phone. Her arm jerked to a halt, stopping in midair.

Jesus! Such a simple thing! Why can't I do this? Noise, loud and scratchy, muffled her thoughts. Her heart thundered. Tension tightened her shoulders. Panic returned, stealing her breath. Her hand found the solution even as reasoning said *No*, and then, *maybe*.

Unscrewing the lid, she carefully cut the tablet in two, placing the remaining half back in the bottle. Her fingers trembled as she popped the half tablet in her mouth. Susan pushed the bottle away, licking her lips. It wasn't that big a big deal. Not really.

It was only half.

And it was only this one time.

Chapter 8

Miranda woke to the sound of the phone. The distant *ring* muffled in the warmth of her cocoon. She'd slept deeply. Her sleep thickened brain barely registering the sound before once more falling back into slumber. Turning on her side she smelled Declan, his scent rousing her to full awareness. Her eyes popped open gazing at the spot next to hers. It was empty. Pain swooped back in. Miranda absently stroked the cold sheet next to her. It was nowhere near as comforting as the warmth of his flesh was.

"I've got it bad baby." He'd whisper into her ear, sending little shivers up and down her spine.

Her toes curled as she whispered back, "Me too."

It was true. She'd lost herself completely. Her thinking had changed and she'd done things she'd never done before. It was like temporary insanity, she'd been completely under his spell. Honestly, she would have done anything he wanted. And she did.

A gurgle from her stomach interrupted her thoughts, reminding her she'd skipped dinner last night. Declan's face floated before her eyes as she made the bed. She pushed it away. It popped back up. His image wouldn't stay gone. She hesitated tugging the quilt into place, she really needed to wash the bedding, but she couldn't do it. If she did, she'd be washing away the last little bit of him left.

Jesus, what was happening to her?

Intelligence and a level head was something she prided herself on. In school she'd been at the top of her class. Miranda could achieve anything she set her mind to. Anything, that is, except *this*. Miranda thought back to when Declan first began getting sick. She was so worried sure he had cancer or brain tumors, or some other terminal disease. In a way she supposed he did. She'd been so naive. His lies still echoed in her mind. *It's a migraine headache baby. I've had them all my life.*

"Baby?" He croaked.

"Declan?" She whispered, sure he was going to tell her he'd just been in a car wreck.

"I need your help." He mumbled, sounding like he was speaking through a mouthful of broken glass.

She'd panicked, as he asked her to take a pill from the bottles of medications she was making up. It was 'just one pill.' She could take away all his pain. "Please baby," he whispered, his tone pleading.

At first, she'd been horrified. Of course she couldn't! It was illegal. It was unethical. It was immoral! But as she listened to him retching, the pain in his voice got to her and she changed her mind. She'd been so scared, at first. Any moment she expected John to yell, "Stop!" catching her red-handed. She was positive John would see what she was doing and report her to the police. But John hadn't even noticed. She'd mixed and measured the powerful concoction right under his nose. The prescription called for thirty pills and she made thirty five by changing the formula ever so slightly. With an 'on purpose-accidental spill' of the narcotic ingredient, she managed to make it look like an accident. Miranda sure hoped the spill would explain the missing ingredients.

John glanced at her over the top of his computer just as she was wiping up the last bit of the spill, glaring at her. He grumbled, complaining about the mess and inconvenience she was causing him. They were on a triplicate prescription system for narcotic medications and the paperwork was exact, with no room for error. It was a newer system and one John didn't easily prescribe to. He was from a bygone era and still held the ability to order what he needed, via telephone. Lucky for her and lucky for Declan, at least that's what she thought then.

Jagged Little Lies

Each time it got easier. Declan was always so thankful and as weird as it was, it felt kind of good to be needed like that. It never even entered her mind that what she was witnessing wasn't normal. It didn't occur to her his problem weren't migraines, they were something much, much bigger than that. Caught up in helping Declan to feel better, she was oblivious to everything. Really, there wasn't anything she wouldn't do, to see him smile. A sharp, bitter laugh escaped as her eyes narrowed. *Huh, she bet he wasn't smiling now.*

The day in the courtroom she'd made a vow. She promised. It was over. She was done.

An image of Declan not so vibrant as he sat shackled and sweating. *Oh God he must be in agony!* Her heart quickened. Her stomach churned like she'd just been kicked in the guts. A large achy feeling was left by Declan's absence. The intensity of it surprised her. The day stretched before her, seemingly endless. It was her day off, a day that used to excite her. Now it just filled her with dread. Too many hours with nothing to do, nothing that is, except obsess over Declan.

Come on Miranda! Get it together! With renewed resolve, she stripped the bed. What she really needed was a new start, one that came without the scent of Declan. Quickly, before she could change her mind, she filled the washing machine, adding her favorite scented laundry softener to the load. Her finger hovered over the start button for a second, before she pushed it watching as the sheets swirled inside of the front loader.

There. That was it. The last little bit of the two of them together. The last time they'd touched or made love, the last time she'd held him, it was all there swirling inside the machine. *Oh God, what had she just done!* Miranda reefed on the door pulling the sopping sheets from the machine. With a whimpered, *no, no, no* she inhaled the soapy fragrance.

Oh God! It was too late! He was gone.

Stupid. Dumb. Now look what you did! Dazed Miranda lowered herself to the floor. Amidst the wet linen she wondered if she was losing her mind. Lately, she'd become very unstable. Her emotions were all over the place. Was she bipolar? She'd never acted this way before, ever. *Why had he done this to her?* If only she could just hate him. It would be easier, but she couldn't. All She did was miss him and each new minute he was gone added to her agony.

Maybe she should take a pill. Maybe this would all go away. It always seemed to work for Declan. But no, she'd tried it before and it was disastrous. She remembered how sick she'd been. Declan had been bugging her for days to try it. "Come on," he wheedled. "Take one with me." He'd begged her, implying if she'd loved him she would. Declan wanted her to know how good it felt. He also wanted to make love, and would caress her until she couldn't think straight. So she did it.

They each popped a pill, one which was usually prescribed for cancer patients. She hated it. The room spun and she vomited. Declan was so attentive and caring as he rubbed her back and fetched cool clothes. He'd assured her she was fine. It would all be worth it.

It hadn't been.

It was the worst experience imaginable. Her tongue didn't work right and she hadn't been able to speak clearly. It terrified her. Declan laughed, as if there were something humorous in the situation. Her neck was rubbery, her head felt too heavy to hold up and it drooped and sagged. She'd been like a rag doll, her motor skills highly impaired. She couldn't wait until it was over.

Dampness from the cold wet sheets snapped her back from memory lane. Miranda got up off the floor putting the sodden sheets back into the washing machine and stripped off her night wear, adding it to the load. She pushed the start button grimly. The phone rang and her dour mood fled. Her pulse skyrocketed.

Jagged Little Lies

Maybe it was Declan! Wide awake and coursing with energy she ran for the phone. *Please don't let him hang up.*

The number on the call display stopped her dead in her tracks. Her shoulders slumped and her excitement turned to dread. *Oh shit.* It wasn't Declan. It was his mother. Disappointment overcame her. Her hand hovered just above the phone daring to pick up. Miranda snatched it back not wanting to talk with Susan. As a matter of fact, she was probably the last person on earth she wanted to speak with. Susan didn't like her and she wondered why she was calling.

Maybe something happened to Declan? Did he ask Susan to call? Uncertainty overrode her dislike. She picked up the phone. "Hello."

Her own voice echoed back at her. The call had gone to voicemail. It was probably for the best anyhow. But what if something really did happen to him? She wouldn't be able to live with herself if she didn't at least listen to the message.

Wait. What about the promise she made, her vow to have nothing more to do with Declan? Just the thought of never seeing him again brought on a fresh wave of anxiety. She squirmed in discomfort, wanting to do the right thing.

What was the right thing?

Maybe she could just ask Susan how he was doing. Just in case. It wasn't like they were getting back together. No, no, nothing like *that*, at all. She would find out how he was doing and then, she could put him out of her mind once and for all.

After all, she promised.

Miranda smiled, feeling better than she had all morning, and hit play.

Chapter 9

"Hey! Wake up! Come on, sit up, you need to drink this."
Steve the male nurse towered over the infirmary bed.

The bed's occupant was a filthy mess, his hair wet and
stringy, either from grease or sweat, or both. His skin was gray
and his breathing shallow. His face was covered in stubble and
his lips were cracked from dehydration. The clothes he wore
were long passed needing a wash. The stench caused Steve's
eyes to water. *Christ these guys were disgusting.*

Steve tried again. "Wake up!"

This time he got a response. Declan moaned.

"Here, drink this. It'll make you feel better." Steve said,
placing the small tumbler of light red liquid between Declan's
lips.

Declan gagged at the intrusion of bitter tasting, cherry-like
liquid and swallowed automatically. The after taste was sweet,
sour and sickly. His tongue snaked out between dry, cracked lips
searching for any droplets of moisture it could find.

Steve withdrew the tumbler, amazed the guy could even
drink from it. Sometimes these men were just too far gone and
then he'd need to use other methods. *Jesus, would you just look
at the guy.* The disgust he'd been feeling raised another notch as
he watched Declan's tongue. *Huh! Even half dead they still
wanted to get high.* Steve pulled off his gloves with a practised
snap, hoping the sick young man he was attending didn't have
any diseases he might catch. Oh yeah, the gloves were supposed
to protect him but he still worried.

"Hey, buddy," he said, pushing on Declan's shoulder. "I'll
be back in awhile to check on you. You'll feel better shortly."
Steve shook his head and left for his coffee break, but first, he
needed to wash his hands. With a backwards glance at the bed he

59

wondered about Declan. *Why in the hell would a guy want to end up like that?*

Declan lie on the bed vaguely aware of Steve's attention. In a world of pain, he briefly wondered what the nurse gave him. He barely noticed his new cell and had no recollection of moving from his previous one. A shaft of cold climbed his spine. He pulled the blanket closer. He drifted off in a sea of agony, made just a little more bearable.

The large male nurse entered the room, helping Declan up off the infirmary's cot and back to his cell. He held his arm as if grasping a large venomous snake and asked, "How are you feeling?"

Declan croaked "better" and then, "what did you give me?"

Steve slowed his steps replying, "Methadone, it's a better option than what you've been using."

Declan tried to stare him off, but he was in no shape to do so. Instead he played dumb. "I don't know what you're talking about," he insisted.

Steve snorted. "Yeah you do. We did a blood test on you and the results came back positive. You passed with flying colors." Steve laughed before saying "No pun intended."

"I didn't give you permission to do any blood work on me."

Steve looked at Declan incredulously and laughed. "Get over yourself princess, you're in lockup. We don't need your permission!"

The walk back to his cell seemed endless. Declan's legs throbbed with aches and pains the entire way. He peered into the cells as he passed. There were some really big, bad-ass men in here. He attempted to stand taller but his legs were just too rubbery. One big ape stood up close to the bars. When Declan passed him, he reached out almost touching him.

Steve barked "Pete! No touching!"

Jagged Little Lies

Ape man stared at Declan rubbing his genitals. The meaning couldn't be any clearer. Declan averted his eyes. *Jesus, I need to get out of here.*

"Uh Steve, I need to make a call, where's the phone?"

Steve grinned as if he'd just told a joke, instead of asking a question. "Where's the phone! Ha, you crack me up kid."

Declan stopped suddenly in the hallway feeling the stares and stared back. His anger was building and he wanted out. *Now.* "The phone," he insisted.

Steve stopped grinning and asked, "Is this your first time in the big house?"

"What?"

"Jail," Steve drew the word out as if he was speaking to a child. "Is this your first time in jail?"

The hallways grew eerily silent. Steve looked at Declan as he became aware their conversation was fodder for sick minds. Steve shook his head and said "never mind."

With a firm nudge, Steve led Declan away. Declan kept his head down as he walked beside Steve. He avoided eye contact and further conversation. He got the message. He better be careful. Steve stopped outside an occupied cell and unlocked it, turning to Declan he smiled a sarcastic grin. "Home sweet home buddy."

"This isn't my cell," Declan argued, staring at the huge man sitting on the lower cot.

Steve steered Declan inside the cell assuring, "Yes it is. I'll be back to see how you're doing in a few hours." The cell doors banged shut with a loud clang behind him.

Declan stood with his back to the bars. The bed he'd been in such agony on previously was now occupied by a giant. The giant glared at him and said, "You smell like shit. Wash up and get rid of those clothes." He nodded indicating the tiny sink against the back wall.

Truth was, he did smell like shit and he felt like it too. His new bed held a folded pile of linens and the blue jumpsuits they all wore here. With stone-like features, he stripped off his dirtied clothing and took a bird bath. The towel wrapped around his midsection, Declan wondered what to do with his soiled clothing.

"Pick up your clothes *boy!*" the giant bellowed.

Declan obeyed bending to pick them up and then not knowing what else to do, he climbed the ladder leading to the top bunk. Changed into clean prison clothes, he made the bed and stuffing his old dirty clothes under his pillow, he lay back thinking. There had to be a way that he could make a call. He'd figure it out. He just hoped it didn't take him long. *What the hell was in that red liquid anyway?* He'd heard about Methadone but never used it before. What he'd heard was you didn't get high from it, so there was no point in wasting his time trying it out. At the moment he didn't feel *high* exactly, but he sure as hell felt better.

The giant got up from the bed beneath him with a groaning protest. Standing, he looked even bigger. He eyed Declan for a moment causing his sphincter muscle to spasm. Towering over Declan he roared, "What's your name *boy?*"

Declan turned his head away, avoiding the shit burger this guy must have eaten for lunch. "Declan," he answered to the wall.

"Declan? What the hell kind of pansy assed name is that?" he snarled. "Think I'll just call you *boy.* You hear that *boy?*" He poked one of his oversized fingers into Declan's shoulder. Not getting any response he poked harder. "I say, you hear that *boy?*"

It felt like he'd been poked with a sledgehammer. Declan winced in pain. He'd like to tell the giant asshole to eat shit, but apparently he already had. And he wasn't stupid either. He needed to leave here in one piece. So instead he grunted and said, "I hear ya."

Jagged Little Lies

The giant seemingly satisfied with his answer, asked, "What are you in here for boy?"

"Robbery, but I'll be out soon."

Laughter greeted his words, a deep-twisted bray. "Sure you will be boy, won't we all!"

Declan hesitated before asking, "And you?"

"Homicide, but I'll be out soon," the giant snorted, another burst of laughter following his words. "Yup, I'll be out soon!" The giant's face convulsed, as it twisted with laughter growing purple. He fought for breath coughing and hawked up a greenie, and spit it into the sink.

Declan cringed. *This guy was fucking gross.*

"Clean that up *boy!*" the giant demanded, his eyes bulging.

Declan, fighting the urge to tell him what he could do with his mess, climbed back down the ladder. Cold water dribbled from the tap as he used his hands as a cup, rinsing the disgusting mess down the drain pipe.

"Make sure you get it all now. You don't want to make me get up."

Declan looked in the sink. The only thing looking back were a few drops of water, but just to make sure he used his sleeve to clean them away, and then glanced at the giant. The hulk had settled back on his bed and was bent over inspecting a toe.

He looked up from his inspection to inform Declan, "They're gonna need cutting soon."

Declan scurried up his ladder. He hoped the last comment was just casual conversation, but he didn't think so.

Animals awoke from their afternoon naps. The noise outside his cell grew. The beating of the bars began. Cat calls and taunts were joined by the falsetto voice he recognized from before. "Hey, pretty boy, welcome home."

Declan closed his eyes hoping to block them out. It didn't work. His eyes popped open as he lay staring at the ceiling.

There was muck clinging to it. *Jesus Christ, he didn't want to know what that was!*

"Pretty boy come and play!"

The bed below him squealed as the giant climbed out. With just a few steps he reached the bars. His giant hands fisted at his sides. The noise stopped immediately. He stood for a moment before returning to his bed. His presence intimidated all who were near. He never said a word. He didn't have to. His body language said it all. Satisfied he lay back down.

Who the hell was this guy? Declan's body tensed. His aches returned. What they'd given him hadn't been enough. Not even close.

He was going to need *more*.

And fast.

Chapter 10

Lyndsey awoke to Drake's hand on her breast. Grinning at him, she said, "Good morning!"

Grinning back, he said, "It's about to get better."

They made love slowly, neither of them in a hurry for a change. Lyndsey marvelled at how easily she could let go of her inhibitions now. She'd always been so ashamed of her body before and was grateful it wasn't the case any longer. She remembered the first time they'd made love, years ago. After coming home from the bar one evening and quite a few drinks, he'd teased her, bathing her in champagne. It was easy then. Drunk, her inhibitions never bothered her. Sober, it was a different story.

Sober, she had been stiff and uptight. She'd been so anxious about it. Not even really sure if she could enjoy sex without a few drinks. But he'd been patient with her. Just like he always was and soon, she'd learned to relax. Lyndsey moved closer snuggling Drake's back. It was warm and she nestled there content.

Beneath her cheek the muscles in his back tensed. She knew what it meant. "You hungry?" he asked.

Drake liked big meals, bacon and eggs for breakfast, meat and potatoes for dinner. She, on the other hand, was OK with a bowl of cereal, or piece of toast. Drake liked cooking when he had the time, so they'd worked out a system. He cooked and she cleaned. Unfortunately, his cooking added a few extra pounds to her waistline, while seeming to have missed his entirely.

The warmth of his back retracted and the hard edge of a shoulder bone took its place. She felt irritated suddenly and snapped, "No. I'm not."

"What's that for?" he asked, meaning her tone of voice.

Her back to him, she got out of bed reaching for her housecoat. "What's what for? "She questioned back.

Drake's eye narrowed. "Let me know if you change your mind."

Lyndsey made the bed they'd just lain in. It was still warm from their bodies. She really wished they were still laying there. She needed it. Human touch, his. *Why couldn't he understand that?* She knew he couldn't read her mind. Still, she hadn't wanted to tell him she really needed those extra moments. It just wouldn't have been the same if she had. For her, being held was always more important than being made love to.

The wedding picture standing on the night table caught her attention. They looked like a couple of grinning fools. Their smiling faces peered back at her, their joy easily apparent. Now that had been a night to remember!

"Hon," Drake hollered from the kitchen, "one egg or two?"

The black cloud evaporated leaving her grinning. *Did he ever have her number!* "One please," she hollered back.

Her moods never lasted long and Drake knew it. If they did, she was the one who needed to do something about it. It was what she preached at work and she wouldn't preach it without practising it. Besides, she hated hypocrites and she knew a few.

Over breakfast, they fell into old familiar banter. "Do theses eggs remind you of anything?" Drake asked, holding up two eggs he'd picked out of the carton. His face wore a wolfish grin.

"No Drake, they don't. Yours are nicer," she assured him.

Lyndsey tossed Meelee a scrap of bacon. The little dog caught it midair swallowing it whole. "Jesus Meelee, at least chew it!" she said, tossing out another scrap.

The phone rang causing them both to groan. It was their day off and a ringing phone usually meant their plans for a lazy day were about to be cancelled. "You get it, please Drake."

Wagging his finger at her he grinned, sure he'd just scored another IOU. He picked up the receiver all traces of his former

Jagged Little Lies

teasing self vanished as he answered officially. "Drake speaking," he frowned listening, his face serious and pinched.

Oh this can't be good. She studied him as he gripped the phone. His eyes found hers trying to relay the message. Her body tensed getting ready for the crisis.

A shoulder shrug and eye roll warned her. This was not good news. Drake tried stalling, "She's a little busy right now. Can she call you back?" Lyndsey heard the sobs from where she stood. Drake pulled the phone away from his ear rubbing it.

With his hand covering the phone, Drake mouthed, "It's Dee."

Her heart kicked up a notch at Dee's name. The few calls she received from Dee in the past never brought good news. She dreaded hearing about her latest crisis, taking the phone from Drake she said, "Dee?"

Through the phone's receiver, she heard a child crying in the background. Dee was making soothing sounds. A pause and then, "Oh Lyndsey, thank God you're home!" Dee shushed the child close by and then burst into tears.

"What's wrong Dee? Whose child is with you?" Lyndsey questioned. Just the thought of Dee with anyone's child caused her grave concern. Dee couldn't look after herself, let alone a child.

"Lyndsey, I need you, PLEASE! You have to come right now! They're gonna come back and hurt me. I mean, *really* hurt me!"

"Dee, slow down. Who are *they*?"

"Lyndsey, I don't have time to explain! Please, hurry!" Dee screeched, as the child wailed in the background.

Listening to the child's cries, she made up her mind. "OK, I'm coming. Where are you?" Lyndsey jotted down the address assuring Dee she was on her way. Christ Dee sounded bad. But then, she always did.

Worry etched her brow as she turned to Drake. "Sorry love. I guess our laid back day will have to wait."

Drake nodded. "You go get ready. I'll clean this mess up." He said, indicating their breakfast dishes. "But I'm coming with you."

Lyndsey knew he hated it, going with her on calls like this. A rush of gratitude warmed her. He was her rock. She truly appreciated his ever present support. "Drake you don't have to. It's OK. I do this for a living you know."

"I know you do, but this could be dangerous. You know Dee hangs out with some pretty sick characters."

Lyndsey did know. She was actually amazed Dee was still alive. She'd been working the streets for a very long time. Most didn't last that long. It was a brutal world, one filled with violence and death.

It was just too bad Dee couldn't stay sober. This wasn't the first time she'd called Lyndsey for help and this call was probably just a waste of time. Still, she needed to know the child was safe.

She remembered the last time Dee called. It was years ago, and Lyndsey found her in a seedy motel room. She'd been a mere skeleton, with hollowed-out eye sockets. Lyndsey had driven her to detox praying this was Dee's bottom. She'd dropped her off at the center. Dee had been profusely thankful, promising she'd do whatever it took to be well. But it hadn't lasted long. Once Dee began feeling better, the willingness she had faded, replaced by complaints and reasons why staying at the Detox Center was a bad idea. Of course in Dee's mind, she wasn't as sick as the rest of the people, and it was all just a government money grab. Lyndsey had heard it all before. Addiction loved excuses and *always* blamed somebody, or something, else.

It was like Dee had turned to stone as her pleading fell on deaf ears. She'd tried so hard to convince her, telling her it was going to get worse. Much worse, but Dee wouldn't listen. Her illness had all the answers and Dee didn't have a clue her *best thinking* was going to kill her. So Lyndsey let her go, one more time.

There but for the grace of God go I. She first heard the phrase in early recovery. At first it didn't make any sense, but then it did. She could so easily have been in Dee's shoes now. She was certainly headed there. Her best thinking had been killing her too. Zipping up her jeans the phone rang. *Jesus what is it with the phones today?* "Dee?" She asked, clicking on the speaker button so she could finish dressing.

"Lyndsey?" Jan questioned.

"Oh Jan, hi, I wasn't expecting you, I thought it was Dee. She just called with another um... crisis."

"Oh Lyndsey, you're not going to go over there are you?"

"I am. Drake and I are leaving shortly."

"Oh Linds, I don't think that's a very good idea." Jan hesitated and then said, "Do you remember the last time?"

"I do. Clear as a bell. And I agree with you, I'm not sure it's a good idea either," Lyndsey replied somewhat impatiently.

"Then why are you going?" Jan asked.

Lyndsey buttoned her top, her impatience growing and tried to stay calm. "I'm going, because I heard a child crying."

"A child? Whose child? Dee doesn't have children." The mother in Jan worried.

"Look, I'll call you back later. Dee didn't sound good and neither did the child. I really need to go."

"Lyndsey maybe you should just call social services instead. I mean it's your day off and..." Jan trailed off not wanting to finish her sentence, but the meaning was clear.

"I know you care Jan and I appreciate it," Lyndsey said, slipping on her cross trainers, "but I'm still going. Once I get there I'll access the situation and if warranted, I'll make the call then. But I've really got to go now. I'll call you soon." Lyndsey hung up the phone and went in search of Drake.

Not finding him in the kitchen, she poked her head out the back door and hearing the car warming in the garage she smiled, *yup her rock.* Lyndsey locked the door behind her and joined Drake in the car.

"Which way?" he asked.

As she gave him the address he winced. It was a bad part of town, known for its homeless and mentally ill/addicted population. She was glad Drake was with her. This part of town always scared her. The people there played by entirely different rules. They were unpredictable and took what they wanted, when they wanted.

The ride wasn't a long one, but seemed longer due to worry. Drake slowed as they reached the area. The streets were littered in garbage and filthy looking, strung-out people wandered them. Lyndsey scanned the buildings looking for the address Dee gave her. Most of the buildings looked abandoned, with their cracked window panes and nailed up doors. Graffiti covered other buildings making it difficult to find the numbers she was looking for. She spotted an address that was close and Drake pulled into an area advertising *All Day Parking.* The chain link fence surrounding the park canted slightly to the left.

"Do you think the car will be safe here?" Lyndsey wondered out loud.

He glanced at the area again. The parking area housed three other cars. "Not sure, but those ones look OK."

They locked the doors hoping the car would still be in one piece when they returned. "OK here we go," she said, reaching for his hand as they walked side by side.

The air was rich and abundant with misery. "Oh Drake..." She couldn't even finish.

Drake squeezed her hand reassuringly. "It's just up ahead," he said, pointing to a brown two-story building.

Jagged Little Lies

The building was ancient, advertising *Room and Board* in cracked and faded painting. They entered through the main doors. The foyer held a stained, overstuffed couch and an empty reception area. Thick, rope-like grey webs decorated the ceiling and walls. The floor was littered with cigarette butts and garbage. The place looked like it needed to be demolished. They wandered down the hall in search of room 112. Careful not to touch anything Lyndsey peered closely at the doors.

The door to Dee's room was open, hanging crookedly in the doorjamb. Placed directly in its center was the reason why. A large hole, most likely from a kick, gaped wide open in the split wood. Sobs greeted them through the open doorway.

"Dee?" God the place was a mess. The furniture overturned. Plants were tossed, spewing dirt everywhere.

"Lyndsey?" Dee called. "I'm in here, please come." Dee's voice cracked and hiccupped.

Lyndsey stepped carefully around the door with Drake closely behind her. Memories of another time and place raced through her head. Her chest filled with anxiety at what she would find, hoping Dee hadn't tried to kill herself again.

Dee was upright in bed, holding tightly to her side. Lyndsey stopped dead in her tracks, her mouth open in amazement. Never would she have recognized her. On the street she'd have walked right passed her and not known. Dee winced again. Her face was bloated and swollen, her eyes black and blue, the right eye swollen shut.

"Oh Dee," Lyndsey moaned, taking in her badly beaten body.

The blankets she was swathed in squirmed and moved. Lyndsey looked again. "Dee?"

Drake cleared his throat, placing an arm around Lyndsey.

Dee stroked the squirmy blanket while holding firmly to her side. She murmured "Sshhh to the squirmy mass. Frail cries muffled by the weight of the blankets, caught Lyndsey's attention.

"Dee!" Lyndsey demanded.

Dee shifted removing her hand and freeing the little bundle. A small, tousled head of dark hair popped up revealing a tiny little boy. The covers squirmed again and a rail thin arm appeared. An arm dotted in bruises.

"Oh My God Dee," Lyndsey moaned picking up the child without even thinking. The little boy's diaper sagged off his bottom, heavy in the weight of going too long without a change. The smell of rank ammonia hung suddenly thick in the air.

The child cried as he looked at Lyndsey. Dee looked up at her still wincing and said, "Meet Billy."

"Dee, whose child is he?" Lyndsey cried horrified.

With flat, deadened-eyes, Dee replied. "He's mine Lyndsey, and I want you to have him."

Chapter 11

The waiting room was plush and elegant. The receptionist glaring, not happy Susan had shown up without an appointment. With pursed lips she assured Susan her chances of speaking with Declan's lawyer were slim to none. Susan argued, insisting on staying and paying all of Declan's legal fees. With the mention of money the receptionist looked torn, saying only, "Please excuse me," as she disappeared from the reception area momentarily.

Susan stared woodenly at the glossy magazine cover she held in her hand thumbing through it, but not really seeing it.

The receptionist returned, her cheeks a stained red as she asked "Would you like coffee or water while you are waiting?" The smile froze on her face, her over painted, bright red lips, bowed in displeasure.

"Water would be good," Susan replied, hoping to chase away the dryness in her mouth and the fogginess from her head. She probably shouldn't have just shown up like she did, but she worried if she didn't come now, she might not get here at all.

Her anger helped too. After hanging up the phone with Miranda she wasn't able to sit still. With gritted teeth she'd forced herself to be polite on the phone and it cost her. The idea of grovelling enraged her. She still felt the burn of humiliation. It was so frustrating. She might need her, but sure as hell didn't like it. If the only way to Declan was through Miranda, well, she guessed she was willing to go that route. For now.

The receptionist placed a glass of water and another stack of glossy magazines next to her. "He shouldn't be too long," she said, straightening the pile.

It was funny how money could change things. "Hmmm," Susan replied, too tired to make idle chit chat.

The receptionist walked stiffly back to her desk, clearly insulted by the audacity of the woman and yet unable to do anything about it. Her frustration showed as she picked up a stack of papers on her desk and began angrily rifling through them.

Susan took a sip of water and thought about Declan. *How could this have happened to them? Where did they go wrong?* She was pretty sure it was Dick's fault. If only he had been a better father. The familiar burning twinge accompanied the thought of Dick. She still couldn't believe they were over and she experienced a fresh wave of pain every time she thought about him. Somehow Dick had managed to carry on with his life as if they'd never been. She'd tried calling him over the years and asking for help. But his solution was always the same, to let Declan deal with it. *Jesus how was that for support!*

Bitter acid crawled up her throat. Maybe she was getting an ulcer. Worry creased her brow as she made a mental note to mention this new symptom to the doctor on her next visit. The tall glass was cool and slippery. It trembled in her hand as she took another swallow. Her mouth had a tangy, bitter, metallic taste. It left her feeling queasy, opening her purse she searched for a breath mint. Her hand hesitated, pushing past the little bottle of pills to the mints underneath. God it was tempting, but she better be careful.

"Susan?" The receptionist looked at her inquisitively. "Are you OK?" she asked.

"What?"

"I've called your name twice and you didn't respond." The receptionist looked at her strangely; perhaps security guard was in her job description as well. Apparently satisfied she had Susan's attention she continued, "Mr. Briggs can see you now," standing she motioned to Susan. "Follow me please."

Susan followed her down a long hallway. Their footsteps muffled in the soft, plush carpet, underneath. Opening a thick,

Jagged Little Lies

wooden door, she said, "Please have a seat. Mr. Briggs will be with you shortly."

Two chairs sat facing the desk. She chose one and sat down. The walls were adorned with diplomas and degrees. Apparently Mr. Briggs was very well-educated. Did the multiple glass enclosed frames, mean he was a good lawyer? She hoped he knew what he was doing. She wouldn't accept anything but the best, when it came to Declan.

Mr. Briggs entered the room shortly after she did. He was dressed in a dark blue pin-striped suit and black glossy shoes. To her eyes he looked elderly, most likely past retirement age. Anger sharpened her tone as she demanded, "What have you been doing to help my son?"

"Hello Susan," he replied. "Do you mind if I call you Susan? Or would you prefer Ms. Ahh?" He searched his papers looking for her last name.

Before he could find them, she interrupted with, "Susan's fine, now about my son."

Mr. Briggs gave her a long look, over his shaggy brows and said, "Can I be blunt with you Susan?"

"Please."

"It's not looking good." Mr. Briggs said pushing a long strand of thinning hair off of his forehead. "They caught him red-handed. He's been sentenced to two years, plus one day. Susan, he pled guilty, end of story."

Incensed by his words, she bolted from her chair and began pacing his office, trying to curb her anger. "Mr. Briggs, my son is most definitely NOT guilty. He clearly has had inept misrepresentation at his trial, which I might add, I wasn't even informed of!" She stood a few feet back from the man's desk not quite trusting herself to go any nearer.

"Susan, your son is an adult, albeit a very young one. He didn't require his mother's permission to obtain a lawyer. The court appointed him one and I can assure you I've done

75

everything necessary to get your son the fairest judgement possible, given the circumstances."

"Why wasn't I informed of any of this?"

"Like I said, your son is an adult and it's *he* who is my client. I'm sure you've heard of client confidentiality?"

"Then why are you talking to me now?"

"Because your son called me today and gave me permission."

"What?" Pent up anger rushed away on a tide of relief, just knowing Declan called and was thinking of her, she felt better. Back in the chair she asked, "How's he doing? What did he say? Does he need anything? Is he hungry? Can I visit him? When can we get him out?"

"Slow down Susan. He didn't speak about how he was doing, or if he was hungry. He needs money and was wondering if you would send him some."

Her stomach dropped, the relief turned to disappointment. "He didn't say anything else? Just that he needed money? "Her words quivered and she swallowed, trying to keep the screams inside.

"That's about it," he nodded sadly.

Susan opened her purse once again reaching for the cheque book. Her hand brushed the little plastic bottle. The few remaining pills rattled in their container. Her voice sounded funny, low and quiet, as she asked, "How much?"

Mr. Briggs bushy eyebrows lowered, resembling two furry caterpillars. "How much what?" he asked, not following her line of thought.

"Money." *Jesus, no wonder her son was rotting in a jail cell.*

"Oh, that. He mentioned two hundred dollars. He said it should be enough for now."

She wrote a cheque for five hundred. She'd need to move some money out of her line of credit, but she could do that tomorrow. She mentally added yet another item on her growing

Jagged Little Lies

to do list. Handing the cheque to Mr. Briggs she said, "See he gets this immediately."

Mr. Briggs stared at her clearly perplexed. "He'll have it soon." He cleared his throat before saying, "There are certain policy and procedures in place you know."

She snapped, "I don't care about your policies, Mr. Briggs. What I care about is my son. And I suggest you do too. Now, what can we do about getting my son released?"

"Ahh, like I've mentioned Susan, your son pled guilty. There is nothing we can do."

The man was ridiculous! Of course there was something he could do, pointing a shaky finger at him she threatened, "We will see Mr. Briggs. We will see!" As she turned her back on him she left the room slamming the door far harder than she'd intended. Her heart ping-ponged uncontrollably in her chest and her blood boiled. She wanted to scream, or cry, or kill something.

Not wanting the receptionist out front to see her just yet, she ducked into a nearby washroom. Without bothering to turn on the lights she sat on the toilet. Years of frustration and pain boiled within, swirling throughout, consuming her, eating her alive. Hot tears coursed down her cheeks. Her throat closed making it hard to breath.

She was so alone. Why couldn't she make anyone understand? Was she crazy? What was wrong with everyone? Panic stole her breath, whistling in her tightening throat. A soft knock rapped on the door scaring her further.

"Is someone in there?" the receptionist asked from the other side of the door.

She didn't want to answer. She couldn't, maybe she would just go away.

"Susan, is that you in there?" The receptionist repeated followed by another knock.

Shit, she wasn't going away!

"Susan? Are you OK?" The receptionist asked sounding alarmed.

Damn it! "Yes, I'm OK. I'll be right out." She assured in a voice made squeaky by her tightened throat muscles.

"Well... OK then." The receptionist replied, not sounding at all convinced.

Salvation and it was right in front of her. Susan withdrew the bottle, retrieving the half pill she'd cut earlier. With the decision made she felt relieved before she'd even swallowed it.

With the bathroom door half cracked she took a final glance in the mirror. Her eyes locked on the mirror's image for a second, shrugging off the concern growing within, she reasoned. *This was it. No more.*

This would the last time.

She wouldn't do it again.

She promised.

Chapter 12

Speed helped to numb the growing voice in her head, but not for long. Turn *around! Turn around this instant! What the hell are you doing?* Miranda white knuckled the steering wheel. It was like she'd split in two. One half remained rational, horrified at what was happening. The other half had gone completely mad and was driving the car. The two sides of her fought briefly, the steering wheel jerking in her hand. A car sped by in the opposite direction giving her a warning honk. She continued to drive. The mad half was definitely winning.

As the trees rushed by, she thought about Susan's phone call. She'd been *sweet as pie* when asking if she'd heard from Declan recently and then to top it off 'wouldn't it be nice for the two of them to go for a visit?' *Ha! Ya right!* She couldn't think of anything she might like to do less than visiting her former boyfriend in jail *and* spending time with his mother, who, just happened to loathe her. *Oh yeah, good times had by all.*

There was no way she was gonna phone her back. She didn't owe her a damn thing, but still, guilt nagged her. Not that it was anything new. Guilt seemed to accompany her most places these days. It really wasn't a comforting companion. Miranda touched the duffle bag beside her. She'd packed Declan's socks and underwear in it. Then added a couple of muscle shirts hoping he could wear them under his prison garb. She hadn't been able to help herself when packing his things, liberally spraying her citrusy body fragrance on his belongings. Still not satisfied, she'd packed books and paper, pens, envelopes and stamps. She even placed a picture of the two of them together, smiling at each other and clearly in love.

A sign advertising gas stations at the next exist caught her eye. Her gas gauge hovered at a quarter of a tank. The prison was still another hour or so away. Exiting the highway, she found the station a little farther up the road. Too bad she couldn't fill her tank. She didn't like worrying about running out of gas, but she was limited on the amount of cash she could spend. Declan, unfortunately, had done more than just breaking her heart, he'd ruined her finances too. She was left paying the Visa and rent and the "buy now, pay later" toys he accumulated.

"Fill her up miss?" A fresh faced attendant asked.

Miranda fumbled in her purse looking for her wallet. "Just a minute please," she said as she found her wallet and searched inside. The billfold was almost empty, holding only two twenties and some change. God, she'd be running on fumes by the time she was done. Should she get cigarettes for Declan? *What the hell*, the mad one insisted, plucking an almost maxed out credit card from its snug pocket as she said, "Fill her up."

Leaving her car to the attendant she wandered into the convenience store. She needed coffee in the worst way. Her eyes caught on a fishing magazine she knew Declan would like. She pulled it off the shelf along with another magazine featuring monster trucks. The coffee smelled delicious and as she was pouring a cup, she spotted the chocolate bars Declan loved. With a giddy laugh, she added half a dozen bars. Next to the chocolate bars were the jelly babies. *Why not?* Miranda tugged three bags from the rack to add to her growing pile. On her way to the counter she saw the chewing gum he never seemed to be without. There was only five packs left of his favorite kind, she took them all.

Her arms full and not able to hold anymore without spilling her coffee, she waited in line. "Did you find everything you were looking for?" The cashier asked, giving her a curious stare.

Her cheeks reddened. "Oh this isn't for me! It's for my boyfriend, he has a sweet tooth and he's -" she broke off horrified, almost blurting out he was in jail.

"Is there anything else?" The woman inquired.

Jagged Little Lies

The display of cigarettes lined up on the shelf behind the cashier beckoned. He would need them, he must be crawling the walls by now. *Well maybe just one pack.* She pointed to the brand he smoked. "Those too," she said

The cashier added the package of cigarettes to her items. "Will this be all?" She questioned.

One pack wouldn't last him very long and then what? Torn, she hesitated.

"Miss?" the cashier said, losing some of her patience at the growing line behind Miranda.

The crazy half reached a decision. "Plus a carton," she said as she held her breath as the purchases plus gas was totaled, hearing the amount she winced. As she handed the clerk her credit card she prayed *please let it go through,* trying to appear calm waiting for the approved sign and breathing a sigh of relief when it did.

The small amount of money left on her card was what she kept for emergency. Now she wouldn't be able to use it again. She was surprised the amount had gone through, gathering her purchases she hurried out the door. The clerk called "Miss" and Miranda quickened her steps. Maybe it declined after all, starting her car she expected to see the woman running after her and drove away looking in the review mirror.

The bag rested on top of the duffel and her hand went in search of the coffee, finding only an empty spot where she usually kept the cup, she glanced around the car hoping it wasn't spilling. With one hand she opened the bag. *She wouldn't have put it there would she?* No, nothing in there but her purchases for Declan.

An image of her coffee flitted through her thoughts. She'd left it on the counter. She was so worried about Declan's cigarettes and the card not going through, she'd forgotten it. *Damn you Declan!*

Settling instead for a stick of gum she drove off. At least she didn't have to worry about gas anymore. What did he look like now? Had he changed? Would she would be able to tell if something had happened to him? You heard such awful stories about what went on in prisons. The thought of another man touching him made her gag.

It really wasn't that long since she'd seen him last, but it seemed like a lifetime. A day without him was an eternity, a few weeks a death sentence. A few years... Incomprehensible, shaking her head to clear it she wished again for the cup of forgotten coffee. Miranda focused concentrating on the road. The turnoff should be coming up any second.

Up ahead, she saw the sign announcing her turn off. Another ten minutes down the road and she was pulling into the prison yard. Miranda parked in visitor parking. The lot was full. Observing the cars she thought about the poor souls who, unlike her, had tied their lives to these prison bars.

Grim, she gathered up Declan's belongings, shaking her head at the rows of cars. Some held toys and infant seats. Miranda shook her head again. She was surprised at the number of people coming here to visit and bringing their children into an atmosphere like this. What were they thinking? Thank God she wasn't that far gone.

A woman exited a car nearby holding a toddler by the hand. The toddler pulled a small carrying case behind her, while her mother adjusted the baby who was riding her hip. The baby dropped his soother and whined.

Miranda followed her back to the front gates. The toddler struggled with the carry case and the woman bent, baby dangling in mid air as she snatched it from her. Juggling the baby and the carrying case, she glanced back at the toddler barking, "Hurry up!"

Well at least she could be thankful for small favors, she thought, eyeing the family of three. The woman in front of her

Jagged Little Lies

had it far harder than she ever would and besides, she wouldn't be coming back here to visit again.

Impatiently she waited for the large gates to open. Miranda entered the prison yard thinking it was a good thing she'd bought all the purchases she did today. This way she wouldn't have an excuse to come back. Declan would be set now and anything he might need in the future sure as hell wasn't her problem.

With the rational side of her now leading the way, Miranda felt stronger. Her resolve returned, preparing for her final visit. She hardened her heart.

She wouldn't be back.

Not ever.

Her citrusy scent wafted through the air.

LORELIE ROZZANO

Chapter 13

Declan lie on the top bunk afraid to breathe. The giant beneath him was fast asleep. The man's snores kept him awake, but it was his farting that really pissed him off. The guy was rotten to the core. Maybe he was decaying. Declan thought about stifling that rotted gut forever, but knew he was no match for him. The bed, a hard concrete slab, was the worst he'd ever slept in. He shifted positions trying to find a more comfortable one. Sleep was too strong a word. He'd barely slept at all and was hurting. His cellmate tossed in his bed causing Declan's to tremor. His words, thickened by sleep, were incoherent as he gave off another obnoxious blast of anal air.

The animals around him stirred. Soon, it would begin again. Declan closed his eyes. His bladder was full to bursting. His legs ached, his stomach churned. He gritted his teeth thinking, his lawyer was supposed to stop by with some papers for him to sign and to bring money. He was pretty sure he'd be able to find something in here, something *more* than just the cherry red liquid they were giving.

On the verge of pissing himself, he crept down the ladder. Quietly, he sat hoping to muffle the splatter of urine hitting water. Declan stared at the massive lump of flesh just a few feet away. His urine mingled with the stink of the man's breath, creating the most hideous of odors imaginable. He took in the colorful tattoos and meaty forearms. His bowels cramped and he winced, feeling the sweat gathering on his brow.

With a final shake he thought about flushing the toilet, but decided not to. No use spending one second more in the company of this guy awake than he had to. Creeping up the ladder once more he settled into his bed with a sigh. With the blanket covering his nose he used it as a breathing mask, hoping he could get back to sleep. Sleep. He'd probably be doing a lot

85

of it in the next few years. If he was lucky that is. The bunk rocked underneath him, he felt the tremors in his spine. His pulse quickened and he listened intently. The snoring stopped. He could *feel* the guy. The room was heavy with him. The hairs on the back of his arms raised and he held his breath. *Shit! His cellmate was awake.*

The bunk moved again and Declan opened one eye. Over the side of the bed he could make out two, block-like hairy legs, protruding. *Jesus the guy's feet must have been a size fourteen!* His roommate stood exposing a massive back decorated in a large, colorful rooster. He took a step in the direction of the urinal Declan just used and stopped. His head turned in Declan's direction faster than a rattlesnake. Without time to close his eyes he just stared, while the big guy barked, "Boy, what in the hell is that smell!"

The big guys face twisted with rage as he gave him the stink eye. With a ferocious yank he pulled the blanket from Declan's face and stabbing a meaty finger into his chest roared. "Boy, where in the hell are your manners? Were you born in a barn? You always and I do mean *always,* flush the toilet."

With his face just inches from Declan's, his spittle flew landing on his cheek. Declan flinched. His breath was beyond anything he'd ever smelled before. Declan's eyes watered from the rancid odor. His long, greasy graying hair, hung swinging in his face. Declan tried not to flick it away. The old guy hadn't seen a dentist in a very long time. Declan noticed at least two rotting stumps in his mouth. The other teeth were long, yellowed and fuzzy. *Christ when was the last time this guy brushed his teeth or his hair for that matter?*

A large, callused hand slapped his cheek as the giant emphasized his point. Declan's head snapped back from the impact. His jaw clamped shut and he bit his tongue. "You hear me boy?" the old goat demanded.

Jagged Little Lies

Declan nodded his head indicating he did. The meaty arm retreated from view. The massive mountain of a man hovered over the urinal emptying his bladder as Declan studied his back. The rooster was large and colorful with a puffed up chest and attitude indicating *don't mess with me.* Briefly, he wondered why a guy would get a rooster tattooed on his back, but he sure as hell wasn't going to ask him.

"Clean yourself up boy and make your bed."

Declan pulled the blanket tight over his bunk and brushed his teeth at the sink, brushing them longer than necessary hoping the big ape would get the point. What he really needed was a shower, but then dismissed the idea. He'd heard too many horror stories about what happened to guys in jail when they showered.

With nothing left to do, he climbed back up the ladder and sat cross-legged on his bed, his back resting against the hard wall. He wished for a book, or TV, anything to take his mind off what was happening.

The cell doors opened up and down the hallway. Inmates wearing blue jumpsuits filled the halls. Snatches of conversations were heard, in angry aggressive tones. He hopped off his bed joining the line of inmates just outside the cell. Managing to not touch or bump anyone, he studied those closest to him. He could usually tell just by looking, who might have what he might want.

He caught the stare of a pimply-faced guy behind him. The stranger closed the distance between them asking quietly, "What are you looking for?"

Declan looked again, this time more closely, still suspicious the guy might be a Narc. But he didn't look like one. He was lean and twitchy. Ahh twitchy, it said he'd been using and *recently.* Willing to take the chance he whispered back, "Oxy, or something close."

Twitch seemed to think for a moment before saying, "You want crystal?'

87

"Uh, uh," Shaking his head no Declan said, "It's not really my thing. Can you get me heroin?"

They entered a dining hall. He stood behind Twitch and grabbed a tray. The line was long and Declan watched the others jostling one another. A guard stood nearby with a serious face. Cameras were recessed in the ceiling. Another guard stood by the back wall.

Once passed the guard Twitch muttered, "Maybe, but it's going to cost you."

Declan, really hoping the guy was talking monetary asked, "How much?'

"I'll have to get back to you on that."

Declan filled his tray with something looking like a mixture of glue and porridge. He added a little carton of milk to the mix hoping it would ease the ache in his bones. A couple slices of white bread and a scoop of anemic looking scrambled eggs joined the mix. Sticking with Twitch he followed him to a nearby table.

The type of men he usually avoided sat at the table. Declan studied the crowd through lowered lids trying to mimic the attitude. The inmates ate as if starving, wedging great forkfuls of food into bulging cheeks. Declan picked up his fork trying the eggs first, his stomach rolling. The eggs were on the cool side and congealed in his mouth. Man he felt like shit and wasn't sure he could eat.

With a glance at Twitch he decided to push it. "How soon?" He asked, trying the gluey porridge hoping he might have better luck. He swallowed the sticky mass. Ooohh...Christ the food was bad.

"Depends."

"On what?"

"Just depends." Twitch repeated, narrowing his eyes.

Declan took the hint and shut up. Maybe they'd give him another shot of methadone soon. He pushed his tray away opening the milk. His hand shook clasping the carton. The milk was cold, but it didn't sit well. Another cramp hit. It uncurled in his midsection wrapping around his bowel and stomach. The pain pierced his gut as if he'd just been stabbed. Declan's legs bounced, bringing a fresh sheen of moisture to his face.

Twitch narrowed his eyes before commenting, "You're in a bad way."

The table around him quieted. Vulture-like eyes feasted on him, like they would with any dying prey. Grim, he willed the shake out of his hand before tossing back the rest of his milk. Using the back of his arm to wipe his mouth, Declan stared at Twitch before replying, "Nah, it's nothing."

With the focus of a surgeon, Declan managed to pick up his fork and eat his eggs. All the time aware he was being watched. He ate every bite fighting the acid burning in his throat, hoping to appear nonchalant, as if this were just an ordinary occurrence for him. The eyes still following his every move. The table was silent, hair stood up on the back of his neck. Yup, he was most definitely being watched and he wouldn't give them a goddamn thing.

The table remained cloaked in a stony silence, and Declan avoided their hostile stares. He stared past them, focusing on the clock and willing his face to remain impassive.

He could feel their eyes, staring and hungry as they watched, waiting for just the right opportunity to pounce. *Come on, come on,* he stared at the clock, willing the hands to move just a little faster. The hands seemed frozen in time.

The vultures remained vigilant.

Chapter 14

The little boy grasped her finger and grinned. The sight of his smile broke her heart even more than his eyes did. She pulled the boy closer, wrapping her arms around him, wanting to shield him from the hell this room encompassed.

Dee gasped as she tried getting out of bed. Lyndsey stood gripped in an eerie déjà vu as Drake crossed in front of her. Dee held tightly to her side obviously in pain.

"What happened?" Drake asked Dee.

Wincing as she pulled up the dirty t-shirt she wore, she showed him. "They beat me up pretty good this time." Holding her rib cage, she said, "I think my ribs are broken."

"Oh Dee," Lyndsey cried, echoing the words she'd spoken many times before. Horrified, she stared, taking in the black and yellowed bruising covering her entire side.

Dee winced, stifling a sob.

Lyndsey barely recognized her. Gone was any trace of warmth or humanness. Dee had crossed the line from living to merely existing. It was an existence that was void of anything real, or anything worth living for. It was a realm, which many of the walking dead existed in.

The little boy pulled on her finger bringing it to his mouth. He suckled for a moment before replacing her finger with his thumb. Her attention caught, torn between him and his mother. Dee was fumbling with the bedside drawer and looking at Drake beseechingly. Drake stepped forward and pulled the drawer open. Inside was a pharmacy of pills. Scattered amongst the bottles was a junkie's haven. Needles, spoons, cotton swabs and other paraphernalia littered the drawer.

A groan escaped between her pinched lips as Dee groped for the bottle. Her face was a deathly, anemic white. Her nostrils

91

flared and breathing heavily, Dee grimaced again, this time in frustration or pain, or perhaps both.

Shoulders slumped she passed the bottle to Drake and said, "Please."

With a solemn glance in Lyndsey's direction Drake took the bottle from Dee's hand removing one of the pills and handing it to Dee.

"No Drake," Lyndsey whispered.

He shook his head, his frown implying *does it really matter?* "Lind's, she's in pain," he rationalized.

Dee took the tablet, not bothering with the glass of water standing on the night table nearby. Her jaw moved back and forth chewing the tablet as she swallowed quickly. "Gimme another one," she ordered, holding out her hand.

"Uh, uh," screwing the lid back on the bottle Drake wagged a finger. "One is enough for now. We need to talk."

Dee's gaze returned to the open drawer and Drake pushed it closed hoping to keep her attention long enough to gather more information.

Billy squirmed in Lyndsey's arms, his thumb no longer satisfying him. "Dee, when was the last time this child had anything to eat?" She eyed the old fast food container suspiciously.

Ignoring Lyndsey Dee begged Drake. "*Please*, just one more."

Drake turned away from Dee looking at Lyndsey. "You know what we have to do Linds," his eyes lingering on the child in her arms.

"No," clasping Billy even tighter she implored, "Please Drake, not yet."

Dee coughed a long, wet gurgle. "Oowww," she moaned.

Lyndsey tried again. "Dee, whose child is he?"

Billy squirmed again wanting to get down. Lyndsey bounced him on her hip to afraid to put him down. The carpet was dirty and stained. She worried he might get his hands on something sharp, or a forgotten pill.

"Dee!" Her voice was louder than she intended and Billy's lip trembled.

Dee still eyed the drawer and Lyndsey felt her patience evaporating. Drake noticed the problem and removed the drawer. He placed it on the counter behind Lyndsey.

Dee's face twisted and she snarled, "Jesus Christ I just want one more," pulling the covers back even further she got out of bed. Her legs were matchsticks and bore the imprint of older bruises and welts. She stood in her t-shirt and underwear. Her T rode her belly, a belly that bore the marks of a child. The stretch marks crisscrossing her stomach like a spider web.

Lyndsey's jaw dropped open at the obvious answer.

Dee still focused on the drawer behind Lyndsey, lurched past her, moaning as she went. Lyndsey and Drake watched as Dee stumbled almost falling, then regaining her foothold. After a few shaky steps she reached the counter retrieving the pill bottle. This time she managed to open it on her own.

Billy's eyes were huge as he watched his mother stumble around. His lips pouted and he squirmed. His face scrunched up before he let out a cry. Lyndsey patted his back trying to comfort him. "It's OK. You're all right. There, there," she whispered into his ear.

Dee, no longer interested in the drawer, looked at Billy and shouted, "Stop that noise!"

Billy froze in her arms, his wailing stopped immediately.

Lyndsey handed Billy to Drake and grasped Dee by the arm, sitting on the edge of the bed with her. "Dee please, we need to talk," she insisted.

Dee slumped next to her and moaned. Lyndsey helped her into a more comfortable position. "Dee, you need to go to the hospital."

"No," she shook her head. "Lyndsey there's nothing they can do for me. They don't cast broken ribs. The pills will help. That's all I need."

"What happened to you Dee?"

Dee laughed, a broken rattle edged in hysteria. "One of my johns wasn't very happy with me Linds. He got a little rough. So I took a couple of pills and when the next one came by I was a little, um..." Dee hesitated. "Well let's just say he wasn't into necrophilia. When I wouldn't give him the money back he got mean. Thing is he said he'd be back, and he's bringing company. I didn't really feel it then, but when the pills wore off, I couldn't even move."

"Is that why you phoned me?"

Dee nodded continuing, "Billy is getting too old for this. I usually book the johns at night when he's sleeping. If he wakes up, well, he's probably too little to know what's going on. But... lately, I think he knows. I can tell by looking at him and I just..."Dee hesitated, "Can't work with him here anymore."

Drake stepped forward with Billy curled in his arms. Billy looked terrified at the man holding him as he reached for his mother. Dee never even noticed. Lyndsey scooped him up and said, "Dee you need help and this is so... so unfair to Billy."

"I think I'm a little past help, don't you Linds?" Dee cocked an eyebrow. "And I agree, it's not fair to Billy, that's why I want you to take him. Please Lyndsey. He needs someone better than me to care for him."

For the first time she saw a flicker of something *human* cross Dee's eyes before hardening again. "Dee, I can't just *take* your child." Drake nodded in agreement.

"Why not?" Dee insisted. "I'm giving him to you."

"Dee, you can't just *give* children away. We need to phone social services and go through the right channels."

"I don't want him in foster care Linds."

Jagged Little Lies

"It's for the best right now, Dee. He will be cared for and safe." She adjusted Billy's weight from her hip to her chest. Billy snuggled into her, wrapping his thin, bruised arms around her neck. His head fit perfectly into the hollow of her shoulder. A shudder rippled through his thin little body

Shaking her head, Dee pulled on a pair of jeans. "I know you Linds and you'd never do that. I still remember the little animals you were always saving. I trust you, please Linds! It's just for a little while. I'm going to get help this time. I mean it. I ahhh, I just need a little more time."

The pills must be working. That was fast. Dee hopped first on one leg, then the other, as she pulled on her jeans. Lyndsey felt so powerless with Billy in her arms, and Dee on her way out to do it all over again. She shivered. This could have been her life. Without a doubt she'd be in just as bad shape as Dee by now, or worse. If she'd lived, there wouldn't be anything *alive,* left about her.

Billy's warm body was soft as he snuggled deeper into her. The weight of him was comforting. He didn't weigh much really. Of course his mother's addiction had already added a ton of extra weight to him. Lyndsey wondered how long it would take to show.

She'd seen it way too many times, others, just like Dee, fighting the very treatment that would save their lives. Fighting to the bitter end, as they continually denied the reality of their shattered existences. She shivered, holding Billy closer. Sometimes she forgot. It was easy to dismiss just how insidious and powerful this disease really was. It was in the room with them right now, as Dee applied lipstick to her lips. It was looking, always looking, for *more* and if she wasn't careful it would consume them as well.

Dee brushed her hair and twisted it in a knot on top of her head. Her sunken features looking back at her in the glass and

Lyndsey wondered if she could even see them anymore. Patting her hair and spraying on cologne she muttered, "That's better."

Drake moved closer to Lyndsey, putting his arm around her and Billy. *So he could feel it too.* There really were no words to describe it. Dee getting herself ready to "go to work" while her bruised and battered child lay sleeping in Lyndsey's arms.

With a brief glance in their direction she opened the door with a "see ya" and was off. No cuddles for Billy, no promises for Lyndsey and Drake. She was on a mission and it owned her.

"Wow," Drake whispered, humbled by the powerful presence.

"I know," she whispered back. The hairs on her arm stood up as she watched Dee cross the threshold without a backwards glance.

Billy moved in her arms again. His thumb found his mouth in his sleep and made soft, sucking sounds. Drake reached over and pushed a strand of hair out of the child's face. His fingers caressed the softness of Billy's cheek.

They stood facing the wreckage of the room wondering what they should take, if anything, for Billy. Lyndsey couldn't see anything looking like diapers, or clothes that might fit him. She wondered if he had a special blanket or a favorite toy, but she couldn't see those either. She spied a pile of dirty clothing, but wasn't going to touch them. A baby cup sat on the counter, but the milk had curdled long ago and she wasn't even sure if the cup was salvageable. The only precious thing this room held was resting safely in her arms.

Her eyes took in the room a final time, just in case.

But in the end there was nothing left to take. It had all been taken before. Other than tragedy there was nothing left, nothing but broken dreams and promises. And they wouldn't take those.

"You ready?" Drake asked, the meaning far larger than those two little words implied.

"Yes," she nodded, understanding.

96

Jagged Little Lies

"OK then." His breath hitched a little, as he looked at her and smiled a crooked grin.

Lyndsey smiled back, her lip trembling. Tears blurred her sight.

With a kiss to her brow he reached for her hand, and together, they left the room.

Chapter 15

Jesus! Susan slammed on her brakes narrowly avoiding the car in front of her. *Concentrate Susan, concentrate!* It was tempting to go back home and crawl under the covers. When had it all turned into such a chore? She took her foot off the gas pedal slowing down and letting the car in front of her gather distance, thinking about the group she'd promised to start. Maybe she could cancel it. She'd say she was sick or something. The tires jarred as they traveled over the yellow line. *Shit!* She sat up straighter slowing again. Her fingers found the knob and as she reset the cruise control, she spotted her exit. Her heart raced as she put the turn signal on. *How did she get here so fast?* She couldn't remember driving this far. Something was seriously wrong with her and it was affecting her memory. Maybe she had a brain tumor?

With a hard left, she pulled into the grocery store and parked the car. Her hand reached for the door handle and stopped as she debated whether to get out or not. She really needed a few groceries. Then again, she hadn't been very hungry lately. Too bad there were people inside the store. *Maybe I should just phone an order in? Then I won't have to see anyone.* She hated seeing people right now, especially families. *Dear God, why is everything such a fight within my head?*

This is ridiculous, yanking open the door she remembered to click the lock button on her key fob. Her feet dragged as she crossed the parking lot. She couldn't remember feeling as tired as she had in the last year. It was like each new day brought an extra little bit of tired.

Susan looked longingly at the shopping carts. They were so much easier to push than carrying the damn basket she picked up now. But she'd never been able to place just a *few* groceries in the cart. Instead, she'd filled it just as she had back in the days when they'd still been a family. It felt so good pushing the cart around, adding item after item. She'd go home to her empty house and put the food away, and for a moment, feel comforted by her full cupboards and refrigerator. The comfort didn't last long though, and when the food inside started to rot she would chide herself. Adding ridicule to her misery hadn't left her with much of an appetite.

Eyes downcast, Susan moved quickly, not wanting to invite conversation. Her heartbeat raced with her footsteps as she scanned the aisles for people she might know before entering them. On a mental list she added *milk, butter, yogurt, coffee, bottled water, and laundry soap.* The little basket filled quickly. Susan stopped and reorganized the items trying to get them to fit. The weight of the basket hanging from her arm pinched, hurting. The produce aisle was empty and she stood contemplating the lettuce and tomatoes, suddenly feeling a wicked craving for salad. Her mouth watered at the colors and shapes before her as she gathered up tomatoes, lettuce, cucumbers and peppers, and carefully balanced them on top.

Hungry for the first time in a long while, Susan thought about adding chicken breast to her salad. She could barbeque it at home. The smell of the fresh baked bread was intoxicating. She wandered into the bakery momentarily forgetting her vigilance and stood fixated on the cinnamon buns. *What the hell* a few extra pounds wouldn't hurt she reasoned, adding the icing topped buns, to her overflowing basket. Just as she was reaching for a loaf of bread, a tap on the shoulder stopped her and she jumped.

"Susan?"

Her heart lurched recognizing the voice as she turned. *Oh Christ just what she needed.* Lori stood facing her a scowl wrinkling her brow and looking concerned. "Oh hi Lori," she replied listlessly.

Jagged Little Lies

Lori's concerned look faded, to be replaced by one of incredulity. "Jesus Susan! I've been trying to get in touch with you forever! Where have you been?"

At one time Susan and Lori were inseparable. Lori and her husband lived next door to Susan. They spent countless hours together raising their kids, camping, eating family dinners, playing cards and indulging in hours of gossip, over cups of coffee. After Dick and she had ended their marriage, she and Lori's friendship started to change. It felt awkward, stifled, with Lori asking too many questions. Personal questions, questions Susan did not want to answer. Lori was way too critical of Declan, suggesting Declan should do more around the house, or why was she mowing the grass when Declan could be doing it? Susan grew tired of the questions and eventually started avoiding Lori. After a period of time, they just drifted apart.

For some reason, Lori had taken to calling her again and leaving messages Susan never bothered returning. Lori had even knocked on her door a few times, but Susan, not wanting to speak with anyone, ignored the knock. Caught, she blurted the first thing that came to mind. "I've been out of town."

Lori looked unsure before saying, "Well, it probably did you good with all that's going on."

Susan back stiffened, "What do you mean?"

"You know with Declan and all." Lori trailed off for a moment, and then added, "How's he doing?"

Nosy bitch! Angry at the woman in front of her she snapped "What do you mean by *how's he doing?*"

"Jesus Susan, I *mean* how is he doing? I heard what happened - that he's in jail. I tried calling you. I came over a few times. I'm worried about you."

Ha! Susan stared at Lori thinking of the endless gossip they'd filled their coffee cups with over the past years. Her nostrils flared as she replied, "How in the hell do you think he's doing? How would you be doing, if you were sitting in jail for something which wasn't even *your* fault?"

The look on Lori's face changed yet again, her eyes grew big and round, filling with sadness. Susan wished she could slap the pity right off of her face. She knew what they were all thinking, and she hated them for it.

Lori twirled a short strand of hair before asking, "Are you all right?"

"Of course I'm all right. Why do you ask? Are you all right?" She quizzed back.

"We used to be friends Susan, and I thought you might need a little support with all you're going through," Lori replied, sounding wounded.

"Well, as you can see, I'm just *fine*. I really don't want to discuss Declan, and I certainly don't want him to be the topic *du jour* at one of your little neighbourly get-togethers! Besides, you'll all see, he really didn't do it. His lawyer's working to overturn the charges as we speak."

Lori looked dubious and switched topics. "Michael was asking about him. He thought he might go up and visit."

Yeah right! That was all Declan needed, his incredibly *successful* friend coming to visit him in prison. Michael had gone on to university after graduating, and Susan was sick to death of hearing about all the scholarships and top marks he was receiving. "I'm not sure that's such a good idea." It was all she could come up with.

"Well, I guess they can figure it out. I keep forgetting they're grown boys and they probably don't need their *mothers* making decisions for them." Lori laughed for a second before clapping a hand over her mouth, her eyes wide.

"Oh Susan, I'm sorry. I didn't mean..."

Jesus was Lori implying Declan's being in prison was her fault? Not bothering to ask she juggled the basket on one arm,

Jagged Little Lies

her purse on the other, and glancing at her watch replied. "Look Lori, I've got to go. I'm running late."

The tension eased and Lori smiled. "I'm so glad I ran into you. Say hi to Declan for us. And Susan, if there's anything we can do, please don't hesitate to give us a call."

Lori's tone oozed sympathy and Susan recoiled from it. "Ya, well ah, thanks." Her blood boiled as she watched Lori pushing her overfilled shopping cart to the cashier's checkout. She thought about putting her basket down and just walking away, getting in her car and driving, and leaving it all behind. But where would she go? Fatigue settled over her, suffocating the impulse.

The trunk opened with a soft *click.* Placing her groceries inside, Susan wondered if Miranda had left for the prison yet. The thought of her baby behind bars once again brought tears to her eyes. She drove home wiping the tears away while fighting the urge to scream or go crazy. An image of Lori, pushing her big cart of groceries, played in her mind.

It was so unfair! Did Lori even know how lucky she was? Or did she take it for granted? Was she oblivious to her blessings? To her overstuffed grocery cart? Lori still had a *home,* with a family waiting inside for her.

The car found its way home without Susan seeming to notice. As she pulled into her driveway, she noticed the lawn was overgrown and choked with weeds. They'd always prided themselves on keeping a spotless home and a well-groomed yard. She needed to prune the flowers, pull the weeds, and mow the lawn. The job seemed enormous and she felt even more defeated.

With a grocery bag on each hip, she stopped to check the mail. A handful of bills and fliers looked up at her from inside the box, adding these to the bags Susan opened the front door. The house yawned, echoing in its vacancy. She stood in the doorway, overcome by the vast emptiness awaiting her.

103

Silly bugger, just go, shaking her head she crossed the threshold, glad to put the groceries down. She eyed the mail opening an overdue electric bill demanding money. A telephone bill two months behind its due date came next, followed by a Visa bill, which was at its limit. The discarded envelopes littered the countertops. Dick had always taken care of the bills. They'd arrive in the mail and she'd hand them to him, not even bothering to open them. She wished she could still give them to him.

A small smile played upon her lips as she imagined resealing them and marching down to the post office with Dick's address stamped on the front of the envelope. Susan chuckled as she thought about forwarding the mail. She could picture his face when he opened the letter, his amazement quickly turning to anger, thunderclouds crossing his face, as he thought of her. Anger was the only thing left between them anymore.

Laughter died on her lips as quickly as it began. Tears welled, spilling down her cheeks. Her body gave into exhaustion and slumped against the granite counter tops. Deep shudders tore through her chest. The ghost of the family they'd once been danced behind her closed eyes.

She'd lost it all, everything that ever mattered, gone. And she couldn't get it back. Panic flared and her stomach burned. Her heart raced uncontrollably, knocking wildly in her chest. Her throat tightened. *Was she dying or having a heart attack?* Susan spied her purse and reached for it.

Twisting the cap off the bottle, she shook out a pill. It landed on the countertop in front of her. *Should she cut in half?* She hesitated as she placed the pill on the cutting board. It was silly to cut it in half.

After all, it was just a pill.

One, tiny, little, pill.

Besides, if she was dying, it didn't really matter.

Chapter 16

The pats were rough. The female guard looked right through her, not noticing her discomfort. Her cheeks grew hot. She cringed in embarrassment. The female guard seemed bored as she continued her intimate slide over Miranda's body.

What had they done with her bag? A big, stone-faced guard, took it when she'd come through the first set of steel doors. Prison wasn't the kind of place, which invited a lot of questions, and looking into the guard's face, she wasn't about to start asking any now. The roughly intimate hands gave her a final pat and directed her forward. Behind Miranda was the woman she'd seen in the parking lot. The woman's face remained impassive as the guard turned to her. Shocked, Miranda noticed even the baby and toddler were searched.

Not wanting to look, but unable to stop, Miranda shook her head wondering what kind of a person you'd have to be to bring kids here. The toddler stood bravely, her face stoic, as the guard patted her little body. The baby wasn't as brave and screamed at the guard's cold hands. The mother sighed, shifting the crying baby on her hip with a defeated look, one that spoke volumes about silence and suffering.

With nothing amiss, the guard turned to Miranda and gave her a dismissive nod indicating she could go. Miranda followed the small crowd down a long hallway to a large, open room. The 'visiting' room was stark and institutional, holding only tables and chairs. She glanced around not sure where to sit, finally choosing a small vacant table. Miranda noticed the woman from the parking lot struggling as she claimed a table next to her. She fought the urge to offer her help. The baby whined and fussed. The woman, oblivious to the baby's cries, unpacked the carrying case taking out crayons and a coloring book. Then, picking up the toddler with her one free hand, she sat her in the chair placing a crayon in front of her. "Sirsty mommy," was her only thanks.

How does she manage it? Miranda wondered.

"Mommy" settled herself and the baby into a chair next to the toddler and Miranda watched in amazement as the woman flipped up her top exposing a large breast, crowned in a massive nipple. The whining baby eagerly latched on and the room filled with suckling sounds.

Miranda squirmed in her seat, uncomfortable with the intimate scene in such a hellish place. Picking at a cuticle she wondered what in the hell she was doing. The adrenaline high, or whatever it was she'd been on, wore off, leaving her feeling antsy. The door swung open to reveal the guard who searched her earlier. In her hand was the bag Miranda brought for Declan. She marched with purpose in Miranda's direction. Her heart sped up at the look on her face.

Jesus Christ now what?

The guard with her finger up and pointing at Miranda dropped the bag on her table. It landed with a loud "Thwack!" The baby next to her stopped suckling and let out a startled cry. The guard stood above her looking down at her with a pinched face. Her pointing finger wagging in Miranda's face, she announced, "There is no smoking in here! You may pick them up when you leave. "

It took her a minute before she clued in. "Oh you mean the cigarettes. I didn't know. Ah sorry," She stammered.

The guard removed her finger from Miranda's nose giving her another ferocious look. Maybe she was wondering if she was carrying more than just cigarettes. An image of latex gloves crossed her mind and her pulse skyrocketed. She saw the woman next to her watching with interest. Even the toddler stopped coloring, as the guard loudly declared to all in the room, "Make sure it doesn't happen again, or you might be doing more than just *visiting* next time."

Jagged Little Lies

"Whew! She's one nasty piece of work."

Miranda nodded in agreement. She didn't want to encourage conversation with the young mother since she wasn't sure if the place was bugged. She could see the guards sitting on the other side of the glass walls and didn't want to risk upsetting them further.

With practised ease, "mommy" took the baby from her breast continuing to talk, not seeming to notice Miranda's reluctance to engage. The baby squirmed on the woman's shoulder before giving off a loud burp. "You can't bring them in." She said, looking at Miranda. "I'm surprised they're giving them back to you. They don't usually, you know. They just keep them and smoke them too." With a final pat to the baby's back she placed him back on her breast.

Her breast was bigger than the baby's head and Miranda felt her eyes drawn to it. The woman looked up and caught Miranda looking. Horrified to have been seen looking at the woman's breast, she felt her cheeks redden once again. Not knowing where to look, she stared at the ground.

The woman, not at all concerned asked, "You have children?"

Miranda shook her head still staring at the ground.

"This be your first visit?"

Jesus she was persistent. "Yes, first and last. I won't be coming back." Her tone sharpened as she emphasized the *coming back.* She really hoped the woman took the hint and didn't keep bringing these poor children back either.

"Hah! Sure!" The woman chuckled, mimicking Miranda's words *I won't be coming back.* The baby raised his head and wailed. The mother stopped laughing and scolded the baby. "You hush now!"

Miranda bit back her retort. Getting into an argument in the visiting room at the prison, was probably not the smartest thing to do. But then again neither was coming here. *Jesus when was*

Declan coming? Did he even know she was here yet? With nothing else to occupy her time she opened the bag and took out a piece of gum.

The rustle of the bag caught the little girl's attention and she got off her chair and wandered over, standing next to Miranda she reached for the bag. Miranda pushed the bag farther back on the table saying, "No honey this isn't yours."

Great long eyelashes and a beatific smile, peered up at her. The little girl determined, reached for the bag again, this time saying, "Pease."

Miranda looked to the child's mother for help, but she was busy with the fussing baby. The child really was adorable, maybe just one stick wouldn't hurt her. The toddler grinned up at her, Miranda grinned back, taking off the wrap from the stick of gum she offered it to her. The little girl's face lit up, as if she'd just caught her first glance of Disneyland. The stick of gum looked too big for the child and Miranda tore it in half instructing, "Now don't you swallow it."

The gum almost made it to the child's mouth before being snatched out of her hand. "Mommy" glared at Miranda. "Don't you ever give my chile gum. She too little for that," and throwing the offending piece of gum at Miranda, she marched back to her table, toddler and baby in hand.

Gum wasn't good for her? What in the hell did she think taking her on prisons visits would do? Miranda sighed, cringing at the ignorance of some people as she tried to ignore the crying baby and toddler. Her head was starting to pound and she was hungry. Turning her back to the little family she wolfed down a chocolate bar, licking her fingers she glanced up and spied Declan through the glass windows. He was dressed in a blue jumpsuit, his face serious, as he stood next to the other inmates.

His eyes scanned the room looking for her. Miranda thought he looked sick, pale, drawn and *hardened*. It looked like he'd lost some weight since the last time she'd seen him. The weight

Jagged Little Lies

loss made him look meaner, edgier. His eyes met hers. Her heart lurched at the impact of his stare. A look of relief washed over his features.

The door swung open allowing the inmates access to the room. Miranda felt off kilter as time slowed. She watched Declan cross the room. It seemed to take forever. She stood with open arms, and felt a brief touch.

"No touching!" A loud, hostile voice blared, blasting them apart. The guard pointed at them through the glass.

Declan withdrew his arms, but not before Miranda was given the opportunity to get a full, heady inhale of him. Her body responded, wanting, needing, *more*. They sat awkwardly across from each other. Miranda's hands clenched in her lap, it took everything she had not to touch him. Their eyes made love and she felt the tingle in places only he could ignite. Her body grew warm.

Declan *devoured* her with his eyes. "Oh baby, you're killing me." He groaned.

She licked her lips knowing what she was doing. She liked that she was *killing* him. It was intoxicating.

"I didn't think you would come." He whispered.

His words broke the spell she'd been under, bringing back the harsh reality of the prison walls. Anger replaced the heat. "Neither did I."

"I'm so sorry." He said, his face twisting with regret.

"How have you been?" She asked, knowing he would understand what she really meant.

"Pretty sick, you know... they um, don't have much to help me in here."

"Well that's good." Miranda eyed Declan. "You can clean up in here and maybe, when you get out, you'll have a chance to do it differently."

Declan's baby blues searched her eyes intently, trying to decipher the meaning behind her words. She willed her face to remain impassive. She didn't want to give him the wrong idea, breaking eye contact she pushed the bag across the table. "I brought you a gift."

Still looking at her, Declan opened the bag and selected a candy bar. He tore off the wrapper and ate half in one bite. As if remembering his manners he offered her a bite. Miranda smiled, shaking her head no and said, "I brought you cigarettes but they took them from me."

Declan stopped chewing and frowned. "You can't bring them in to me. Next time leave them in your purse, just pretend they're yours. I'll find a way to take them from you once you're in."

"Declan," Miranda shook her head, "there won't be a next time."

He balled up the chocolate bar wrapper and threw it in the bag. His leg reached hers under the table, brushing up against it. A jolt of electricity shot up her thigh from their touching limbs. The door to the visiting lounge swung open and a guard walked in their direction. "They're coming to get me," he said solemnly.

Her heart sunk. She flailed, the wind knocked from her. Tears sprang to her eyes. "Why? You just got here."

"It's an unscheduled visit, baby, and it's my first." Declan trailed a finger up her arm before snatching it back. "If I don't make a stink this time, the second visit will be longer."

The guard reached their table standing beside them. "Time's up, say good bye."

The world stopped once more. The strangeness of the situation unnerved her. She felt her resolve fading as she searched his face.

"Please, come back," he begged.

The guard took Declan by the arm. He looked frantic. "Please Mandy!"

Her body convulsed, she felt frantic too. She couldn't let him go like this. It wouldn't be fair to just leave him hanging. And he looked tortured. She hadn't even gotten the chance to talk with him!

The guard steered him away from the table. With a backwards glance at her Declan shouted "Miranda!" His eyes looked wild.

She couldn't bear it any longer. "I'll come next weekend." She assured him.

"I love you." He called to her, less frantic now.

"I love you too." She called back, watching as he disappeared through the doorway and then from the glass.

"Mommy" snickered. "*I won't be coming back.*" Her words sarcastic as she turned to her partner laughing.

Miranda left the lounge with the woman's words echoing in her head. *She can laugh all she wants, but we'll see who has the last laugh. At least I don't have to raise two kids on my own.* Driving away from the prison, she thought about Declan.

There was no way she'd been able to accomplish what she'd set out to do. The visit was just too quick and she hadn't the opportunity to say what she needed to. That's all it was. Closure, she needed closure and she would get it on the next visit. And then, she would start over.

Start fresh.

Start anew.

Yes, she vowed, her next visit would most *definitely* be her last.

The sound of the woman's laughter still played in her head.

Chapter 17

Declan followed the guard back to his cell. He carried his bag of goodies and wondered why in the hell she'd put the cigarettes in there. *Damn it!* He'd only been able to bum the odd butt by trading his food for it. Anger sparked briefly at her stupidity, but it faded just as quickly as it came. *Christ she was beautiful.* He still couldn't believe she'd come. It took everything he had just to keep his hands off her. Now that was torture, seeing her, being so close, but not able to touch. Next time he'd find a way. Maybe he could get one of the inmates to distract the guards, but he'd need more money to barter with.

Money, lots of money. Cash was king here. With it he'd have a pretty soft couple of years. Without it, well... things would be rough. *If* the lawyer was doing his job the money should be here soon. No doubt his mom would have sent some. Trouble was, if he didn't get it fast, he'd be forced to call her. Declan winced, *God he dreaded hearing her voice.* She seemed on the verge of tears when he phoned, trying hard not to let him hear just how desperate she was to talk with him.

His bag of goodies banged against his leg catching the attention of the inmates he passed. Hungry, predatory eyes watched him, wondering what was in the bag. It was a dog eat dog world, and the inmates wanted everything you had, and then some. Declan wracked his brain trying to come up with a good hiding place. Not an easy task when your cell is only six by eight, *with* a giant rooster occupying it.

Falsetto voice noticed the bag he was carrying and sprang to the bars. "Pretty boy... what do you have in the bag? Can I see? Pleassseee. I *love* playing with bags."

Laughter filled the hallway. Such a sick sound, like the laughter you might hear at a school ground when a big kid tortures a smaller one. In a way that's just how it was here. Only

113

the big kids had grown up. *Kind of.* They'd grown up mean and bullying anything smaller than them. Declan knew he'd need to grow a set of bigger balls and fast, by the looks of the eyes following the bag he held onto.

Back in his cell, Rooster waited. "What you got there, boy?"

Declan made it half way up the ladder before a meaty fist clamped onto his leg. The hand like vice-grip squeezed painfully.

"I said, what you got there boy!"

Rooster released his leg and Declan climbed back down. They stood facing each other, without much room to spare in the tiny cell. Rooster towered above him, nearly toppling him with his hot garbage breathe. With the two of them standing, the room shrunk even further, leaving nowhere to turn. Rooster sat on his bed extending his hand. Declan knew he wasn't going to win this one and handed the bag over.

"Boy, I got me a sweet tooth and you brought me the solution." Rooster laughed, giving Declan a fond swat and sending him crashing into the bars.

The room spun wildly as he straightened up. His head hurt and a little goose egg was starting. He rubbed at it, while standing as big and tall as he could. *No time like the present.* "It's mine. My girl brought it for me. You can have one if you like."

A smile played across Roosters grotesque features. He stopped pawing through the chocolate and magazines looking over at him. "Boy you amuse me. I like that." He bundled the bag up taking a single chocolate bar from it, and placed the bag under his pillow as he continued, "And because I'm feeling so generous, I have a little something for you." Rooster left the bed stepping in front of the urinal.

Jesus Declan cringed thinking, *what in the hell is he going to do now?*

Jagged Little Lies

With a grunt the old goat lowered himself to his knees. Declan's heart kicked up a notch, eyeing him suspiciously. Rooster fiddled with the flange on the urinal, one massive arm reaching around to wiggle and tug at the back side of it, as he lifted it just a crack. With his finger nail he pulled a small plastic bag out from under. Still on bent knee he released his grip on the urinal using it to help him stand.

With a look of accomplishment, he turned to Declan grinning. "Rumour has it you were looking for a little something." He said, dangling the little plastic pouch, holding the pills Declan would do anything for.

Declan swallowed. His need greater than his fear, he reached for the pouch.

Rooster swatted him again, this time landing him on his ass. "Wait your turn boy!"

Barely registering the new bruises, Declan got up from the floor. His eyes remained fixed on the giant loosening the pouch. Rooster withdrew a single tab and placed it on the counter in front of him. Declan glanced at the pill. His mouth watered. He'd never wanted anything as bad, as he wanted this pill. It was the answer to all of his problems.

"What cha willing to do for this boy?" The giant asked softly.

Declan hesitated. There was really only one thing he *wouldn't* do. *At least he hoped he wouldn't.* "What are ya thinking?" he asked.

Rooster picked up the pill and sat on his bed. He patted the spot beside him indicating that Declan should sit. Grinning slyly now he said, "Thought you'd never ask."

Declan sat down next to him, his side touching Rooster's. His body was warm and wreathed in its own special brand of stink. The small area seemed cloaked in it and he fought the impulse to gag. The giant pig sure as hell better not have *that* in mind. Maybe he could knock the guy out somehow and then grab the colorful little pouch of pills. Declan looked again at the pill. It was only a twenty, not one of the more potent ones. The pill looked miniscule in the Roosters giant hand. The tiny round pink shell beckoning.

"What I want boy," Rooster murmured, "is someone I can trust."

"Hmm," He didn't know what to say to that, so he didn't say anything.

"You following me?" Rooster questioned, the smile sliding from his face as he glared at Declan.

Declan stammered, "Not sure that I am."

"Jesus boy, what's wrong with you? Are you stupid or something?"

Declan waited, not sure where any of this was headed.

"I need to be able to count on you boy." Rooster rumbled. "I've got something in mind which might benefit *you* and *me*."

Declan wondered if he could swallow the pill. It had to be slimed with the stink of the man holding it by now. *When was the last time that hand had been washed?* His stomach turned at the image the old goat's smell conjured up. He raised his eyes from the pill and nodded.

"You got any experience with running these pills boy?"

Declan laughed, but only on the inside. *Yeah he had experience, and it got him here.* But he didn't say it, instead he nodded, "A little."

"See, I got a way we can *both* be happy." Rooster's tone turned smooth and deadly.

Declan wished the old guy would just get to the point. His eyes travelled to the tantalizing pink orb. *Maybe he should wash it? No, it might damage it. He could tear off the coated shell and would have, if he had another waiting. But that would make it go to fast and he didn't know when he could get his hands on another one. No, better just to swallow it the way it was.*

116

Jagged Little Lies

"You see, I can get these little beauties just about anytime I want. You know that boy?" Rooster cuffed Declan upside the head to make his point.

Declan saw stars. His head buzzed.

"Getting these pills isn't the problem." Rooster stated, replacing the pink pill back into the plastic pouch and dangling it in front of Declan's face.

Declan hypnotized, was unable to take his eyes off the little pouch. His mind raced with ways he could get his hands on it. Only inches from his face it dangled, calling for him, everything else around him fading. His focus entirely rested on the little bag only two inches from his nose. *So close.* His muscles tensed ready to spring into action. Adrenaline and *need* joined forces. He eyed the Rooster pretty sure he was capable of homicide if the opportunity arose.

Rooster moved pulling the bag away, placing it under his pillow with Declan's goodies he continued. "Of course the real problem is delivery."

Declan's eyes roamed the cell. Maybe he'd missed something. Hard walls and smooth surfaces met his gaze. His eyes fastened on his toothbrush and stopped. An idea came to mind, it would take awhile. *But it might work.*

"See, what we have here is a supply and demand problem." Rooster spoke softly, shifting his weight, leaning up off his buttocks ever so slightly. The air ripped with an ear splitting fart. The old goat laughed, seemingly amused by his own grotesque bodily functions.

Declan leaped off the bed trying to avoid the stink.

"I've got the supply, now we need to meet the demand." Rooster stopped talking for a moment probing in his ear, and pulling out a wad of wax he wiped it on the wall.

Declan's stomach heaved at the sight of the greasy, yellow ball of wax.

"And boy," Rooster continued, "in here we've got a shitload of demand. Now what I'm thinking is you just *might* be able to help me out. Not neglecting his other ear, Rooster probed it too.

Declan watched as half Roosters finger disappeared into his ear canal before surfacing with yet another yellow, greasy, ball of wax. This he added to the wall as well. Jesus, his skin crawling with revulsion, he thought he'd never met a nastier piece of work. Still, this nasty piece of work had something he wanted and he could play the game. After all, he'd been playing it most of his life.

With eyes mere slits and adapting a tougher persona, Declan played up to the sick fuck, hardening his tone he asked, "How so?"

Rooster smiled, patting the bed beside him. "Come here boy."

Declan squatted lowering himself to the giant's level and the stink hit him.

Rooster shook his head, and mouthed, "Closer."

Breathing through his mouth Declan inched closer, sitting on the edge of the bed.

Rooster eyes narrowed, his tone mean. "Closer," he repeated.

Declan shifted moving an inch. Stink coat his tongue. He thought about the pills. *Maybe he could use the pillow and try to suffocate him with it?*

Rooster's leg touched his and he tried not to recoil. The pillow beckoned only a few feet away.

Declan, still holding his breath, sprang into action.

Chapter 18

Billy slept most of the way. With no car seat, Lyndsey strapped him in beside her as best she could. Her arm ached from using it to hold Billy firmly in place during the drive. A police car passed them and she held her breath. Christ that was all they needed. A ticket for no car seat, and how would she explain the bruises on Billy?

The police cruiser sped passed them. Drake glanced over at her, the stress on his face a clear indicator of the situation they faced. "We need to get him to the hospital Linds. He needs to be seen by a doctor."

"I know. But can't we spend a little time with him first? Please Drake! Just for a few hours? We can bathe and feed him, maybe read him a story. The bruises look older and I think he is fine. Well, I mean as fine as he could be, given his horrendous living situation. And it's not the bruises I'm worried about. Those will heal. It's the emotional bruises that worry me most."

"I'm worried about him too Linds. This kid is going to need a lot of help if he even stands a chance at a normal life." Drake ran a shaky hand through his hair.

"I know, but if we take him to the hospital right now, it will add to those bruises. Christ, Drake, he's been through enough today already, without adding to it. He'll be terrified when they examine him. I just wanted to get him a little more settled, before he has to face yet *another* bout of terror."

Billy squirmed, cringing in his sleep. Lyndsey pulled him closer to her. "God only knows what his demons are. Jesus Drake," her voice broke as the enormity of Billy's sad, little life hit, "it's just so goddamn unfair."

"I know it is honey." He said reaching over and giving her knee a squeeze.

The rest of the drive was silent, each of them deep in thought. *Why in the hell should Dee be able to have a child and she couldn't?* Looking down at Billy Lyndsey felt sick. She had wanted a child so badly and they had tried for years. She and Drake had been to all sorts of specialists. The best any of them could come up with was that she'd done some damage to her body with the birth of her first child. It left her with a tilted uterus.

For a while she'd been obsessed with it, trying to get pregnant and taking her temperature. Lyndsey kept track of when she was ovulating and charted it like a sailor plotting his course. She read everything she could get her hands on, trying and discarding different methods. It had been such a rollercoaster, as each month she held her breath waiting, waiting to see. With each new month and proof she wasn't pregnant arriving, she crashed, wondering *why?*

Why could she get pregnant when she wasn't ready and had no chance of giving a child any kind of life? Why couldn't she get pregnant now, when she had so much to offer a child, Why, why, why? It had taken a toll on the both of them and Drake eventually called *stop*.

She'd gone seeking spiritual advice. After all, she knew enough to know her quality of life and happiness were her responsibility, *hers and hers alone.*

With hard work and working the steps, she slowly began moving away from *why*. So much had changed for her beyond just not using drugs anymore. She'd learned instead of asking *why* to use *why not?* Why not her? After all she'd been given so much. She had fingers and toes and food and shelter. She had a job she loved and a man she adored. She had a beautiful home and a family of origin that was healing. She had great friends and an amazing life. *So why not her?*

Finally able to count her blessings, not her sores, they'd moved passed it. Not that the longings went completely away,

Jagged Little Lies

she just didn't *live* in them anymore. Seeing Billy today brought it back.

Drake parked the car effortlessly in the garage. He parked as he did everything else, with ease and a natural talent, reaching for Billy Lyndsey stopped him.

"Let me carry him. I think he is afraid of men Drake." Gently, so not to frighten him, Lyndsey stroked his face. "Billy," she called in a soft voice, "Billy honey wake up."

Billy's body tensed beneath her finger tips, rousing from the safest place he knew, he looked up at her cautiously. Lyndsey unbuckled him, scooping him up. *Oh god those eyes.* How did such a young child get eyes that old? Not even wanting to know the answer to that question, she followed Drake inside.

Drake disappeared into the bathroom briefly, running a warm bath while Lyndsey undressed Billy. "We don't have any clothes or diapers for him Linds." He pointed out, his cheeks flushed from the bath water.

"I know honey," she nodded. "Would you mind running to the store and picking up a couple of things? It doesn't mean anything Drake, other than Billy has a right to be in clean clothes and diapers."

"Linds?" Drake gave her a hard searching look.

"I know what you're thinking and I'm okay. Really, Drake," she said as she placed Billy into the bath. She stood and gave Drake a quick reassuring kiss. "I just want to clean him up and give him a little love. God knows he needs it. And then we can take him in. Okay?"

Not convinced, Drake gave her a long, hard stare before leaving. Lyndsey sat on the edge of the tub. "You need some toys don't you Billy?" She lowered her little yellow ducky from its perch on the shelf above into the water. Billy's face lit up. His bruised arm reached out stopping just before the duck, looking up at her to gage her reaction, his fingers encircled the plastic toy.

121

"It's Ok Billy, you can play with the duck," she encouraged him. Billy picked the duck up placing it in his mouth. He chewed for an instant before smashing it back down into the water. The water splashed up getting Lyndsey wet and she laughed.

Billy's little body stiffened his eyes bugging out.

"It's OK Billy see," Lyndsey smiled at him reassuringly. She splashed him back with a tiny wave. Droplets of water sprayed the duck and he smiled, using the duck once more he slapped at the water. Waves of water splashed around him as he sat closing his eyes. Time stopped, and for a moment, he was just a sweet little boy, having a bath. His grin was infectious and Lyndsey felt her own responding.

They played splashing water and each other. Lyndsey washed Billy between splashes. His little body was riddled in bruises, his bottom raw from to much time spent in between diaper changes. But at the moment, none of it mattered.

They played until the water cooled and wrapping Billy up in a fluffy towel she dried him as he clung to the rubber ducky. With nothing to dress him in, she swaddled him in an extra towel mindful of his un-diapered bottom. Lyndsey snuggled Billy, hoping he wouldn't pee on her. She went in search of her old teddy bear. The middle of her bed looked as good a place as any and Lyndsey plopped Billy there while searching the back of her closet. The old one-eyed bear was stuffed far back in the corner and she grasped its arm pulling it free.

Lyndsey smiled. "Look Billy I have a surprise for you." Billy looked back at her intently, a cautious little smile wavering. Just like a magician making a big show she counted, "One, two, three!" She pulled the bear from behind her back to surprise Billy.

His smile faltered as he chewed on the duck and froze. Billy's eyes widened as he screamed. It was agonizing to hear, the sound filled with terror, setting the bear on the night table she scooped him up murmuring, "Shhh, it's OK Billy, it's just a toy."

Jagged Little Lies

Billy's body trembled violently in her arms. His shrieks stopped to be replaced with great racking sobs. His crying was loud and violent. Lyndsey feared he might choke on his tears. His body stiffened and he pushed against her. She put him back down on the bed not knowing what else to do.

On the middle of their bed, wrapped in towels and holding the rubber duck, he looked so small and alone. Her heart flip-flopped in concern. Lyndsey sat on the edge of the bed, not wanting to get to close. She'd done something wrong and lost some ground with him. His fist waved rubbing at an eye, his sobs lessened to be replaced with shudders, his little chest moving with each one.

What in the hell had happened? She noticed Billy's eyes locked on the bear. *Had it scared him? Maybe it was the missing eye?* Lyndsey picked up the bear and placed it back in the closet. She looked back at Billy. *Oh my sweet little boy, what has been done to you?* What were you suppose to do with a terrified little kid? Worried he might pee on the bed and wanting to comfort him, she picked him back up. Lyndsey held Billy, sitting in the rocking chair she'd been waiting years to rock a child in. The rocking motions were comforting and soothed them both. Soon she felt him relaxing against her.

A forgotten melody came to mind. Hush little baby don't you cry. Not able to remember the words she hummed most of it. Lyndsey stroked his head and cheeks, her fingers tracing circles as they caressed. Her touch was feather light as it smoothed his hands and little feet. His skin was soft and he smelled of soap and shampoo.

The warmth of Billy grew heavier, as he settled in her arms. His breathing changed, growing slower. His warmth and weight reminded her of a different time and place. Memories of other little boys flashed before her. A tiny babe she rocked in her arms, his little head smelling of baby powder and sweetness. A little boy carrying a tattered blanket with the smell of fabric softener and laundry soap in the air. A little boy she'd never seen before, with a profound message. Git wel son.

Then there was Billy. Broken little Billy, and she already felt fiercely protective of him. Maybe this was why she had never had any more children

As she stared at Billy Lyndsey thought about Dee. She wondered what she was doing at this moment. Looking upon her son she vowed to her old friend. *I promise Dee.* I will take care of him and keep him safe. I will love him, until you can. She'd already overcome some incredible obstacles. She was sure they could overcome this.

Guilt plagued her. She knew it wouldn't be easy to convince Drake. He was such a good man and she prayed he would do the right thing. Billy moaned in his sleep, his fingers curling tightly around hers. Lyndsey gathered him close and snuggled his warm little body. The soft click of the clock was barely noticeable as time passed.

The rocker slowed and then stopped.

The duck fell to the carpet, unheard by either of the room's occupants.

Chapter 19

Susan's fork stopped in mid-air. A piece of broccoli dangled from the tines, she studied it for a moment before plunging it into her mouth. Her plate was almost empty. *How had that happened?* She'd been thinking about Declan and not noticed what she was eating. She shrugged, speared a piece of chicken and focused on chewing it. The food tasted like rubber.

Chicken used to be one of her family's favorite meals. They would have it every Sunday. She'd coat the chicken pieces in bread crumbs and parmesan cheese and then bake them in the oven. A pot of whipped, creamy potatoes accompanied the chicken. Declan always talked her into baking a cake. He would help her by licking the spoon and the bowl.

Susan looked up from her plate full of memories. A longing for yesterday pushed her up from her chair. After scraping the remaining food into the garbage, she rinsed her plate. Her insides felt bruised, as if her memories had beaten her heart leaving it broken. She felt like a shell, a hollowed-out husk, of what she once was.

The dishcloth was warm and soapy, strangely comforting, as she swiped up and down the counter tops cleaning away the last traces of her meal. *Maybe a walk would make me feel better?* There was a time when she walked every evening. Sometimes she walked with Dick, or Declan, but most of the times alone. And she'd loved it, a brisk walk around her neighbourhood after dinner. It would be *her time.* She liked looking at all the homes she passed. Susan studied the exteriors of the homes making mental notes. The neighbors' homes gave her ideas for her own. If the curtains were open, she'd wave to the families inside smiling. Back in the day, it was fun to run into a neighbour on the street and chat for a minute or two.

Now she walked under the cover of darkness. But it wasn't the same, and she was always afraid. Her mind turned the rustle of a leaf into a mad rapist or serial killer. She sighed, tired, deciding the walk required too much effort, and settled for the bills instead. As she typed in her password, her mind returned to Declan. She'd finally learned to do online banking. Declan had bugged her for years to learn. He was good with computers and wanted to show her how. She'd resisted at first, worried at the instant access of her personal line of credit. But he persisted, laughing, saying *don't worry Mom.* With just a few clicks he'd shown her how she could move money out of her own account into others. Like paying bills and credit cards, and of course, transferring money into his account.

The password came up wrong. Susan stared at it blankly. She'd changed it so many times over the years. She remembered the first time it happened. She'd been paying bills when she noticed there was money missing from her account, thinking the bank must have made a mistake she phoned in reporting it. The bank traced the transaction and it showed the missing money had been transferred into a savings account, one which held the name of her son.

At first she'd been furious. *How dare he steal from her!* Susan waited impatiently for Declan to come home, her anger rising with each passing hour. Finally he walked in the door and she landed on him, hurling insults and accusations. She'd been out of control. Declan sat calmly not defending himself, and eventually she'd run out of steam and cried.

Declan was so sweet and forgiving, comforting her with his words. He admitted it was him and he was sorry, but he really wanted to buy her something special for her birthday. He felt bad for doing it, but it meant so much to him, to be able to give her a birthday present. So he'd taken the chance and was going to pay it back, of course. And he was sorry. *So sorry.*

Jagged Little Lies

He always was. *Sorry.* It was a word she'd come to dread. Thing was, he meant it every, single, time. So she'd changed her password again and again, but he'd always figured it out. And he was always, so *sorry.*

Her hatred for Dick surfaced. How dare he just walk away from it all? He had abandoned her and Declan. Jesus, what kind of *man* did that? For a moment she wished she could kill him. Just rid the world of his cowardly little body. At least then there'd be a real reason for his, *not getting involved.*

Seething, she tried another password. *Denied access* flashed across the screen. She tried again, nalkced is Declan spelled backwards, *denied.* Susan tried her name and then the name of their street. *What was it?* Frustrated she tried to think. She noticed the little box above *forgot your password* and clicked on it. A question appeared. *What is your son's middle name?* Oh thank god! At least she hadn't forgotten that, typing Richard into the space she finally accessed her account. Anxiously, she clicked on her personal line of credit.

The numbers blurred in front of her eyes, putting on her cheaters she looked again. *Oh Dear God!* Six numbers stared back at her. More than three hundred thousand dollars gone, vanished, spent. For the life of her, she couldn't tell you on what.

She'd first taken the line of credit out when they'd split up, borrowing against the house was easy. Dick told her it was foolish and she needed to get a job. But she'd dismissed his words as just another way to shirk his responsibilities. She had no intentions of working. Besides, with his alimony and child support payments, she really didn't need to, *if* she was careful.

But she hadn't been. She'd gone on a buying spree wanting everything new. At first it was fun and exciting, as Declan and she travelled from place to place buying whatever they wanted. She hoped the traveling and her purchases would help to make things better. Maybe it would stop the pain she was in, and it did, at least momentarily. But the pain always came back. She lived with it each and every day.

With a click of the mouse Susan transferred the last ten thousand dollars into her chequing account and clicked on *pay bills*. The ten thousand wouldn't even cover the visa bill. Only paying the minimum requirement she paid her bills. Her fingers drummed the granite counter tops as she subtracted the money spent on the lawyer representing Declan. To the best of her calculations, there would be enough money left over to get her through the next week or two.

Christ. She was going to have to call Dick. She loathed the idea, but she needed help and God knows he owed her. Maybe he could pay the lawyers bill. He made enough money to, that's for sure. Her anger fueled impulse dialed the familiar numbers.

As the phone rang, she wondered if Dick ever missed her, even just a little. He certainly didn't act like he did. His tone, when speaking with her, implied coolness and caution, there was nothing warm, or friendly, about it. And she was pretty sure he was screening her calls. They played telephone tag most of the time and their conversations seemed to come through, via Declan.

Declan passed messages to his mother, from his father. Or if Susan needed something from Dick, she'd get Declan to call asking his father for it. It hadn't been the best way of communicating by any means, but it was better than Susan and Dick speaking. Whenever they spoke it almost always, ended in name calling and hang ups.

However, Declan was no longer here and so she waited, listening to phone at her ear ring.

A female voice finally answered, sounding winded. A breathy "Hello" greeted her.

Startled Susan said, "Oh I'm sorry, I've got the wrong number."

Jagged Little Lies

The woman on the other end asked "Who are you looking for?"

"My husband, I mean ah, Dick," she replied, feeling strangely rattled.

"This is Dick's place."

"Oh well ah," *who was she speaking to?* "Can I speak with him please?"

"Sorry, he's a little busy at the moment. Can he call you back?"

"NO! He can't! It's an emergency and I need to speak with him right now." Susan didn't mean to sound so urgent, but the thought of waiting for a phone call back was more than she could bear.

"Oh, well um..." The woman covered the phone and a muffled conversation followed, then, "Just a moment please."

"Susan!" Dick's voice full of alarm, "is Declan okay?"

Is Declan okay? What an ass! If you had anything at all to do with your son, you'd know he wasn't! "No, he is not okay," she snapped.

"What's wrong? What's happened?"

"Who was that on the phone?"

"What?" Dick asked, not following her.

"The phone Dick, the phone, who was I just speaking to?"

"Susan, what in the hell does this have to do with Declan?" Dick shouted.

"Watch your tone Dick or I'll hang up." She knew she had the upper hand, but only for this moment.

"Please Susan." Dick tried again. "Is Declan OK?"

"The woman Dick, who is she?"

"Her name is Laurie, Susan, now how is Declan?"

The fear she'd first heard in his voice changed, sounding more impatient now, than scared. *And she still needed the money.* But hearing Dick say Laurie's name twisted something inside of her and she foolishly blurted out, "You're not seeing anyone are you?"

A gust of pent up breath blew through the phone. "Jesus Christ Susan, if there's something wrong with Declan tell me now, or I'm going to hang up."

Wow they really had this hang up game down to a science. "Don't Dick. Declan needs help."

"What kind of help?"

"Well... I saw his lawyer today."

"And?"

"And, he's going to see Declan. Dick I've asked him to try and get the charges overturned."

Dick sighed and Susan could imagine him, rubbing a weary hand through his greying hair. "Susan what does this have to do with me?"

"Jesus Christ Dick! Last time I checked you were his father. It would be nice if you remembered this and supported him just a little. Do you have any idea what it must be like for him in there? What he must be going through?" Her throat clicked shut on the last sentence strangling the words. She was close to tears and her thoughts turned homicidal.

"Susan," Dick said, "Declan "plead guilty. For once in his life he did the right thing, and you want me to step in and *fix* it?"

"You know it wasn't his fault! If he hadn't met that *woman,* none of this would be happening."

"Stop it Susan. We've been done this road a million times before. I will not go down it with you again. Now I'm going to hang up." His tone softening just a little at his next words, "You need help. Please, for Declan's sake Susan, get it."

The phone clicked softly in her ear. "Dick? Dick!" She tossed the receiver across the kitchen and wailed. The bastard! She hated him! Why couldn't he just die! She wished him to hell and *Laurie* too.

Jagged Little Lies

The thought of him with anyone else shredded what little sanity she had left. Pouring a glass of water Susan reached for her purse, and twisting the cap off the bottle she looked inside.

Only three left.

Shaking out two, she swallowed them.

Chapter 20

"Hello, earth to Miranda!" Lisa teased.

Miranda smiled shaking her head. "Sorry Lisa what did you say?" They were talking about Lisa's stagette, when the image of Declan's face distracted her.

"I *said* I hope you're going to wear the hot little red number you keep in your closet for *special* occasions." Lisa's giggle implied she thought this might be one.

Miranda winced. She hadn't been able to work up the nerve to tell Lisa she wasn't going. At least she didn't want to, but as her bridesmaid she felt obligated. They'd been best friends since elementary school. Inseparable too, that is until she met Declan. Lisa never liked him or thought he was good enough for her. And she wore an "I told you so" smile when Miranda informed her of their break up.

Miranda looked away from Lisa, not wanting to upset her and said, "I think it's a little too soon for the red number."

Lisa snorted. "Yeah right! You know what they say to a cowboy who's been thrown from their horse. Get back on and *ride*." Lisa laughed, thrilled at the idea of Miranda hooking up with a new prospect.

"Yeah well, I'm not sure I'm ready for that." She omitted most of the why, not wanting Lisa to know about her recent prison visit. *God she kept so many secrets these days.*

Lisa's laughter stopped as she looked more closely at Miranda. "Are you OK? What's up?"

Miranda forked a bite of salad stalling for time. She wished she could tell Lisa. The pressure of keeping secrets was exhausting, but she already knew what Lisa would say if she told her. And she didn't want to hear it. Not again.

"Miranda?" Lisa quizzed.

133

"I'm all right Lisa. Just tired, I'm not sleeping very well." *At least that part was the truth.*

Lisa speared a tomato wedge from Miranda's plate waving it in the air. "Is this about Declan?" she asked, her lip curling as she pronounced his name.

"Ah no, well sort of, I guess," Miranda stammered, to tired to think up anything more.

"Jesus Miranda, you should be up dancing on the table right now. This is good news! I'm so glad you finally got your head on straight and were able to see him for the *loser* he really is!"

Miranda's eyes narrowed in anger, she hated it when Lisa talked about Declan like this. Needing to defend Declan she took her friend on. "You never really knew him Lisa. Not like I did, and you were *always* looking for faults."

"Miranda, it wasn't like I had to look very hard! His *faults* were so visible! Everyone could see them. Jesus Miranda, the guy couldn't even keep a job and he was always mooching off of you, or somebody else."

"Yeah well... He ah, just ah, seemed to catch a lot of tough breaks." Miranda stumbled, confused, her thoughts not easily described.

Lisa's face flushed with indignation, her forked tomato wedge getting dangerously close to Miranda's eyes. "Jesus Miranda! Are you serious? He was going to let you take the fall for him. He's a snake. *A coward*! And he was using you! You were the only one who couldn't see it!"

As if just noticing her tomato, Lisa shoveled it into her mouth and chewed, raising a hennaed brow she scowled. "Don't tell me you miss him Miranda."

OK she wouldn't. Tell her that is. And she did. She missed him badly. But she wouldn't tell her that either. Instead she said, "I think it would be normal to miss him. After all Lisa, we lived together and I thought I'd be spending the rest of my life with him. *You* never liked him in the first place. Not even in the beginning, when things were good."

Lisa's fork dropped to her plate with a clatter. "Oh my God Miranda, things were never good! Don't you remember?"

"Of course I remember!" And she did. There were some hot memories, especially when she was lying alone in her bed. Memories that left her squirming in need and missing him more than words could ever describe. But she wouldn't be sharing those memories with Lisa either.

Miranda poked at the salad on her plate and said. "He always tried Lisa. Even after all the shitty breaks he kept getting, he tried."

"What? Wow! Who stole my friend's brain? I'd like it back please! Are you serious? Please tell me you don't believe this!" Lisa looked intently at her.

She clenched her fork feeling furious. "Stop it Lisa. That's enough! I won't listen to you bully Declan anymore. You've always been jealous of our relationship and it's not like I pick apart your love life."

"Jealous? Is that what you think this is? Jesus Mandy, you're further gone than I thought!"

"Name calling is not helping things Lisa. I just wish you would try and understand."

"What's to understand Miranda? The guy is a jerk. A loser. *Period.* But what I don't understand is, what's happened to *you?*"

"Me? What do you mean me?"

"It's like you're on drugs too Mandy. I mean it isn't hard to figure Declan out. He's a drug addict for Christ's sakes! What's happening to him makes sense. It's you I'm worried about. As far as I know you don't use drugs and yet your thinking is like it's, I don't know, *impaired* or something."

"That's absurd! My thinking is not impaired. How dare you say that?"

"It is, Miranda. Something is seriously *wrong* with the way you're thinking. It's like you have blinders on when it comes to Declan."

"For Christ's sakes Lisa, and to think I called you my friend! Seriously, do you think this is helpful?" Miranda couldn't stand sitting at this table another instant, pushing her half filled plate away she rifled through her purse.

"Don't go. I'm just trying to help. *Please.*" Lisa reached across the table touching her arm.

Miranda stiffened. "You know, I really wished I could be honest with you and that you could be supportive, like a *real friend*. But I can see it isn't going to happen. Maybe you better think about getting yourself another bridesmaid. One who's brain isn't quite as *impaired* as mine!"

Lisa pulled back her arm, recoiling from the hostility in Miranda's tone. Her face wore a look of sadness and horror.

Miranda stood tossing money on the table. "Thanks for the great lunch. It's been a slice. Let's do it again sometime soon. *Not!*"

She stormed out of the restaurant, opening the doors a little too roughly in her anger. The doors slammed shut behind her, leaving the plates to rattle in her wake.

Miranda never even noticed the tears rolling down her best friend's face.

Chapter 21

Adrenaline jackknifed his system. Declan sprang at Rooster knocking his head against the cement wall. To get better leverage, he moved onto the giant's lap and pressed his knee into the old guy's crotch. Grabbing a handful of greasy hair, he banged his head against the wall. *Once, twice, three* times, he smashed the old goats head.

The rooster's eyes bugged from his purpled face. He pushed against Declan's chest. Declan rode him like a like a rodeo clown, refusing to be dislodged. Rooster gave up trying to extricate him and instead grabbed Declan by the throat.

His throat slammed shut, his windpipe sealing tight under the steel hands. Declan let go of the greasy hair he'd been holding. *The pressure was unbelievable.* The giant's fingers felt like screws as they ground against his windpipe. With both hands, he tried to pry open Rooster's vice - like grip from his throat.

Rooster shook him, holding him by the throat. "You gonna be sorry now boy. Gonna have to teach you a little lesson."

Not able to reply Declan bent one of Rooster's fingers, yanking as hard as he could on the digit. Nothing budged. Panic raced through his body as he struggled for oxygen.

Rooster, not seeming at all concerned over his deathly grip continued. "Yup, it's a real shame boy. I had such high hopes for you."

Declan gave up on Rooster's fingers, thinking furiously. He needed to stay calm. *You don't have much time left so you better make it count!* Star bursts of color exploded behind his eyes. Declan slumped in Rooster's grip, hoping it looked convincing.

Rooster crowed. "What's a matter boy? You had enough?"

Declan jerked, slamming Rooster in the jaw with his head and driving his finger into Rooster's eye. The sliminess of the

137

great bulging orb made him gag. To his dismay his finger did not penetrate the orb, instead sliding smoothly off of it to catch on the skin below. His nail tearing the skin at the corner of the old goat's eye as it slid downwards. Declan watched it all, as if in slow motion.

Rooster howled, furious, shaking Declan by the throat.

Declan's head bounced back and forth violently. The cell spun in front of his eyes.

The giant threw Declan across the room.

Declan crashed into the bars, his head and elbow taking the worst of it.

Rooster stood, bloodied from the torn skin around his eye. Picking Declan up from the crumpled heap he lay in, he shook him again.

Declan's jaw slammed closed and bit his tongue.

Rooster grinned insanely, and slapped Declan's face and head as he rumbled, "That's it boy. Fight back. I can see we're going to have to toughen you up some."

Declan's head snapped back and forth from the impact of the *slaps*. The starbursts of color morphed into a symphony of fireworks, exploding behind his eyes. Strangely, he'd stopped feeling the pain. He heard the *thwack* of his flesh as it was hit, but no longer felt it. He hung limply as Rooster played with him.

"You had enough boy? Well? You ready to hear my plan?" Rooster gave him a final shake before releasing him.

Declan stood up on rubbery legs. His throat was swollen and making whistling sounds, as he tried to gulp in great breaths of air. He thought his elbow was probably shattered. He winced before feeling his head, sure it too was cracked, and running a hand through the hair line just above his ear he noticed the beginnings of one mother, of a goose egg.

"I *said* you ready to hear my plan?" Rooster's tone implied he was done playing and ready to get serious.

Jagged Little Lies

With nowhere to run Declan faced him. "What plan?" he wheezed.

"Now you're talking smart, boy. Like I said, I got a plan what'll benefit you and me. Think of it as a *mutual* package." Rooster roared with laughter, slapping his leg at a joke only he thought funny.

Declan cringed. The adrenaline was wearing off and the pain was getting worse. His elbow throbbed wickedly and he worried there was a bone chip floating in it. The egg on his head pounded and he was pretty sure he had a concussion.

"I'm gonna need you to be my distributor. I'll supply the stock and you can sell it." Rooster stared off over his head thinking. "And of course, I'll let you sample some of the merchandise."

Declan moaned. He hadn't meant to, it just happened. His body shook and his stomach rolled. He made the toilet just in time as his last meal came up.

Rooster scratched his head and continued talking as if he hadn't noticed. "Of course, how much you get will be up to you. The more you sell, the more you get, plain and simple, hey boy?"

On hands and knees, Declan crawled away from the toilet, resting his back against the bars.

Rooster fished under his pillow, pulling out one of the magazines intended for Declan. The glossy cover held a big, beautiful, shiny truck. Rooster thumbed through it slowly taking his time.

Declan rested against the bars to broken to get up. He stared at the giant and seethed. Hatred so great it blackened his vision bloomed inside of him. His eyes wandered the cell, looking. He saw the toothbrush again and stopped. It would work. He'd make it.

The giant snorted picking his nose, "Why boy, this magazine ain't nothing but sissy - girl trucks! What they really need are hogs. Get me a *real* magazine next time. Tell your girl I want one with hogs! Hogs and chicks." Rooster used the cover like it was a tissue and tossed the magazine to Declan.

It landed cover side up. The gelatinous mass of snot stared up at him. Furious, he tore the cover from the book and avoiding the mess, crumpled it into a ball. Declan stared at the torn magazine his and heart seized. Just knowing Miranda touched this magazine and the pig on the bed had touched it too hurt him more than the giants fists never could.

Rooster slouched, munching one of Declan's chocolate bars. "Boy it's time to get to work." He retrieved the pouch from under his pillow and he counted the pills. As he palmed the pink pill he said, "Now listen up, here's what we're gonna to do."

Declan listened and as far as he could tell, it might work. Of course it was him taking all the risks. But still. The thought of being in this jail cell for two more years was more than he could handle. Without a doubt he'd be insane before his time was halfway done.

Rooster flicked the pink beauty with a giant thumb. Up and down it went. Just like the toss of a coin. All he had to do was say yes, and it was his. As for the rest of it, well, he'd worry about it when he got there.

"Well?"

Declan nodded, his throat to sore to answer.

With a final flick, Rooster caught the pill and tossed it to Declan.

Declan's arm shot out catching it. His elbow screamed at the sudden movement. His mouth watered in anticipation.

With the tiny pill in his hand he debated, hating the thought of putting something into his mouth that Rooster just touched.

His head pounded. His elbow screamed.

Fuck it.

Declan swallowed. The pill and the stink of Rooster left a nasty after bite.

Chapter 22

Billy's screams woke her. Disoriented, Lyndsey looked wildly around the room, expecting to see something alarming. Billy's body tensed in her arms and he screamed again. His eyes sewn tightly shut as he thrashed about. Her heart pounded in terror. She had never heard screams like this before.

A long shrill scream stopped abruptly and Billy relaxed. Confused and scared, Lyndsey held him close. Billy's breathing slowed into a deeper rhythm. *Was he still sleeping? What in the hell?*

Drake's concerned face appeared in the doorway. With finger to lip, Lyndsey tiptoed to the bed and lowering Billy she surrounded him with pillows. The throw at the end of the bed was soft and fleecy, as she carefully tucked him in, not wanting to wake him. Billy made a smacking sound with his lips before snuggling deeper into the throw. His little hand curled around the soft material bringing it, and his thumb, to his mouth.

Lyndsey watched for a moment as he suckled his thumb. Sighing with relief she edged away from the bed. She wasn't a psychiatrist, but she was willing to bet Billy suffered from PTSD and night terrors.

"Wha ...?" Lyndsey shushed Drake before he could finish his sentence.

With the door ajar, they left the room quietly. Once in the kitchen Drake turned to her saying, "What in the hell was that all about?"

Her hands shaking slightly, Lyndsey poured a glass of water. She noticed the parcels. Drake had brought home more than just a *few* items. "I don't know what his screams were about Drake. But they sure scared the hell out of me! I must have fallen asleep and his screams woke me up."

"Poor kid, I wonder what's been done to him?" His forehead crinkled. "Are you all right?"

"Yeah... I think so. It was just so *scary* to wake up like that. I thought someone was in the room with us."

"Jesus Linds, it sounded like he was being tortured. Was he really asleep? How could he sleep through all that noise?"

"I don't know. I couldn't. Drake what did you buy?" Lyndsey said wanting to change the subject. "I need to get him into a diaper."

Still scowling, Drake opened one of the bags pulling out two packages of diapers. "I wasn't sure what size he'd be, so I bought both."

The diapers were wrapped in a colorful plastic wrap, with smiling babies on the packages. The babies were cute, and plump, and looked nothing at all like Billy. Lyndsey opened the package with the pull ups in them saying, "I think these should fit him."

Drake opened the other bag grinning, "Look at these Linds. I couldn't resist." He pulled out a pair of blue, sleeper pajamas, with little yellow ducks. "I used to have pajamas like these when I was a kid."

"They're adorable honey." Lyndsey said, wishing she could smile for him, just a little. To show how much she appreciated him. But she couldn't. She was on the verge of tears.

Drake folded the sleepers. "I think..." His words trailed off as he noticed the expression on her face. "Aw honey. It will be okay." He said, putting the sleepers down and folding her into his arms.

Lyndsey rested for a moment against his chest. The steady reassuring beat of his heart was like an old and familiar friend. It comforted her through many a difficult times and it comforted now.

Hugging him back, she agreed. "I know we'll be okay Drake, but what about Billy?"

Jagged Little Lies

"Billy will be okay too. It's just going to take awhile."

"But that's the problem Drake. If he doesn't get the right person to care for him, they could do more harm than good. If he gets an impatient or exhausted care giver, it'll be a disaster."

"Lyndsey, there are some great foster families out there."

"That's right Drake, there are. But Billy will be a full time job. He can't go to a family who already has a bunch of other children. Let's face it, most of the kids going into the system have multiple problems. And, if the problems are too great, or they're too disruptive to the fostering family, then they're simply given a higher designation and moved elsewhere."

Drake's forehead wrinkled. "You've lost me Linds. Speak English, not counselorease."

Counselorease was Drake's word for clinical language. Lyndsey laughed the first time she heard the expression from him, but she wasn't laughing now. "Drake, a designation defines the type of care a child will need, and then matches the child with a suitable foster family. The higher the designation, the more difficult the care for the child is, and it also brings a higher amount of pay."

"Huh," Drake snorted. "You couldn't pay me enough to do this kind of work. It must be heartbreaking."

"It is, but it's rewarding as well. At least sometimes, but mostly it's just frustrating. The system is flawed, but it's the only one we've got."

"Well," Drake sighed, "Maybe Dee will finally get her act together."

Lyndsey gave Drake *the look.* "Now I know you're just trying to make me feel better. She has even less of a chance than Billy. I'm not even sure if she can get well. Did you see her eyes?"

"Yeah, what's left of them. She's looking pretty bad huh? Can you imagine having a mother like that?"

Lyndsey thought about her own mother. A mother who buried her head in the sand and kept secrets, but she done the best she knew how at the time. And it hadn't been her mother giving her the bruises, although she'd known about them.

God she hoped it wasn't Dee who was giving Billy the bruises. "No Drake, I can't imagine. I know the bruises look bad, but don't underestimate the psychological damage. It's easy to focus on the physical marks. They're bad, hideous even, but it's all the rest of it I worry about."

"What do you mean?"

"It's hard to explain. My words won't do it justice, but I'll try. When children are little *everything* they learn about the world, and themselves, come from the people caring for them. In my case it was my parents. If your caregivers are filled with tension and worry, or anger and rage, then you absorb it. It's like you're a sponge. Or a blank tape. And your caregivers program in, what you soak up."

"Jeez Linds, I'm not sure kids are like sponges!" Drake teased.

"In healthy family systems children soak up love and acceptance, developing self worth, and self esteem. Problems are acknowledges and sometimes solved. They can communicate and they have empathy and compassion for others. Their differences are celebrated and encouraged. They are *all* of equal value and each individual can get their needs met."

"Sounds like my family."

"It does. You were very lucky. Not all of us are, certainly not Billy, have that privilege. What happens in *unhealthy* family systems is very different to what you experienced as a child. In unhealthy families children learn they are to be seen and not heard. Sometimes they're not even to be seen. They learn expressing their own opinion, or disagreeing, gets you a cuff upside the head, or a belt across the back side. They learn feelings are *dangerous* and to be kept a secret. Problems are

144

Jagged Little Lies

never acknowledged, simply covered up. Children from unhealthy families learn they're a pain in the ass, and develop low self worth and low self esteem. They become emotionally starved and needy, particularly in their relationships with friends, or boy-girl relationships. They become hyper vigilant and-"

"What's hyper-vigilant?" Drake asked interrupting her.

"It's like you have this antenna, " Lyndsey paused blowing a piece of hair from her face, "and you can tell how others are feeling without them ever saying a word. You can just *sense* it. If they're in a bad mood you know how to make them feel better, or you just walk on egg shells around them. What you really want is for them to be in a good mood, because if they are, then well...then, it's great." Lyndsey said, scratching her head wishing she could do a better job of describing it.

"Why? What's so great about it?"

"Well, it's like if this person's in a good mood, then the whole family is in a good mood. But if he or she isn't, look out! You end up spending a lot of time trying to make other people happy and you never really feel equal to them. You always feel sort of less than, and *different* somehow. Apart, like you're standing on the outside looking in."

Drake looked solemn. "Sorry Linds," he whispered in her ear.

"It's okay Drake, really."

"I just wish it could have been different for you."

"It wasn't meant to be honey and I'm okay, *now*. In unhealthy family systems you learn never to disagree, or voice your opinions. And that's a real problem for children, because then they grow up not able to ask for what they need. And their *needs* become greater.

"Well I think Billy will be a lot better off without Dee. I sure hope this doesn't screw him up for life."

"The thing is Drake, he needs her. He needed her touch to help develop part of his brain. Touch is so important, especially

145

in the first six months of life. It helps to develop the limbic system, a part of his brain which doesn't develop like it should without it. "

"What happens if it doesn't develop properly?"

"He can have a difficult time cognitively and socially, to say the least." Lyndsey admitted.

"English please." Drake reminded her.

"His thinking could be somewhat impaired and he'll probably struggle with impulses and fitting into society."

"Jesus! All of that just from missing a few cuddles?"

Drake's chest was warm and hard, snuggling against him she bit his ear lobe. "Hah! Don't ever underestimate the value of a few good cuddles, mister!"

He snuggled back for a moment before tilting her chin up. "We need to get going soon Linds. You can't just *keep* him."

"Please Drake I-" Lyndsey stopped in mid sentence by the shrill piercing shriek of a scream.

She stiffened in Drakes arms and Billy shrieked again.

Jesus it sounded like Billy was in pain!

Without a backwards glance at Drake she broke free from his arms and bolted from the room.

146

Chapter 23

Come on, come on. Susan glanced at her watch for the thousandth time, as she fidgeted in her seat. The waiting room was warm and stuffy. People of every age slumped in chairs, sneezing and coughing. Her ten o'clock appointment was already thirty minutes late. With the sleeve of her shirt used as a breathing mask, she looked around the room. Her legs bounced up and down with impatience noticing the old fellow across from her blowing into a soiled hanky. *Wasn't this great! She was sitting in the middle of a flu and cold epidemic.*

God she hated germs. The old man's soiled hanky caused her to shudder and she reached into her purse searching for the bottle of hand sanitizer she always carried with her. Susan squeezed a generous amount into her palm, rubbing her hands together vigorously. With the germs taken care of, she spotted the empty pill bottle in the bottom of her open purse. Only a few hours ago she'd taken her last pill.

Her last pill!

She almost gone without it, but the thought of going into the doctor's office feeling anxious was more than she could bear. Lately, her medication didn't seem to be working as well. Maybe some of her pills were placebos. Was that even possible?

A touch on her shoulder interrupted her thoughts. "Excuse me, do you have the time?"

An elderly woman sat next to her clutching her purse and cane. Susan glanced at her watch. "Ten thirty." She informed her.

The woman released her grip on the cane long enough to clutch at Susan's arm. "If they keep me waiting any longer, I might not make it to my own funeral!" she snorted. "At my age, you don't have much time left."

Startled, Susan tried pulling her arm free of the woman's grasp, but the woman's arthritic fingers remained firmly entrenched in Susan's shirt sleeve. Hoping the woman wasn't carrying the plague she managed to assure her. "I'm sure it won't be long now."

The elderly woman snorted again. "My hip's been acting up, my son says I need to get in and see the doctor about it. I know they won't do a damn thing, but to satisfy him, I'm here. He's always threatening to have me put into one of those *care* homes. Ha! Care home my ass! More like warehousing for the nearly dead."

"Well I ah... Susan hesitated, not sure what to say.

Finally releasing her arm, the woman picked up her cane and slammed the ground with it. "You know, the only good thing about growing old, is when you're running out of time it really forces you to speak your mind. You say what you mean, because it might be the last thing you ever say. No more bullshit!"

Susan's eyes widened as she looked at her again. She'd always thought you became somewhat *less* as you aged. Less forceful, less spirited or temperamental, less able even, strangely, she found the woman beside her interesting.

The wrinkled face peered at her for a moment. "I've shocked you haven't I?"

"A little" she agreed.

"My son says I'm always doing that, shocking people. He says I need to stop it and it's probably a sign of dementia."

"Well, I'm not sure. Ah, you could probably ask your doctor about it."

"Well I'm sure! There's nothing demented about me. If anything is demented, it's the society we live in, and our politicians, and the fact the media promotes fear and horror, and anything *good* isn't news worthy. My husband, God rest his soul, would watch the news every night and bemoan what our world was coming to. Of course he never did anything about it. He just watched and moaned. And that's what it's come down to. We're a society of watchers and moaners. Nobody wants to get involved anymore. They all just sit back and complain. Our country is in a fine mess, and it's getting worse every minute." Her cane hit the ground twice as if to emphasize her point.

Susan glanced at her watch again. She was feeling jittery and anxious, and the woman's thumps weren't helping any either. Each *thwack* nearly caused her to jump out of her skin.

"I'm sorry dear. It looks like I've upset you. Are you okay? How rude of me. Are you very sick?" The elderly woman asked her face wrinkled in concern.

"Oh no I'm fine. Really." trailing off she realized that fine people probably did not sit in doctors waiting rooms. "I, ah, just have the flu, or something."

"Well it might be menopause. It looks like you're the right age for it. God knows, nothing can ever prepare us woman for that!"

A young nurse with a sheaf of papers in her hand interrupted their conversation. "Susan, please come with me."

"Nice to meet you," Susan said relieved to put an end to their conversation.

The woman grasped her hand. Her grip was firm as she squeezed Susan's hand between her own. "We're all running out of time you know. Make the best of what you have left." She instructed.

Susan pulled free of her grasp and nodding at the strange old woman turned to follow the young nurses departing back. *We're all running out of time* echoed in the recesses of her mind.

The young nurse bounced down the hallway stopping in front of a closed door and opened it. She turned to Susan with a smile saying, "The doctor will be with you shortly."

Just like a ballerina, the young nurse swivelled as she gracefully exited the room. Her youthful body needed nothing more than its rightful age to portray art in motion. Susan thought about the old woman's hands as she glanced at hers wondering if they would bend and twist too. Life. It was so damn cruel. When you were young and beautiful, you never really knew it. You were never satisfied with the way you looked, always wanting to be prettier or thinner. Then one day you look back, realizing you were gorgeous and you'd give anything to have nice tight skin again.

Susan heard footsteps nearing in the corridor and her heart raced. She hated these appointments and having to ask for the pills. It felt like she was begging, or a drug addict, for God's sakes.

The door swung open revealing her doctor. "Hello Susan." She stated sitting down. "Just a moment please."

Dr. Carter tapped the keypad on her computer, her fingers flying over the keys. She looked up and noticed Susan's interest. With a little frown she shifted the computer blocking Susan's view. Anger flared. How dare the woman block the screen! After all, it was her patient files she was looking at.

"I see you're overdue for a pap smear." Dr. Carter said giving her a long stare before turning back to the computer screen. "You'll need to book a longer appointment next time." With a final tap she clicked a key putting the computer to sleep and then turned her chair to face Susan.

Susan squirmed. She hated eye contact, particularly today as she sat feeling like a criminal.

"What can I do for you?" Dr. Carter asked.

Susan cleared her suddenly dry throat. "I um, well, I was hoping I could get another refill on my prescription."

Doctor Carter scowled. "Susan we discussed this before. This medication was only temporary. Did you make the call I asked you to?"

"I did, Susan nodded. "I start tomorrow. I don't think I can even get through the doors without the medication though.

150

Jagged Little Lies

Things seem to be getting worse. I think they made a mistake with my last refill."

"How so?" Dr. Carter frowned, staring at her intently. "What do you mean, they made a mistake?"

"Well the medication doesn't seem to be working as well. I wondered if maybe the pharmacy was adding placebos."

Doctor Carter's brow shot up. "The pharmacy would never put in placebos. They only do that on studies, never prescriptions. No, what's happening Susan, is you're developing tolerance."

"What kind of tolerance?"

"Susan, like I explained to you on your past visits, this medication is a temporary fix to get you through a short period of time. It's highly addictive and over time, you develop tolerance. It means you need a higher dosage than the one you started with."

"Oh."

"I'm going to write you out this script, but only as a tapering off measure. I want you to follow the instructions *exactly*."

"What exactly is a tapering off measure?"

"It means you'll be doing less, not more, of this medication as you wean off. You won't need it. The group you'll be attending will help you deal with your pain in a much healthier way than turning to medication." With a furious scribble on her script pad Dr. Carter tore off the piece of paper and handed it to Susan.

"I'm not sure how attending a group can help with my pain and -" Susan stopped as Doctor Carter interrupted her sentence.

"Look, I'm not going to argue with you Susan. Just follow the instructions and book the appointment for your pap on the way out. Good luck with your group." She smiled briefly before leaving the office.

The door closed leaving Susan alone. Anger and resentment boiled within. She seethed with it. Sometimes she just hated people, looking at the blank computer screen she wondered if she could pull up her file.

It was so tempting. *What did the doctor write about her?* Clicking the mouse she stared at the blank screen hoping to wake it up. Her heart raced with fear. *Dammit!* What were you supposed to do? It didn't look like any computer program she was familiar with.

The prescription pad to her left beckoned, calling her name. Susan glanced at the piece of paper she held in her hand. *Twenty pills that was all.* Her heart sunk. *They wouldn't last long and then what?*

A cheery laugh warned her someone was drawing near. She recognized the pert steps of the young nurse.

No Susan, don't! Her conscious warned her.

The footsteps grew nearer.

Her purse yawned, wide-open.

A need far greater than anything she'd ever known before, reached out and snatched up the pad.

Chapter 24

Miranda reprinted the label for the third time. Jeez she better get it together. Coffee, maybe it would help. On her third cup from the pot she made earlier she entered the reception area. "John, I'm ready for you."

John was in his favorite place. Main stage in front of the cash register as he preened accepting accolades from his aging clientele. "About time Mandy!" he declared, chuckling with his *good old boy* humour.

Her back stiffened and she snapped "It's Miranda."

John looked over at her in surprise. His mouth hung in a perfect O, before changing to a look of stern disapproval. She had just broken the golden rule. Never *ever* let your customers see anything other than smiling faces and pleasant attitudes.

She withered in his gaze for a brief second before he returned his attention to Mr. Thom. His face morphed once again changing from stern disapproval to beaming sunshine. John spoke eloquently as he instructed Mr. Thom in the taking of his medication.

Mr. Thom grasped John's hand shaking it frantically. "Thank you John. Thank you."

John stood in the glow of Mr. Thom's praise as if it were nothing more than his due before returning once more to Miranda. With their one customer now departing the building he returned to his usual countenance. The one that she knew was the *real* John.

His lip curled in disdain as he spoke to her. "Don't you ever correct me in front of customers again *Mandy*."

"Yes John." The words came easily. She knew there was no point in pushing it and she did snap at him.

John started calling her Mandy after Declan came to visit her at work. He overheard Declan saying it and he'd been calling her

Mandy ever since. Only her closest friends and family called her Mandy. They were people she loved and John was most definitely *not* in the same category.

"Did you finish the labels?"

"Most of them," She replied nodding her head. "Well enough you can fill the next batch."

He eyed her shrewdly. "You're not as sharp as you used to be young lady. I don't care what personal problems you might be having, I won't have it affecting your job."

Needing to do something, she took a sip from her coffee cup. Miranda averted her eyes and looked at the floor. She wished she could tell him what she really thought. Instead, she bit her tongue.

John pointed a finger at her. "Consider this a warning. Now get back to work."

The telephone beside them rang, bringing an abrupt end to their conversation. Miranda sighed with relief as John picked up the phone. In his radio announcer voice, he greeted the client at the other end.

She had only taken two steps away from him when she heard the sunshine in his voice turn to ice. "Miranda, it's for you."

John's face looked like he'd just sucked on a lemon as she grabbed the phone from his hand. Unless it was an emergency she wasn't suppose to receive personal calls. "Hello?" she asked.

"Miranda," her mother launched right in. "I just got off the phone with Lisa. She is absolutely devastated. Tell me you didn't really mean what you said."

Her back burned with the heat from John's eyes on it. "Ah... mom, I'm sorry I can't talk right now. I'm sure everything will be fine. Don't worry. I'll call you when I get home."

"Miranda, Lisa says she thinks you might be seeing Declan again. Dear God Miranda, please tell me this isn't true!"

Jagged Little Lies

Good lord, her mother sounded like she was on the verge of tears. "Everything will be fine mom, now I really have to go." Miranda hung the phone up and turned to John.

"Sorry about that. My mom just found out my uncle is being admitted to the hospital."

John relaxed a little, the cold look fading from his face. "Back to it then," he said.

"Right," she agreed.

Miranda busied herself printing out the labels. John's presence in the back room helped to keep her mind focused. He sat at his desk one eye on her, the other on his computer screen, while playing a game of solitaire. In a way it was a relief to work and not think. Miranda finished bottling and labeling the medications.

"Okay John, they're ready."

John stretched, his gaze fastening on the row of bottles waiting for his approval. He was supposed to take a final look at the labels and medications inside the bottles, to make sure none were mixed up or mislabelled.

"Why don't you do it? I will supervise." He said, turning back to his game.

"Oh... well, I guess I could." Miranda eyed the labels and their contents. Using the computer program, she cross-referenced the client's medications with the new ones being bottled. The last thing she needed was a client having a reaction to a medication because she hadn't researched it properly.

Her eyes scanned each word and bottle. Searching vigilantly, Miranda checked and rechecked, before she was satisfied. The bell above the door chirped announcing their next customer.

John tapped the keyboard closing his game. "Good timing. I just won." He mumbled as he left to enter the reception area.

"Arnold! Great to see you, you're looking well," he purred, lying through his teeth.

Miranda bagged Arnold's medication while standing next to John. She rang up the purchase before handing the bag to John.

With Arnold's money in his hand, John explained the importance of taking his medication with food.

Arnold stood starstruck as John continued with his speech. Miranda watched, awed, as always, at how easily John could turn it on and off.

But John wasn't the only one who knew how to play the game. It seemed she was learning fast, too. The lies were coming so much easier now. Miranda thought about Lisa. How dare she call her mother and get her involved in all of this!

Why couldn't she catch a break? It wasn't like she went around telling everyone who they should and shouldn't spend their time with. She was an adult for Chrissakes! It was nobody's business but hers, who she spent time with. She wasn't a dummy. She knew it was over between them. They just needed closure and she was going to make sure they got it.

With a wave and "goodbye" to John, Miranda left for home. *Maybe Declan would call tonight.* Just the thought hurried her steps. Miranda wondered what he was doing at this very moment. Maybe she could bring pizza on her next visit. God knows, he sure looked like he could use more meat on him. She'd have to phone the prison and find out if she was allowed.

Home sooner than she realized, Miranda briefly wondered how she'd gotten there so fast. The phone was ringing as she neared her door. *I knew it!* Miranda smiled and raced across the linoleum.

Declan! Declan! Her heart soared.

The receiver almost slid out of her sweaty hand as she shouted, "Hello!"

"Miranda?" a worried voice said.

Winded and disappointed, her heart plummeted.

Chapter 25

Warm, it was so warm. Declan floated in a sea of bliss. *This must be what heaven feels like.* His body was swathed in soft clouds. He'd never felt so good in all of his life. His physical body faded to a non-existence. He was somewhere between sleep and wake. He drifted in an euphoric haze.

The bed below him trembled. The rooster crowed, "Hey boy, time to get to work."

Declan laughed, floating off again. Time faded, in and then out, meaningless, until an earthquake shook his bed.

"Let's go boy."

Rooster's grumble penetrated his bliss-soaked brain. Declan sat up looking around his small cell and noticed things he'd missed on previous viewings. The crack just off of the tiny window spoke to him of profound possibilities. He gazed at it in awe, losing all sense of time once more.

"They'll be opening our cells anytime now boy. You remember what we talked about?"

Declan nodded, the motion caused him to giggle.

"Jesus boy," Rooster said eyeing him. "You're higher than a kite. We need to bring you down a little."

Declan's vision blurred and his head spun, as Rooster gave him two quick slaps on his cheeks. "Hey." He protested.

"That's better boy. I can't have you going out there looking like a blubbering fool, now can I? You wouldn't last two minutes."

The shininess wore off. The cell changed back into a prison of bars, the blissful seas fading somewhere distant. Declan still felt the smooth pull, but it warred with the giant in front of him.

"I'll start you with one." Rooster mumbled something Declan didn't quite catch and then spoke clearer, "And remember boy, its cash or cigarettes. You got that?"

157

His head started to throb. He winced, knowing it was a sure sign the pink pearl was past its peak. "Yeah," he replied. *Maybe he could pocket one.* He could always say he'd lost it.

"And don't try any funny stuff." Rooster made his point by wagging a finger at him. "I might have something for your efforts when you get back."

The noise outside their cage grew as feeding time neared. Rooster offered him another plastic wrapped package. Declan palmed the package, admiring the satiny-smooth feel of it. He placed it inside his sock. He felt better just knowing it was there.

The bars slid open and bodies jostled against each other in their brief attempts at freedom. Declan joined the swarm of lost humanity, relieved to be free of the Rooster, he moved with the crowd. Blue jumpsuits and ink, flowed down the hallways.

Twitch sidled up next to him. "I hear you might be carrying."

Man word really gets around, Declan thought. But he didn't say it. Instead, he grunted a noncommittal "maybe."

Twitch took it as a yes. "I might be able to help you out, for a little *something* of course."

Christ, they all wanted a piece of you in these shark-infested waters. Ignoring Twitch, Declan followed the crowd into the dining hall. Picking up a tray, he stood in line. Twitch stood behind him and whispered into his ear.

"See that guy over there? He's a nasty piece of work." Twitch said nodding to indicate the muscle bound inmate further up the line. The inmate's body bulged within the confines of the blue material. His head was bald and smooth.

Declan wished Twitch would shut the hell up. His whispering was like sandpaper rubbing in his ear. The sea of bliss drifted further out, becoming a distant memory on the horizon.

"You don't want to mess with him." Twitch said twitching beside him.

Jagged Little Lies

Christ what was this guy on? "Shut the fuck up." He hissed.

The line moved forward at a snail's pace. Declan's stomach rumbled in response to the smell of food. *I better eat while I can.* It wouldn't be long before it would all begin again.

"I mean he is one," Twitch stopped abruptly, as the man he spoke of turned in their direction.

The big man stared Twitch down, shooting him a *look* that said it all. Declan tried to appear nonchalant as the muscle-bound ape took in his measure. With feigned ignorance Declan stared at the food. He turned to Twitch and said, "Mmmmm this smells good."

Twitch blanched and ignoring Declan hung his head

The muscle-bound man still stared at them. His face looked chiselled from granite. His lips pulled back in a sneer as he made slashing motions over his throat. His message was clear.

"Oh jeez... we're dead." Twitch muttered his leg jerking as his body shook.

"What do you mean, *we*? What's his problem? What does he have against you anyways?"

Muscles filled his tray with enough for three and joined a table of look-a-likes. Smooth, bald, shiny heads turned as Declan and Twitch walked by.

"I ah, sorta ratted him out." Twitch admitted.

"What do you mean by, *sorta*?"

"I overheard some talk about him giving the shank to one of my buddies." Twitch said under his breath. "And I ah, kinda let my buddy know, for a price of course."

"Where's your buddy now?"

"They've got him over in protective custody."

Declan was beginning to clue in as to why Twitch, twitched. And he had a pretty good idea what Twitch's *price* was. He wondered where Twitch kept his stash.

"We can sit here." Twitch announced as he joined a table of lean, dark haired men.

The table grew quiet upon their arrival. Declan sat down and began eating. He could *feel* the eyes upon him. Mean, hungry, viscous eyes. He raised his head staring back, the pink pill giving him a sense of false courage.

"Hola amigo. Como esta?" Twitch said breaking the ice, just before all hell broke loose.

The lean, dark haired men, all spoke at once. Declan didn't understand what Twitch had just said, but the body language around the table was easily discernible. Harsh tones, in rapid fire, circled the table excitedly. Declan continued eating.

Twitch gulped, his tone pleading, as he conversed. The conversation grew louder and after a short pause Twitch's face paled. With his eyes nearly bugged out of his face he rose from the table with his tray in hand and looked at Declan. "They want me to leave."

Declan started to get up too but was restrained by the largest of the lean, looking at Twitch for guidance, Twitch merely shrugged.

"They want you to stay." He said turning his back on Declan.

Twitch hadn't gone more than a few steps when a blue suited leg shot out tripping him. Twitch landed hard. His tray exploded off the smoothly polished floor, with his dinner landing a few feet away.

The noise stopped instantly. The silence was eerie and filled with threat.

Twitch got to his knees.

The guard nearest their table sauntered over, looking at Twitch with an amused expression he asked, "What seems to be the problem?"

"No problem." Twitch assured him.

The guard smiled, eyeing Twitch and the table. "Right, clean it up then."

Jagged Little Lies

Twitch stood smiling. He cleaned up the mess with his napkin. He placed the remnants of his dinner on the tray and left quietly.

Twitch walked in the direction of the trash cans, his receding footsteps signaling an *all clear*. Conversation returned edged in laughter, as the inmates pointed at Twitch's departing back.

Declan pushed his tray away, no longer hungry. The familiar twist of his bowels had begun. Nausea crept up the back of his throat. His leg tapped, beating out an old familiar tableau, one of angst and misery.

The table of inmates quieted, staring at him intently.

The largest of the lean smirked, holding out his hand expectantly.

Declan didn't need to speak their language to know what they wanted and placing his hand palm-side up, he spoke in a universal language. *What are you gonna to give me for it?* The words remained unspoken, but the meaning was clear.

The largest of the lean glowered, his eyes wide open and un-blinking. Declan's leg rat-tat-tatted underneath them.

They stared deadlocked, each with an open palm waiting for the other to give.

The lean man finally blinked and smiled. His teeth were great white chicklets against his dark skin.

Sweat gathered on Declan's brow. He willed his body still. Moisture gathered under his arms, and on his forehead.

A drop of sweat rolled down, stinging his eye.

Declan narrowed his eyes and sat up straight, fighting the urge to blink.

161

LORELIE ROZZANO

Chapter 26

Billy stiffened. He screamed. Lyndsey stared down at him writhing in her arms unsure what to do.

Drake circled them rubbing his hands together. His face twisted in worry and helplessness. "Maybe he has the flu or something," he offered hopefully.

Hopefully, because to Lyndsey's untrained ear, it sounded like Billy was dying. "I don't know what to do Drake!" She wailed.

"Here, give him to me." He said, opening his arms wide to receive the screaming bundle.

Lyndsey placed Billy's stiff body into Drakes arms. "Why is he getting all stiff? Is that normal?"

"I don't know Linds. It doesn't look *normal.*"

Billy's face turned a darker shade of red than before. His eyes screwed tightly shut as he shrieked again. Drake paced with Billy in his arms, speaking softly to him, "Shhh little Billy, you're okay, everything's all right. There, there." He said, patting Billy's backside hoping to dislodge the gas, *if* this was the problem.

"Is gas really that painful?" Lyndsey wondered, thinking the same thing as Drake. "Maybe he's just hungry?" Lyndsey chewed her fingernail helplessly. "Do you think he still takes a bottle? He looks a little old. What should we do?"

Drake bounced Billy before saying, "Try warming some milk. Maybe it'll help."

"I wonder if he's ever had just *regular* milk before. Lyndsey said filling the cup halfway with milk and pushing start on the microwave.

Billy's shrieks quieted for a minute, his body stiff and his chest heaving from exhaustion. A tear slipped down Lyndsey's

163

cheek as she stroked his head and crooned. "Oh my sweet, sweet little boy, please be okay."

Billy's puffy eyes opened and he reached for her. Lyndsey picked him up and Billy shrieked. Handling him as gently as she could, she looked at Drake. "It's like he's made out of glass. Just touching him seems to hurt him."

Drake nodded, opening the microwave to retrieve the cup of warm milk. After a quick hand wash, he used his finger to test the milks temperature. "This should be fine."

Billy buried his head in Lyndsey's chest. His hands plucked at her shirt, as his mouth sought her breast. "Oh oh, we might have a problem here Drake."

"Huh?" Turning from the fridge he shot her a questioning look.

"Look." she said, pointing to Billy.

Drake's jaw dropped open as he watched Billy fretting with Lyndsey's shirt. Billy squirmed, his legs kicking and screamed. Lyndsey pulled Billy away from her shirt, sitting him on her lap. Billy screamed louder, his face turning purple.

"Here Billy, try this. Num, num." Drake said, pretending to take a sip of the milk and offering it to Billy.

"You don't think Dee would still have been breast feeding him, do you?"

"I don't know. He's a little old for it. Damn!" Drake said grabbing for the paper towel, as Billy spit warm milk over the front of his new pajamas. "He sure doesn't seem to know how to drink out of a cup though."

"He must. I saw one in their room." Lyndsey moved Billy shifting him away from her blouse.

Drake threw the paper towel into the garbage. "It's easy to see what he wants Linds, and it's something you can't give him."

Lyndsey gently pulled Billy's hands away from her blouse again and tried to distract him with the cup of milk. Placing it to her lips she said, "Look Billy, num, num!"

Jagged Little Lies

Billy pushed the milk away his body stiffening once more. He screamed bloody murder. His shrieks were so loud she almost dropped him. Trying not to panic she whispered, "Something's really wrong Drake."

Drake took the cup from her hand and emptying it into the sink said, "I know."

Billy's cries grew louder making further conversation impossible. Billy's body no longer folded into her lap. Instead, he lay plank-like in her arms. Lyndsey got up from her chair and holding onto him the best she could, she gave Billy to Drake, not trusting herself to carry him.

She quickly gathered up her keys, purse and the throw blanket for Billy. Drake followed and they headed for the car. Lyndsey got into the back seat and together they strapped Billy into the seat belt. His screams echoed off the car's interior. Lyndsey strapped her own seat belt on while sitting next to Billy, as Drake backed the car out of the garage.

Her heart raced with anxiety and she felt shaky all over. *What was wrong with Billy? Did they do something wrong? Was he was allergic to milk? Was he dying? Please God, please, please, please, don't let him be dying.*

The motion of the car seemed to soothe Billy. He sagged against her hip, his body releasing from its plank-like state. He shuddered and she held her breath. His shrieks lessened turning to sobs.

Lyndsey gasped, the pent up air leaving her lungs. Listening to Billy, her heart broke. If there was ever a sound for pure, unadulterated sadness, this was it. *It was just so dammed unfair. Why did little, innocent babies, have to hurt like this? Are you listening God? Why?*

Billy sobbed with gusto, choking on his mucus. Lyndsey hadn't felt this helpless in a long time. It was agonizing.

"Almost there honey," Drake reassured them from the front seat.

Billy's sobs slowed with hiccups. His head bobbed against her. Drake pulled into the emergency entrance. "I'm going to drop you off first and then park," he said as he pulled up to the front doors.

Drake parked next to an ambulance. He put the car in park, and opened the back door to let Lyndsey out with Billy. Billy was asleep and looked peaceful.

Drake raised an eyebrow. She nodded. Drake unbuckled Billy, waking him in the process. Billy's shrieks started immediately. Lyndsey got out of the car reaching for Billy. Drake helped to hold him in place as she reached for her purse.

"I'm not sure what I'm going to tell them." Lyndsey worried.

"You'll figure it out." He said giving her a quick kiss. "I'll be right in."

Drake drove away looking for a place to park and she turned with Billy in her arms. The emergency entrance doors swung open and she entered the building.

The lights overhead were bright and Billy turned his face into her shoulder muffling the volume of his screams. Lyndsey's eyes scanned the interior of the building looking for an admitting counter. People of every shape, size and color, stood or sat, waiting to be seen. Head wounds, twisted limbs, punctures and bloodied bandages, all announced she'd come to the right place.

Fingers crossed, Lyndsey stood in line. An argument broke out as a man in line yelled about having to wait. Billy stiffened in her arms hearing the loud voices, and then added his wailing to the volume.

The doors opened and she saw Drake hurrying through them, his eyes searching. Relief washed over her as he neared, and standing beside him, she borrowed some of his strength.

The man at the front of the line banged his fist on the counter shouting, "I'm a taxpaying citizen and I want to be seen *now!*"

166

Jagged Little Lies

Billy jumped in her arms, shuddering in response to the bang. Lyndsey nuzzled his neck and marvelled at the softness of his skin. Drake tightened his arm around them as they stood waiting.

A pretty nurse came around the corner and greeted them. "Please come with me." She said softly, her face mirroring the concern furrowing her brow.

Lyndsey stepped out of line and turned to follow the nurse, when the argumentative man noticed, "Hey! We were here first!" He shouted.

Billy jumped whimpering. The nurse shot the man a look scowling. The enraged man seemed to come to his senses, his cheeks reddening. With a final look at the newly embarrassed man, the nurse turned back to Lyndsey and Drake and said, "Please follow me."

Holding hands, Lyndsey and Drake followed the little nurse into the bowels of the building. Stretchers lined the hallways with patients lying prone. Lyndsey flashed back to a time when she'd also been on a hospital stretcher, in one of the sheet-like gowns. It was devastating to lie there, hopeless and broken.

Billy stiffened in her arms, pulling her from old memories. "He's doing it again Drake."

The nurse stopped at a cubicle and pulled open the curtains, which held a crib. Lyndsey lowered Billy into it as the nurse pulled up the aluminum rail bars. Lyndsey gently wrapped the throw blanket around Billy. Billy didn't seem to notice, lying elongated and stiff.

"How long has he been like this?" The nurse asked.

"Just since he woke up from his nap, at least I think..." Lyndsey trailed off not sure where to begin.

"He's not ours." Drake interjected. "His mother is a friend of ours, and she um, gave Billy to us."

The petite nurse lips formed an O, as her eyebrows raised. Lyndsey knew exactly what she was thinking. Only this time she was on the other end of it.

Her tone neutral, the nurse said only, "The doctor will be here shortly and we'll need a blood and urine sample."

"Why do you have to take blood? Won't that hurt him?" Lyndsey cried, her old paranoia of needles resurfacing.

The nurse probed Billy with gentle fingers starting at his head and working her way down his body before replying, "A little, but it's necessary."

Lyndsey stood at Billy's bedside. Billy stopped whimpering. He lay stiffly, his big beautiful eyes, glazed. He looked scared.

Lyndsey's heart lurched knowing that this *help* was adding to the overall damage of Billy.

"Can you please get him undressed?" The nurse requested, satisfied there were no broken bones.

Drake helped Lyndsey get the sleeper off Billy's rigid body. The air grew chilly as the nurse noticed the discolored bruises over Billy's body. She said, "I'll be right back."

Lyndsey covered Billy with the throw as she noticed the nurse departing the cubicle on quick steps. She caught a glimpse of her face just as she grasped the curtain, before pulling it firmly closed behind her.

The nurse's face was pinched, her nostrils flared in anger.

Worried she turned to Drake. "You don't think -" Shouts and yelling erupted down the hallway stopping her mid sentence.

Drake opened the curtain peering out. He noticed policemen coming up the hallway, and pulled it closed it again. To Lyndsey he said "Jesus, it's a zoo in here!"

"Drake, I don't want him to get a needle."

"Linds, it's just a little poke. He probably won't even feel it."

"What are we going to tell them Drake?"

"I don't know honey. Let's just see what they ask us."

"They'll give him back to us, won't they?"

Jagged Little Lies

"Lind's we can't -" Drake stopped, as the curtain was yanked open.

They turned expecting to see the doctor. But they were wrong. Two angry looking policemen entered the room. The nurse stepped in behind them.

Billy screamed at the sight of the uniformed men. The nurse wrapped Billy in the throw blanket and lifted him from the crib.

Billy reached for Lyndsey and she moved. The policeman blocked her way and grabbed her by the arm.

"Hey!" Drake protested, trying to protect her. The larger of the two police officers shook his head frowning at Drake, as he held firmly to his arm.

"What the hell!" Lyndsey exploded.

The nurse carried Billy from the room. His face was red from screaming, as his legs kicked while his little arms reached over the back of the nurse for her.

The curtain parted and the nurse carrying Billy left the room.

Chapter 27

Susan glanced in the rear view mirror. Nothing. *Calm down, calm down.* Her hands shook on the steering wheel, expecting to see the police any second now, as her eyes searched the rear view mirror yet again. *Were the police already at her house? Should she go to a hotel, or leave town? But then what about Declan?*

The thin thread of reasoning she'd held to seemed to have snapped, leaving her feeling completely out of control. Her hands wobbled and she stared at them as they locked onto the steering wheel. *Whose hands were these?* She wondered, still shocked at the act they just committed. It was like her hands belonged to someone else. A stranger, or criminal, certainly not her, for she'd never done anything like this before.

Back in the doctor's office, her mind said *no.* She heard it, clear as a bell. But her hand snaked out anyways. Then a quick knock at the door and it opened revealing the pert nurse asking, "All done?"

Susan nodded her head not trusting herself to speak, and standing on shaky legs the nurse gave her a questioning look. "Is everything okay?"

"I'm fine." She insisted, clearly not.

With her heart in her throat she'd left the building. *What in the hell possessed her?* She kept waiting for the call. *Thief!* With every step she took, she expected to hear it. The word rattled in her skull.

Odd, she made it to the car without incident. A moment of panic came when she reached into her purse and couldn't find the keys. She was worried she left them behind. But no, there they were in the bottom of her purse, with all her other odds and ends she hoarded these days. Susan glimpsed the large white pad while pulling the keys free and terror seized her again. Her hand trembled violently and she dropped the keys. As she bent to retrieve them, she noticed the missing key fob. *Dammit it, she'd grabbed the wrong set of keys!* With trembling hands she tried inserting the key into the lock. Her hand shook wildly and she missed, scratching the car's paint. "Please, please." She whimpered, fearing at any moment someone would run from the building yelling, *stop that woman! Thief!*

With a wild look over her shoulder *just in case,* she noticed a young man watching her from a nearby car. She turned, but not quick enough.

"Here, let me help you." He offered, through the open window and crossing from his car to hers, took the keys from her shaking fingers as he opened the door.

"Thanks," Susan mumbled, sliding into the car.

"Bad news?" He questioned.

"Could be." She affirmed, closing the door and driving away.

Now she was a criminal. Except that she wasn't. Jeez she wanted to see Declan on a *visit*, not be his cell mate! After driving aimlessly, she decided it was just too risky to go home right now. With a jerky right she pulled into the shopping mall. Shopping was something which had always soothed her in the past, but she was way beyond soothing today.

The script in her purse needed filling. She wouldn't be able to function without it. Need overrode fear and steeling herself for what was to come, she climbed out of the car. The mall doors opened with a loud *whoosh* and Susan walked through glancing at passersby.

God she hoped she didn't know anyone. This wasn't her usual shopping spot, or pharmacy, so she *should* be alright. There was no way in hell she could fake normal right now. The trembles wouldn't still and she felt worse than anxious, she felt *paranoid.* Susan glanced nervously at the passersby once again sure they were whispering and pointing at her, somehow aware of the crime she just committed.

A group of young teenagers pressed against her as they passed, snickering and pushing each other. One stopped to mumble "sorry" as he passed by.

She snarled, "Watch where you're going!"

The young man retracted his *sorry* with a one-fingered salute as he joined his buddies. They looked at her and snickered before moving on, pushing their way down the malls corridor.

A pharmacy sign blinked *open* in bright neon up ahead and she stopped, sitting on the bench provided for weary shoppers. *Should she go in like this?* She needed a moment to unwind. Her shoulders sagging against the hard bench and wiggling her jaw trying to lessen the kinks from grinding her back teeth, she sat opening and closing her mouth. Somewhat embarrassed, but not really giving a shit, she imagined what a strange sight she must be. On the edge of hysteria, sitting on a bench and looking like a newly landed cod fish. Her jaw popped as it loosened. With deep breaths she tried calming her frazzled nerves, while picturing the little white pill.

Soon, she'd feel better.

"Susan?"

Her eyes popped open and she closed her mouth. Lori stood in front of her with a curious look on her face. Anger flared inside her chest. *Of all people, why did it have to be Lori?* Forcing a smile she said, "Hi Lori."

"Wow, what are the chances? I don't see you in forever and then *twice* in one week." Lori sat down next to her on the bench and Susan's heart sunk.

Lori transferred her purchases onto the bench beside her and turned to Susan taking a closer look. "You don't look so hot. Are you okay?"

"I'm fine. Just run down. I must have caught the flu or something."

"Oh Susan! That's awful. I can bring over some of my chicken soup, if you like," Lori said, smiling at the implied memory.

At one time Lori had been a godsend. Declan was really sick and she'd been up all night. The next morning there was a knock at the door. Barely able to keep her eyes open she'd answered and there was Lori, with a big pot of chicken soup *and* a shoulder to lean on. Together they nursed Declan back to health and finished off the soup.

Susan looked at Lori for a second before shaking her head, "Thanks Lori, but I'm good."

A frown replaced the smile and Lori reached out her hand. "Susan, I wish you would let me help."

Anger flared again. "For Chrissakes Lori, I don't need your pity."

Lori withdrew her hand. Her eyes shrewd, she searched Susan's face before asking, "What's happening to you?"

Not able to play the game any longer she didn't try. "I would think that would be obvious. Don't pretend you don't know. Everybody *knows*. I'm sure my family has been the topic of *neighborly* discussion many times. And I'm sick to death of it."

Lori's eyes widened. "But what's happening to *you* Susan?"

"What do you mean *me*?"

"*You*, it's like you're not even the same person anymore."

Jesus what kind of idiot was this woman? "Of course I'm not the same person *Lori*, she said sarcastically. I don't live in fairy tales, like *some* people I know."

Lori blinked and looked shocked. "You know very well I don't live in a fairy tale. That was hurtful Susan. The old *you* would never have said anything like this."

Susan stared into Lori's wounded eyes. She felt nothing. No remorse, no guilt, nothing, except suspicious. Her eyes narrowed. "Yeah, well the old *me* is long gone Lori. She left with the rest of my family."

Jagged Little Lies

Lori rose off the bench rather stiffly and gathering her purchases and shaking her head said, "You need help Susan." Lori paused, thinking for a moment as if considering saying more.

Susan met Lori's eyes and any thought of further conversation resolved.

As Susan watched Lori's retreating back she smiled. *You're right about one thing Lori. I do need help.*

And entering the pharmacy she went in search of it.

Chapter 28

Miranda yawned while washing her face with cold water. She hadn't slept well at all. And the sound of her mother's voice playing *over* and *over* in her head hadn't helped any either. If only she hadn't picked up the phone. Jeez, listening to her mom go on and on about Declan was the last thing she needed. Seriously, she wished she could tell them all to go to hell.

An ice cube dripped between her fingers, as she stood in front of the mirror hoping to repair the damage. Her eyes were puffy and she closed them as she pressed ice cubes to her lids. Images of Declan surfaced. Declan just out of the shower. Declan in bed. Declan, running on the beach, chasing her. Declan laughing, always laughing, until he wasn't.

Hot tears mixed with ice and the cube soon melted. God she really couldn't remember ever having hurt this badly. It felt like she was dying.

Damn you Declan! She thought it would get easier. But it didn't. Who knew time would induce such great, gaping holes. She'd been so numb in court. The words were just words. There was no way to realize how the slam of the gavel would change her world. That day her happiness had been imprisoned just as surely as Declan had.

At first, she was so angry it was easy not to miss him. Miranda blamed him for everything that happened, but it wasn't long before her anger turned elsewhere. She started doubting herself. Eventually she grew tired and then numb.

Ha! Her face twisted contemptuously. She wished she were numb now. With brisk movements she towelled her face dry and peered at it again. The ice cubes hadn't worked. Dammit! She would just have to go into work looking this way. A bottle of foundation repaired some of the damage. She spread it on thick.

Why do you put that goop on? You don't need it baby.

Get out of my head Declan!

After a final dab of makeup and a generous squirt of her citrusy body spray, she was ready. With a last look in the mirror she flicked off the switch. *Maybe she should move?* Every room in the house reminded her of Declan. But where would she go? Just the thought of packing up exhausted her. Not to mention, she was broke.

Stop it! Her brain noise rattled on incessantly as she put the kettle on. Music, that might help, she turned on the stereo and sat down to eat stale oat flakes. What she needed was a plan, a way to take back her life. A list would be helpful. Lists were something she'd been making since childhood. She felt more organized with them.

Her cereal finished, she rinsed the bowl and began mentally creating *The Plan.* She *would not* let Declan haunt her every waking moment. She *would* go to Lisa's staggette and she *would* enjoy herself. She *would* pick up her paycheck today and she *would* put some in savings. She *would* go and visit Declan this weekend and she *would* say goodbye. She *would...*

With a 'to do' list fresh in her mind and feeling somewhat better, she decided to walk to work. It was a beautiful day and for once she had the time, leaving the house she headed for the pharmacy. The bright sunshine brought out walkers. Miranda glanced at the others she passed wondering, *are their lives as messed up as mine?* She'd gotten lucky with one thing though. The police never put it together and Declan hadn't said a word about where he was getting the pills.

Would it have gone easier for him if he had? Was the punishment the same if you committed a crime while not in your right mind? Declan was high as a kite when he committed the act. She, on the other hand, had been cold stone sober. Really, they'd both been guilty of robbery. She might not have held the knife, but she was every bit as guilty.

Jagged Little Lies

Her lip curled downwards. She still couldn't believe she'd taken people's medication and given it to Declan. *Wow. Who does shit like that?* She first thought of the idea when she'd gone home for lunch one day. Declan hadn't been feeling well and she was worried about him.

He'd been in bed, white as a ghost. The garbage can stood next to the bed and Declan was in the process of using it. At the time she thought his *sickness* was due to migraine headaches and she was angry he wasn't insisting on a MRI. As she approached the bed he'd looked up at her. She's never seen him so sick, and he was cold and clammy to her touch. With a hot water bottle and a few aspirins, she'd done her best to make him feel better, but it didn't help. Back at work she worried about him all afternoon. John had left early that day, asking her to dispose of the medications which were dropped off due to no longer being used, or expiring.

A medication prescribed for migraines caught her attention. It was a powerful opiate often prescribed to cancer patients. She wondered if it would help Declan. She pocketed the medication and disposed of the rest. That was the start of it. Declan responded instantly and she felt so good being able to help him.

Of course she never saw it coming. It had kind of *grown*. Each time she took just a little bit more. At first one bottle and then two, eventually she took the whole lot. The two of them would spend hours at the kitchen table, going through other people's medication. Some they kept, some they threw away. It seemed like such a game at the time, albeit a very addictive one. It was a game of secrecy and risk and played only by them. When the pharmacy stopped receiving bottles of unwanted medications, she found other ways to help Declan. Ways that left them both devastated.

A terrible weight burdened and she wished she could change what happened. Miranda rounded the corner and was startled to see the parking lot up just ahead. She stared, looking at the cars

179

and feeling uneasy. She hadn't realized she'd walked this far. *How had she not noticed the streets she trod on? Jesus Miranda! Get it together.*

She stepped through the door of her favourite coffee shop. The familiar smells greeted her, an intoxicating blend of coffee and cinnamon. The small shop was crammed with people. The place was a goldmine and charged a fortune for their lattes and mochas. But despite, or maybe because of the price, business was booming.

While waiting her turn in line, she remembered the first time she'd come here. Declan insisted and he loved the cappuccinos. He'd asked her to find them a table while he ordered for them. The tables were small and crowded with occupants. But she managed to find them a seat at the bar, wedging herself in between the laptop-tapping customers. The cafe seemed exotic with its spicy smells and loud music. They sat for hours that day, people watching, listening to music and drinking coffee. They'd been so carefree, with nothing more important on their minds than whose coffee tasted better, while discussing the various ways they could play with their whipped cream.

She smiled at some of the images the whipped cream brought to mind. They even tried one of their ideas as soon as they'd gotten home and –

"Miss?"

Miranda's cheeks flooded with color as she looked at the fresh faced barista standing in front of her. "Ah sorry, I was ah daydreaming. What did you say?"

The barista smiled before replying, "It must have been some dream."

Miranda's cheeks grew even hotter as she paid for her purchase. "Thanks," she mumbled placing a sleeve on her cup.

Nervous now, she felt like everyone was looking at her as she exited the shop. As if somehow they'd been able to read her mind, seeing the imagery of her with Declan and the can of

Jagged Little Lies

whipped cream. The coffee stung her mouth as she took a sip, willing the erotic images from her mind. *God she was so scattered these days.* She couldn't stay focused and it was starting to scare her.

With another addition to *The Plan,* Miranda mentally checked off *stay focused.* The back door to the pharmacy drew near and she opened it cautiously. Oh no. By the looks of it, it was going to be a long day. The back room looked as if a bomb had just gone off in it and John would expect her to clean up the mess.

John always worked this way. He referred to it as his 'unorganized masterpiece.' She just called it messy. No sense getting bent out of shape over it, picking up bottles and replacing them in their rightful cupboards she got busy. While wiping down counters and cleaning the sink, Miranda hummed a little tune playing in her head. John poked his head in just as she was sweeping the floor.

John glanced at her, his big molded smile disappearing and said," You're late!"

"Uh uh," shaking her head no to negate his comment she protested. "No I wasn't late. As a matter of fact I was early. I've been cleaning." She said holding up the broom to prove it.

John studied the room for a minute scowling. "Don't forget to make up the blister pack for Mrs. Rier."

"I thought you were making it up?"

"I've been busy. You'll have to do it. Oh, and wash the floor while you're at it, I spilled some sucrose by the sink."

The sound of the bell at the front counter interrupted any further conversation. John muttered, "Oh great," before stalking off.

Miranda stuck out her tongue and made a face at his departing back. She muttered, "And a very good morning to you, too," as she got busy with the mop. Laughter bubbled from her throat at the ridiculousness of her life. She was broke, her boyfriend was in jail and she was *sort of* a thief. She hated her job, she hated John and she was losing her mind. And, for some reason, it seemed hilarious. Maybe she was becoming bipolar? She laughed again as she listened to John out front.

"Oh good morning Mrs. Rier and how are you today?" He purred.

Miranda recognized the gravelly voice of Mrs. Rier asking if her medication was ready. Mrs. Rier was a very cranky old lady and John usually sent Miranda to attend to her. Miranda loved her, especially because she was one of the only customers who didn't seem to bask in John's spotlight.

"Of course it's ready." John lied through his teeth. "Mandy, can you come out here please."

Don't call me Mandy, you ass. Pasting a smile on her face she joined John at the front counter.

"Mandy, I'm going to get Mrs. Rier's medication. Please help our next customer."

"Of course," She replied. "Mrs. Rier, have a seat please." Mrs. Rier scowled at her for a moment before moving to the bench.

Miranda faced her next customer. The woman's graying head was lowered as she fumbled in her purse. The purse trembled with the force of the woman's hand crashing around inside of it as she fought the contents before freeing a white sheet of paper and thrusting it at her. Miranda picked up the prescription and giving it a quick glance asked, "Have you ever taken this medication before?"

Miranda raised her eyes from the prescription. A look of pure hatred met her gaze.

She gasped.

Susan's lips peeled back, her finger pointing at Miranda as she snarled, "You, you little bitch. It's all your fault!"

Horrified and frozen Miranda stood rooted to the spot.

Jagged Little Lies

Susan glared, howling "You!" Her eyes were dark pinpoints of madness, before rolling up into her skull.

Miranda watched helplessly as Declan's mother crumpled to the floor.

Chapter 29

Declan patted the bulge in his crotch once again. It was a good thing his prison suit hung loosely or the contraband would be easy to see. He still couldn't believe he'd been able to pull it off. The stare down at the table was intense. A deadly game of cat and mouse, only he was the mouse. Christ he didn't belong here. Not among these players, he didn't. He was *way* out of his league.

There was a second when he'd almost blown it. It took everything he had not to look away or show fear. Any sign of fear in here, would be like bleeding into shark-infested waters. The inmates developed a keen sense of smell and could spot fear a mile away. Only the thought of his next pill kept him going.

He hoped he would get one soon. He was prepared to take on the Rooster if need be. His face remained stoic as he gritted his teeth. Man he hurt. His legs throbbed like they were broken. His meal wasn't sitting well either, and if he didn't get something into him quick, it would be coming back up

A hand slammed into his back, almost knocking him to the floor. Declan turned, searching for its owner amidst the departing crowd. A dark-haired member stood slightly to the side revealing himself, and nodding, he passed. Not sure what else to do, Declan nodded back.

Back in his cell, he climbed the ladder to his bunk. *Should he?* The Rooster wasn't here. Now would be a good time to search for his stash, eyeing the hallway he looked for the cameras. They were all over the place, they must be, but he couldn't find them. *Nah, better not,* wiping sweat from his forehead he decided to put the search off for another day.

Besides, he was starting to hurt. *Bad.*

One of the older guards poked his head in the door. "You've got a visitor."

185

"I do? Who is it?" He asked, slowly climbing down the ladder.

"What?" the guard snorted, "Do I look like your fuckin secretary." He laughed while circling Declan's wrists in steel.

Jesus, why were they were all so difficult? He followed the guard not saying another word, aware he was being watched.

Eyes of every shape and color watched his passing.

Declan followed the guard to a section of the prison he'd never before entered. He was ushered into a small room that held a round table and two plastic chairs. The guard eyed him and pointed to the chair, indicating he should sit. "Don't try any funny stuff." He warned. "I'll be right outside."

Yeah right! He tried not to smirk. Jesus he could take the old guy with one hand tied behind his back. His stomach rumbled and he winced. On second thought, he sat, his knees popping. Nausea uncoiled as his intestines gurgled.

The guard heard the gurgle and laughed. "What, the food in this joint doesn't agree with ya?" He snickered.

Declan closed his eyes, lowering his head and ignored him.

Not at all put off, the guard seemed to be having fun. "Enjoy your suite at the Ritz." He laughed as he left the room.

His finger nails drummed the table top impatiently. His bones ached in a way he'd come to dread. Nausea moved from deep within his belly, starting its climb. He searched the room for a garbage can, but didn't see one. Declan swallowed. It was bitter, hot and sour. Footsteps echoed down the hallway getting closer.

Just outside the door murmured voices and then the old guard spoke, "Be careful, you have a dangerous criminal in there." He laughed sarcastically, indicating Declan was anything but.

The door opened and Declan raised his head.

"Hello Declan." His lawyer said.

Declan's heart lurched. *Was he being released?*

Jagged Little Lies

Mr. Briggs sat down, joining him. With a poker face he stated, "You're probably wondering why I'm here."

Declan nodded, trying not to move.

Mr. Briggs looked at him questioningly. "Is your neck stiff?" His long grey brows wiggled as he spoke.

"A little." Declan agreed.

"Did you fall? Are you hurt?"

"I'm fine, just a touch of the flu."

Mr. Briggs backed his chair up, obviously worried about catching it. "Well then, I'll make this quick. Your mother came to see me. She wants me to try and overturn your charge."

"That's impossible."

"I know. I told her the same thing," Mr. Briggs agreed, rubbing an eye. "It's very difficult to get a charge overturned when the accused has already pleaded guilty."

"Why does she want to do that?"

Mr. Briggs harrumphed. "The woman, your mother, is obviously in some distress. She has the misguided notion her poor son can do no wrong."

Dislike dripped from Mr. Briggs' tone and Declan heard it loud and clear. "I will remind you, Mr. Briggs, you work for me." Declan spoke up trying to sound assured, but it didn't come off well. His teeth were starting to chatter and he was freezing.

Mr. Briggs' brows joined together. He peered at Declan with concern. "I say, you really don't look well. It's not catchy is it?"

"I'm not sure." Declan eyed him. "It might be."

"Well then, let's get right down to it, shall we? As I said, your mom wants me to petition the court and ask for a new trial date. I was hoping you could talk some sense into her."

Christ his mom. He could just imagine her. She must be going nuts about now. He should probably call. But it was the last thing he wanted to do. He just wasn't up for it. As far as talking some sense into her, why in the hell would he do that?

187

"Mr. Briggs," Declan said cutting to the chase. "Did she give you any money for me?"

Mr. Briggs scowled. "Young man, are you in the least concerned for your mother's well being?"

Acid burned the back of his throat. It was hot and mixed with bile, swallowing the foul mixture he scowled back. "Mr. Briggs I hired you as my lawyer, not my therapist. It seems your age is catching up to you. It might be a good idea to think about retirement."

Mr. Briggs stared at Declan. The look of dislike had been replaced by one of repulsion.

"So," Declan repeated. "I will ask you again. Did my mother give you any money for me?"

Mr. Briggs sighed and stood up breaking eye contact. He looked down at Declan and shook his head. "Would you like a few words of advice young man?"

"Just answer my question."

"Well then, I won't waste my breath." Mr. Briggs turned. "Guard," he yelled.

"Hey!" Declan protested.

The guard entered the room his face stern. Declan's stomach gurgled and he gagged.

Both men froze. The guards face blanched. "You better not make a mess in here!"

"Well?" Declan managed.

Mr. Briggs reached the door. His expression was dour as he looked at Declan for the last time. "She did, may God help her poor soul."

A knifelike pain tore through his intestines. His stomach clenched and he tightened his sphincter. *Oh no!*

With the cheeks of his ass clenched tight, Declan followed the guard back to his cell hoping he'd make it in time.

His bones grated, his stomach rumbled, and the pressure in his intestines built.

Jagged Little Lies

Declan squirmed and clenched. Sweat beaded his brow. He would make it.

Each step was agony. *I can make it. I can make it.*

His bowels quivered, a long, loose, wet sound, trailing in his wake.

Chapter 30

"So, you're saying your friend just *gave* you the child?" The officer asked for the thousandth time.

Lyndsey inhaled. Patience was an attribute she learned to develop over the years of her internship, but it was still difficult. "That's exactly what I'm saying." She agreed.

Clearly confused the officer asked, "And you didn't think that was a little strange?"

"Not really, given the circumstances. Look, I've already answered your questions and I'm-," she broke off as the nurse opened the door.

The nurse poked her head in pointing to the officer. "I need to speak with you." She said, nodding her head in the direction of the hallway.

Lyndsey stood alarmed. "How's Billy?"

"I'll be back in a minute." The officer said glancing at her. "Wait here."

Something was wrong. Where was Billy? What had happened? Where was Drake? Worrying she chewed her inner lip bristling. *How dare they ask her to stay in this room? Billy needed her. Jesus she hated being treated like a criminal. Still she could understand...* trailing off, she stopped.

She hated waiting. Her mind spun worse case scenarios.

The door opened again, this time the entrance way was crowded. The police officer, the nurse, a physician and a frazzled looking Drake stood by the opening.

"Please sit." The physician instructed walking into the room and waving at the rest. "I'm Dr. Garret."

Drake sat next to Lyndsey joining her at the long table. He gave her leg a reassuring squeeze. She groped for his hand.

The doctor cleared his throat looking solemn, speaking directly to Lyndsey and Drake. "I'm afraid the little boy you

191

brought in, is very sick. He's undernourished and underweight. The ecchymosed, or bruising, will fade over time, but his dependency will need immediate attention."

Lyndsey's heart sank.

Drake not understanding the implications asked "What dependency?"

Lyndsey held her breath praying she was wrong.

"We did a routine blood and urine screen." Dr Garret said his eyes deep, dark pools, of sorrow. "The results are rather, well, disturbing."

"What did you find?" Drake asked still not getting it.

Lyndsey cringed, *please don't let it be.*

The nurse inhaled sharply, her nostrils flaring.

The officer stared his pupils little black dots in his eyes.

Dr. Garret glanced around the table before answering. "The blood and urine analysis tested positive for opiates."

"What!" Drake stood looking horrified

Lyndsey tugged on the back pocket of Drakes jeans sending him a silent message. Drake snorted and spun around to look at her. "Could this be true?" He asked incredulously.

"The tests don't lie honey." She said thinking of Billy's screams.

Dr. Garret cleared his throat and carried on. "The child was in distress and clearly uncomfortable. We have given him a small dosage of morphine to help with his symptoms. He will need to be weaned off the medication *slowly.*"

The police officer pulled out a small pad of paper and pen from the front pocket on his shirt. He began scribbling furiously.

Looking uncomfortable Dr. Garret said. "Of course we have called MFCD. A social worker is on her way. Billy will need to stay with us until we have weaned him off the opiates. He will also require a special diet."

The officer stopped scribbling and asked. "What's the address of the perp?"

Jagged Little Lies

Drake jerked a hand through his hair. "Are you saying Dee just *gave* drugs to Billy?"

Meeting the glare of the officer, Lyndsey replied. "She lives in a hotel. She doesn't have a fixed address. We picked Billy up at the Lions Head Motel on Terminal Avenue."

Turning to Drake, she said. "No honey, I don't think she just *gave* them to him. I think she had still been breastfeeding and he got them that way. Although I guess it's the same thing."

"Is that possible?" He asked the doctor.

Nodding, Dr. Garret replied. "It is. If the mother is using opiates they transmit to her baby via breast milk. We see it all the time in the neonatal ward, babies who are undernourished, born to mothers who are addicted, or alcoholic. Of course most of those mothers don't keep their children. But if they did, the children would probably be in the same predicament Billy is in now."

"How is Billy?" Lyndsey asked on the verge of tears.

"Right at the moment he's resting comfortably. But he's got a long road ahead of him." Dr. Garret shrugged.

Replacing the pad and pen the officer rose. Nodding at Dr. Garret and the nurse, he glanced at Lyndsey. "I'll be in touch. You're not planning on going anywhere are you?"

"Other than work and home, and of course here, I don't think so."

"Guess it means were going to have to cancel that Caribbean cruise huh Linds?" Drake replied sarcastically.

The officer shot Drake a dark stare.

Nudging Drake and shooting him a glance that said, *"this is not the time,"* Lyndsey backpedalled. "He's just kidding," she said, looking at Officer Scowly.

The patrolman frowned, nodding and left the room.

Drake muttered, "Jeez, I think he must have seen one too many episodes of Cops."

Jesus Drake, shut up. "Can we please see Billy?"

Dr. Garret stood offering his hand.

Drake shook it a little too hard and Lyndsey grimaced.

"You've got one hell of a grip." Dr. Garret smiled at Drake patting him on the back.

The nurse joined the trio at the door. She looked at Dr. Garret for confirmation and said, "Follow me."

Lyndsey offered her hand. "Thank you Dr. Garret. Will you be overseeing his case?"

"To start with, and then we'll see," he said releasing her hand. "Don't worry, he's in good hands."

They followed the little nurse down another hallway to the elevator. "He's on pediatrics." She said punching the call button.

The elevator door opened with a soft chime, and they stepped into the already crowded ride. They rode up in silence, each lost in their own thoughts. The door chimed again, the automated voice announcing the sixth floor.

"That's us." The nurse said crooking a finger.

The sixth floor looked very different than the one they just left, with its yellow painted walls and bright rainbow. In one corner was a big green, leafy tree, with bright red apples clinging to the branches. Toys scattered an area that looked like a playroom. Parents sat with their sick kids on cushions, or little chairs, playing with Lego blocks or trucks.

"This way," The nurse said side stepping the play area.

Lyndsey tore her eyes away from a little boy who'd lost his hair and had tubes in his nose. His big blue eyes followed her as she passed. She longed to turn and give him a hug, or an ice cream, or something. If only she could brighten his world for a moment.

The hallways were dotted with colorful pictures and followed a nursery rhyme theme. They passed Humpty Dumpty and the three little pigs. The nurse's steps slowed. "He's in here. You have five minutes."

Jagged Little Lies

The room they entered was darker than the hallways. It held a crib that looked more like a prison cell than bed. A Spiderman lamp sitting on a table, gave the room a soft glow. Lyndsey could just make out the outline of Billy.

They tiptoed over to him. He lay on his back. His cheeks were flushed and rosy. His hand clutched the throw from the bottom of their bed. His dark hair curled around his ears.

With the chair pulled up as close to the bed as she could get it, she put her arm through the bar and stroked Billy's hand. He felt warm and soft. Drake leaned against the windowsill watching. Poor Billy, he hadn't asked to be born, or to be a drug addict. But here he was. And just like she did, he was getting treatment for his addiction. It might look different, but it was still treatment. First he'd need detox and then intensive therapy. Billy's help would come in the form of play therapy, Dee's, if it ever happened, would be different. But the end result was still the same. It was all geared towards a successful outcome, for healthy individuals, free from addictions and other destructive behaviours.

Drake left the window and stood next to Billy's bed. Looking down he whispered. "He looks like a doll."

"Yeah, but he's missing some of his stuffing." Lyndsey whispered back.

Drake sighed, already weary, they weren't on the same page and they both knew it.

"We better go." He whispered again.

Billy stirred opening his eyes. He sat up looking at Lyndsey and Drake, his little fist still clutching the blanket.

"Oh oh," Drake mumbled.

"Hello sweetie," Lyndsey said reaching into the crib, her fingers moving the hair out of Billy's eyes. Billy gave her a big smile, his grin reaching from his eyes to her heart. Holding out his arms, Lyndsey picked him up. Billy cuddled against her, his small arms wrapping around her neck.

She cooed. "You feel better don't you sweetheart. What a special little boy you are."

Drake cleared his throat. "Linds." He warned.

The nurse returned with a red headed woman. She looked at Billy before saying, "This is Carol and she will be Billy's social worker. Carol this is Drake and Lyndsey. They're friends with Billy's mother and brought him in."

Carol shook hands with them. Her hand was warm and firm. And her eyes met theirs without hostility or judgement.

Carol spoke gently, "I'm sure you have a million questions. Here's my card, you can call me anytime. Turning to Billy who peered at her over Lyndsey's shoulder she said "Hello Billy."

Billy hid his head playing shy.

The nurse picked up a blanket in the crib folding it, before looking at Drake and Lyndsey."Sorry folks, but time is up, you'll have to leave now."

Holding tighter to Billy Lyndsey asked, "When can we come back?"

The nurse and social worker glanced at each other. It was Carol who spoke first. "Are you sure you want to do this?" She asked her voice tinged with concern.

Lyndsey's blurted "Yes."

Drake remained silent.

The nurse reached for Billy. "Why don't you wait a little while? It will help us to get him settled."

Billy wailed holding tight to Lyndsey's neck.

The nurse frowned and pulled Billy free. He wiggled in her arms pushing against her, screaming again as she tried soothing him with rocking motions. Billy reached for Lyndsey, his eyes filled with terror.

"You better go now." The nurse insisted.

Drake reached for her arm. "Come on Linds."

Lyndsey turned away from Billy, allowing Drake to steer her.

Jagged Little Lies

She stumbled from the room, leaning on Drake. Her eyes swam with tears leaving her momentarily blind.

Her world tilted as Billy's cries followed them down the hallway.

Chapter 31

Susan drove home mortified. For a moment there she'd been sure the pharmacist would call the ambulance. *Christ that was all she needed!* She'd have likely found herself a guest in the hospitals psychiatric ward. Not that she could blame them either. Seriously, she must have looked like a crazy person. The urge to reach over the counter and throttle the little tramp had almost gotten the best of her.

She'd seen Miranda and just... snapped. One minute she was about to launch over the counter and the next she was waking up on the floor. *What was wrong with her? Did she faint?* The last time she fainted, she'd been going through in vitro treatments. Back then Dick and she were having sex so often, it become *almost* like a job. But she certainly wasn't having sex now. Maybe she was just hungry. When was the last time she'd eaten anything?

A vicious cauldron of rage and pity burned in the back of her throat. Susan gnashed her teeth. Never before would she believe herself capable of hate, but now, things had changed. And *never* had she hated anyone more than she hated Miranda, except, well, maybe Dick. But that was different.

Oh God. Now Miranda knew her dirty little secret. Would she tell Declan? And what about the pharmacist who made such a big deal over helping her up, as he fetched water and fawned all over her. By then, a small crowd gathered around to watch. Never, in her entire life, had she felt so shamefaced or disconcerted.

Finally, because she really couldn't go any lower, she glared at the crowd and shouted, "Show's over folks." She must have looked crazy because it worked. The crowd dispersed instantly. Too bad she hadn't been able to do the same with Miranda.

Susan winced. If she could have, she'd have left right away. Sitting there was tortuous. But it would mean *no more pills*. She'd been torn. Stay and face the humiliation, or flee. Every fiber of her body wanted to flee, but something even stronger urged her to stay. So she stayed, sitting on the bench and doing her best to look invisible.

The pharmacist asked Miranda to accompany him into the back room. Miranda followed looking shellshocked, her face white as she nodded. Thankfully, it was the last Susan saw of her.

It wasn't long before the pharmacist returned, alone, with her little white bag in his hand. Susan glanced at it again riding beside her in the car and shook the bag. She really liked hearing the pills rattle around inside. The sound was comforting. But what if Miranda put something in it? Would she have done that? Maybe she added another ingredient, like say arsenic, or some other kind of poisoning.

No, she wouldn't have, besides the pharmacist was in the back room with her the whole time. Still, she might just try half a pill to start. At least she'd be ready for group. Yes, she'd give it a try. Really, she'd do anything, as long as there was a chance it might help Declan.

Pulling into her driveway, she breathed a big sigh of relief. Thank God she made it! No police following her, no psychiatric wards, just home. It was bittersweet. She put the keys in her purse and saw the white pad. She couldn't keep it in her purse. *Should she bring it inside?* What if the police did show up and went looking for it? The pad was incriminating evidence and clearly pointed out her guilt. Would the doctor even notice? Yes, she was sure she would. Her shrewd eyes missed nothing. Susan just hoped she didn't notice it immediately. Maybe then she wouldn't know who took it.

What the hell was she thinking? And who the hell was she? Changes were happening in her, and not for the good. The strange thing was, she cared less and less each day. Maybe she should just throw the pad away. Then they couldn't prove anything.

Yes, that's what she would do. Just throw the damned thing away. Maybe burn it in the fireplace. She shoved the little white bag into her purse as she slammed the car door. Plucking the mail from its box she entered her house announcing, "I'm home."

She was met with silence.

Pain twisted beneath her breastbone. Susan gasped. *Maybe she had a tumor, or a bleeding ulcer?* Damn, she'd forgotten to mention the pains to her doctor. Jesus, she would need to start writing lists, adding the fainting spell to the very top.

Susan got a glass of water and opened the pill bottle. Twenty pills that was all. She'd need to be careful. Calculating how long she could make them last, she swallowed one. *Just to help me sleep.* And yes, she really needed a good night's sleep. This time she would even go to bed. *No more couch.*

She thought about Declan as her dinner heated in the microwave. What would she say if he asked her about the pills? Or was Miranda under the same confidentiality clause a doctor or lawyer might be?

Careful not to burn her fingers, she peeled off the clear plastic cover on the package. Steam wafted up, smelling of cardboard and wax. The package advertised Schezwan Chicken. The chances of finding any *real* chicken in it were slim to none, and the carrots looked freeze-dried. Oh well, picking up her fork she shoveled it in her mouth

The meal was tasteless and bland. Rinsing the tray under hot water and placing it in recycle, Susan thought again about Declan. She heard prison food was horrible. He must hate it. Declan was used to nothing but the best. She remembered their shopping trips and his expensive tastes. He wouldn't settle for anything but the most expensive items. A whole wardrobe could be bought for the price of just one pair of jeans! Things were always so important to him. What he looked like, and what people thought of him, mattered to him a lot.

The Visa bill was enormous and she'd hidden it from Dick, hoping to chip away at it in small increments. But he found out one day anyway, after trying to use his Visa card at a gas pump. The card was maxed and he hadn't been able to get the gas he needed. To make matters worse, there wasn't enough gas in the tank to get him home. After running out of gas, he'd been forced to ask for help from a passing motorist.

Furious, Dick took the card from her. For a few days neither of them spoke, finally it was she who broke the ice by saying Declan needed clothes. This started another argument which ended with Dick insisting on going shopping with them.

Their shopping trip was a disaster. Dick, stern with Declan, had not agreed to spend "the absurd amount of money" on one pair of jeans. Declan sulked stating he "would not be caught dead" in the clothing Dick wanted him to wear.

They all left the store barely speaking to one another. Dick bought a pair of jeans and a t-shirt for Declan that he swore he'd never wear. The ride back was tense, and once home they'd all gone their separate ways. Dick left to work on a project he needed to finish up, and she and Declan finally had a chance to talk.

In those days, they talked a lot. She'd been able to confide in Declan, telling him how unhappy she was with Dick. She was sorry he was so strict. Back then it was always the two of them against the world.

Her throat burned with pain. Somewhere, it all just went so *wrong*. Forcing the thoughts aside, Susan dried her hands. The closet in her beautiful bedroom was huge, but she barely even noticed it as she searched for something to wear the next day. She wanted to look confident and hoped the right clothing would make her feel that way. Susan placed her choice, a blazer with cream-colored pants, on the chair next to her bed. She winced as she set the alarm for 6 o'clock the next morning.

A tremor of anxiety filled her chest. She hoped she could sleep. She avoided looking in the mirror as she brushed her teeth. What did they do in this group? She wouldn't have to talk about herself would she? Maybe it was like school, with lectures and homework. She hadn't been told much when she registered, other than being informed everything she needed would be provided.

With an extra layer of face cream, she patted her cheeks. Maybe the cream would help with the pinched, drawn look, her face wore these days. Climbing into bed, she marveled again at the comfort of her mattress. It came with a lifetime warrantee. At the time she never guessed it would outlast their marriage. But the mattress, true to its word, was just as comfortable now as the day they bought it.

Of course she didn't spend much time in it anymore. It brought back to many painful memories. But she hadn't been able to get rid of it either. She just avoided it most of the time, choosing instead to sleep on the couch.

Dick had been a great lover, so tender and caring. She'd been a virgin and in the beginning she'd been so stiff and awkward, but he'd been patient, always wanting to ensure her needs were met before meeting his own. She hadn't noticed it at first, the missing caresses and cuddles. Or even that the time between their lovemaking was growing longer, until finally it ceased altogether. And she never knew the last time they made love was *the last time.*

She wished she'd known. But she'd been so wrapped up in Declan. She was angry that Dick didn't see things her way. It drove a wedge wider than the Grand Canyon between them. She remembered the nights of lying next to Dick wide awake, shoulder to shoulder, and a million miles apart.

Now she had lost him. At least she was pretty sure it was over. She wondered if Lori was staying with him tonight. Had they slept together yet? Did Lori spoon with him the way she did, nuzzling his shoulder and inhaling him?

A sob tore from her throat. The thought of anyone else experiencing what she did with Dick sickened her.

He said he loved her. How could he touch someone else if he meant that? Hot tears flowed down her cheeks. *How many times could a heart break before it stopped beating?*

Please stop. Please stop. Past memories tormented her, keeping her awake as she stared at the clock. She was going to look like hell. Her eyes would be puffy and she'd be exhausted tomorrow, fluffing a pillow Susan tossed in the bed trying to get comfortable.

The clock *clicked* and the icemaker churned adding ice to the tray. A car drove by. A dog barked.

Wide awake she stared into the darkness.

Chapter 32

He wore a cowboy hat, cowboy boots, a gun holster and nothing else. His bronzed body glistened with oil as he gyrated in front of their table, with his fingers firmly intertwined behind his head. His bronzed hips rolled in time to the beat of the music. His flexed pecs did a little dance of their own.

Lisa reached across her with an oil-soaked hand, trying to gain the attention of the male dancer. Pointing she said, "Your turn Miranda."

The dancer, taking Lisa's cue, gyrated his way over to Miranda.

Shaking her head while eyeing the bronzed god undulating before her, Miranda said, "No thanks Lisa think I'll pass."

The dancer slowed as he took a bottle of oil from his gun holster and poured a generous squirt into his palm. He smiled a delicious invitation, while rubbing his dancing pecs and six-pack.

A round of girlish sighs could be heard coming from their table. The ladies giggled, intoxicated from more than just the drinks they were being served. Lisa shot her a dirty look before standing to join the dancer. Lisa was dressed in a negligee, fish-net stockings and high heels. Crude language scrawled on the negligee left no doubt this night was her stagette. Lisa teetered, holding on to the dancer for support.

Miranda looked at her friend. *Man was she drunk.* Lisa was never much of a drinker, but tonight she consumed shot after shot as it arrived at their table. Lisa giggled as she massaged the stripper. Her hand *slipped* and she howled.

The table of girls howled back and egged her on. The dancer smiled, taking a step backwards. Lisa smiled, taking a step forward and then teetered. She stumbled and fell. The table howled with laughter at the sight of Lisa landing on her derriere.

Miranda looked at the shot glasses lined up in front of her. She hadn't been able to keep up. She picked up one and tossed it back. A sickening-sweet licorice taste flooded her taste buds. Grimacing she put down the empty glass. The girls howled louder and she glanced over at Lisa. She was trying to stand but couldn't quite master it.

The bar maid stopped at their table. Unloading her tray of another round of shooters, she jerked a thumb in the direction of the only two other males in the club. "It's on the house ladies." She informed them. The male bartenders waved and blew kisses at their table.

The drunken table of girls twittered and waved back. Susan's hateful eyes played in her mind and hoping to erase the image, Miranda picked up another shot glass. This one was three layered. She got most of it down and gagged. The sweetness was even more intense than the last one. A long swig from the bottle of beer she'd been nursing helped wash it down.

Lisa finally managed to get back up, but she wobbled. Miranda laughed. The girls and Lisa made their way to the dance floor.

The bronzed dancer joined in too, bumping and grinding against each of them, leaving oily smears on their clothing. The music blared and the strobe lights flashed. Lisa fell again and Miranda reached out for her, nearly toppling onto the floor herself. Helping Lisa up, Miranda fought a wave of dizziness.

The strobe flashed another bright light of swirling bodies and her head swam. Miranda held onto Lisa's arm as she led them back to the table. Lisa could barely walk and murmured "No."

Ignoring her she kept walking. Lisa lost a shoe and staggered beside her. "Come on. I think we've had enough," she said, wondering if they could get a cup of coffee here.

Back at the table, Lisa reached for another shot. Miranda grabbed for it, but missed. Lisa spilled most of it down the front of her negligee before consuming the rest. Miranda polished off the rest of her warm bottle of beer, her thirst still not quenched.

Looking at Lisa she asked. "Had enough?"

Lisa's thick-lidded eyes drooped. "Jsst about." She said, slumping beside her.

After throwing a few bills onto the table, Miranda waved at the girls still on the dance floor. The girls swarmed the bronzed dancer, barely noticing their departure.

Miranda stumbled, barely able to navigate the short distance to the door. Lisa was incoherent, hanging like a dead weight from her shoulder. Hoping the cold air would help sober her up, she left the club. The thick doors closed behind them, leaving them in an eerie silence.

Lisa lost her second shoe between the table and door and now stood only in her negligee and stockings. She shivered beside her. "Cold," She complained.

Miranda spotted a taxi up the street and hailed it. "Hey!" The cab remained parked. Miranda steered Lisa closer to the side of the street before shouting again. Lisa wobbled, falling off the curb.

The taxi did a u-turn and pulled up next to them. The driver got out of his cab shaking his head. "She better not make a mess." He said, glaring at Miranda.

Miranda struggled trying to help Lisa up. "Jesus! Could you give us a hand here?"

The taxi driver remained immobile, arms crossed, studying them.

"She'll be fine." Miranda insisted.

The driver reached a decision and bent down to help. Between the two of them, they managed to get Lisa into the back seat. Miranda clicked in Lisa's seat belt hoping it would help keep her upright. The taxi shot off, throwing Miranda across the seat. "Whoa, not so fast," She complained.

The driver shook his head but slowed.

Righting herself, Miranda clicked in her own seat belt. The scenery outside the window blurred and the cab's stuffy interior cloyed. The driver's last meal hung in the air, adding to the cab's thick atmosphere.

Lisa squirmed beside her and then stilled.

The darkness outside the window reminded her of Susan's pupils. Black pinpoints of insanity. She'd known Susan didn't like her, but she never guessed to what extent. So, Declan wasn't the only one who liked his little pills. Funny, he never mentioned *that* before.

Lisa moaned and the driver turned his head.

"She better not get sick!"He exclaimed.

"She's fine." Miranda assured him, hoping he would put his eyes back on the road.

The driver turned away from her and facing the road drove even faster. Clearly, he wanted them out of his cab and quickly.

She thought back to Susan. After she fainted, Miranda feared she had died. As Susan lay crumpled on the floor, her first thought was for Declan. Not that he was really close with his mom or anything, but she was still his mother. Then Susan had stirred and Miranda scampered into the back room. John took over without ever realizing what was truly taking place.

Should she tell Declan his mother was crazed and on pills to boot? But if she told him, she could lose her job and then what? It wasn't like there was another job to go to, or even a little money put away for a rainy day. Hell, she'd be lucky to cover this cab ride.

Lisa squirmed against Miranda and mumbled, "Sick."

The driver glanced in his rear view mirror meeting Miranda's eyes.

Miranda smiled, holding up her finger and thumb and forming OK.

The driver scowled again before looking away.

208

Jagged Little Lies

Miranda sighed closing her eyes. She felt so stuck and hated it. Life used to be so much easier. It was more fun and well, less *heavy*. At least Declan didn't have to worry about a roof over his head, or three squares a day. Lately, she wasn't even sure if she could feed herself. A spark of anger surfaced. It wasn't fair! She hadn't really done anything wrong and she was left with the mess.

It was stupid to have come out tonight, but after Lisa called, she hadn't been able to say no. And besides, she didn't want Lisa to know how serious her money problems really were. So instead she'd thrown bills on the table as if they were of no concern. Bills, that were meant to go to her food budget.

Sighing again, Miranda figured she would worry about it tomorrow. Maybe she would wake up and all her problems would be gone. Poof, all her troubles just magically disappeared and life would be back to the way it used to be. Hah! Yeah right. That was the problem with growing up, you really couldn't kid yourself anymore. She wished she still believed in fairy tales, with knights in shining armour on white charges, coming to her rescue.

In the beginning, that's what she thought Declan was. Her prince and her soul mate. He would stand beside her, forever and ever. But it sure didn't turn out like any fairy tale she ever read. Her prince turned into a con. His armour was a prison jumpsuit, their kingdom, a jail cell.

Miranda rested her head on the cool window glass. She really wished she could find her *happily ever after*, but lately it just wasn't happening. Maybe this was why grownups always looked so tired and miserable. Was this what it was all about? Living paycheck to paycheck and never making enough money. Or working at a job you hated day after day, with tiny moments of fun, to be later glossed over by the guilt you felt for having it.

Lisa moaned shifting restlessly in her seat, breaking Miranda's train of thought.

The taxi driver's eyes narrowed in worry and concern, as they met hers in the mirror once more. He shook his head letting out a long sigh.

Miranda opened her mouth, another assurance ready, but before she could get the words out Lisa's body convulsed beside her.

The driver swore in a foreign language, as the air filled with a hot, sour stench.

Miranda shrugged, numbed beyond caring.

It looked like the driver had a mess to clean up after all.

Chapter 33

"Oh pretty boy, are you in there? Come out, come out, and plaayyy!"

The bed beneath him trembled as Rooster pounded his meaty fist on the backside. "Stand up boy! You gonna take that?"

Declan grinned blocking it all out. The oxy Rooster gave him made it so easy to do. He loved this feeling. He was boneless. Maybe this is what it felt like to die. Your body was no longer present, but your mind was wide awake.

The bed shook underneath him. Rooster growled, "Stand up!"

Declan grinned and threw himself off the bed. He landed on his feet. *What in the hell was Rooster getting all riled up for?* Grasping the bars between his fingers he peered down the hallway seeing the mirrors and other reflective objects being thrust between the bars. The inmates had it all worked out, as they angled for a glimpse into each other's cells.

"You wanna play pretty boy?" The falsetto voice trilled.

Actually, he did. Declan grinned not grasping the idea. He laughed. *God he felt great.* Amazing even and he loved *everyone,* even the Rooster. Declan ran his hands up and down the bars liking the smooth, satiny feel of them.

The Rooster crowed, having risen from his roost. "I'll give you something to play with!" He roared, threatening the unseen voice.

You could hear a pin drop, it was so quiet.

Satisfied, at least momentarily, Rooster turned to Declan and pointing at the sink said, "Clean up that mess."

Declan laughed. Rooster scowled.

The warm water was nice. Declan filled the bowl sponging the sides. Rooster's facial hair floated in the swirls of soap.

Declan happily scoured the aluminum bowl, rinsing it with fresh water. Like a little kid, he splashed in the warm water, humming.

"Stop that racket! We've got business to attend to and I don't need you caterwauling while we do it." Rooster puffed.

Drying his hands on his jumpsuit Declan grinned. He almost liked Rooster. He never realized how funny the guy could be.

"And wipe that idiot smile off your face boy. People are gonna think you're simple-minded for Chrissakes!"

"Yeah right," poking a finger in Rooster's meaty arm Declan replied, "Look who's talking, with a name like Rooster-" Declan stopped abruptly as Rooster's meaty hand clamped over his mouth, stifling the rest of his sentence.

The old bird's eyes nearly popped out of his sockets. He leaned in close and whispered into Declan's ear. "Boy, you don't want to be crossing the line. Not now. Not ever. There is only so much I can do in here to protect you, and then, it's out of my hands. As long as there's something in it for me, I've got your back, but make no mistake, we ain't friends. And I will stick you just as surely as the next guy, if you step out of line. You hear me?"

Rooster released his hold on Declan and gave him a push. Declan spun, landing hard against the bars.

Not seeming to notice the hurt he just inflicted on Declan, Rooster continued. "Now here's what we're gonna do."

Declan listened as he outlined a plan of action. Rooster wanted Declan to give him a slice of the money the lawyer was depositing into his account. Rooster would take that money and pad his supply. Declan would help move the supply and Rooster would keep him in the little pills he so dearly loved. It would be a win - win for each of them. Rooster would make the cash he needed for his release next year and Declan, well for him, it would just be one long party.

Up off the floor Declan grinned. "Sounds good to me. If I run out of money, I can always get more." He bragged.

Jagged Little Lies

Rooster cleared his throat, "We'll see. From now on you come to me *before* you do anything. I want to know what you're thinking and who you're talking to, capisce? You make no decisions on your own. None, zip, nada, you got it?"

Whatever big fella, Declan smiled, saying nothing.

"And right now I want you to come with me. You need to beef up a little." Rooster continued.

Declan followed Rooster down the hallway, past the cages. It really wasn't that bad here. What with the cherry flavored juice he was getting and the little pills, a guy could *almost* have a regular party. He hastened his steps, catching up to Rooster. *Christ the old guy could really hoof it. What the hell was he on? You couldn't be that old and fast without something, could you?*

In the prison yard, Declan glimpsed men huddled in groups. Some lifted weights or played basketball; others hung out and watched. The yard felt sinister and Declan tried to appear cool.

"Hey, Tiny, Rooster called to a mountain of a man. Tiny turned in their direction and gave Declan a flat-eyed stare.

Declan stared back and Rooster cuffed him upside the head. "Show some respect boy!" He growled.

Declan lowered his head staring at the ground.

"Tiny, we're gonna to need to toughen this little fellow up. I think you might be just the right guy to do it."

Tiny's lifeless eyes looked Declan over. Declan shivered. You just knew this guy was in for something *really bad.*

"Hmm." Tiny rumbled.

Declan's warm floaty feeling diminished. Rooster cocked an eye at him and asked. "Do you think it can be done?'

Tiny scratched his chin. Declan stared intently at a pebble. Tiny removed his hand and gave Declan's bicep a hard squeeze. "How long's he in for?" He asked Rooster.

"As long as we want him to be, isn't that right boy." Rooster crowed.

213

Declan remained mute, sensing this was the best response. He really wasn't feeling so hot. The floaty-feeling drifted away. Christ it didn't last long. What he needed was his own personal stash. And Rooster was right. He did need to beef up. In here he still looked like a little kid among the men. A little weight lifting would probably be a good idea. And maybe Tiny would have some ideas of his own on how to enhance his stash. Declan wouldn't relax until he wasn't worried about where his next fix was coming from.

Rooster and Tiny were deep in conversation about the best way to beef him up. Tiny poked a cucumber sized finger in his direction. "He's gonna need a lot of work." Tiny flipped Declan's arm around like a rubber snake before letting go.

Declan winced. Maybe he could get Miranda to bring him some of the pills they discarded. *No better not.* It wouldn't be fair to ask her to do it. Besides this was how the whole thing started. Still... She did have access and man could he use them. Maybe he could just talk to her about it. See how she felt. He wondered how closely they checked the visitors on visiting day. He knew they checked their bags and their belongings, but they didn't search their bodies did they? He would need to ask around.

Tiny picked up a large black ball and tossed it to Rooster. Rooster caught it with an "umph."

I guess he isn't as tough as he looks. Declan tried to hide his smile. His thoughts returned to the one place they never strayed far from, as he wondered if he could talk her into it. He could get the odd pill off Rooster, but it wasn't going to be nearly enough. Maybe he would give her a call tonight and kind of feel it out. Just sort of mention it, casually. Not like he was asking her to do it or anything. He could probably say he met a guy whose girlfriend was bringing it in and it wasn't a problem. He'd make some sort of bullshit up and then see how she reacted.

Jagged Little Lies

Tiny laughed as Rooster caught the ball. Rooster's face turned a deep red, with little beads of sweat starting on his brow. He grunted with effort as he threw the ball back.

Jesus, the old guy was really starting to show his age. Declan smirked hiding his head. His stomached rumbled and his smirk fled, with the quivering of his bowels. *Shit!* This was ridiculous. There had to be a way to get his hands on what he needed. He'd always been able to figure out a way before. The players had just changed a little. That was all.

Maybe he could just sneak away and risk going back to the cell? Declan took a step backward. If he were caught, Rooster would surely kick the shit out of him. And he wasn't sure how he could avoid all those Goddamn little mirrors up and down the hall way. All he needed was one of the inmates to see him going back into the cell and the gig would be up. He knew someone would rat to Rooster for sure. *Maybe he could just check?* You never knew, the coast could be clear and if it wasn't he wouldn't take anything. But if it was, he would just take a couple of pills and get the hell out of there. He could always pretend like it wasn't him, he'd gotten pretty good at acting. He was pretty sure he could pull it off. He could say he needed to use the bathroom and instead go back to their cell. He would have to be quick though, really quick. Hell, he wasn't even sure how to get back there.

Taking another step backward he calculated the odds. It was risky, but then it always was. His intestines rolled and he bit his lip. Deep in thought, he faintly heard someone yell, 'Heads up!"

Instinctively his head rose.

A large black ball sped towards him. Time slowed and then sped back up. Before he had a chance to get his arms out, the ball hit with a *whoosh*. For a moment he thought he'd been shot in the gut, so great was the impact.

Declan heard their laughter as he fell.

The wind left his body as he landed on the hard concrete, his head snapping against the pavement with a vicious *crack.* He wanted to scream with pain, but he couldn't breathe.

He tried to sit up, but was unable to. Instead Declan thrashed on the ground gasping for air like a newly caught fish.

Above him, the two giants towered.

Chapter 34

Lyndsey wrote the lecture notes on the board and stopped. Dammit she'd done it again. With a weary sigh she erased the paragraph she'd just written. *It was going to be a really long day.* She and Drake stayed up far too late last night, trying to come to terms on what to do about Billy. They hadn't been able to agree and decided to call a truce. Both recognized they were tired and going in circles

Looking at her papers, Lyndsey tried to concentrate on the task at hand. Shortly she would be joined by a room full of people she had only spoken with on the telephone. She owed it to them to be prepared *and* present. She was lecturing on *the essential symptoms of the family disease* and needed to be on her game.

She made sure she had plenty of tissues after she arranged the chairs in a circle. She grabbed one and dabbed her own eyes, thinking about Billy. Strangely, it was the little box with the tissues that most people avoided when first entering the room.

The water jugs were full. The coffee percolated giving off a heady aroma. The scene was set, and she was as ready as she ever would be. With a last glance around the room that would be home to this next group of people, at least for a little while, she was *almost* ready.

Lyndsey closed her eyes traveling to a different realm. Quieting her thoughts, she listened with her heart and then began. *Dear God, please use me as an instrument of your will. Please allow me to be free of my expectations and judgements. Please still my tongue should I use it in anger or harmful intent. Please give me grace and empathy. Please walk with me and help me to carry the message. For I teach nothing without your love. Amen.*

She squared her shoulders and went to meet the group. Her heels made comforting noises as they traversed the familiar tile hallways. In the waiting area she glimpsed her first look at the small crowd of people. She saw faces wreathed in worry. She was a stranger to them and a scary one at that. She wouldn't be for long though, by this afternoon they would all begin to feel like family. They already were; they just didn't know it yet.

The glass was cool to touch as she pushed through the doors smiling, hoping to reassure. "Hello and welcome," Lyndsey greeted. "We will get started with your orientation shortly, but before we do I'm going to ask each of you to sign a confidentiality form." Lyndsey said handing out the forms attached to clip boards. "If you need a pen there are some on the counter, please help yourself."

The small group eagerly busied themselves, glad for the opportunity to be doing something with their hands. Pens scratched across paper and then stilled. Tension filled the air once more. Gathering the clip boards Lyndsey said, "Please follow me."

Holding open the door, she waited for the crowd to enter the main building. One woman held back not joining with the others. Her face was pinched and drawn. A thousand years of small hurts flickered across her countenance. "I think I've made a mistake." She whispered.

Lyndsey indicated *just a moment* to the group of people waiting on the other side of the glass. She turned to the distraught woman and said in her most gentle tone, "I think the mistake would be in getting here and *almost* going through the doors. You would be left with never knowing if you made the right choice or not. Only what ifs? What if I had gone? What if it would have been helpful? What if I found a way to be happy? What if I found a way to be at peace? What if...? You have nothing to lose and *everything* to gain. And besides, if you really want to leave, you can. But don't you want to at least know if this *is* a mistake, before just assuming it is?"

The woman's mouth opened as if to argue the point and then closed. She nodded giving a weary sigh and rose to her feet. For the briefest of seconds she wobbled before steadying herself. Lyndsey flinched inwardly. *The depth of the woman's pain was enormous.* Lyndsey watched her, her brow furrowed in concern, as she joined the group looking subdued.

"This way please." Lyndsey instructed.

The little group obediently followed staying close as they passed others in the hallway. The building was deceiving in its looks and was far larger than it appeared. Lyndsey toured her group showing them where they would be eating their meals. A tentative tug caught her attention stopping her.

An elderly woman stood frowning as she held onto her sleeve. Cane in hand she said, "I'm already lost. How will we ever find our way back to the door?"

A middle age man snickered before replying, "Maybe that's part of the plan. They don't want you to be able to find the door."

Oh dear. This guy was going to be a problem. It was still too early to introduce feedback so instead she assured the elderly woman. "If you get lost just ask one of the passersby for help."

Shocked, the woman let go of her sleeve and cried. "But what if it's a drug addict I'm asking?"

Problem man snickered. "You better watch your purse."

Lyndsey shot the man a look encouraging him to knock it off. Misinterpreting the meaning he smiled and winked. With a mental *later*, she continued her tour saying, "It's important to remember the people in this building are here to get better. Just like you. They are learning how to have healthier lives."

Lyndsey wrapped up the tour. The twelve new members filed into the group room. Conversation ceased and the air thickened with apprehension. All eyes fastened on the box of tissues.

"Please take a seat." She said breaking the spell.

Alliances were already beginning to form as people sat next to each other. Lyndsey handed out the binders and pens. "Before we begin how about a round of introductions, I'm Lyndsey and I would like to welcome you to the family program. I know it hasn't been easy getting here, but I hope your experience this week will help you change that."

Problem man smiled charmingly and said, "I'm Eric."

Next to Eric sat Sandra and then Charlie, Shelly, Terry, Shawna, Kim, Russell, Rick, Marge, Irene and Susan. Lyndsey focused as they introduced themselves, wanting to address them by name.

Irene gripped her cane clearly agitated. "Why don't we have name tags miss?"

"Please call me Lyndsey. We don't have name tags because we're not attending a conference. And if you forget someone's name, then just ask them."

Irene snorted thumping her cane. "Well I think that's ridiculous!" Turning to the woman beside her she said, "Don't you?"

Susan blanched and shrank back into her seat. Irene thumped her cane again as Susan sat mutely at her side. Irene quickly changed topics. She looked at Susan frowning. "What did your doctor say?"

Susan's face went from white to red as she glared at Irene, "None of your business!" She hissed.

Lyndsey sighed as her pulse kicked up a notch. Sometimes she really missed working with her old clientele. *Give me the addicts and alcoholics any day.* At least you always knew what to expect with them. Now the families, they were different. They attended these programs in hopes of supporting 'the sick one' in the family. Not understanding 'the sick one' was them.

Jagged Little Lies

Her hands were sweaty. Lyndsey wiped them dry on her skirt. She began talking about her lecture. "I'm going to be talking with you today about The Essential Symptoms of the *family disease*. Some of you may be able to identify your own families on this board. If you would like to take notes please do so. I will have hand outs at the end."

Eric spoke up before she could continue. "Why don't you just give us the handouts now and save yourself the speech?" He snickered again clearly amused by his wit.

Lyndsey eyed him shrewdly. She was going to have to play hardball sooner than she'd anticipated. Glancing at the rest of the group she took their temperature. Susan glowered at the old woman next to her. Eric smirked confidently in his seat. Irene sat upright, oblivious to the hostility being directed her way. The only telltale sign she was nervous was the white of her fingers, as they held tightly to her cane.

The others were a little harder to read. They avoided eye contact by flipping through their binders. *Too soon.* She'd derail them at this stage if she addressed Eric's gamey tactics. No, she'd have to wait a little longer, otherwise she would have the classic *them* against *her* and it would be too difficult to undo.

Tension hammered her shoulders. She took a deep breath trying to lessen it, thinking about Billy for an instant. *God she hoped he was feeling better today. What in the hell was she doing here? She should be with him. She would go and see him right after work. How long would he have to be in the hospital for? Did they find Dee yet? Maybe she could get Dee to insist Billy be placed with her, but then what about Drake?*

Suddenly realizing all eyes were on her, Lyndsey blinked. Number one rule, *stay focused* but her mind had wandered. Heat burned her face and she drew a blank. Aiming for a demeanor of confidence, she turned her back to the group, picking up the felt pen and hoping to buy some time. She eyed the board trying to remember where to start.

221

Tension clawed leaving her thoughts a blank canvas.

Forget it. Lyndsey turned away from the board and back to the group, deciding to go with what she knew. Eyeing each of them she said, "Before I begin I need to tell you I'm feeling nervous. So as you can see, I too, can relate to how each and every one of you must be feeling. And I know whatever brought you here hasn't been easy. I hope together we can get past this and become a little more comfortable with each other."

Her tension lifted fading away. She felt lighter and her mind cleared. The familiar words came flooding back and the blank canvas filled.

This time eyeing the group, she smiled.

The feeling in the room turned bringing with it one of inquisitiveness, rather than hostility. Lyndsey turned once more to the board, her felt flowing freely.

The group breathed a collective sigh of relief.

Only Eric remained frozen, scowling, as he stared at the board.

Chapter 35

Susan stared open mouthed.

"Be careful you might catch a fly." The old woman chuckled.

Oh great, just her luck. Of all the people who had to be in this stupid group thing, she gets the old lady from the doctor's office. Susan thought back. *Had she seen her leaving the office?* She'd been so panicked she couldn't even remember.

"What brings you here?"

"Mmm, not much." She lied.

The door buzzed and another person entered the waiting area. Susan took the opportunity to busy herself in her purse. Maybe the old woman would take the hint and leave her alone. She fumbled inside the silk lining her hand automatically reaching for the little bottle. Her thoughts were scrambled and she needed a coffee in the worst way. If she hadn't overslept she would have had one too. The alarm must have been buzzing for an hour by the time it finally pierced her sedated brain.

Minutes crawled by as the hour grew later, and she found herself growing more and more alarmed. In the end she'd given up and gotten out of bed, breaking yet another vow. She'd lost track of how many times she'd done this recently. By the time the bottle was in her hand she was so frenzied all she could think of was sleep. So she'd taken two of her precious little tablets. The pills worked immediately finally allowing her the sleep she so badly craved. And for a moment she found bliss. But she was paying for it now.

"It's a little ridiculous don't you think?" The new arrival asked her.

Not following she asked, "Pardon?" Her voice sounded flat and old. Not at all like hers.

His brows raised and he waved his hands indicating the room they were sitting in. "This. We shouldn't have to be here. After all, it's not like it's *us* with the problem. Now is it?"

Susan was parched, her head thick. She needed water. She had no idea what this guy was talking about and didn't care. She wasn't going to to ask him to please explain himself, because she didn't want to listen. So instead she just grunted sliding her eyes away from his.

Obviously not getting the message, he continued. "I haven't seen you on visiting days before have I?"

Susan shook her head. *Ouch,* something slogged within her skull feeling wet and heavy. She wished for her sunglasses. The light in the room felt too bright and her eyes watered. *What time was it when she'd finally gotten to sleep?* Way too late by the feel of it. She hoped this group thing wouldn't take long. She really wasn't feeling up to it.

The old woman thankfully seemed to have forgotten about her, as she chatted with the newest arrival. Susan tried sizing him up. He looked about her age. He was dressed in khaki trousers and a golf shirt. His face wore a perpetual smirk and she disliked him instantly, looking down at her own cream colored trousers she sighed. They were too big and hung off her backside like an old man's pants. She hadn't had the time to put anything else on, so instead chose a longer jacket. It wasn't as becoming on her as the blazer was, but in a rush, she didn't have much choice.

Now sitting here with her eyes puffy and her big clothes, she felt embarrassed and ugly. Her hand curled comfortably around the bottle sitting inside her purse. *It would probably help,* sneaking a look around the room to see if anyone was watching she snuck her other hand inside the purse. With as little noise as possible, and praying the bottle wouldn't rattle, she undid the lid carefully fingering one of the tiny tablets free. The snap of the purse's clasp echoed off the waiting room walls, garnering

Jagged Little Lies

unwanted attention. Conversation stopped, inquisitive eyes turned in her direction.

Susan coughed. The tiny pill lay in her sweaty palm. Praying it wouldn't dissolve she murmured, "Just a little cold."

Curious heads turned away not wanting to chance infection, except for one. The old lady eyed her shrewdly. Susan coughed again bringing her hand to mouth. As she covered the forced cough, she managed to mouth the pill. She glared at the old lady, hoping she got the silent message. *Mind your own business!*

The woman was either too old, or too daft, to understand and continued watching her. Susan licked the inside of her palm making sure to get anything which might have dissolved. The bitter taste flooded her mouth adding a pasty coating to her tongue. The old lady finally turned away when a confident-looking woman entered the room and asked them to sign a confidentiality form. Susan easily signed the form knowing she would never see anyone here again, since she never planned to admit she'd been here in the first place.

As she listened to the woman collecting the signed forms, she recognized the voice as the person she first spoke to on the phone about her son. The lady was far too cheery and confident given their current situation. With an inviting wave, she welcomed them to the building as if it were the House of Miracles, or something like it. Susan hoped it wouldn't be her leading the group. She didn't like her on the phone and she liked her even less now.

What could she possibly know about pain and suffering? She needed someone who'd been there, not the Susie Homemaker standing in front of her. It was a mistake. She shouldn't have come. Panic flared and she wanted to bolt.

The group of people stood with an expectant hush, following the woman through the door. Susan sat glued to her seat not moving. The woman turned to her holding open the door with a curious look on her face. Susan wished she were invisible and

225

anywhere but here. "I think I've made a mistake." She whispered.

Instead of leaving, the woman stayed. The small group waiting on the other side of the glass watched as the woman spoke to Susan of what ifs. Susan cringed, feeling like a specimen on display and barely heard the woman who spoke with such passion and conviction. And finally, just to get her to shut up, Susan rose following her through the glass doors.

On the other side of the door, she stared at the tiles, avoiding the curious stares. The building they entered was beautiful. Strange, she never thought a place like this would look nice. She pictured it looking seedy and more, well, institutionalised. Feigning interest in the decor to avoid any attempts at conversation, she studied her surroundings. At one time she'd been great at designing and decorating. Dick always said she had a natural gift for putting color and materials together. Her home was a showplace filled with friends and family. For awhile they'd been the envy of the neighbourhood, but things changed...

Jesus. Susan angrily flicked a tear away, wishing Declan were here instead of being stuck in some tiny little prison cell. She made a mental note to call the lawyer as she pictured her son. Of course Declan wasn't a *real* drug addict. He didn't put needles in his veins and he wasn't homeless. He just used pills, and it wasn't like they were illegal. After all, millions of people were prescribed medications every day. She should know.

The fog she'd been swathed in started to lift. The overwhelming hopeless feeling dissipated and she walked with more purpose. Maybe this week wouldn't be as awful as she thought. She might even learn a thing or two about helping Declan in a more effective way. Who knew, there might even be a lawyer in the group? Khaki pants kind of had the *look* about him and maybe she could pick his brains about some new ways to get Declan out.

226

Jagged Little Lies

It all came down to asking the right questions, that was all. Of course in order to ask the right question, she needed a clear head. Thank goodness for the little pills she carried with her. There was no way in hell she could do this without them.

For a moment she was torn, not really understanding why she was making such a big deal over how many pills she was using. Silently vowing for the rest of the week she wouldn't worry about it, she relaxed. After all they were being prescribed to help people, not harm them.

The beige walls blurred as she picked up speed. No more worry! It seemed like it was all she ever did these days. Worry, worry, worry!

Well, she was done with it! No more!

Determined to find answers, Susan caught up to her group.

Chapter 36

Miranda winced and her head pounded something fierce. How much did she drink last night? Hmmm, skipping dinner wasn't the smartest idea either. And was she ever thirsty. Dragging herself out of bed, she stumbled into the kitchen filling the largest glass she owned with cold water. With her thirst taken care of Miranda popped a Tylenol. Thank Christ she didn't have to work today.

Free time wasn't something she had much of. What should she do with her day? Her pounding head solved the problem and she opted for going back to bed. Might as well wait for the Tylenol to kick in and then figure it out. The bed was heavenly and she sank gratefully into its soft folds. She was just drifting off when the phone rang.

The call display flashed *unknown number*. Oh God, she really didn't feel like talking, but what if it was Declan? Then again, the pharmacy number came up unknown. Maybe it was John calling her in. Torn, she hesitated.

The phone rang once more and she made her decision muffling her voice just in case. "Hello." She croaked.

"Miranda? What's wrong with your voice?"

"Oh thank God it's you Declan. I thought maybe it was work and I really wasn't up to going in today..." she trailed off realizing she said too much.

"What do you mean you *aren't up to going in today*?" Declan quizzed, his tone sharp.

Oh shit, me and my big mouth. "It's nothing, really. I'm just not feeling great, that's all."

"Are you still in bed? You sound sleepy. What did you do last night?"

Declan didn't like Lisa and he hated it when she went out with the girls. Not that he had any rights to be making decisions

229

about her life anymore. She felt a spark of anger and huffed. "Not that it's any of your business, but I went to Lisa's stagette." An awkward silence hung in the air.

"Declan?"

"How could you Miranda? While I rot away in here, you're out having fun!"Declan whined and Miranda bristled.

"I'd like to remind you Declan, I don't owe you *anything*. We aren't even in a relationship anymore. What I do with my time is my business! I don't even know why I'm talking to you right now. So be nice, or I'll hang up." Miranda threatened, hoping he'd be nicer because she really didn't want to hang up.

"Whoa Baby, please don't hang up. You're killing me, you know. It's just, the thought of you out at the bar with all the guys drooling and me in here, well..." Declan trailed off.

Miranda's heart melted. Her anger dissipated. *It must be so hard for him in there.*

"Mandy, thinking of you is the only thing that gets me through the day. Please don't be mad babe. I couldn't stand it if you were."

"Then don't tell me what to do Declan. I listened to you before and look where it got us."

"Sshhh baby, please be nice. I know it's my fault. I'm sorry. I wish we could go back and do it all over again. "

"So do I, but we can't. I don't know what to do anymore Declan. I keep waiting for John to find out it was me taking the discarded medications. I expect the police to show up at work, or here, anytime. I'm broke trying to pay off *your* bills. I barely have enough money for food or rent. I don't even feel like myself anymore. I feel old."

"You're not old," Declan cut in. "You're beautiful and don't you ever forget it. As soon as I get out, I'm going to make it up to you. You'll see. I'll make it better. I promise."

"I don't feel beautiful Declan. I feel *changed*. I'm not even sure who I am anymore."

Jagged Little Lies

"Why you're Miranda the marvelous, mouth-watering muffin," Declan teased.

"Jesus Declan, I'm trying to have a serious conversation with you. This isn't the time for jokes. In case you haven't noticed, my whole fucking life is falling apart here!"

"OK, OK jeez. I was just trying to lighten the mood a little."

Miranda sighed, reached for her glass, and drained the last drops of water before replying. "Well don't. I'm sorry if you can't handle a grown up conversation Declan. But I'm trying to tell you how I feel and I don't appreciate your jokes."

"Okay." Declan said quietly, sounding subdued.

Guilt blossomed as she listened to Decaln's tone. What was she doing? "Look, I'm sorry. I'm a little testy today. How are things going for you in there?"

"Um, all right I guess."

"What do you mean, you *guess*?"

"Well you know... I'm still pretty sick."

Miranda sighed. "I thought they were giving you medication to help?"

"They are. It's just..." Declan didn't finish.

"Just what?"

"It's not really enough, that's all. I'm still feeling sick. I need to find other ways of trying to feel better."

Miranda felt the chill run up her back. Dread spread through her body. "What do you mean by *other ways*?"

"Nothing much, I um shouldn't be talking about this on the phone. Are you coming to visit me tomorrow?"

"I don't know." She hesitated. Her head said run, her heart said go.

"Please come, *please*." He wheedled.

She couldn't disappoint him. The thought of him there, waiting for her- she just couldn't do it. "Declan, you need to start dealing with this *problem* of yours."

231

"I know honey. And I have. I'm going to this group. A twelve step meeting group, it's supposed to help me get better. I'm only doing it for you."

Hope flared inside Miranda. "That's good Declan. I'm so glad to hear it. What do you do in these twelve step meetings?"

"Well, ah Mandy, I can't really talk about it. They're confidential."

Miranda's eyes narrowed. "Are you sure you're really going Declan?"

"Jeez Mandy, I wouldn't lie to you. At least not anymore, I promise. Trust me baby. Okay?"

God she loved the sound of his voice, and the way he whispered *baby* into her ear. Her body responded, wanting him badly. She wanted to trust him more than she wanted anything else.

"Please Miranda, say that you'll come. Please, I need you."

The last bit of resistance she been holding melted. The thought of seeing Declan brought light to her world. She smiled, "Well, okay. Do you need me to bring anything?" She asked more from habit.

"Uh yeah, could you bring me some smokes?"

"What! You've gone through all your cigarettes already?"

Declan laughed. "Yeah, well, not much else to do here. The thing is I ah, lent most of them out. And when you bring the cigarettes in a bag the guards go through it. Sometimes you don't get them back for days. Plus they take some. So I was wondering if you don't mind, could you just bring them in your bra or something?"

"Are you crazy? I can't bring cigarettes in my bra! You want me to end up in jail too?"

"Well find someplace else to put them then. You'll think of something. And you can't end up in jail Mandy, they aren't illegal.It would really help me. *Please*."

"Jesus Declan, I can't believe you're asking me to do this!"

Jagged Little Lies

"Don't worry. I checked it out first. I got a buddy in here whose girlfriend brings them in all the time. But if you don't want to, I'll understand. I'll just have to go without, that's all."

"Well you'll just have to go without then! I'm not bringing them in like that. I'll bring your cigarettes in a bag, same as last time and you're lucky to be getting them at all."

"OK OK. Do whatever feels right. I just want to see you baby. I think of you every second."

"Yeah, well, maybe spend a little more time thinking about how you're going to get us out of this mess."

"I will. It's all I think about. Look my time is up. I have to go. I'll see you tomorrow?" Declan questioned.

"I guess so."

"K love you baby. Bye." Declan said hanging up the phone.

Miranda stared at the receiver in her hand. At least she hadn't said it back. She still didn't know what she felt for him, other than crazy. And she most definitely would *not* be smuggling cigarettes into jail.

How dare he ask her to do such a thing! What in the hell was he thinking?

She nibbled a finger nail as she thought about their conversation. Declan sounded disappointed. What was it like to not have freedom? Not to be able to come and go as you pleased? To live behind bars, scared for your life? It was bad enough he was sick all the time, but to have to go without cigarettes too?

And it wasn't only him who'd done wrong. She played a huge part in it as well. She was just lucky she wasn't sitting in a cell someplace too. The guilt she'd been feeling earlier grew heavier. She chewed her index nail furiously. *It was only one pack of smokes.* He really wasn't asking for much.

Eyes wide Miranda pulled her finger from her mouth gazing down in surprise. Her nail was ragged and chewed to the quick. Dammit! She'd stopped biting her fingernails years ago.

233

Guilt spread like wildfire as she thought about Declan. It strangled her with its suffocating hold. Her mangled finger hung in mid-air as she appraised the damage.

Oh to hell with it.

She might as well have a matching set.

Chapter 37

Jesus he was such an asshole. Problem was he really didn't seem to care enough to change it. Well... that wasn't *quite* it. He did care, but seemed *unable* to change. Or was it unwilling? Why would you want to change something that worked for you? Declan groaned, his arms trembling, as he hefted the bulky weights above him.

Muscles vibrated in parts of his body he never before knew existed as he set down the bar. Wet with sweat, Declan replayed the call. She was still half asleep and she'd sounded sexy as hell, her words throaty and deep. Just hearing her voice brought back memories of the times he'd lain awake in bed watching her sleep. He stiffened, groaning. You sure as shit didn't want to be walking around at half mast while here.

The bar hovered just above his head. Declan gritted his teeth pushing aside thoughts of Miranda. His arms screamed and his shoulders howled. He managed ten more repetitions before setting the bar down. His hands trembled as he sat up. His arms felt weird, like they wanted to float away. He flexed his biceps hoping to see an improvement.

Not bad. But then his build was pretty good naturally. He might not be as muscle bound as some of the guys here, but he had a pretty good V. Miranda sure thought his muscles were sexy as hell.

Determined, Declan picked up the bar forcing another ten repetitions. It was a good thing he hadn't asked her to smuggle in the pills. He might really have blown it. He figured the best way to see how far she would go was by starting slow. If she smuggled in cigarettes a few times, she'd get more comfortable with it and then he could ask her to bring in the pills. Contraband was coming in somehow.And he was pretty sure it was the ladies

235

who were bringing it in. Miranda just needed to grow a set-that was all.

And what the hell was she doing out at the bar? Jesus it pissed him off. Her friend Lisa was a real piece of work. Wouldn't she be happy now? Lisa never liked him. Always bitching to Mandy about what a lowlife he was, and how she could do better. I mean, what kind of friend would do something like that? It was too bad he couldn't introduce Lisa to Rooster. Maybe her idea of *lowlife* might improve. He'd bet Rooster could show her a thing or two.

She better come to see him. He'd be pissed if she didn't. He needed to straighten her out. No more going out to bars. He better be careful though. He was pretty sure she wouldn't leave him for good. But still, he didn't want to chance it. When it came right down to it, most people were full of shit. They threatened, but in his experience, they didn't really mean it. Still, Declan didn't want to lose Miranda.

There were vultures, just laying in wait, at the bars and clubs. He didn't want her anywhere near the scene. No way. He wanted her at home, waiting, until he got out, safe where she couldn't get into any trouble, or be tempted by another guy. Besides, a good woman belonged in the house, not out at the bars. And she was good. She just needed a little tweaking.

Yeah she'd come. Of course she would.

Glad to have resolved the problem, Declan thought about Twitch. The word on the row was he'd scored a shitload of dope last visiting day. Lately, the mood changed from one of threats and violence to one of vacant stares. Declan wondered why the guards didn't seem to notice. It wasn't hard to tell. Hell, half the guys were on the nod in here. Mind you, it was probably easier to guard a sleepy lot than it was a hostile one. Maybe they just didn't care.

Rubbing his bruised abdomen in anticipation, Declan hoped he could weasel a couple little beauties off Twitch. He might not be the sharpest tool in the shed, but he always seemed to have a good supply of dope. And Declan was going to help him out by lightening his load. After all, what was a buddy for?

He spied the dreaded ball being tossed by two of the larger goons. What in the hell did they stuff the ball with anyways, concrete? Before anyone could get the wise idea to throw it at him again, he left the recreation area. Declan cringed, remembering their howls of laughter from the last time. It felt like he'd been shot. He was sure he was dying. When he was finally able to breathe again he heard their laughter. By then he'd gathered a crowd. He wouldn't live that one down anytime soon.

On the way to his cell, Declan tried to appear confident. He passed others, nodding at a few, but mostly trying to look as if he was minding his own business. In here it was best not to speak unless you were spoken to, and even then you better be careful. Guys were always looking for a fight and you never wanted to give them opportunity. Then there were guys like Twitch who you could talk to, but even with him you needed to be cautious. Twitch types, were everybody's boy. And he would sell you down the road faster than you could shake a stick.

Declan entered his cell. Rooster was nowhere to be seen. His heart rate soared at the rare opportunity and glancing over his shoulder saw the hallway was vacant. *It was now or never.* Quickly he tossed aside Rooster's pillow freezing at the familiar cat call.

"Pretty Boy... Oh pretty boy. Where have you been? I've missed you." Falsetto called, taunting.

Declan dropped the pillow as if he'd just been scalded. He put it back exactly, and pulled a clean jumpsuit from the shelf. Nonchalantly he left his cell, not even giving falsetto a glance. Oh well, he needed a shower anyways. He knew he stank, but Jesus he hated those communal showers.

Damn, he'd been so close. Would Rooster be stupid enough to keep his stash there? Declan knew he was going to find it. It was just a matter of when. Still trying to visualize Rooster's stash, Declan entered the shower area. It was a big open acoustic pit. He chose the shower farthest from the two others inmates showering. Declan adjusted the water, closed his eyes and lathered his body with the soap from the dispenser on the wall. At one time his soap and hair products were the best money could buy. His shower at home was loaded with every product under the sun. Now he used prison soap.

Out of the shower and toweling off, he stared past the other men. It was hard not to look. The first time he showered here he'd been horrified to find his eyes wandering to the guy in the shower stall, comparing. He always wondered how he measured up in that department. Now he knew. As far as he could tell he was average, but just to be sure he was constantly checking. He'd never been all that interested in a guy's equipment before, but now he was morbidly curious. That kind of curious could get him killed, if he wasn't careful.

The shower energized him and he went in search of Twitch. Not like he looked very far. Declan knew where to find him. Declan passed guards and inmates as he looked for Twitch. It was getting easier. It was weird, everybody wanted respect here, demanded it even. As if being in jail was the highest ranking a man could achieve.

The day room was loud. Declan wandered by tables where inmates played cards, or hung out watching the tube. He spied Twitch right away, slouched against a pillar watching television. Declan poked him in the shoulder. "Hey, what's up?'

Twitch jumped. "Jesus man, don't sneak up on me like that!"

"Whoa, chill out."

"Pretty hard to do when there might be a hit out on you. Don't you think?" Twitch sniveled his large Adams apple bobbing as he spoke.

"Yeah, you got a point." Declan conceded.

"Man I'm messed up." Twitch confessed.

Jagged Little Lies

Declan stared at Twitch. His hair hung greasy and limp. His skin was pale and waxy, with big blotches of red erupting in large pimples. His body twitched and jerked spastically. "What are you on?"

"I got a shitload of meth and I haven't slept in a few days. It's a bad trip man, but I can't seem to put it down." Twitch's cheek jumped and then stilled.

"Maybe you need to try something else. I can get you a couple oxy's. That should help."

Twitch shot him a red eyed stare. "Downers have never really been my thing man, but I guess I could give it a try. I sold all the horse Jenny brought in."

"Yeah, I can tell." Declan snorted. "Christ half the guys in here are on the nod. You'd think they'd notice." Declan said nodding at the guards.

"As long as everybody behaves, it's all they care about. Besides, these guys aren't dangerous when they're nodding; it's when they aren't you have to watch out." Twitch jerked a hand to his face and then changing his mind, lowered it to his side.

Declan watched Twitch; glad he was nowhere near as fucked up as this poor bastard. "I've got some cash I'm looking to rid myself of. I was wondering if we might make a deal."

"Well, like I said, I sold it all except for the meth. I didn't think up was your thing." Twitch picked a pimple staring at Declan.

Declan smiled. "Let's just say I'm broadening my horizons."

"How much you want for the pills?"

"How much you want for the meth?"

Twitch thought for a moment and reached in his pocket. "How about we call it even, I'll give you half a gram, and you give me two of the forties."

"Nah, how about I give you one forty milligram and you give me half a gram like you said. Besides, by the looks of you, I'd be doing you a favor by taking it off your hands."

239

Twitch fidgeted. His cheek twitched. His knee jerked. His eyes blinked, his lids closing rapidly.

Declan waited.

The dope slid from Twitch's pocket as he handed it to Declan from behind the pillar. "Deal," He spoke softly.

With his newest treasure carefully stashed, Declan left Twitch before anyone could notice what they were up to. He couldn't wait to get back to his cell. Shit he hadn't done meth in a long time.

Declan fingered the oxy still left in his pocket. It was going to be a *good* night. A wide grin split his face. It was party time. The grin faltered for a second as he thought about the cash he was burning through. Oh well, easy come, easy go.

And there was always more where that came from.

Whistling, Declan hurried back to his cell.

Chapter 38

Lyndsey walked her group to the door, smiling inwardly as she observed them. Each of the twelve walked with purpose. To get the hell out of there! The day hadn't been easy for any of them. The people leaving were not quite the same as they'd been entering the building and their somber faces reflected the changes.

"I'll see you tomorrow morning at 8:30 am sharp." Lyndsey reminded her group.

Eric groaned. "Can't we start a little later tomorrow seeing as we did so much today?"

Lyndsey raised an eyebrow and Eric grinned, backing off.

Irene was moving slowly. Lyndsey was concerned this week was going to be too much for the elderly lady. "How are you doing Irene?"

Irene's cane canted to the left as she leaned heavily upon it. She nodded sadly, "I just wish I learned all this years ago. It would have made such a difference for Harry and me." She commented wiping a tear from her cheek.

Lyndsey smiled at her encouragingly. Irene was one of those precious people, where what you see, is really what you get. She was sweet and feisty and vulnerable, all rolled into one. With a gentle squeeze to Irene's hand, Lyndsey said goodbye.

There was still one missing. Lyndsey turned looking for Susan hoping she hadn't managed to slip through the doors without her noticing. She asked her group of twelve to refrain from using any mood-altering substances this week. Only her antenna was picking up signals from Susan. Lyndsey stood by the door and spotted Susan coming from the washroom.

Susan walked with her head down, and passed Lyndsey without noticing.

Lyndsey tapped Susan on the shoulder and she jumped. She noticed once again how pale and thin the woman was. "I'm sorry; I didn't mean to startle you Susan."

Trembling, Susan attempted to make light of it. "It happens all the time." She murmured.

Should I wait until tomorrow? Lyndsey wondered. After all, their day was long and she really wanted to see Billy. Torn, but knowing she couldn't just ignore her intuition, Lyndsey decided to voice her concerns. "Susan, I'd like to speak with you for a minute."

Susan blanched, her lips thinning with disapproval.

Inside her office Lyndsey asked Susan to take a seat. "I know it's been a long day, but I'm concerned about you. I noticed you stopped talking to the other group members and when anyone asks how you're doing, you say *fine*. Susan, you're not fine, and it's written all over your face."

Susan scowled. "How I'm doing is really nobody's business but my own. I didn't come here to talk about myself. I came to learn how to help my son."

"I understand that was your motivation, but how you're doing *does* affect your son."

Susan's fingers whitened as they gripped the arms of the chair. Her nostrils flared. The air filled with distrust and hostility. "I will not be gossiped about over coffee. What I think and feel is not your, or anyone's, business. And quite frankly, I think you're misleading people. I would never have come if I knew this was about me."

Hard, black eyes, stared intently at her. It was unsettling. The woman was sick and miserable. Her world was one of darkness, and hurt. She trusted no one. It wasn't that long ago she'd been there herself. No way was she going to be able to get through to her tonight.

The tough love approach out the door, Lyndsey tried penetrating the blackness of Susan's gaze with empathy. "Well

Jagged Little Lies

I'm glad you came. I know this doesn't make sense to you right now and it shouldn't. But I can tell you this, the more you put into your week, the more you'll get out of it. If you can, try and stay open to the process. It will get easier."

Susan shook her head clearly not believing her and locked eyes with Lyndsey. "All I want to know is will this help my son? I want your word or I won't keep wasting my time. If you can't guarantee me being here is going to help my son, I won't be coming back tomorrow."

And that would be the worst mistake you ever made, because then you'd continue to live in your self-induced misery, growing more bitter and resentful with each passing year. Of course she didn't say it out loud. Susan wasn't ready to hear it quite yet, but Lyndsey hoped she'd stay. Soon enough she'd be ready to hear the truth. *And the truth shall set you free.*

It was going to be a long road. There was a lot of hurt and damage to unravel, before becoming well could ever enter the picture. *Love her until she can love herself.* It was a motto she learned in her earlier years, when first entering the rooms of twelve step meetings. Back then Lyndsey was filled with bitterness, hurt and resentment. It was a poisonous existence and she hadn't been at all loveable, looking at Susan now took her back there. She was so close to death, living in apathy. Numbed out and toxic, Lyndsey dwelled in a dark, lonely and hopeless place. The women in her support groups had shown her love and empathy, in spite of her nasty ways. They loved her, until she could love herself.

And to whom much is given, much is expected. "Well then, if that's what you need. I can guarantee you this week will help your son. But only on one condition."

"What do you mean by *condition?*"

"In order for me to guarantee this program to succeed, I will need your full cooperation. That means when someone asks you

243

for your input, you give it. You start opening up and let us get to know you. The other group members are taking risks too."

Susan frowned wiping a strand of thinning hair from her brow. Her voice was cool, but her fingers trembled giving away her true emotional state. "I don't see how my feelings have anything to do with this, but... I'll try." She complied.

Lyndsey grinned. "That's all we require."

Now for the tougher part, the grin slipped from her lips. "Susan, there was another issue I noticed. I would like to address it with you." This would be a prickly subject. She wished it got easier over the years, addressing difficult situations, but it never did.

Round shoulders stiffened as Susan looked at her blinking, her nostril flaring as if smelling smoke.

"I ah," Lyndsey stammered, "couldn't help but notice you seemed very tired when you first got in this morning." *Christ what an understatement! Susan was almost nodding off in her chair.*

"So? What, you're not allowed to be tired in this group either?" Susan argued.

"Of course you're allowed to be tired, but *tired* isn't what I was picking up. I'm going to speak bluntly with you, please keep in mind this is in your best interest."

A sharp, gasp-like breath met her words. Susan's head lowered and she stared at the ground waiting.

Lyndsey cleared her throat. "What I saw wasn't so much *tired* as it was *sedated*. Are you taking any medication?"

"You already asked me this question and I answered you no. I'm not taking any medication. Like I said, I was just tired, that's all." Susan looked up defying her to mention it again.

She's bullshitting me. This must be a bigger problem than either of us knows. Lyndsey inwardly winced, *great, an addict in the family program.* It wasn't supposed to happen. There was no point in explaining to Susan people who didn't have addiction issues didn't lie about taking their medication.

"Can I go now? I'm *tired.*" Susan dragged out the word, as if talking to a two year old incapable of understanding.

Well Linds, be careful what you wish for, because you just might get it. She thought back to earlier in the day when she wished she might be working once again with her addicted clientele. Lyndsey nodded at Susan. "Yes, you can go."

At the front door, Lyndsey whispered "goodbye" to Susans' disappearing back. Susan moved quicker than she had all day as she escaped the building. Not bothering to answer back, she scuttled out the door and down the walkway. Lyndsey watched her retreating, understanding that for the moment, Susan felt free.

Free, because soon she would use again. She would be looking forward to it. Free, because for the moment, Susan could breathe and not hurt. Free, because the pills would bring temporary comfort to a women who so desperately needed it. Free, because sedation would temporarily ease her thoughts.

But nothing was free for long. Soon the freedom Susan experienced would turn into something far, far, different. It would become a *need*, something dark and evil and alive, coiling inside your spirit and robbing you of all things worthy. Susan didn't know it, but she harboured a deadly guest. One who wasn't satisfied until its host was nothing but a hollowed-out, empty husk.

With a sigh Lyndsey retraced her steps, picking up her coat and purse she locked the doors. She really needed to go and see Billy. *But maybe she should call Drake first?* A quick glance at her watch and she decided against it. It was getting late and she wanted to get there before Billy was asleep for the night.

Once in the car, Lyndsey put the phone on speaker. The car purred, starting up right away. Lyndsey smiled remembering another, older car, years ago. People might not understand her appreciation of something as miniscule as a car starting, but when you've lost everything dear to you and lived to tell about it, you look at it differently.

The speaker echoed the ringing of the phone, bouncing off the four walls of the car, as the tires ate up the miles to the hospital. "Hello," Drake answered, in his deep, sexy voice.

Her heart fluttered. The feeling was intense and euphoric.

Now this was true freedom.

Content, Lyndsey pulled into the hospital parking lot, hoping to catch a glimpse of Billy.

Chapter 39

Just who in the hell did Lyndsey think she was talking too? Susan seethed, opening her purse to extract a pill. Dry, she swallowed it, liking the bitter aftertaste it left in her mouth. With an eye on the rear view mirror she backed out of the parking lot narrowly missing another car. *Asshole*, she swore at the near miss. What a waste of time, this was such bullshit. It was all she could do, sitting in a group of strangers and white knuckling the chair. She didn't belong there. She wasn't anything like *those* people. And did that Lyndsey person really think she was buying the caring attitude? Christ she wasn't that naive. The others sure seemed to be eating it up though. Why in the hell would some strange woman even give a shit about her?

Was it was the money? Maybe Lyndsey earned a lot of money pretending to care about others. And how dare she talk to her about medications! She wasn't a doctor and she certainly had no right to be asking those questions. Of course she could ask all she wanted, but Susan had no intention of telling her the truth. Not that she had anything to hide really, it just wasn't her business. Maybe the next time she saw Lyndsey she would ask her if *she* was on any medications. Come to think of it, the woman looked entirely too happy. She probably was on something.

Pedal to metal, Susan drove furiously. She felt so torn, caught up in something she wanted no part of and yet, if there was a chance it would help Declan...

The flash of blue and red in the rear view mirror caught her attention breaking her train of thought. Glancing down at the speedometer she groaned. *Shit!* She was speeding *and* she was caught! The police car narrowed the distance between them tailing her bumper. The flashing light lit up the interior of her car. Heart thundering, she pulled over to the side of the road and glanced down at her purse. Her hand jerked spastically on the steering wheel causing the tires to skid in the gravel. The pills! The prescription pad, Shit!

She wasn't even supposed to drive on this medication. Dammit! What in the hell was she going to do? This was all Dick's fault! Straightening out the car, Susan turned her blinker on while waiting at the side of the road.

Was she supposed to hold her hands in the air? The blue and red lights lit up the highway in front of her. She prayed none of the passing motorists recognized her car.

Not sure what to do with her hands she folded them in her lap, entwining her fingers. The folded hands vibrated. Susan quickly pulled them apart hoping to still the shakes. Why was she shaking so much? Was she getting Parkinson's, or some other dreaded disease?

Hands now resting on her hips she thought about her purse. The police officer wouldn't ask to see inside of it, would he? *Her driver's license!* He would want to see that! She glanced in the rear view window watching as the driver's side door opened. She snatched up her purse and fumbled inside, trying to pry her driver's license from the wallets plastic sheaf, but it stuck. With a furtive glance at the car behind, she saw the officer climb out of his vehicle.

The purse yawned open on her lap, the prescription pad peeking up at her. With as little movement as possible and trying to appear calm, Susan carefully removed the pad from her purse shoving it far beneath her seat. While trying to decide what to do with the pills she stole another panicked glance in the side mirror. *Shit! He was almost at her car!*

Her hand, acting of its own accord, removed the bottle from her purse and placed it behind her back, pushing until it disappeared into the seats crevice. The purse still gaped open and her fingers fumbled once again trying to remove her driver's license.

Jagged Little Lies

A blinding beam stilled her frantic hands and she glanced up blinking.

A knock on the window followed by a muffled, "Open the window please ma'am."

Obeying the officer Susan pushed the button, rolling down the rear passenger's window instead. "Oh shit." She mumbled.

"Ma'am?" The officer questioned.

"Ah, just a second please." She said trying again, this time hitting the right button.

The beam of the officer's flashlight swept the interior of her car, before coming to rest on her face.

"Jesus that's bright!" She snapped. "Do you mind?" Susan ground her teeth together trying to rein in the rage coursing through her nervous system. She was just so sick and tired of people for Christ's sakes.

The bright light slid off her face lowering to the purse in her lap.

"Did you know you were speeding?" The officer asked.

"I was in a hurry to get home," she admitted. "I probably was going a little too fast."

"It was more than just a *little too fast* ma'am. You were doing a hundred and forty in a hundred kilometer speed zone. That's excessive speeding."

"Yes, well, I'm sure I wasn't the only one. I was just keeping up to traffic." She said waving at the empty road before her.

The flashlight beam circled the car once more.

"Have you had anything to drink tonight ma'am?"

"No, well some water and coffee, if that's what you mean." She laughed, trying to appear calm.

The officer wasn't amused. His tone was without a trace of humor or friendliness. As he leaned into her car she got her first good look at him. "I'd like to see your driver's license and registration."

Jesus! He wasn't any older than Declan! He was just a boy. He looked far too young to be an officer. Mind you, everyone seemed to look younger these days. The tightened grip of fear she'd been experiencing relaxed now that she knew she was dealing with a child. Susan tried pulling the license free once more.

The flashlight beam followed her attempts. Susan gave up finally offering the officer/child her entire wallet.

"Registration please ma'am." He said prompting her.

The papers slid from the glove box and she handed them over as well. Her hands shook only slightly. Susan hoped he didn't notice.

With a step backwards away from the car, the officer advised. "Please wait in your car ma'am."

Susan watched through the side mirror as he took her driver's license and registration papers back to his vehicle. The cop/child would be checking to see if everything was legit, and it was thank God.

Minutes ticked by. Her fingers drummed a tune of impatience and frustration on the steering wheel. *What in the hell was he doing in there?* A car passed, slowing as it saw the flashing red lights. Susan lowered her head, praying she wasn't recognized.

There was a time when she knew everyone in this town. She used to love it when a neighbour or friend passed by in their vehicle, or on the street and waved, or stopped by for a chat. But that time was long gone and all she wanted now was to be left alone.

Her leg twitched impatiently jerking. Her body vibrated. She gnashed her teeth. Anger burned, leaving acid in her throat. Really nothing had gone right since Dick left. Her world had slowly fallen apart. Each year, another little piece of it floated away leaving her on shaky ground. They'd made a vow. Till

Jagged Little Lies

death do us part. Not, I'll leave you when I don't get my way, or I'll abandon you and find someone else.

No, they solemnly sworn to love and cherish one another in sickness and in health, for richer or poorer, forever and ever, until death do they part. They had taken their vows in the eyes of God, as well as friends and family.

And she meant it, with every breath in her body. She thought Dick did too. Susan wished it was death that parted them and not this. It would have been easier visiting his gravesite than knowing he chose to abandon them and moved on with his life.

Bile burned in her throat, so bitter and hot it caused physical discomfort. She instinctively reached for a Tums and then stopped. A glance in the side mirror revealed the outline of the officer sitting in the car behind her. *I'm sure a Tums is fine.*

With a practised move, she peeled back the foil thumbing out a tablet. Her teeth crunched the chalky pills, her thoughts once again returning to Dick. She wished she wasn't so gutted when it came to him. She hated him more than anybody she'd ever met, but it was bittersweet. There were so many sweet memories too. They'd shared moments of pure, ecstatic bliss. There were times of closeness in their marriage when they were like one person. At one point, they'd even finished each other's sentences.

Dick even got sympathy pimples. Every month, just a few days before she got her period, sure enough there was Dick, sprouting a new crop of zits. Like clockwork they were. They laughed, knowing to get in an extra night of lovemaking while they could.

A soft bubble of laughter escaped with the memory. Her smile faltered and then stopped abruptly, her laughter curdling in her throat. Tears flowed hot, down her cheeks. *Get it together girl!* She warned herself glancing once again into the side mirror.

The child/officer was getting out of the car.

Finally, at least now she could get going. God she hoped she could sleep tonight. She didn't think she'd attempt the bed again. Maybe a nice cup of hot tea would do it and then zone out in front of the TV. Mindless chatter could be so comforting. Really, she just couldn't bear the silence another night.

Fingers tapping Susan waited.

The officer approached the car, his flashlight lighting the way. Her hand snaked through the driver's window expecting her belongings back.

Her palm remained open and empty.

Instead of returning her belongings the officer said." Please step out of your vehicle ma'am."

Hesitant and not knowing why she was being asked to do so, Susan obeyed leaving the driver's side door wide open.

The officer's flashlight once again swept the interior of the car.

Susan's breath hitched as she spotted a tiny trace of white staring up at her from between the seat's crevice.

Chapter 40

Miranda clicked off the TV to restless to sit still any longer. Incessant mind chatter plagued her thinking, leaving an ominous pit of dread in her stomach. The fingernail she'd been gnawing on was wet and shriveled as she wiped it on her jeans. *Dear God, dinner with her family, at least the Tylenol helped a little.* It wasn't something she was looking forward to. Not at all, but when her Mom called she couldn't think of a way to say no.

The blush brush stopped in mid-air, as she pictured it. She could already see them. Her family, sitting around the table asking a million questions about her life. Her brother would be there with his wife and kids, her Mom and Dad in their usual chairs, and her, the odd man out.

Miranda sighed. *Might as well get this over with* and adding an extra touch of color to her cheeks, took a final look in the mirror. Her reflection stared back. Miranda cringed. Big pouches of flesh sagged below her eyes, leaving her looking tired and *changed.* Hopefully her family wouldn't notice

Purse in hand, she briefly debated walking, but it was too far. It would have been nice to clear her head though. It was still a little foggy from last night. If she felt this awful, how did Lisa feel? The caring thing to do would have been to call, but she just wasn't into talking. Not today.

Let the performance begin! What a performance it would be, acting as if everything was just peachy. With her mother's eagle-eye it wouldn't be easy. Miranda steeled herself for the upcoming event as she pulled into the old familiar driveway.

Her brother's van was already there. Looking at it she shuddered, remembering when her brother owned a Harley and a jacked up pick-up truck. They'd been close in those days, always conspiring against their parents. They were rebels, each with their own dreams about how to live free and independent of society's rules. They laughed at their parents, with their self imposed bars, vowing they'd never end up like them.

Miranda shook her head looking at the minivan. Two cars seats sat behind the driver's seat. A *minivan,* never in her wildest dreams did she see that one coming. Her brother had bought into the great North American dream. A wife, a home, two kids, a dog and a god damn minivan. He was exactly like her parents, and now, they all wanted her to be just like *them.*

As she opened the front door, a delicious smell greeted her. Her mouth watered and her stomach rumbled. Her mom was a good cook. It smelled like she prepared one of Miranda's favorites. The smell of roast beef and the sound of children's laughter mingled in the air. This house represented so much of her life. For a moment she stood in the hallway blinking, trying to clear the tears, overcome by the sudden onslaught of emotion stepping through the front door brought with it.

She'd grown up in this home, her bedroom just up the staircase. Countless hours were spent imaging her life when she moved out. Certain she'd be a rock star, or an executive with an important title. Maybe she'd be a nurse, or a doctor, or a veterinarian. For sure she'd be a humanitarian making a difference, travelling to third world countries and volunteering her services. Of course she would be confident and smart. The possibilities were endless; she could be anything she wanted.

Back then she didn't doubt herself for one second. She looked longingly at the staircase. If only she could go back. Start over. Climb the stairs and go back to her room, back five or ten years.

"Hi sweetie, I didn't hear you coming in."

Miranda startled, looking up from the life she hadn't lived. "Oh hi mom, I was just coming to find you."

Her mom looked closely at her. "You look tired, is everything all right?"

Jagged Little Lies

Oh oh, here we go. "Of course, I'm just feeling a little under the weather."

"Well then, come with me. What you need is a good home cooked meal." Her mom said, wrapping her arm around Miranda and steering her into the heart of the house, the kitchen.

Miranda's mother believed a good, home-cooked meal solved all your troubles. She put all the love she carried into her cooking. The results were always mouthwatering.

In the kitchen, Miranda spied her four-year old nephew, Toby, pushing his truck around the floor. *Vroom, vroom* he said, as he ran over the feet of any who happened to be in his way.

Tucked in a corner was his two year old sister Emily, busily eating in her high chair. She had more food on her face than in her mouth. When she saw Miranda she gave her a big, messy-mouthed grin and waving her chubby little hands in the air she cried, "Randa, randa in her high-pitched squeal.

Her brother glanced away from Emily and shot her a dirty look. "Please Miranda. We're trying to get her to eat her dinner."

Biting back a swear word Miranda replied sarcastically, "And hello to you too."

Her brother barely acknowledged her presence. He was focused on his youngest not making a mess and eating every crumb.

What happened to you and who stole my brother?

But she already knew the answer to that question. Her brother met Marley and forgot everything, and everyone, else. He changed from a free-spirited guy to a lovesick puppy. He followed Marley around 24/7 and even adopted Marley's beliefs and lifestyles. They got married and the rest was history. Her brother was just a memory, except for the odd glance from time to time.

For something to do she poured a glass of water and asked her mother, "Can I do anything to help?" If she appeared busy, maybe she could avoid the conversation sure to follow at the round table.

Her mother smiled shaking her head. "No Miranda, it's all done. Just sit and visit please." She said waving her hand at the vacant chair.

Her brother, eyeing her water glass, shot her another dirty look. "Thirsty?" He quizzed. He very much disapproved of her lifestyle and wasn't shy about voicing his opinion.

Her mother spoke for her. "She's a little under the weather Vince. Leave her alone." She said stepping into an old familiar role.

"Ya right!" He said, eyeing Miranda and snorting. "What you got the flu? Probably the 24-ounce kind," He laughed apparently amused by his wit.

Marley came to her rescue, looking at Vince she frowned. "Knock it off Vinny."

The smirk on Vince's face disappeared to be followed by one of hurt. "I was just kidding. Can't anyone take a joke?" He complained.

Toby roared over her foot stomping her toes. "Vroom, vroom," He shouted.

Emily copied with her own version. "Rmmm," she said, squirting a mouthful of peas into the air.

Vince's face paled and he mumbled, "Jeez," jumping up from his chair.

Miranda's father took a sip of his coffee, adjusted his glasses, and asked, "What's new?"

Oh not much. I'm just debating on whether or not to smuggle some cigarettes into the prison for Declan and yes, I'm going to visit him. Lisa drank so much she puked in the cab on the way home last night. Oh, and I rubbed oil on a stripper and really kinda liked it. By the way I might be losing my job and going to jail, well that's if anyone finds out I was taking medications from the pharmacy. And let's not forget I don't have enough money to pay my rent and could be facing bankruptcy and eviction...

Her dad knuckled an eyeball before setting his glasses back in place. He looked at her waiting for a response.

Her shoulders bumped up shrugging, as if to indicate nothing much, but just in case he didn't get the message she voiced, "Not much." She said, while reaching down to grab the truck.

Toby glanced up from the floor his little face all scrunched up and looking more like his dad than ever. "My truck," he insisted, before snatching it back.

Her brother glared at her frowning once more.

Intervening yet again, her mother announced, "Dinner."

Chapter 41

Jesus that was close. Declan hurried out of the laundry room, and managed a nod as he passed the guard. The broken glass he pilfered pressed against his leg. As far as he could see you couldn't tell. He sure as shit hoped the guard wouldn't notice the slight bulge.

Declan held his breath. The guard stared through him as he passed on by.

The meth he scored was burning a hole in his pocket. Rooster better not be in a late-night mood.

Entering his cell, Declan found Rooster sitting upright on his bed reading a book. He looked up from the novel with a smug grin. "You got something for me?"

Declan nodded, fishing in his pocket careful not to dislodge the glass, or little paper wrapped package, and pulled out a wad of cash setting it beside Rooster.

Rooster's meaty hand remained palm side up and Declan fished inside his jumpsuit again. This time he held out two, shiny-round, yellow pills. "I got rid of most of them. Twitch is royally messed up and he took one. A couple of the guys from B block wanted them too."

Rooster raised his eyes and squinted. His face resembled a sunken Halloween mask. "Did you get *all* the money? I don't want any fronts."

Declan bent sifting through the bills, counting, he calculated. "I sold four of the forties. That should be about a hundred bucks I owe you." He said, pulling out the right amount of money and pocketing the rest. "The guys are bitching they want something stronger, they're hoping I can bring the eighties next time."

Rooster snorted. "Yeah well beggars can't be choosey now can they?"

"Probably not, but I think you'd move more of em with a higher dosage."

Rooster's eyes bugged. "Listen boy, if I wanted any shit from you I'd squeeze your head. I'll be doing the thinking around here."

"OK," backing down Declan agreed. "I didn't mean anything by it. Just trying to help out is all." He fidgeted wondering how he could ask for his payment.

Rooster's eyes retracted back into their sockets. "Why didn't you get rid of them all?"

"I tried, but Twitch's girl brought in a shitload of horse and there's not a real high demand at the moment. I'll try again tomorrow," he said, eyeing the little yellow beauties.

He hoped Rooster would get the hint and offer them up as payment. He could have himself one hell of a party, what with the meth to go up and the oxy's to come down. Uppers had never really been his thing. The crash coming down was way too brutal, but with the help of the two little beauties Rooster held in his large sweaty palm, he was looking forward to this night.

"You bet your ass you will," Rooster growled. "Here, take this and we'll call it even," he said, offering Declan one of the yellow orbs.

Declan reached for the pill, his revulsion for Rooster lessened by his need. Rooster walloped him in the arm as he palmed the yellow orb. It was like a sledgehammer being drilled into his bicep. He was going to have another bruise. His hatred for Rooster raised another notch.

Waiting, it was all about the waiting. Oh he'd bide his time. But he'd get him. One day, sure as shit, he would. This knowledge soothed his aching arm.

Rooster laughed. Pain was the old guy's drug of choice. Pain and demoralization were what made the Rooster tick.

Tick tock you freak. It's coming your way.

260

Jagged Little Lies

Rage burned as Declan climbed the ladder settling onto the bunk.

Rooster made a harrumphing sound with his throat and got up from his bed to spit a disgusting mass into the toilet. He stood at the bars glowering, just looking for a fight.

Muted voices of the inmates settling into their bunks could be heard up and down the hallways

Rooster sighed, not finding what he'd come for and climbed back into bed.

Declan relaxed reaching into his pocket. *Soon*, he whispered, fingering the glass and reaching beneath his pillow as he retrieved the lighter. God he was tempted to light up now, but the risk of getting caught was high. Thank Christ meth didn't leave a smell. He knew the guys smoked dope in here, but he'd never been able to figure out *how?* Weed left a tangy, sharp, skunk-like smell in the air.

Declan strained his ears listening for any sign Rooster maybe asleep yet. *Waiting, waiting...*

Shit, he'd never been any good at waiting. He withdrew the paper package with bated breath and pulled the little flap free. He wouldn't be able to cut it up, but he could snort a little hit. Declan licked the end of his index finger and dipped it into the white powder, then putting the white tipped finger to his nostrils edge, inhaled, coughing, hoping to mask the noise.

His head exploded in a sudden rush. *Whoa.*

Rooster's breathing slowed.

Bam! Fuck that was good! Electricity sizzled throughout him.

The noise outside the hallway grew quieter still. Rooster let out a soft snore.

Almost time. Declan fingered the lighter careful not to make a sound.

Rooster's breathing grew deeper. The kind that said he was out.

Declan grinned removing the glass. A small dab of the white powder went on the under-curve and he lit it. The noise from the lighter ricocheted off the walls stopping his hand. He listened.

Rooster snored. The hallways were quiet.

Declan torched the pile of white powder. It smoked an odorless trail. He sucked greedily, inhaling as much as he could get of the intoxicating smoke into his lungs. On the verge of bursting, he almost gasped. His face grew red with the effort until finally he let go. A gush of smoke exhaled as he sank back against the wall.

Pleasure of the most intense kind flooded his brain, tunneling down his spinal column. His head buzzed. His toes tingled. He stiffened, aroused and ready. The broken glass still in his hand he re-lit the scorched little pile. The buzz was on. The dragon awoke. And he wanted *more*.

Hours passed. His thumb grew callused.

Declan re-lit the glass for the thousandth time. A small stream of smoke spiraled up. The straw he'd made from a piece of paper was bent and darkened. He held it in his mouth like a scuba diver might, inhaling from his apparatus as much of the precious smoke as he could. Finally satisfied, he put the straw down.

Hold it, hold it. Very little smoke escaped his sore, achy lungs.

Good one.

On auto pilot, he added another pinch of the white powder to the piece of broken glass he swiped in the form of a light bulb. Declan relit his makeshift pipe. *Better slow down.* He warned himself, taking in another massive lungful of smoke.

Rooster snored loudly beneath him.

His heart raced. Euphoria soared. *This was good shit.*

Footsteps at the end of the hallway penetrated his euphoric haze. As he hid his pipe and stash Declan swiped his face. His eyes stung. A greasy film covered his skin.

Jagged Little Lies

He recognized the footsteps. They belonged to a guard. Click, click, the sound echoed off the hallway floors strangely musical.

A sock yanked from his foot was a good hiding place. Declan wrapped his most precious belongings in it. With the dope safe inside its new home he thrust it underneath his pillow and wiping his slimy face once more, lay down. The prickly blankets pulled up to his chin he feigned sleep.

His heart slammed against his rib cage beating out a powerful tableau of dopamine overload. His toes curled. His body vibrated.

The blankets were itchy and prickled his chin. Declan fidgeted not able to lay still. The veins in his body were engorged, the blood rushing, like a swollen riverbed in the spring.

Rooster mumbled something incoherent in his sleep.

Declan twitched wide awake.

The guard's footsteps drew closer.

Man was he ever wasted.

Chapter 42

Twinkle, twinkle... Lyndsey hummed the rest of the lullaby. Sleep-heavy eyes looked up at her. Billy's eyelashes were gorgeous, long and black as he blinked repeatedly, fighting to stay awake. His cherry lips puckered in a bow turning upright smiling at her. His little hand held tightly to her finger. He smelled clean. Like powder and sweet baby boy.

A well-used recliner held the two of them as they rocked next to the hospital crib. Billy was warm and soft. Supple, not stiff, like he had been. With Billy in her arms she thought about Dee. She must be going through hell. Lyndsey knew what it was like to give up your child. In Dee's mind, she'd done the best thing she could for Billy.

Anyone without the disease of addiction would know the best thing for Billy was for his mother to get clean and sober. But addiction didn't work like that. It never told the truth. Instead it whispered words of deceit, planting them just as expertly as any horticulturist would. Next it hijacked your common sense and reasoning. What was left was a very sick person, with impaired judgement, incapable of rational behaviour or honest thinking.

In Dee's mind it made perfect sense to give up her child. As a matter of fact, she was probably boasting about her accomplishment right this minute. Dee would stand on her pedestal, avowing love for her child and how she would do anything for him. Well, anything but getting clean that is. This was the part Dee couldn't see, simply because she was no longer capable of *honestly* looking. So instead she would boast, and in the wee hours of empty arms, perhaps take comfort she'd done the right thing. Of course she was going to need larger amounts of mood altering substances to keep up the pretense, but this is what her illness desired all along.

265

And in the meantime, Lyndsey held her sweet baby boy, yet another casualty of this damned disease. Lyndsey kissed the top of Billy's head. It smelled of baby shampoo. With her cheek resting on top of Billy's soft hair, she knew there was going to be some tough days ahead.

Not that she was afraid. She wasn't afraid of anything really, other than going back to the life she once lived. The memory of it was still fresh. Humans were never meant to live in that much pain, deluding themselves they were having *fun*. Thank God for treatment centers and twelve step meetings.

Billy stretched and yawned loudly. Lyndsey marveled at the life she held in her arms. There was an energy and vibrancy to Billy now. She didn't think he would need to stay much longer. He looked so much better than the last time she'd seen him. Soon, they would need to decide.

*And speak of the devil...*Decisive footsteps approached just outside the doorway. Lyndsey tensed and Billy stiffened. Lyndsey relaxed her body, aware Billy was picking up her emotional cues.

A nurse wearing a serious expression entered the room. "Visiting hours are over." She stated.

Lyndsey nodded. "Thanks, I'll be just a minute. I was hoping to leave when he fell asleep."

The nurse frowned. "His chart says he's to go into foster care. Are you his new foster mother?" she inquired.

Not lying exactly, Lyndsey replied, "I'm hoping to be."

The nurse plumped up Billy's pillow fussing with his blankets. Satisfied with the arrangement, she turned and looked at Billy and Lyndsey. Her frown was replaced by a look of curiosity.

The nurse looked like she had something on her mind. Lyndsey waited.

The nurse fidgeted with the call button before putting it down. "Do you mind me asking you a question?"

Jagged Little Lies

Lyndsey stroked Billy's hair. "No. I don't mind."

Her eyes big and round the nurse looked down at Billy. "How do you do it? I mean I know it's not my business or anything, but how can you sit there, loving this child and knowing it's just going to break your heart. No good ever comes of it you know. His mother will either waltz back into the picture and cause more devastation and chaos, or he'll be so badly damaged no home will be able to care for him. Most likely he'll be bounce from foster home to foster home, until he's old enough to be on his own. Chances are slim he's going to end up anywhere other than jail."

Unfortunately, what the nurse said was so often true. It was just one more reason why she needed to make the decision she did, because it didn't have to be this way. But it took a particular person, or family, to raise a child who'd been damaged. A person who didn't quit when the going got tough, and who would give love unconditionally.

Poor Billy, he hadn't asked for any of this, but then neither did she. And rather than dwell in what *was,* the solution lie in what *is*.

Lyndsey shook her head and replied simply. "I think we do it because we can."

The nurse shrugged casting her dubious look. "Well I don't think I could do it. It's just too painful."

"What's a little pain?" Lyndsey laughed. "If I let my emotions make the decisions for me, why I'd never come out of the house again. And besides, we never know unless we try. And speaking of pain, I imagine your job would come with a considerable amount of it."

With an emphatic shake of the head indicating no, the nurse shook her head. "You'd be surprised. Most of us learn to shut off our emotions early on in our career. The ones that don't, well, they don't last. They burn out too quickly."

"See I disagree with you. I think there's a way you can do your job *and* feel your emotions. I mean if you're turning off your emotions here, you're probably turning them off elsewhere. Without emotions we're only half alive."

"Uh, uh," shaking her head again, the nurse argued. "You'll see. If you walk around feeling the pain of others, it's just too difficult."

"I imagine it would be *if* you felt it. But we can't really feel other people's pain. What we feel is our own response to it. It's *our* pain we feel and as long as we have healthy coping mechanisms in place, the pain doesn't consume us."

The nurse looked at her skeptically. "You must be new to this."

Lyndsey laughed quietly. "You're probably right," she agreed.

"Well it's been nice talking with you. Visiting hours are over. So I can tuck him in." She said reaching for Billy.

Lyndsey hesitated wanting to tuck Billy into his little bed, but the nurse reached for him instead.

Billy shrieked and stiffened at the nurse's touch, reaching for Lyndsey's neck as he clung to her. Lyndsey tried lowering him into bed, but he wouldn't let go of her neck.

With a grim face, the nurse managed to undo Billy's hands from her neck grabbing him away. She scowled at Lyndsey saying, "He will wake all the other children."

Billy's face purpled. Lyndsey wanted desperately to snatch him back. The health system they worked in was so broken and obsolete, but the nurse was just following orders. She had to play by their rules in here, even if it wasn't in Billy's best interest.

Not wanting to make a bad situation worse, Lyndsey complied. With a kiss to Billy's brow she promised to return. A final pat to his back and she forced herself to turn away. She hoped the nurse would stay with him until he fell asleep.

Jagged Little Lies

As the elevator doors slid open, she could still hear his cries. *One more wound for Billy.*

Determination hardened her jaw. She was about to even those wounds, even if it meant inflicting a few on herself.

Inside the elevator Lyndsey punched L for lobby.

Billy's cries followed her to the ground floor.

Chapter 43

The flashlight beam travelled past the small white lid and stopped. Susan watched in horror as the beam of light returned, shining brightly on the exposed lid.

The officer peered inside the car. "And what do we have here?"

Maybe she could say they were Dick's and she hadn't known they were there.

Officer-child reached over and wiggled the bottle free of the seat. He shone his bright light on the bottle reading the label.

Oh shit! Her name would be on the label! She couldn't say they were Dicks now.

With a questioning looked he turned to her. "Are these yours ma'am?" He asked.

Of course they're mine you twit, as you very well know. My name's right there on the label. Playing dumb she squinted. "I'm sorry young man. I don't have my glasses on." She caught her mistake as soon as it left her mouth, but it was too late to do anything about it.

"Your license doesn't indicate you need glasses to drive." Child-officer said stroking the peach fuzz on his upper lip, and glancing at her license again.

"I don't," she assured him, although she probably did, driving at night she was almost blind. "They're just reading glasses. I don't need them for driving at all." She said, hoping she sounded convincing.

The officer scowled giving her a penetrating look, and peering at the bottle again shook it rattling the pills. "This is a powerful medication ma'am. You shouldn't be driving while using this medication. It says it right here on the label."

Susan looked closely at the bottle he held, this time letting recognition dawn. "Oh, that's where they are. They must have fallen out of my purse. I wondered where they'd gotten too."

The beam of the flashlight took another swipe at her face. Her eyes closed instinctively. *She wondered if he could tell by looking at her eyes. She'd heard you could. Were her pupils bigger? Maybe playing dumb wasn't the right approach after all.*

Susan switched tactics hoping to intimidate him with her age. "Young man, if you don't take that light from my face this instant, I will be forced to report you."

The child-officer slowly withdrew the light. He handed her back her bottle of pills along with her driver's license still nestled inside her wallet and the registration papers. "You might want to put these in a safe place." He said indicating the medication he'd handed her.

"Yes. I will." She agreed.

With a wave of his hand at the open car door, he indicated she should get back in. A pad produced from his jacket pocket held his attention for the next minute. Child-officer bit his lower lip as he wrote.

Susan put her wallet back inside her purse along with her little bottle. Opening the glove compartment, she thought it could have been so much worse. *Thank God he didn't get down on his knees and looked under the seat. There was no way in hell she could have explained the prescription pad.*

Through the half-opened window, the young police officer handed her the ticket. Susan stuffed it into her purse not even bothering to look at it.

The boy child explained if she wanted to appeal she could go to the court house, in person, within so many days. Susan stopped listening to the legal jargon. She wasn't going to appeal anything. It would take way to much effort.

"Do you understand ma'am?"

"Yes."

Jagged Little Lies

"Well then have a good evening and a safe ride home."

"Thank you." She cringed, not in the least thankful. But what were you supposed to say in situations like these?

For the first time a grin appeared on the boys face and tipping his hat he replied. "You're welcome ma'am," as if he'd just held the door open for her, or some other small favor.

Not sure if she should just drive away, she waited.

He waved his hand. "You're free to go."

"Ah, well, thanks." She winced inwardly before carefully steering the car back onto the road.

For the next few miles she drove cautiously under the speed limit, continually peering into the rear view mirror to see if he were following her. She didn't think so. There weren't any headlights way back on the road.Not unless he was driving with his lights off. But he wouldn't do that, would he?

Finally sure she wasn't being followed, Susan increased her speed. She needed to make it to the pharmacy before it closed. There must be something she could use for sleep. With only a few pills left, she didn't want to dip into them, in the middle of another sleepless night.

With a look in the mirror, she shuddered. The darkness felt *sinister*. Was she becoming paranoid? What was happening to her? She was changing from the loving stable woman she'd been, to the one who now sat in her car worried something was out to get her?

Is this how people go crazy?

God, her life was crumbling before her very eyes. The pretentious mask she'd clung too for so long was beginning to crack. She seemed helpless to stop it. Stranger still, she wasn't even sure she wanted to. With Dick gone and Declan in jail, it all seemed so pointless anyways.

Confused, she thought about the medication she was using. It was created for exactly this purpose, to help people cope in difficult situations. And if this didn't qualify as a difficult situation, she didn't know what would. The truth was she liked these pills. She liked the way they made her feel and how they took away the pain. They comforted her making her life bearable. She could breathe with them.

As she pulled into the pharmacy's parking lot, she felt better. Maybe she just needed to relax a little. Not make such a big deal about every little pill. Susan shifted the gear into park and looked around. It was late and there weren't many cars. *Please don't be closed.* The lights were still on inside the building, but it looked empty. She ran from the car huffing as she crossed the pavement.

With a ferocious pull on the front door she yanked on it. The door swung open easily in her hand.

The cashier looked up from her till. "We're just about to close."

"I won't be long." Susan assured her, hurrying down the aisle before she could say anything else. With the signs overhead directing her, it didn't take long to find what she was looking for. Not sure what brand of over the counter sleep aide worked best, she grabbed both.

Back at the cashier, she glanced over her shoulder praying Miranda wouldn't be working this late. She wasn't. At least not that she could see.

Susan thought the cashier was giving her a funny look. "My husband asked me to stop, but I couldn't remember which kind he wanted." She laughed, shrugging as if two bottles of sleeping pills were no big deal.

Careful to follow the speed limit she made it home. Suddenly the night didn't seem quite so gloomy. Once inside she set her purchase on the kitchen counter.

Relieved at not having to face another night of endless misery and woe, Susan chided herself for not having thought of this before. She could have saved herself from so much agony. The directions on the bottle said to take one or two tablets before bed.

Jagged Little Lies

Not sure which bottle to take from, she took one tablet from each. Susan hummed while washing her face. She even put on a little silk teddy. One she hadn't worn in years. It was Dick's favorite. *Eat your heart out baby.*

Crawling into bed Susan plumped her pillows and fluffing the covers, settled into the soft cloud. She closed her eyes waiting. *I wonder how long it will take.*

The pillow didn't feel quite right and she plumped it again.

A vision of a three-year-old Declan crossed mind. He'd been lying in bed between Dick and her. "I want to pump it mommy!"

Declan plumped the pillows, his chubby little fists hammering up and down. He was so adorable. Dick reached over and mussed them up. It started a big tickling fest. The bed was destroyed. They three of them laughed until their stomachs hurt, eventually curling into a great big family ball, as they drifted off to sleep.

Susan blinked, fluffing her blankets, noticing once again how big the bed was. Eyes closed, she waited. She tried counting sheep, but their faces kept turning into Dick and Declan.

She tried meditating, but didn't get far.

Frustrated and anxious, she got out of bed. She must not have read the label right, walking through the darkened hallways she entered the kitchen. The childproof lid stuck for a moment inducing panic, before she twisted it off spilling one more tablet into her hand.

There, that should do it.

Back in bed she yawned. Her body felt warm and fuzzy. Her eyes felt heavy and she relaxed against the pillow top.

Her hand shot across the bed, grasping for the family no longer there.

Minutes ticked by. Her body loosened and relaxed.

Sleep and its sweet release finally found her.

Chapter 44

The car door slammed loudly in the quiet neighborhood, sounding like a gunshot in the black night. A startled cat jumped off the fence with a fierce yowl. A light came on in the window next door and curtains moved. Her skin prickled as she hurried to the front door.

Dinner with her family left her rattled. She couldn't get out of there fast enough. It was torturous sitting in their old chairs, in exactly the same spots, and pretending everything was fine. How many times did she bite her tongue? And her brother, she could have walloped him, watching as he smugly shoved food into his thickening body all the while acting as if his life was so much better than hers. Too bad she couldn't talk to him anymore. If she could, she'd ask him what happened. Why was he so sarcastic and bitter? Was he completely miserable? Because it sure looked like it. Why didn't he do something about it?

It was too bad she couldn't talk to any of them, at least not about anything important, or true. They wouldn't understand what she was going through, or how she felt. They'd tell her to stop it and what was she thinking? But they wouldn't understand. Not that she could blame them. She really didn't understand either. She just knew when she was with Declan, she felt alive in ways she didn't when she was with others. Declan understood her completely. She could tell him anything and he'd get it.

The worst part of the night was talking with her dad. He was a man of few words, but she got the feeling he knew a lot more than he was letting on. Not by what he said. More by the way he looked at her. She felt really bad about lying to him. But what else could she do?

Miranda put the plate of leftovers her mother sent home with her into the fridge and changed into her flannel pajamas. They were a gift from her family. Her mom gave them to her for Christmas last year. Declan hated them. He teased her about being dressed up like Nanook of the North, as she crawled into bed wearing them. It didn't take him long to get her out of them either. He preferred her to sleep naked, but she'd never been completely comfortable with it.

Now that he wasn't here, she needed the fleecy comfort and sent a mental thank you to her mother. The twinge of guilt returned. She really wished it didn't have to be this way. It was easier to avoid her family than face all the questions and disappointed looks. If she ever stopped answering their calls they'd be over in a heartbeat. So instead she played the game, even though it was getting old and tiring.

Miranda absentmindedly took the wrapper off the large slice of chocolate cake she'd been unable to eat earlier. It looked delicious. Her thoughts returned to Declan. Would he be asleep by now? She wondered if he slept a lot, hoping to while the hours away. God she felt bad for him. It was pretty harsh to send him to jail. Maybe it would help though. It wasn't like he was a bad guy, but he'd done some bad things. Is that how it was with all the inmates in there? Good guys doing bad things?

She finished off the cake with a gulp of milk and licked her fingers. Declan did bad things to get the medication he needed. She wasn't sure about the other inmates, but they didn't look like good guys. They looked mean and nasty and huge. She hoped Declan didn't get like them. Her finger traced the rim of the plate chasing crumbs. She patted her stomach.

Was she getting a gut on her? Declan wasn't interested in chubby woman, as he'd always been quick to point out. He'd adored her body. The one time she'd spoken to him about children, he reacted with horror. She'd been teasing, but he didn't know it. His eyebrows drew together and he frowned looking very serious, saying he never wanted her beautiful body to become marred. She continued teasing him, telling him it

Jagged Little Lies

might be too late, she might already be pregnant. His eyes grew wide. His face paled.

For some strange reason she had felt compelled to keep up the pretense and the next day Declan disappeared. It was the first time of many and she'd never forget the agony of wondering where he was, or who he was with. That night she'd berated herself as she lay wide awake in bed staring at the clock.

He hadn't come home until dawn. She heard him coming through the front door, the soft click of the door jamb announcing his presence. On tiptoes he'd come into their room, carrying a handful of wildflowers. With her eyes closed feigning sleep, she watched him through slits as he undressed, placing the flowers into a glass of water on the night table.

He'd climbed into bed ever so quietly whispering her name. With his arms wrapped around her, he had whispered words of undying love, and he was sorry and he'd never do it again. She lay stiff and enraged. How dare he worry her by staying out all night? Why didn't he call?

Other than sorry, Declan didn't seem to have an excuse. Miranda became so frustrated she hit him. Tired and frazzled she'd slapped him across the face wanting to shut him up, wanting to hurt him, like she'd been hurt.

He didn't try and stop her. Not once. He never even protected his face. Instead he faced her not flinching until she'd come to her senses. And once she did, she was horrified. She'd collapsed into his arms, and they'd both sobbed, each devastated. Their tears mingled and their bodies joined in the only way they knew how to make things better. Afterwards, they'd talked for hours, and Miranda felt closer to him than any other human on the planet.

For awhile it was good between them. They eventually got out of bed. Declan cooked brunch. They howled with laughter looking out their window at the neighbour as she scratched her head wondering where her missing flowers went. Declan was always doing things like that, bringing her flowers from somebody's garden, or a planter she coveted from a drive they'd been on.

Weird, but she found herself drawn to the danger of being caught. It was a little like getting high. Well not quite the same. The few times she'd used with Declan she didn't like it at all. But it was a rush getting away with things, and she liked how Declan adored her. As if she was the most important person in the world.

Why did it hurt so much? It was physical, the pain of missing him. Maybe she'd been too hard on him. Maybe she wasn't supportive enough. She'd been so sure her love could change him, save him even. Maybe she hadn't loved him *enough.*

Maybe leaving him was the wrong approach. Maybe what she needed to do was love him *more.*

Her pulse accelerated at this thought. It certainly felt right. If she really got honest with herself she couldn't wait to see him. She'd get up extra early tomorrow and go for a run. Maybe she could make a dent in the chocolate cake she'd just eaten. A long hot shower and makeup were just what the Doctor ordered.

She bet Declan would drool when he saw her. It was probably kind of mean, but she liked the power she held over him. It was intoxicating. She loved being needed by him. She might even smuggle in his damned cigarettes. After all, it wasn't like they were illegal. She would have to think about it, see how she felt in the morning.

Wishing it was morning all ready, Miranda picked up the book she was reading. Lying in bed she thumbed through the pages. The words blurred. She couldn't focus. Her mind kept returning to Declan.

Who was she kidding? She wasn't over him in the least. Without him, she felt halved. Like she was only half alive, and missing a vital ingredient.

Jagged Little Lies

Stop it Miranda you're driving yourself nuts! Think of something else. Okay what would she wear tomorrow?

Out of bed again, she found her favorite pair of skinny jeans and a tiny top she was too embarrassed to wear. She added a pair of black stilettos to the mix, placing the ensemble on the dresser.

Satisfied she climbed back into bed and turned off the light. Ensconced in flannel Miranda smiled in the dark. There wasn't much covering in the tiny top. Her stomach and cleavage would be on display for all to see. She'd seen strippers dressed in more clothing. *Oh well might as well use it, before I lose it.*

Anticipating the look on Declan's face, she drifted off to sleep.

Chapter 45

Footsteps stopped in front of his cell. Goosebumps broke out on his skin as he felt the guard's eyes searching the darkened interior where he lay. A droplet of sweat trickled into his eye and he almost blew it. His heart quivered. *Was he having a heart attack?* His toes jerked and his calves' spasmed. Declan's jaw clenched tightly, the muscles twitching.

A beam of bright light played over the wall beside him. He closed his eyes, willing his body to relax. Rooster snored loudly below and the flashlight beam lowered. Declan opened his eyes a crack, peering through the slits. The guard's face was pressed between the bars as he concentrated his search, the flashlight beam sweeping the bed below.

A grinding noise escaped his jaw and he froze. The flashlight beam rose hovering over his bed. *Fuck.* The beam hung there, just over his bed, for a second which felt like eternity. It was all he could do to lay still. Wisps of something crawly traced across his skin, as if ants walked on him. The urge to itch was unbearable.

The guard withdrew his face and the beam bounced along the wall before coming to a rest on the hallway floor. Declan ripped off his blanket looking for the ants. Other than his boxers, he saw nothing. The crawly feeling left him panicked. Not sure what to expect he looked more closely at his limbs. He couldn't see any bugs, but then again it was pretty dark. *Maybe they were under his skin?* Panic seized him again as he scratched his legs. The relief was instantaneous. He scratched harder, this time including his arms and face.

His fingers came away wet and he looked at them in surprise. He was barely able to make out the darkened smudges on their tips. The bed below him creaked. *Oh shit.*

Rooster roared. "Stop that boy! You're like a dog with fleas. Don't make me get up."

Declan played possum. It didn't work.

"Did you hear me?" Rooster threatened as he got out of bed.

"Yeah I heard you." He quickly agreed.

Rooster rose to his full height rearing his arm back and cuffed him in the ear.

Declan's head spun with the impact. A high ringing noise echoed inside his skull.

Satisfied, Rooster turned to the urinal. Not wanting to witness the old goat's bathroom habits, Declan turned his head. The urge to itch was driving him mad. It was time to take the little yellow beauty. He just hoped it would do the trick.

The smell of urine was strong. Rooster didn't believe in drinking water and his piss stank. The trickle stopped for a moment before starting again, this time followed by a ripping fart. *Jesus the guy was a pig.*

The bed shook under him as the Rooster settled back in. About the only time he really felt safe in this joint was when everyone else was asleep. For a few short hours he could relax his vigil and breath. It was too bad he shared a cell with such an old goat. One who got up every few hours to take a leak. *Who did a guy have to blow to get a cell change?*

The euphoric high he'd been experiencing earlier wore off some, to be replaced with a dark annoyance. Declan popped the yellow pill into his mouth and swallowed it easily. The ants crawling on him had sharp teeth, nipping over and over. Only they weren't really on his skin, more like *inside* of it. Not wanting to risk another shot to the head he tried not to scratch.

Come on, come on. He urged, willing the pill to hurry. The crawling sensation continued. He wondered if it would drive him mad. Christ he needed more meth, or more pills. Where he was now, was hell. His flesh housed great raised welts running along his arms and legs.

284

Jagged Little Lies

God he wished Miranda were here. She was a great scratcher. She'd scratched his back for hours leaving him ecstatic. Her fingernails were just right and she was tireless. Maybe he could get her to give him a scratch when she came tomorrow. Hell, maybe he could get her to give him more than that. Declan smiled at the thought. He'd give anything for a little privacy. He craved it almost as much as he craved the pills. He'd never lived in such close quarters before. And he'd never do it again.

For the thousandth time he went over where he'd gone wrong. He was pretty sure one of the guys he was dealing to, had ratted him out. That must be it. He'd been so smooth, so careful, even if he was wasted when it happened. Man they'd had such a sweet deal for awhile, Miranda unknowingly supplying him with a very profitable business. One he'd taken full advantage of.

The day was a blur. He wished he could remember it better. In a blackout and up for days the parts he could remember were hazy. He'd been living large, but then that was nothing new. He'd always lived large. It was something he felt entitled to. And when he got out of this hell hole, he'd be living large again. A lot rested on Miranda. Declan wondered if she'd smuggle the cigarettes in for him. A little part of him felt shitty about asking her to do it, but a bigger part of him didn't care.

The crawling sensation faded. The skin he'd itched raw burned. Frustration and rage seethed within. He was not used to being this helpless. He'd always been able to come and go as he'd pleased. Declan contemplated putting his hand under Rooster's pillow for a second, but discarded the idea. He'd get his stash one day, but it wouldn't happen tonight.

The reality of his situation gnawed at him. It was so unfair. It wasn't like he was a big time dealer either. Christ it was discarded medication, pills no one wanted anymore. If they thought he'd learned his lesson from this, they were wrong. All he'd learned was the justice system was a joke. I mean just look at this place. Half the inmates were on something and the guards never even noticed.

Declan thought about his mom. He meant to call her, but had forgotten again. She was probably thinking about him this very second. Declan shuddered wishing she'd get a life, but then again maybe not. He made a mental note to give her a call tomorrow. He'd be running out of money soon, he just wondered how he could ask for it without having to see her. Christ that's all he needed, his mother here visiting, crying and staring at him with her sad, desperate eyes.

The mattress poked his back. It was lumpy and he shifted positions, trying to get comfortable.His legs were beginning to throb and his jaw hurt. The days left in his sentence weighed on him every bit as heavily as a death sentence would. At times like these he felt hopeless. He was nowhere near wasted enough anymore and his misery was driving him insane. He needed something, anything, *more*.

He shifted again trying to relax. No way was he going to do any of this meth shit again. He was going to look like hell too. He hoped Miranda didn't notice. He'd need to play the sympathy card with her and she wouldn't be very sympathetic if she knew he was getting wasted. The pills he could explain, after all they were pain killers. But the meth, no way would she buy that.

Declan wondered what time it was. For once he wished it morning. His thoughts raced. He bit his knuckle hoping the pain would help to clear his head.

It didn't.

His back throbbed adding to the agony. Nausea began its familiar twist. His bowels quivered.

He stared wide awake, waiting, waiting.

It was bad. He was really starting to feel like hell. The cell lightened indicating dawn was near. He wished for his sunglasses, this small amount of light already hurt his eyes. Declan rolled onto his stomach, hoping to get in at least a few minutes of sleep. His head buzzed. The ants had made it to his skull.

Nip, nip, nip.

Declan sat up rocking and holding his head. He wouldn't be getting any shuteye tonight. Not a chance in hell.

Below him Rooster snored.

Chapter 46

"They are only feelings. They won't kill you." Lyndsey assured the group of people in front of her.

Irene snorted whacking her cane on the ground. "This is ridiculous! What do our feelings have to do with anything? We came here to learn and to heal! Not to talk about *feelings*."

Eric nodded in agreement. "It seems infantile really..." He trailed off.

Lyndsey eyed the group. She knew what she was feeling, *frustrated!* Still, she'd need to watch her expectations. After all, this was nothing new. The resistance most people put up when you asked them how they were feeling was surprising. And, they were only on day two.

Susan, with daggers in her eyes, sarcastically asked, "How are you feeling Lyndsey?"

Lyndsey hesitated. *Was it ok to tell the group she was frustrated? Why not lead by example?* Deciding to go for it she replied, "Frustrated. I'm feeling frustrated. Thanks for asking Susan."

The group quieted, startled by this new turn of events. Eric was the first to address the silence. "Um, er, no disrespect intended, but maybe you're in the wrong line of work if you're already frustrated with us. That doesn't make me feel very good. And now, every time I open my mouth, I'll be worried I'm frustrating you."

Heads nodded and the feeling in the room grew tense. Lyndsey felt fear. This was nothing new. It wasn't unusual for her to have an entire group of people turn on her. It was how defense systems worked. But she still felt intimidated by it.

Her eyes firmly locked on Eric's, she hoped it didn't show. "That's why it's so important to talk about feelings Eric. I mean it isn't like they go away if you don't. They simply get bigger

289

and then they come out sideways. My frustration has nothing to do with you."

Irene muttered something Lyndsey couldn't make out. "What did you say Irene?"

Irene scowled. "You're not making any sense. I'm old, my time is running out and I don't want to waste the precious little I have left listening to this gibberish! Of course your frustration is about us. You're frustrated we're not doing as we've been told." Her cane banged the ground twice, *whack, whack*.

We're gonna to have to take that cane away. "Irene I can't blame my frustration on you. It would be like saying you're responsible for my feelings, and that's simply not true. I'm responsible for my feelings, not you."

Susan sat up straight in her chair showing more energy than she'd shown all morning. "Of course others are responsible for the way we feel. Anyone knows that. What kind of BS are you trying to teach us here?"

"It isn't BS. It's true. When I make my emotional wellness dependent on others, I'm going to be very unhappy. Miserable even. My emotional health is *my* responsibility. This is why we're discussing feelings. If I don't know how I feel, I'm doomed to a life of confusion, or feeling victimised and wallowing in self pity. My feelings will become unhealthy actions. If I don't know how I feel, I can't ask for what I need. Instead I'll blame others for how my life turns out and nothing will ever change. Then I'll be stuck."

Susan's face reddened. Her lips thinned. She looked at the group and rolled her eyes.

The room no longer felt safe. It felt like inpatient group. One in which the addicts weren't getting their way. The undertone was one of anger and hostility. Lyndsey accessed the twelve faces. They were all doing their best not to say anything to anger Susan. Their eyes lowered as if suddenly finding the carpet

Jagged Little Lies

fascinating. Only Susan glared around the room, her eyes venomous.

"How does the room feel right now?" Lyndsey asked to no one in particular.

Charlie, one of the quieter ones whispered, "Fine."

Eric looked up from his doodles and replied, "Good."

Irene looked confused and shifted in her seat.

Lyndsey looked at her questioningly, silently encouraging her.

Irene's cane raised then lowered. She cleared her throat and began. "It doesn't feel good to me." She simply stated.

Lyndsey smiled and said. "Can you identify what *doesn't feel good* feels like?"

Irene shook her head and then stopped. "It feels like when I was little and Papa was mad at me. It doesn't feel good."

Irene clapped an arthritic hand over her mouth and Lyndsey caught a glimpse of the young girl she'd once been.

Eric nodded. "She's right, it feels bad."

Lyndsey took her eyes off Irene addressing Eric. "Eric can you identify what *bad* feels like?"

"I'm not sure how to put it into words, but everybody knows what bad feels like."

Lyndsey walked to the board and addressed her small group. "Please face the board."

A sigh of relief greeted her statement as chairs scrapped along the ground repositioning.

Lyndsey divided the board into two, drawing a line down the center. On one side, she wrote *good*. On the other, *bad*. "I want you to tell me the names of the feelings under good."

A few hands shot into the air. Under *good* the group came up with, *happy, content, love, nice* and then *good* once again.

"Ok, now I want you to name the feelings under *bad*."

All twelve hands shot into the air. Under *bad* the group came up with, *angry, fear, scared, lonely, alone, hurt, rage, despair, sick, depressed, shame, hopeless, worried, tired, exhausted,* and then Lyndsey's *frustrated.*

Lyndsey wrote the word *bad* once again in a separate section of the board. "What does the word *bad* represent?"

This time only eleven hands rose. Susan's was the only hand that didn't.

The word *bad* represented, *wrong, mean, brat, criminal, horrible, evil, brutal, not nice, nasty, terrible* and *evil* once more.

Lyndsey eyed her group. 'It doesn't take a rocket scientist to figure out why we might want to avoid our *bad* feelings."

The room quieted other than the odd scratch of a pen.

"Now what if we changed two words?" Lyndsey crossed out *good* and wrote comfortable. Next she crossed out *bad* and wrote uncomfortable.

The tension in the group dissipated to one of curiosity.

"What if we took the judgement out of our feelings and simply called them *comfortable* and *uncomfortable.* Rather than implying there is something evil about me if I am angry or fearful."

Irene raised a hand. "But isn't feeling angry bad?" She questioned.

Lyndsey grinned. "Angry isn't bad at all Irene, its human. It's an uncomfortable emotion for some, for others it's very comfortable."

Eric argued, "But angry is bad. That's when people yell or swear."

Finally. "That's unhealthy behavior Eric. It's an inappropriate expression of anger. Again, this is why it's so important to discuss your feelings. If I can tell you I'm feeling angry, I don't have to act on it. It starts to dissipate. And strangely enough when I talk about my anger, I usually find there's something underneath it."

Charlie scratched his head. "I'm not following this."

Jagged Little Lies

"Anger is a secondary emotion. It's a great cover up for fear, or hurt, or shame. If I can't identify and discuss what I'm feeling, chances are I'm going to act it out. Feelings not identified and debriefed-are doomed to be acted out. They get stored up for too long and come out sideways. This behaviour is inappropriate and keeps others from getting close to us."

Eric was nodding now.

"Of course if I don't take care of my emotional well being, I'll blame you for the way I feel. Then, if I yell at you, it's your fault for making me angry."

Susan nodded.

Lyndsey shook her head. "But it isn't Susan. You're not responsible for my feelings, I am. And it's no wonder if I think anger or fear is *bad,* that I wouldn't want to tell you about it. After all, who wants to feel *evil?* If we take the judgement out of our feelings, we can begin to describe them in a much healthier way. I told you I was feeling frustrated and *could* have blamed you. But then I'd be a victim, and the truth is, I'm not."

Susan shook her head defiantly. Her leg vibrated on the carpet, as the group stole a quick glance in her direction.

"When I'm feeling frustrated it's about *me,* not you. What's usually happened is I've had an expectation. Any time I have an expectation that isn't met; I can expect to feel frustrated. They go hand in hand. This time my expectation was unrealistic. I expected you to be able to talk honestly about your feelings on day two. That was unrealistic."

Irene put her cane down. "Are you saying we're not to blame for your frustration?"

Lyndsey smiled. "That's exactly what I'm saying." She nodded, knowing they were getting it. Well, some of them, anyways.

"Oh?" Irene replied.

God she loved this. Light bulbs flickered as truth dawned. "And just by addressing my frustration I've diminished it. As a matter of fact I don't even feel it anymore. Now what I'm feeling is excited. And I've avoided blaming you for the way I feel. I haven't behaved in a way I feel ashamed of. I took responsibility for my well being, and hopefully, this group feels just a little safer because of it."

Charlie nodded hesitantly, getting a brief glimpse.

Lyndsey sat down as the group repositioned. When all twelve chairs were once again facing each other she said. "Now it's your turn. How are you feeling?"

The room quieted. The tension was back.

Chapter 47

What a load of crap! Feelings, shmeelings. Who gave a rat's ass? Susan wondered again about the credibility of their facilitator. She was beyond impatient and sat grinding her teeth. She still hadn't heard a single thing to do with helping Declan and she was just about at the end of her rope.

"Susan?" Irene tugged at her shirt sleeve. The group of twelve were on a walk. They were supposed to stay together, but Susan managed to keep a few steps ahead.

Irene was huffing. Susan noticed her flushed face. Irene was also very annoying. "What!" She barked.

Irene frowned, "We're supposed to stay together. I can't walk this fast."

Susan shook Irene's arm from her sleeve. "Look Irene, pardon me. But I'm not a big fan of walking in one large group hug. I think our facilitator would be better suited to teaching kindergarten."

Irene laughed. Her laughter surprised Susan and for an instant the black cloud of misery she'd been cloaked in, departed. "I have to admit I was thinking the same thing myself." Irene agreed. "I mean who really cares about the way we feel. But after listening to her, I'm starting to change my mind."

The black cloud was back, settling once again around her shoulders. "Well I'm not."

Irene grabbed her arm. "You know, I spent so many years waiting for my Harry to notice I was having a rough day. I didn't want to bother him with it, but I really needed him to notice. It never occurred to me to tell him. I don't know why it never occurred to me. It was like my feelings were taboo. I shouldn't be having them. As if there was something shameful and weak about them. Oh every once in awhile Harry would notice and then he'd say a few kind words to me. I'd cry and he'd hold me.

I loved it when he held me. It was like he was saying it was okay for me to feel this way. And afterwards I'd feel so special, important even, and life would be good for a little while. Then it would start all over again, with me bottling up something or other and then growing farther and farther away from Harry. I can't tell you how many years I wasted doing this."

Susan shrugged. "Oh." It was all she could muster. *Jesus this was all she needed, Irene's problems on top of her own.* Her headache was back and to make matters worse, she felt shaky and weak.

The ends of her fingers shook with the first signs of what was soon to follow. Susan added the possibility of MS to her growing list of concerns. Whatever the ailment, she knew she'd need another of her little white pills sooner rather than later. She'd have to find a way to slip out to the car. The pills were in the glove compartment where she'd left them. This place was weird and she'd worried about the possibility of her purse being searched.

Irene tightened her grip and her voice wobbled. "Have you ever wanted something so bad, you would give up everything you had just to get it?"

The image of Declan behind bars came to mind, then Dick, laughing, as he lay in bed next to her. It was a powerful vision and it hurt.

"If only I'd known. If only I could go back. I'd never waste another moment keeping secrets from Harry. I see now that when I held myself back, it was so unfair to him. I put so much pressure on Harry to try and figure out how I was feeling. And when he didn't, I wasn't very nice. I'd get all quiet and he'd ask me if anything was wrong. Then I'd tell him no and be all mad when he believed me." Irene's voice grew quiet. She rubbed her eyes.

296

Jagged Little Lies

Susan winced, her aching back adding to her misery. *The old woman must be lonely. It was just her luck to be walking next to her. Christ she hoped she never ended up like Irene.*

Irene slowed letting go of her arm. "I'm sorry. I hope I'm not bothering you. I'm sure you've got your own problems to deal with and here I am, talking your ear off..." She trailed off her face becoming red.

They were passing the parking area where Susan left her car. She really needed to get rid of Irene. "Why don't you go on ahead without me?"She suggested.

Irene's face clouded. "We're supposed to stay together."

The group passed them leaving the two of them behind. Irene pointed at their departing backs and said, "We'll need to hurry."

Susan smiled hoping to reassure Irene. "I need something ah, personal, from my car. I'll catch up to you."

Irene stood her ground. "I'll wait for you."

Oh Jesus.

"What do you need?"

Susan's anger flared. Irene was like Velcro and she couldn't get rid of her. "Well if you must know, I need a tampon." She lied.

"Oh?" Irene looked rather astonished, "You're still having those?"

With her back to Irene, Susan opened the car door. Her hand was definitely shaking now. She withdrew the bottle from the glove compartment. Only a few pills remained. Susan took one and swallowed it.

Irene tapped on the windshield and Susan's hand jerked. The few remaining pills escaped from the bottle and landed on the seat beside her. "Shit!" She screamed.

"What are those?" Irene questioned.

Susan picked up the scattered pills and placed them carefully back into the bottle. She tucked the little bottle into her bra just in case. She felt jittery and her nerves were on fire. She wanted to belt Irene and didn't trust herself.

"We aren't supposed to be taking pills in this class." Irene's cane hit the concrete with a loud *whack*.

Susan jumped at the loud noise and snapped. "It's only a Tylenol, for my cramps. Don't be so Goddamn nosy!"

"Well it doesn't look like any *Tylenol* I've ever seen."

Oh great, the old lady has eyes like a hawk on her.

The group stood in front of them waiting, just noticing they had lost two members. Susan closed the car door and locked it. Irene waited for her. Together they caught up to the others and walked to the front door.

Susan shook her head. She wanted to bolt. It was exhausting trying to rein in her emotions, when all she really wanted to do was scream. She wasn't sure how long she could keep this up.

Lyndsey's promise echoed in her mind and she was torn. There was no way she would go. Not if there really was a chance this could help Declan.

Her steps faltered and then started up again. Every fiber of her being screamed *run*. She hadn't spent this much time around people in years, and now she knew why.

Irene held the door open. The group already through, stood inside waiting. Irene gave her an odd look and asked, "Are you coming?"

Susan glared at her as she marched through the door.

The sound of Irene's cane stopped her. She turned ready to blast her and stopped.

Irene's expression was smug. As if she had a secret of her own. Her cane made *whacking* sounds as it passed by her. She stopped for a minute before giving Susan a knowing glance.

"What now?" Susan barked.

With a smirk Irene said "You forgot your tampon."

Susan seethed as she watched Irene's back disappear down the hallway.

298

Chapter 48

There, that should do it. Miranda stepped back from the mirror. Her cheeks were flushed and her eyes looked like two big black spiders. Her lips were a glossy red. *Had she gone overboard?* Miranda peered into the mirror. She was dressed in a micro mini, having changed her mind about the jeans. The tiny skirt clung to her shapely bottom, and she had to admit, she looked hot!

The only problem was she didn't see how she could smuggle in Declan's cigarettes. There was no way she'd be able to hide anything in her skirt, it was to snug. She pushed the package deep into her cleavage and looked. The top half of the package clearly showed. *This wasn't going to work.*

Miranda stared into the mirror perplexed. She eyed the cigarettes on the counter next to her when she had an idea. Lifting her breast from the bra, she placed the package in first, and then settled her breast on top of it. Her breast spilled over top of her bra, adding at least three sizes to her cup. Wow! She looked like Dolly Parton. Repeating the process with the next pack, she stood back and stared.

The stilettos felt weird and she wobbled in them. Her bust was large and grotesque, with her waistline tiny in comparison. Declan was going to flip when he saw her. She eyed the mirror. She didn't even look like herself. She looked older, harsher and nasty. That was it. She looked like a nasty girl. One who was capable of some very *naughty* behaviour. Miranda smiled. *Eat your heart out honey.*

The tiny beaded purse dangled from her shoulder. It wasn't big enough to house more than a tube of lipstick and her car keys. The stilettos added at least three inches to her height. She felt drunk walking in them. She'd never really like wearing stilettos, although they made her legs look killer. And that was the look she was going for today.

The shoes made driving difficult. Miranda bent and slipped her right shoe off as she drove. The miles flew by. The radio played all her favorite songs and she sang along with them. She hadn't been able to eat anything this morning, but she felt full on excitement and anticipation. The world seemed brighter, shinier. Miranda laughed. Maybe she was full on love.

A sign announcing the prison caught her attention from the side of the highway. She slowed and turned her blinker on. The sign was a sobering reminder of reality and her happiness faded looking at it. The parking lot was full. Prisoners appeared to have many committed family members, if the full visitors parking were any indication. Miranda wondered once again why families would come all the way out here to visit. It wasn't like the prisoners deserved it or anything. By the looks of the dusty cars, they must have come miles.

Of course, it was different for her. Declan wasn't like the other criminals here. He wasn't even in the same class. He'd been sick with no other options. The other inmates however, well, they were a different story. Miranda stretched working the kinks from her legs as she eyed the entrance doors. Her pulse kicked up a notch at the thought of going through the doors.

Maybe they wouldn't check her. They wouldn't put their hands on her breasts would they? With halting steps she joined the line of visitors waiting, eyeing the group warily. The mother and her two small children were here again. The baby she carried was bigger than the last visit and hung heavily on her hip. The woman looked older too. Miranda wondered how she did it.

The baby whined and the woman shushed it, giving her the once over. A smile tugged her lips and an eye brow raised, "New makeover?"

Miranda's cheeks grew hot.

"They don't want working girls in here you know."

Jagged Little Lies

Anger flared at the audacity of the woman. "I'm not a working girl!"

The baby startled, plucking at his mother's top and wailed. The little girl circled her mother's legs and peered at Miranda through them.

With a few choice words on her lips she stopped, spying the little girl watching her. The elderly woman standing in line sighed loudly. "Honey, we all gotta make a living somehow."

The line moved slowly taking forever. With each passing minute Miranda felt more anxious. *What if they did check her? What in the hell had she done?* With a quick peek at her over exposed bust line she shuddered. Sanity returned. *Why didn't she bring a sweater to cover herself up with?* The mother was right. She did look like a working girl!

Time crawled. With each step she was just a little closer to being searched. *Could she go back? Maybe she could just pull the cigarettes free?* With shaky hands she pretended to scratch her cleavage. The male guard watched her every move. Miranda smiled at him hoping it was seductive. Other than disrobing there was no way to be rid of the contraband.

Anger flared as she once again found herself in a perilous situation. It seemed when it came to Declan she developed a type of temporary insanity. The old woman ahead of her appeared relaxed as she stood waiting for the female guard. She must have done this a thousand times. Miranda wondered who she was visiting. Not batting an eye the woman waited as the guard turned to her and began the pat down.

Miranda was next and she watched closely looking to see if they patted you in a general way, or one of a more intimate nature. The guard gave the old woman a few quick pats and sent her on her way.

"Next." The woman guard spoke in monotone.

Her heart lurched as she stepped forward. With her face an impassive mask she stood waiting her turn. The female guard was older than she. Her face bore the lines of having seen it all. Her eyes narrowed as she took in Miranda.

Miranda felt her face grow warm and stuttered. "I got a little carried away. I...don't know what I was ah, thinking." She explained, waving her arms and pointing at her clothes.

The guard's face remained impassive. Her hands were cold as she patted Miranda's body. It only took seconds, but it felt like an eternity and then it was over. The guard nudged her along saying "next."

With a blank face, Miranda followed the group of visitors into the same room they were in before. This time she sat at a different table watching other visiting families, as they settled in getting comfortable. The room was noisy. There were more children this time. A sullen looking young man slouched in a corner joined the old lady. His long dark legs shot out in front of him and his clothes hung on his skinny frame.

The atmosphere was expectant and more appropriate to going on a holiday, than visiting hours in a prison. But Miranda caught the buzz and some of her anger faded as she waited for Declan to join her.

It wasn't long before the prisoners joined them. Laughter mixed with tender words of love as inmates joined their family. The old woman and sullen young man were joined by a middle aged man dressed in a blue prison jumpsuit. He kept himself in very good shape. Miranda marvelled at his muscles as he bent to give the old woman a hug.

Each time the door opened she felt her breath stop. Any second Declan would walk through those doors making it all worthwhile.

And then she saw him. He'd grown too. Muscles he'd never had bulged in places they'd never been. Miranda hungered to run her hands over this new development. Declan stopped when he spotted her, almost to her table but not quite.

Jagged Little Lies

His face was pinched and he looked pale. He didn't look well. Miranda had seen the look on him far too many times in the past. He wore a frown. "Jesus Christ Miranda, cover yourself up."

The smile slid from her lips to be replaced by a matching frown of her own. She eyed Declan with hostility. "How dare you speak to me like that?" Her voice rose and his face paled even whiter.

"Miranda please," Declan whispered. "Lower your voice."

Rage replaced anger as she gathered her purse and rose. "This is what I get for coming all the way out here? Well I'm leaving and you won't be seeing me again!"

With two steps Declan was at her side. "Please baby, don't go. I'm sorry. It's just you look so damn hot in that outfit. I don't want every man in this place drooling over you."

Declan's fingers circled her wrist sending shivers of electricity up her arm. Rage dissipated as quickly as it came and she sat down. With a closer look at Declan she said the first thing that came to mind. "You don't look so hot."

He lowered himself down next to her, his thigh touching hers. The heat from his thigh travelled up to her pelvic region. Declan caressed her cheek briefly before replying, "I don't feel so hot. I had another migraine last night. I didn't sleep much the pain was so bad. Then when it finally passed, the thought of seeing you got me so excited, it was pointless."

Miranda thawed. He was so sweet and she'd never been loved so completely by anyone else in the entire world. She was Declan's world and she liked it. The thought of him suffering worried her. "Are they giving you anything for pain?"

Declan sighed rubbing a hand through his hair. "Not really. It's a good thing you can't die from migraines, although it sure feels like it at the time. By the way, I love your outfit. His eyes bulged a bit, as he leered at her. Have you uh... *grown* since the last time I saw you?"

"Yeah, by about three sizes," She laughed.

Declan looked puzzled. "Is it a special bra?"

Miranda teased, "You could say that." With a quick look around the room she snuck her hand into her bra retrieving the pack of smokes and held them under the table.

"Jesus Mandy," Declan whispered, as his hand joined hers under the table. The cigarettes disappeared as he hid them inside his jumpsuit.

Her breast reduced to its normal size with the other still bulging. Declan eyed her and she almost laughed. It was a heady experience. The fear she'd felt a few moments earlier left her feeling giddy. With her mission accomplished she sat back folding her arms across her chest. She smiled at Declan as he ogled her.

"Wow!" He whispered.

On a roll now she whispered back. "It really wasn't so hard. They didn't even check me that closely. Maybe next time I can bring you a little something for pain."

"Oh baby, I couldn't ask you to do that for me." He replied stroking her arm.

"You're not asking. I'm offering, and I said *maybe*."

The prison walls disappeared as they talked.It was just the two of them. Nobody else mattered. Time flew and before they knew it the guard was at their table announcing the end of their visit.

Miranda's eyes welled with tears at the thought of having to leave. Her mood blackened as she faced the return trip without him. The shine wore off and she felt hopeless.

Declan put his arms around her. "It will be all right sweetheart. I'll be out soon." His face was grey and pale. She knew he wasn't feeling well and it bothered her.

He gave her a quick kiss and left. Without the prisoners the room became somber, like something died in it. The visitors gathered their belongings and left the building. She followed along, her footsteps taking her further and further away from Declan.

Worry stayed with her. Declan's tired, gray face, seemed to follow her to the car. She pondered the idea. It might work. After all, they'd barely searched her.

With a final look at the prison walls, Miranda pulled out of the parking lot still tossing the idea around. They weren't really *drugs*. They were prescription medications. They had a job, and they were legal. If he wasn't in prison he could go to the doctor and get his own.

Now that she really thought about it, it seemed criminal to put him behind bars in the first place. It really wasn't his fault he was in prison. If the judge were more considerate he wouldn't even be there.

With the right medication she'd really be able to help him out. She could just imagine his pleasure and amazement as she pulled the smuggled pills from her bra.

And maybe, just *maybe*, she would.

Chapter 49

Declan's steps dragged on the way back to his cell. He wiped the sweat from his brow and noticed his hand was shaking. *Jesus Christ.* He almost didn't pull it off. Sleep deprived, the crash left him feeling like there were shards of glass in his veins. The urge to itch was driving him mad. Even the cigarettes he carried in his jumpsuit didn't help.

And Miranda *wow*, he had to give her credit. She'd looked like a working girl for sure, but a high class one. The light from the overhead fluorescents pierced his skull stabbing his eyes. Even the cherry juice didn't take the edge off. He'd need something quick and then hopefully, a little sleep.

Rooster glared at him as he entered their cell. "Well?" He asked.

Declan fished inside his jumpsuit retrieving the cigarettes. He pulled out both packs and tossed one to Rooster.

Rooster's thick eyebrow rose. "That's it?"

Jesus the old goat was never satisfied. Hatred flared as he fought to keep his tone neutral. "Hey, it's a start."

A loud snort met his reply. Rooster tossed the cigarettes high into the air and said, "What do you want me to do with these?"

An image came to Declan and he smiled. *Why don't you shove them where the sun don't shine?* Of course he didn't say it. Instead he replied, "I can take them off your hands if it's a problem." As he snatched the pack from midair.

Rooster looked startled and snatched them back. "I didn't say I didn't want them. Watch it boy!"

Declan ducked just in time.

"You talk to her about bringing in something better?"

"Yeah, she will. But right now I'm feeling a little under the weather. You got anything for me?"

The big mole on Rooster's cheek moved up and down. With the hair protruding from its center, Rooster looked like a witch Declan saw in a movie he'd watched as a kid. *Jesus the old goat really got hit with the ugly bat.* He tried not to shudder.

Declan took a step backwards just in case.

Rooster moved forward. His big belly rubbed up against him. Declan stayed still, not flinching or showing how repulsed he was. They were inches apart when Rooster opened his mouth to speak. Declan got a good look inside and wished he didn't. The Rooster's teeth were as ugly as the rest of him. Yellowed and long. The gums were a mix between pink and black, his tongue a yellowish brown.

He gagged. Rooster's breath was beyond horrible. It was putrid, like he'd just eaten from the sewer. It took everything he possessed to stand there. Rooster smiled. It wasn't a nice smile, but one filled with malice. It said I'm bigger than you and I like hurting people. There wasn't anything human in his black pupils, at least that Declan could see. Rooster was pure predator and always on the lookout for his next victim. Right at the moment it happened to be Declan.

Careful not to show fear but *appearing* respectful, Declan tried again. "If you give me a little something now, I'll pay it back twofold on her next visit."

Rooster seemed to be considering this as he scratched a fat finger through his thick oily hair. "I'll tell you what." He said, poking Declan in the chest. "Make it threefold and you have yourself a deal."

At the moment fair wasn't a factor. Rooster could have asked for anything and Declan would've agreed to it. Christ he could've asked for sex with Miranda. When in *need* he'd agree to anything and worry about it later. So it was a no brainer he agreed to it now. Not wanting to appear too eager Declan scowled and then nodded. "Yeah I guess so. You sure cut a hard deal." *There, that ought to stroke the old goat's ego.*

Jagged Little Lies

Breath beyond gross washed his face, as the Rooster laughed. "Stick with me boy and I'll teach you a trick or two."

The tension in the air dissipated and Declan laughed too. *Not a chance in hell you sick bastard.*

A grain of something hard and sharp stopped him mid-itch. His fingers tore into the skin on his forearm trying to dislodge it. Declan pulled it free and stared at it questioningly. The small granule looked like it was made from crystal or ice. He pressed it between his thumb and forefinger wondering what in the hell it was. It was hard, like a rock. A tiny rock, covered in blood. Worry bloomed in his chest as he looked at the strange object he just picked from his skin.

Rooster poked him hard in the back and he jumped. Declan wiped his hand on his prison suit before turning around. His eyes fastened on the mole again. It seemed to have grown and it moved when Rooster spoke. "What in the hell are you staring at boy?" The long-yellowed teeth were barred.

A cuff upside his head came out of nowhere. His jaw slammed together and he groaned. He wondered if his tooth had cracked and ran a finger over it just in case. He must have been doing some serious grinding of them last night. Declan's eyes watered in pain and he lowered his head.

His arm jerked free from his side. Rooster held to it tightly as he inspected Declan's forearm. "What in the hell have you done to yourself? Jesus boy, you better not be playing with ice. I don't want a tweaker for a cell mate. You hear me?"

Declan nodded in compliance.

"Then clean yourself up."

Declan splashed cold water on his wound and swiped it with toilet paper. His other arm itched like hell and he absently scratched at it while waiting for Rooster to give him what he wanted. Tremors ran up and down his spine and the nausea was back.

Not seeming to notice Declan stood on the verge of collapse, Rooster was all business. "I've got six here for you. You can take one. I want three back when your sweetie comes for her next visit. The other five you can sell. Let em know it's me you're selling for. I want seventy five apiece for them."

The pills were green and potent. So the old guy listened to him after all. Declan's mouth watered as he stared at the little baggie Rooster held. He'd only need one and he'd be good as new. Better even. But seventy-five bucks? Declan tried to look agreeable as he said, "Not sure I can get seventy five for them." He noticed Rooster getting ready to cuff him again and said, "But I'll try."

Rooster hesitated, as if wondering whether to cuff him or not, just for good measure. Maybe the old goat was tired, but instead of giving him another cuff, he just passed the baggie to him and left. Declan sighed, relieved to be alone and fumbled a pill free. His hands shook badly and he eagerly swallowed the tablet. He lowered himself onto Rooster's bed. It was a definite no no, but he was to sore and shaky at the moment to try and climb up to his.

He stared at the small round pills. He didn't plan on selling them to anybody. Screw that! He wanted them. *All of them.* He'd just have to figure out something to tell Rooster was all. Warmth crept up his back loosening his muscles. His jaw unclenched. It was going to be just fine. He'd figure it out. He always did.

Declan nodded, almost asleep in a vast ocean of warmth. All his aches and pains vanished. He was in heaven. Or Nirvana? Or maybe both.

He murmured incoherently, entrenched firmly in his blanket of sedation.

In the land of nod he floated, unaware of Rooster's returning footsteps.

Chapter 50

"Come on Lyndsey, we haven't eaten dinner together all week." Drake stated, staring at her with his deep brown eyes. He'd made one her favorite dinners and it smelled delicious.

Drake was a good cook. Lyndsey watched him as he busied himself pulling the chicken from the oven. Each piece was coated in his special blend of parmesan and corn flakes. The result was always crispy and mouth watering. Lyndsey set the table knowing he was right. And besides, they needed to talk. They were far overdue actually.

She smiled, hoping it would lighten the mood and said, "You're right. Is there anything I can do to help?"

Drake put down the oven mitts and sighed. His eyes focused on hers searching. She knew he was trying to gage her sincerity. "Can you mash the potatoes?"

Glad for something to do, Lyndsey opened the cupboard taking out the electric mixer. She added milk, a generous pad of butter and a touch of Miracle Whip, saying screw it to counting calories tonight. The blades whipped the potatoes until they were thick and creamy. Drake gave a final flip to the roasting asparagus and then filled their plates.

On days like today she cut her self a little slack. Fighting calories was the least of her problems right now. When she was tired it was that much harder to worry about the food she was putting in her mouth. Between the group and Billy, she felt exhausted. She picked up a piece of chicken and bit into it without really noticing.

This thing with Billy was getting pretty big for her. Lyndsey thought back to years gone by. She knew she'd done the right thing in giving her child up for adoption. She had nothing at all to offer the baby at the time. It was probably the most mature decision she'd ever made. But then again, there weren't really any other options. But now...

"Linds?" Drake questioned. He spoke the word quietly, his tone soft, concerned.

She turned to Drake trying to put her thoughts into words. How could she tell him she had to do this? It didn't even make sense to her. Billy wasn't her child. Yet he'd come into their lives for a reason and he needed her. *To whom much is given, much is expected.* She'd been given a second chance. There was no way she couldn't do the same for Billy.

"Linds?" This time Drake whispered the word. His big brown eyes were sad. His face worried. He already knew.

"I'm sorry honey. This thing is eating me alive. I feel consumed by it. I'm so torn. I really want to do what's best for us, for you, but I can't. If I walk away from Billy, I don't think I could live with myself."

"Linds, he's not our child. He's Dee's. You're setting us up for a world of hurt if you insist on taking this on."

"I know. I really do. It won't be easy and I'll probably regret it many times. He'll have so many difficulties. Kids born addicted have severe behaviour problems and they need years of therapy, but they do recover Drake."

Drake put his fork down and looked at her solemnly. "Do you understand what that would mean for us?"

Lyndsey placed her hand over his. It was callused and worn. Drake wasn't afraid of hard work, at least not the physical kind. "I think so. Drake, I'm not kidding myself. It won't be easy, but then neither was getting off drugs, or treatment, or the million other things we've faced together since then."

Drake pulled his hand free of hers abruptly, "That's the thing Lyndsey. We've faced them *together*. But I'm telling you, I don't want this. I don't want to raise someone else's child. Do you understand? I don't want to deal with all the difficulties we'll be facing. I don't want to live in the constant worry Dee will return and take him away."

"She won't be able to return anytime she feels like it and just *take* Billy away. There will be safeguards in place to prevent that from happening. And if she ever does get clean, Social Services will monitor her for a long time, before even looking at returning Billy."

Drake's eyes narrowed and his tone changed, growing sharper. "You're not listening to me. I said I don't want to do this. Don't kid yourself, *everything* will change. We've built ourselves a really nice life here. I like coming home and being able to relax. Do you know the few hours I have to unwind each night makes the days grind doable? I like coming home and seeing you after being gone all day. I like the little time we have together. I don't want to give any of it up. Call me selfish, but it's what makes *this* all worth it. Jesus, do you know how hard it is to go and slug your guts out, *every day*? I work my ass off and I don't want to come home to somebody else's screaming kid and more work!"

Anger warmed her insides and for a moment she disliked him intensely. "Do you hear yourself Drake? We're talking about a little innocent boy, not a monster!"

Drake's nostrils flared. The warmth in his brown eyes faded. His tone was biting. "A little innocent boy who is very needy and frankly, I'm just too Goddamn tired for this!'

An old familiar pain rose inside of her, a pain with sharp teeth. She wanted to strike out and hurl insults at him. She wanted to hit him. Lyndsey bit down on her tongue stilling the cutting words wanting to escape. It was something he'd never done. He never belittled or beat her with his words. Hateful, hurting words crawled up her throat. For just a moment she wanted to revert back to years ago, when she used her words to tear flesh. *Be careful Linds. Don't make this worse than it already is.*

Drake pushed his chair away from the table shaking his head. "This won't work Linds. I just can't do it." His tone no was longer bitter, but this time resigned.

"Honey please..." she stopped not wanting to beg.

"Can't," He shook his head and left the room.

A golf ball wedged in her throat. She wanted nothing more than to run after Drake, but instead she picked up their unfinished plates and scraped them into the garbage. Melee, hearing the rattle of the plates, trotted into the room with her tail wagging. Lyndsey made up a little plate for her adding some doggie kibble to it. Melee gave a sharp bark of appreciation before devouring her meal. *Well at least somebody's enjoying it.*

Billy tugged at her heartstrings. *How could she go and see him without starting another argument?* It might be too late, but she wanted to go to the hospital and let him know she hadn't abandoned him.Her home group was tonight. If she went to see Billy she'd miss it.

Anxious about her decision Lyndsey noticed how quiet the house was. The TV was off which was weird. *Where was Drake?* "Drake," she hollered with Melee padding along at her side. He wasn't downstairs in his workshop, or in his office going over the bills. Alarm bells rang and her steps quickened. The bathroom was empty and she hurried down the hallway.

"Drake?" Lyndsey called raising her voice.

Their bedroom door was ajar as she entered the room. The room was dark and she could just make out the shape of him sitting on their bed. Quietly she joined him, hoping somehow, they could work their way through this thing.

His breathing was deep and ragged. She knew he was upset, but just now realized to what extent. Her arms ached to hold him and say the words he wanted to hear. But she couldn't, and for a minute wished she was numb. With nothing to anesthetize her she sat immobile.

314

Jagged Little Lies

Drake drew in another ragged breath. His words seemed huge in the darkened room. "So you've made up your mind?"

She nodded and then realized he probably couldn't see her, so whispered "Yes."

The bed sagged beside her as he got up and flicked the light on. He dragged his suitcase from their closet.

Her heart plummeted. "Where are you going?" She tried not to whine.

His back was to her and she couldn't see his face. His tone was flat. "I'm going to get a room. I need to think this thing through." He said tossing in some clothes and zipping up the case.

"Please," She whispered.

"I'll be in touch." He gave her a wooden peck on the cheek and picked up his suitcase.

"Please Drake... don't go."

His shoulders slumped as he turned to her and she got a long look. His face was resigned. It wore a look she'd seen once before, many years ago, and she knew he meant what he said. Her heart sunk, the words froze in her throat. *He was really going.*

"I have to Linds." Four words which were like blows to her heart. She stared open-mouthed as he left the room.

Dry-eyed the pain stopped. Shock replaced it as she heard the kitchen door close. Drake's truck started with its familiar grumble. Lyndsey held her breath, hoping he would change his mind.

The noise grew softer as the truck receded into the distance, taking her rock with it. She looked around their bedroom stunned. *This couldn't really be happening. He would come back. He just needed a little time to himself.*

Lyndsey picked up his pillow and hugged it, inhaling his smell. Pain erupted from somewhere deep inside. She rocked his

315

pillow as if it were the child she once gave up. Her throat grew sore. Anguish ripped through her and she sobbed.

Why was it so hard to do the right thing? Why couldn't it be easier? Why did Billy have to suffer? Why did she, or Drake for that matter. If this was really the right thing to do, why did it feel so wrong? She fought the impulse to get in her car and chase after Drake. It wouldn't have helped anything. She knew she would still make the same choices.

Sometimes she felt like the loneliest person on the planet. She'd always felt that way when times were tough. It's just they hadn't been tough in so long. Still she knew what she needed to do. Lyndsey got up off the bed. Melee brushed against her leg and she scooped her up giving her a quick cuddle. The brief contact left her feeling better.

She'd go and see Billy and then get to her meeting. And who knew, Drake might even be back by then.

Fingers crossed she drove off into the night.

Chapter 51

Susan rubbed her temple and sighed. Her fork hung listlessly, hovering above the salad. *Would this day never end?* Her brows furrowed in concentration, as she mentally calculated the time she could take her next pill. She'd need one before entering the pharmacy. There was no way she could pull this off without it. With the decision reached, she was going to fill out the prescription herself. She didn't have time to go back to the doctor's office and plead her case, nor did she think she should have to. She wouldn't make it for much, maybe just another twenty pills and then she would see. Determined, Susan speared her cucumber.

Eric glanced at her and blushed. Susan's eyes narrowed daring him to speak. Lately she didn't like people very much. It must have showed because Eric looked away. She still couldn't figure why these people were here. A few, she knew, had to be here. They'd signed up for it when they'd signed their kid over to this place. But the others? Man you must be *really* sick, if this was your idea of a good time.

Lyndsey said there would be a guest speaker tomorrow, one whose story was similar to Declan's. She might as well stay until then. Maybe she could ask him what to do. She certainly wasn't getting any answers from Lyndsey. She'd fill the script tonight and see what tomorrow would bring. Not that she was holding her breath or anything. So far this *group thing* was a complete waste of time.

Irene nudged her. "Not hungry?"

Susan stared at her plate, not wanting to engage in conversation.

"Must be the cramps," Irene muttered.

Not sure if Irene was being facetious, Susan looked up. Irene's face was wreathed in worry lines as she patted her back.

317

Uncomfortable with Irene's attempts at comforting her, she managed, "I'm fine."

The pats to her back stopped abruptly and the moment grew awkward. Susan stood up needing to be away from Irene. She retraced her steps back to the group room and gathered her belongings. Technically, she wasn't really finished for the day, but she'd had enough.

On her way out she kept expecting to hear *stop,* or *you can't leave.* But no one noticed. As usual, the building was bustling with bodies all going different ways. Since Lyndsey had left for the evening, she didn't need to worry about her. It was Irene she was hoping to avoid.

The front door loomed just a few feet away. Outside its glass doors was a very different world, one in which she could come and go as she pleased. Nobody noticed her, she was anonymous. But here, everybody wanted to know you're business, and they called you on it too.

A surge of energy quickened her steps. Her car waited in the parking lot, like a beacon of light, leading her safely out of the storm that was this building. Not wanting to chance being stopped Susan sped out of the lot, almost hitting a car on its way in. She caught a glimpse of the startled driver's face and barked a laugh. Other people's misery had become very attractive to her these days. *Misery loved company.* The idea seemed hilarious bringing with it another bark of laughter.

A thought occurred to her and the smile slid off her face. *Was she bipolar?* She was definitely experiencing some wild mood swings. Or maybe it was menopause, or peri menopause. That must be it. You couldn't just *become* crazy could you?

The idea of being crazy seemed somewhat appealing, and she laughed again. *Who really gives a shit!*

Maybe there was something to be said about having no one in your life after all. Her thoughts turned to the pharmacy and she hoped she wasn't too late.

Jagged Little Lies

At home she scratched her head in confusion. She'd hidden the prescription pad a few times, wanting to be sure nobody found it. The drawer jerked open with a screech and she relaxed her grip. She grimaced at the amount of junk the drawer housed. *Maybe she could add borderline hoarder to her list of growing problems?* Her laughter bordered on the edge of hysteria.

Will they check the signature? The smile slid off her face. She thought she could forge a good likeness. Her doctor didn't have the usual illegible scripture. But she'd need to practise. Finding scrap paper she doodled. Her signature wasn't quite as curly and circular as she recalled her doctor's being, but if you didn't look too closely, it just might do.

Pen in hand she filled in her request. Twenty Ativan, ah yes please. Too bad she couldn't make it for a hundred, but better start slow. Before she could change her mind, Susan got back in the car and drove to the pharmacy praying she wouldn't see Miranda.

The lights were on and people were inside. Relieved, she thought about handing over the script. She would do it nonchalantly. No big deal, just another prescription. Her hands trembled as she reached for the little bottle.

Only one left.

Should she wait? Screw it. She thumbed off the lid and swallowed the tablet. About as ready as she would ever be, she entered the pharmacy. A young girl looked up from the till. "Were closing in ten minutes," She warned.

Susan smiled and nodded her sights on the pharmacy counter. She made her way past the cold remedy medications and mouth wash. A woman about her age was behind the counter counting receipts. She looked up, "Can I help you?"

"Yes, I'd like to fill my prescription." Susan fumbled in her purse before pulling the paper free hoping the tremble in her finger tips wouldn't give her away.

The woman nodded taking the script from her, not seeming to notice the tremble. She glanced at it and smiled. "You can pick this up tomorrow morning."

"What! But I need it tonight."

"I'm sorry, but we are just about to close. You can come back in the morning. Is there a problem?" She inquired peering intently at Susan.

"No, ah... no. That should be fine."She smiled again hoping to convey no problem. Susan walked back to her car empty handed and drove home.

Once inside her house she screamed, venting her rage and frustration. Little things which had been easy before were now hard. Little things, like getting out of bed and eating. Little things like breathing without feeling constant pain. Little things like happiness and peace of mind. Little things like talking to people or filling prescriptions. Just simple, everyday little things, except now they weren't. They were crippling, tortuous, big things and she was beyond tired of it all. And the only thing she'd been able to count on, to bring her any comfort at all, she'd have to wait until tomorrow for.

Curled up in her already there spot on the couch, Susan flicked on the TV. Hostility flickered on with the television and for the first time she felt angry with Declan. *Why hadn't he called? Didn't he care? Did anyone?*

Loneliness hollowed out her insides and she ached with it. Not even the pills seemed to be working anymore. The fleece of the blanket warmed her skin, but not her heart. She could feel it beating through the vein in her neck. It felt cold and dead, moving inside her, keeping her body alive so she might live to suffer another day. If it wasn't for Declan it would be so easy. She would simply put a stop to it. She wouldn't continue to live this way. She wouldn't continue to live.

Memories of times long gone, brought a nugget of comfort. Voices from the TV and the past, mingled.

Jagged Little Lies

Susan's eyes closed, as her body succumbed to exhaustion. The noise in her head quieted and she dozed.

Chapter 52

"No Mom, I haven't seen him."

"Then what else could it be Miranda?"

"I don't know what you mean?" She lied.

A pause and then her mother spoke, her tone soft, worried. Miranda strained to hear her. "You've changed honey. And not for the good. I can see it on your face. I hear it in your voice. And you're avoiding us again. That only happens when you've got something to hide. I know you can't possibly understand this, but you don't have to keep secrets from us Miranda. You're grown and *you* get to make the choices now. If the choices you make are harmful, then I'm going to address them with you. It would be neglectful not to. But it's still you're choice to make."

Oh God, I should never have picked up the phone. Why did I?

"Honey you're an intelligent, beautiful girl. You could have anyone in the world. Why are you choosing a partner who cannot provide for you? A partner who's a drug addict and a criminal? What could you possibly be getting out of this Miranda?"

Her hackles rose. Sometimes she detested her mother's smugness and the way she came across, as if she had it all figured out. "Mom I've told you before, Declan is *not* a drug addict! He uses legal prescription medications, for a medical issue. Unfortunately, the medication is a double-edged sword. It works great for his migraines, but makes him sick when he's not using it. I see it all the time at work. If you want to blame anyone *Mother*, blame the pharmaceutical companies, or the doctors for dispensing it. Don't blame the patients, who are just trying to feel better!"

"Miranda, I swear, when it comes to Declan you've lost your senses. How is it you explain to yourself, and others, that he's in jail?"

"Well *Mom,* I don't. Honestly, no one else is as nosy as you are, and nobody else seems to have a problem with it." Lisa's face appeared before her eyes briefly making her a liar again. But if her mom would stop asking such stupid questions, she wouldn't be forced to lie.

"Honey, we're all worried about you."

"Stop it Mom. You're worried. Don't drag anybody else into this. I don't see anyone else calling."

"You're wrong Miranda, Daddy is worried to. We all are. It's just unfortunate it always seems to be me who gets the difficult job of addressing our concerns. You know how Daddy is. He'd rather not deal with the messy stuff and he hates it when you're mad at him. But he's still worried about you, Miranda."

"You know sometimes I think you get off on this. I mean really..."

"Miranda!" Her mother interrupted, her tone changing from soft to sharp. "This is exactly what I mean. You didn't used to be intentionally cruel. Don't tell me you're using drugs too."

Miranda yanked the phone from her ear looking at it in disbelief. "Jesus Mom! I can't even believe you just said that! Maybe it's you who's using drugs!"

"I refuse to play this game with you Miranda. And I don't appreciate you talking to me this way. I think you're lying to us. I think you're seeing Declan again. And nothing good will come of it. Have you forgotten, just a few weeks ago, you were *never* going to see him again? Have you forgotten how upset you were? How you couldn't even get out of bed? Have you? Because I haven't, and if you think I'm just going to stand by quietly and watch it happen all over again, you're wrong."

There was no winning. She just needed to get off the phone. "Look Mom, I'm sorry. I'm sorry if I've caused you to worry. I really am. But honestly there's nothing to worry about. I know what I'm doing. I'm not seeing Declan again. At least not like *that.* We're just... Friends, that's all."

Jagged Little Lies

"I doubt very much you can just be *friends* with him, Mandy. I think you're kidding yourself and it's hard to see. I wish that you would, oh, I don't know, I'll probably say it wrong, but I wish you would *require* more for yourself honey."

"Okay Mom. I've listened to what you've had to say, and now I really need to go."

"Why? Where are you going?"

"*Mom*," Miranda warned.

"Okay Miranda. But just remember honey. No one will ever love you more than Daddy and I. *No one.* I know you can't understand it right now, but you will one day. When you have your own little girl, you'll want nothing but the best for her. And you'll do anything to make sure she's happy."

"Yes Mom. Now I really need to go."

"I guess... honey. I'm cooking your favorite for dinner tonight. It smells delicious. Do you want to come for spaghetti?"

Miranda glanced down at her exposed cleavage. She could just imagine what her mother would have to say about her new look. Not to mention the fact that she was thinking about how to get in more than just cigarettes on her next visit. At this moment all she really wanted to do was get into her pjs and dream about Declan.

"Miranda?"

"Sorry Mom, I was just thinking about work. They've called me in for the early shift. So I'll have to pass. I'm tired and I'd like to make it an early night. But thanks for the offer."

"Do you want me to make you a doggy bag? I could send Daddy over with it."

No! "Ah, no thanks Mom, really, I'm fine."

"Well... Okay then."

The disappointment in her mother's tone left her feeling guilty. Miranda almost changed her mind, but just couldn't bear the thought of sitting around the table, pretending. And she was already exhausted from their conversation. "Maybe I'll stop by after work for a cup of tea." She offered.

"That would be nice."

"Okay Mom, I really gotta go. Bye"

"Goodbye honey. See you tomorrow." Her mother said cheerfully.

Miranda hung up the phone thinking, *I said maybe.*

Why couldn't her family just let her be? She wasn't telling them how to live their lives. It was like they were trying to make her into the spitting image of them. And that's the last thing she wanted, to be a cut out of her parents. The highlight of their day was dinner and television. They could plan their weeks by the shows they were watching.

Miranda shuddered. No way. She was looking for a little excitement, not dullsville, thank you very much! She couldn't imagine how boring it must be to get up each and every day and do the same thing over and over and over.She'd go crazy.

No way. No thanks. Not for her.

Not that she really had to worry. For her life was *nothing* like her parents.

Not with Declan, that's for sure? *Would he call tonight?* She must remember to ask him how the phone system worked there. Phone in hand, she strolled into the bedroom and undressed. The image in the mirror gave her pause and she wished Declan were here to see it.

Her body responded with a wish of its own. Now that was something she couldn't tell her mother about, but if she could, she might actually understand. For the yearning she felt when she thought of Declan wasn't something anyone else could help her with. It was deep and endless. And right at the moment she ached with it. There was only one cure for this type of need.

Miranda climbed into bed with a sigh. Unfortunately, her *cure* was miles away, in a ten by ten cell. She'd just have to make do herself.

Jagged Little Lies

With the bed covers tossed to the side, she stroked her body thinking of Declan.

LORELIE ROZZANO

Chapter 53

Declan woke. His face felt broken. One eye was swollen shut. *Weird, it didn't hurt.* The cell was dark. His eyes closed and he drifted off once more.

Someone was moaning. The moans were deep, followed by shuddery breaths. It took Declan a moment to realize they were coming from him. At about the exact same time the cause of the moaning rocketed through his drug addled brain, pain washed over him. Immense pain. And then he remembered, at least sort of.

Rooster had beaten him senseless.

He nodded off on the old goat's bed. It was blurry, but he remembered bits and pieces. Rooster had beat on his face like a boxer with a bag. His neck felt all rubbery from the blows. He recalled being bounced off the cell floor like a basketball and remembered Rooster's laughter. He wasn't sure how he'd ended up in his own bunk. Maybe he'd climbed up himself. He didn't know.

Declan tenderly touched his face and winced.

It was pretty bad. His face didn't feel like his. The skin below his fingertips was swollen. It was soft, spongy and tight, all at once. His eye felt as big as an orange. He traced the outline of his nose next. Tears stung his face and he jerked. His nose hurt like a son of a bitch, but he didn't think it was broken. His lips were puffy, like he'd been stung by a bee and his tongue throbbed. He could feel the cuts inside his mouth and his jaw ached. But it was his front tooth that hurt most. The jagged edge sawed at his lower lip. The tooth was cracked and hanging in a jagged shard.

Every nerve in his face screamed. He felt like screaming to. Rage and pain warred within as he sat up. The room spun and his head ached. *Bad idea.*

With stiffening fingers he reached into his sock retrieving the little baggie. The pills weren't his, but it didn't matter. He'd probably earn himself another beating, but that didn't matter either. The only thing that mattered was getting one of these little beauties into him, as fast as possible and then...

His thought trailed off as another wave of pain hit. It was hot, intense. Sweat broke out on his brow. His hands shook as he carefully placed the baggie, palming the pill. Declan managed to get his legs moving and climbed off the bed. His mouth was ruined. No way could he swallow this pill without a little help.

Declan moaned again, this time even louder. With the cup to his lips he swayed, holding onto the edge of the sink. White starbursts floated before his eyes. The water spilled from the cup and ran down his chin. He tried again placing the pill on his shredded tongue. Another mouthful of water, this time he met with success. He felt the small, smooth orb slide, down his throat and waited.

Not able to climb back up to his bed he grasped the cell bars. Rooster was a dead man. He just didn't know it yet. Even if it took him the rest of his life, he'd make sure it happened.

The pain was like a living, breathing thing. Declan closed his eyes trying to make it go away. He heard falsetto down the hallway giving the gears to some new arrival. He'd caught a brief glimpse of him yesterday but hadn't seen him since. The kid was still probably cowering under his blankets and didn't want to come out of his cell. Another wave of pain erupted, this time not quite as intense. *Thank Christ the shit was starting to work.*

You never really knew how long it'd take. Sometimes it happened fast, other times it seemed to take forever. But this must be his lucky day, if you could call it that. Bubbles of warmth, pockets of comfort, mixed with the pain. The screaming inside his face stopped. The aching in his jaw dulled. His tongue, although ragged, felt dipped in warm oil.

Jagged Little Lies

The bars slid free of his hands as they unclenched and he stood tall. He shrugged thinking *might as well get this over with.* With a clean jumpsuit and pair of socks he headed in the direction of the showers. The noise around him quieted as he walked the hallways. Inmates stood staring at him as he passed.

Declan ignored them, head held high. No jeers or taunts this time. He was only stopped once by a guard.

The old guy looked stunned. "What in the hell happened to you?"

"Nothing." Declan replied, stone faced.

"Yeah, well, it sure as shit looks like something happened." The guards stared at him intently. "Now what was it?

Aware he was being watched by more than just the prison guard, Declan tried again. "I fell off my bed, that's all. You got a problem with that?"

The guard, who looked more like grampa than anything else, puffed out his chest. "Listen up son. It's my job to keep order in here. And if I have a problem with anything, you'll be the first to know about it."

Declan stared hard at him, not saying anything else.

The guard shifted his weight from one foot to the other. Declan wondered if he'd make a big deal of it. The guy must be close to retirement and it'd be way easier to turn a blind eye. The guard looked at him again. "You sure you fell out of bed?" He questioned, clearly wanting to do the right thing.

Declan nodded, looking away. "It's what I said."

"Okay then..." Grampa cleared his throat. "Be more careful next time."

Declan nodded moving off down the hallway. He was aware of the curious eyes on him as he walked. He never looked up or acknowledged the stares. It wasn't something you did in here. This place had its own set of rules and they weren't anything like he'd ever seen before. But he was learning and *fast.*

The showers were isolated. The smell of steam and prison soap hung in the air. The last bit of pain uncurled and he moved easily, a well oiled machine. He stripped out of his jumpsuit standing only in his boxers and socks. *Shit.* His socks.

The side of his left sock bulged, disclosing the fact of his hidden baggie. He glanced around making sure no one was watching. He peeled the socks off his feet careful not to open the baggie and jammed them deep within his discarded jumpsuit. Footsteps approached, announcing the fact he'd soon be getting company. He hurriedly rolled the garments into a little ball.

Twitch poked his head into the opening. "I saw you go by."

Declan stepped out of his boxers, turning the water on and making sure he could see his clothing. The water was warm and he relaxed a little.

"What the hell happened to you?" Twitch turned away affording Declan the privacy he desired.

He soaped his head not to touch his face. "I fell out of bed." He said again.

"Yeah right!" Twitch laughed.

Declan continued soaping his body saying nothing. His silence spoke volumes.

"That's your story and you're stickin to it?" Twitch accommodated.

"Yup." Declan agreed.

Twitched scratched his head, his skinny arm rapid firing. "Kay, he mumbled. "Ya need anything?"

Oh I need something alright. An idea began to form, one that he wasn't quite ready to act on. But he needed Twitch's help. "Yeah I might." Declan said. "I'll find you later."

"Okay," Twitch agreed, wandering off.

As Twitch's skinny body left the showers, he was once again left to his thoughts. He wondered what he looked like. With a final sluice of warm water he dried off, wrapping the towel

Jagged Little Lies

around his midsection. Ready to see the damage Declan strode over to the aluminum mirror.

He stared not believing his eyes. Incredulity mixed with rage. Declan renewed his vow. Rooster would pay and *soon*. He looked at his ruined face. One eye was swollen closed. It was going to be one hell of a shiner. His tooth was broken. He had a flash of how he could use the tooth and smiled. His eyes met in the mirror and darkened. He barely recognized himself. More than just his ruined face had changed. He smiled. That too had changed. The smile no longer resembled anything humorous, but something far darker, more sinister.

Declan took a final glance in the mirror before leaving. The image stared back no longer his.

The man in the mirror was a stranger.

Chapter 54

Three o'clock in the morning. Lyndsey didn't mean to look. Really, she'd done everything she could not to. But she did need to use the bathroom. So she closed her eyes as she crawled back into bed, hoping to avoid the bright red numbers on the alarm clock. It was a trick she learned long ago. If she didn't know how much sleep she'd gotten, she could trick herself into feeling less tired. But it wasn't going to work today.

Her body was tense, her heart heavy. At three in the morning it was all very overwhelming. She couldn't imagine how she would go into work today and function. For a moment she wished she were one of the patients. They really didn't know how good they had it. Each of them was being encouraged to open up and share feelings. The trick was to start. The relief you got from expressing emotions was instantaneous and far better than a drink any day.

Her fingers caressed the empty spot next to her. *Was Drake wide awake, or asleep?* She hoped awake. She didn't want to be the only one suffering. It wasn't very nice to wish suffering on him, but she didn't feel very nice at the moment. She was sad and angry and confused, all at the same time. But mostly she just felt alone, even though she knew she wasn't. *Dear Lord please thy will, not mine, be done. Thank you for my sobriety and for Drake. Thank you for my friends and family and everything you've given me, especially this pain. Thank you for Billy and for my son. Please help me to be less selfish and have the courage to do the next right thing. And if it isn't asking too much, please grace me with a few hours of sleep. Yours in service, forever and ever, Amen.*

It wasn't like she was one hundred percent certain there was really a God. Or that she was being heard, but every time she prayed she felt better, less alone, and less burdened. So even if

335

there wasn't a God, it still helped. But she didn't believe that. There was something greater than she pulling for her, or there was no way in hell she'd even be alive right now.

The empty spot beside her seemed to grow and she shifted her thoughts to Billy. Sweet little Billy, it was really hard to leave him, and it was getting harder. When she'd seen him last night his face lit up. They'd played with the stuffed animals in his little bed. He'd even laughed once. It startled them both and his huge grin disappeared, as his lip trembled. Loud noises still caused him to flinch. The sound of his laughter was new and scary. She'd read him a story and sung to him. He fallen asleep on her, his little body all snuggly and warm against her.

Jan was waiting for her after her visit with Billy. She'd been so helpful. Together they'd gone to the meeting. She had so much to say, but felt stifled with a few of her past patients in the room. Jan put her arm around her whispering, "The story doesn't matter, just talk about your feelings."

And she did. Of course it helped. It eased the swirling mass of dis-ease she'd been carrying around since Drake left. She'd come home hopeful, until she saw the empty spot where he usually parked. Her hope diminished as she entered the darkened house. Not even Melee got up to greet her.

Still, she'd managed to fall asleep for a few hours. She could always be grateful for that. The clocked ticked softly. It wasn't the first time she'd been in this predicament, but she'd always had Drake at her side before. Just knowing he was in bed sleeping beside her helped.

Lyndsey reached for Drake's pillow. It was a poor second, but she'd take it. Any morsel of comfort she could get at this moment she'd take, and gladly. *Why did it seem so bloody awful at this hour of night?* The pillow helped. She felt the softness of it, and the silkiness of the sheets below her. Her mind slowed as she used her touch. Sometimes thinking was overrated, especially in the middle of the night. Time passed as she lay

Jagged Little Lies

warm and comfortable. She was never able to fully go under to the sweet bliss of sleep, but she dozed.

Beep. Beep. Beep. The noise came from far away. Lyndsey sat up in bed. She crawled out of her warm nest pushing the off button as she rose. The phone rang and she ran to answer it. *Drake!*

Excitement mixed with her sleep thickened voice as she answered, "Hello."

"Lyndsey? I didn't wake you did I?" Jan said sounding wide awake and pert this morning.

Her heart sunk as she realized it wasn't Drake on the phone. "I... She cleared her throat. I was just getting out of bed when I heard the phone."

"Oh sorry, I didn't want to wake you, but I was worried about you. Did Drake come home?"

Lyndsey's suspicion kicked in. She still didn't trust people, at least not all the way. It was a hangover from her past and she knew it, but it was still there. It was a hell of a predicament too. She didn't want to lie, but she also didn't want to offend Jan by telling her it was none of her business when she'd made it her business last night. Instead she tried to avoid the question all together. "Ah Jan, I'm kind of running late here and I haven't even had coffee yet. Could we talk about this later?"

"Sure Lyndsey, no problem, give me a call when you're ready."

"Thanks, I will. Listen I've got to run."

"Well ah; I guess I'll talk to you soon?" Jan questioned.

"You will. And Jan..." Lyndsey trailed off not quite sure what to say.

"Yes?"

"Nothing, just, thanks for calling."

"Anytime Linds, anytime."

Lyndsey put the receiver down feeling like a bad friend. There were times when it was just easier to have no friends at all.

As her coffee brewed she took a quick shower. She'd have to be careful. She was tired and the thought of the long day stretching in front of her was daunting. A minute at a time, that's how she'd play it today.

The coffee tasted bitter and she grimaced. Drake had bought them this new machine. She'd liked the old one just fine, but he'd insisted. She still hadn't quite gotten the hang of the damn thing and he'd taken over the job of making their morning coffee. She wondered if he'd think about her with his first cup this morning.

Irritation flared as she hurried to get ready. Maybe she would stop somewhere on her way to work and get a decent cup of coffee. With quick strokes, she applied her makeup, careful to conceal the puffiness around her tired eyes. It was a good thing she was working with people consumed in their own torment. Almost always, her patients were so obsessed with their own difficulties they didn't notice others around them. And today she was especially grateful for this.

Suddenly aware she hadn't seen Melee this morning she went in search of her. She wasn't in her bed, or on the couch. "Melee," Lyndsey called.

Nothing, no sound of clicking nails answered her call.

"Melee!" Lyndsey tried their bedroom again.

"Melee?" she yelled as she flicked on the light. Sometimes Melee slept under their bed and she hadn't checked there yet. On hands and knees she lifted the bed skirt and looked under the bed.

"Melee!" Lyndsey could see her. She was curled up in a little ball lying on Drake's side of the bed. Lyndsey got up and walked around the bed getting back down on her knees. Why wasn't Melee coming to her? The poor little thing was getting deafer by the minute.

338

Jagged Little Lies

Lyndsey poked her and then pulled her free from the bed. Melee lay lethargically, not even trying to stand. Lyndsey petted her. "I know it's pretty early girl. Are you not feeling well?"

Melee licked her on the hand and then closed her eyes. Lyndsey patted her again, reassuring Melee. "Don't worry girl. He'll be back soon." Or maybe it was herself she was trying to reassure? Either way, she'd need to make an appointment at the vet for Melee. She was long past due.

Burdened, with yet one more thing to worry about, she left the house. Not even her car started right. She had to try twice before it roared to life. Without Drake to fix things, she was lost. Virtually every aspect of her life these days was linked to his. And in ways she often took for granted.

At least she could still go through a drive through by herself. Lyndsey ordered a coffee and a toasted whole wheat bagel. Licking the last crumbs from her fingers, she pulled into her parking space. The lot was filled to capacity. Even the outside of this building bustled. With a last gulp of her caffeinated brew, Lyndsey exited the car hoping her professional mask was firmly in place.

The caffeine helped. It quickened her heart beat and her steps. She even *almost* felt normal. With her belongings stashed in her office, she gathered the sheets to read from the group members. They were designed to ascertain not only the mood of the group, but the mood of the individual. Sometimes people had less difficulty putting thoughts and feelings to paper. By the looks of these sheets, patience was wearing thin with one of their group members. Susan's name had made the rounds. Now they needed to find their voice and address it.

It was much easier to complain to others than it was to address your concerns and feelings with the individual. She should know. She had done it too. It wasn't until she'd been taught differently that she began to change her ways. Yes, it might be easier, but it wasn't healthier. Talking behind someone's back was a sure sign of cowardice, and it never resolved anything.

A wave of fatigue settled over her and she fought it off. *She could do this day. She could.* She owed it to the people sitting in the next room. She'd give them the best she had. Squaring her shoulders she prayed for the guidance and willingness to see this through.

Lyndsey opened the door and crossed the threshold into the group room. She circled a chair and joined the group, offering up a smile. Focused intently, she asked the question they'd all been waiting for. "How are you feeling today?"

Silence, rich in tension, blossomed in the air. It lingered there for a moment, and then all hell broke loose.

Chapter 55

Susan awoke with a bang, literally. Her heart knocked madly, beating against her rib cage. *Was she having a heart attack?* On weak legs, she rose from the couch making her way to the kitchen. The room was dark, the only light coming from the television.

Bang, bang. She placed a shaky hand on her chest, feeling the erratic pounding underneath her palm. Her mouth was dry. *Maybe it was fear?* She tried to remember the article she'd read, describing the symptoms of heart attacks in women. *Breathe Susan, calm down.*

She reached the kitchen counter and flicked on the cold water. With her glass half filled, she opened her purse and retrieved the pill bottle. It took a second before she understood. With the bottle clutched tightly in her shaky hand, she glanced at it in surprise.

The small, clear round cylinder was empty. She shook it again just to make sure, but nothing rattled back. With trembling hands she sipped her water. The glass knocked against her teeth. Panic flared, accelerating her already speeding heart. Her throat closed making it difficult to inhale and she wondered if she was dying. *Phone 911 you fool!*

But she couldn't. Instead she sat at the kitchen table trying to breathe. It might be stupid, but she didn't want anyone seeing her like this. She just needed to calm down. *Oh God she needed her pills!* With long, deep breaths of air, in through her nose and out through her mouth, Susan managed to talk herself down.

With two hands she managed to get the glass to her lips. The water was cool and soothed her dry, sore, achy throat. She drained the glass.

The kitchen brightened a little. It was time to get ready. She would swing by the pharmacy first and pick up her medication.

Then she would attend group, hopefully for the last time. It was probably silly to think the guest speaker tonight would have any magical words, but she wouldn't leave until she knew for sure.

The large soaker tub filled with warm water and she added floral scented bath gel. The scent reminded her of a trip she and Dick took a long time ago. It'd been just the two of them. Dick insisted and for once she'd gone along with him. They'd gone to the Caribbean. The resort was magnificent, post card perfect, with sun and sand and lush tropical flowers. The sights and scents were intoxicating and Dick was over the moon. He'd chattered incessantly reminding her of Declan. His face grew animated as he pointed out all the beautiful flowers and fauna. But all she could see were the children.Little girls and boys ran in the surf and sand squealing, as they played. She ached for Declan and resented Dick for not wanting him here. Their paradise soon soured and it wasn't long before they were barely speaking. The last few days she hardly even saw Dick. He'd rise early in the morning, dressing in his golfing attire and head out the door. She'd read on the beach, or beside the pool. Her eyes less on the page than they were on the families with their children.

Thoughts of their trip vanished as she lowered her body into the tub. The water embraced her. Susan lay back, twisting her hair into a knot on top of her head. The heat eased her aches. It was nice. Too bad she couldn't stay longer. But there was something more urgent she needed to do. The bar of soap slid hurriedly along her skin and she added a few, shaky strokes of the razor to her legs.

The towel was stiff and prickly, as she rubbed her body dry. Her skin felt prickly too, like it had thinned overnight. She dressed casually in jeans and a t-shirt. Even clothing hurt her skin. Susan discarded the jeans and changed into sweats, hoping the flannel wouldn't chafe. She'd never had achy skin before. *Maybe she'd caught something infectious?*

Jagged Little Lies

The hairbrush tangled in her hair for a moment. With a quick jerk she yanked it free, managing to assemble a passable hairstyle. A little lip gloss and some color to her cheeks, and she was ready to go.

Back in the kitchen, Susan eyed the bananas. She hadn't eaten anything this morning. The thought of food made her sick. Still, she needed something in her stomach. The three, unappealing browning bananas remained on the counter. Susan picked up the freshest looking banana of the bunch, and ate a few bites. Her stomach recoiled, clearly not happy with the intrusion.

The banana wobbled in midair, stopping before it reached her mouth as she fought to keep the first half down. Her stomach lurched. No way could she finish it. Susan threw the banana away and picked up her purse. There was only one thing that would help her now. *Please be open.*

As she backed the car out of the driveway, she glanced at the gas gauge. The needle showed less than a quarter full. She'd make it. It dawned on her as she pulled into the pharmacy's parking lot this would be the *real* test. For some reason the thought never occurred to her before. She'd thought dropping the prescription off was the hard part. Now, she realized, it was actually the easiest part. The real test was going to be picking it up.

Very quickly she'd know if she'd gotten into a one hell of a predicament. She'd either be going to jail, or to group. Quite frankly, right at the moment, jail was more appealing. At least she might get to visit Declan. The image brought an outburst of laughter startling the passenger in the next car.The young man looked up at her his lips forming a large O. Susan scowled at him and locked the door. She never noticed the looks from the others passing her, as she walked into the store head down and mumbling. On the verge of losing it, she wanted to tell the entire world to go to hell.

She made her way down the familiar aisles. Still early, there were no lines as she marched up to the counter trying to appear confident. No clerks stood nearby ready to attend her. The counter was vacant. A little silver bell with a sign reading *please ring for service* was the only customer service provided. The counters were glossy and newly shined. Her palms flattened against the countertops, leaving sweaty streaks. With the corner of her elbow she rubbed the streaks hoping to erase the smears, and rang the bell.

Fingers crossed she wouldn't be face to face with Miranda, Susan waited. The bell's *ring* seemed to hang in the air accusingly. Her chest knocked loudly and her vision blurred. Each second felt like an eternity. Panic flared again. *What was she doing?*

On the verge of bolting, but frozen with fear, she thought she might pass out. The door behind the counter opened with a groan. Susan looked up as if from a great distance. She recognized the man from before.

A flash of irritation crossed his face before it smoothed over. He smiled at her and said, "May I help you?"

Her mouth opened and her throat seized. A squeak rattled forth. The words stuck.

His eyes narrowed as he recognized her. The smile faltered and he took a step back.

Susan licked her lips and tried again. "I'd like..." her throat tightened once more and she stopped. Her hands trembled ferociously and she squeezed them closed, fisting them into little round balls.

With fingernails biting into the cheeks of her palms, she spit out the rest of her sentence. "To pick up my medications... Please." She added for good measure.

John's face remained impassive. "I'm sorry, it's not ready yet. My assistant is late this morning and we're behind schedule. You'll have to come back later."

Jagged Little Lies

What! Was he kidding? Susan felt like hitting him. She wanted to leap the counter and look for herself. She didn't even care if it wasn't *her* medication. There must be something behind those shelves that would help her feel better.

The smile back on John's face, he patted her arm quickly as if to say *there, there,* go *away now.* "It should be ready for you around noon," he said removing his hand. "Why don't you come back then?"

The smile faded as he glanced at her. "No sense waiting." He warned.

Susan managed a nod before returning to her car. *A few more hours, how could she do it?* Out of options, she drove to the one place she least wanted to go.

The building loomed large before her, representing everything wrong with her life. She hated this building with a vengeance. Sick and miserable, she entered through the front doors. She wasn't up to all the questions today. And she had no idea how she'd sneak away long enough to pick up her medications, but she'd find a way. Exhaustion added to her long list of ailments, and her steps dragged.

Bodies jostled against her as she slowed. *Maybe she should just wait in the car?* The familiar sound of Irene's cane floated behind growing louder with each *whack*.

"Susan, wait." Irene's cheery voice called.

Irritation coursed through her at the sound of Irene's cheery voice. Her footsteps faltered and she stopped. Irene grasped her by the arm. Susan gave a hard yank reclaiming her limb, almost knocking the old woman to the floor. Irene looked startled and her eyes welled. "Well, good morning to you!" Her voice wobbled.

With a shaky finger Susan pointed at Irene and snarled, "Look, all I want to do is to be left alone! You got it?"

Irene's eyes grew wide. "What's wrong with you?" She whispered.

"None of your damn business! Now leave me alone!" Susan replied, walking away from Irene as fast as she could, hoping to outdistance the old woman's persistence.

In a world of suffering she entered the group room, sitting heavily in her chair and hoping to avoid eye contact. These people were all idiots. She couldn't stand any of them. The conversation around her slowed and then stopped. Aware all eyes were on her, she willed her shaking limbs still.

Her leg bounced below a *rat tat tat*. Her hands shook like frightened little birds, trembling in her lap. Susan eyed the coffee on the counter needing a hit of something, but worried she'd spill it. Maybe Irene would get it for her? One look at the old woman's face negated the idea.

Her eyes flickered over to the purses hanging on the coat tree. *Would any of them contain medications?* There might even be someone in this group, right now, who held the magic cure. Why hadn't she thought of this before? If the people here were anything like her, they probably had a shitload of medications.

Eagerly she raised her head. *Could she tell by looking at them?* Susan scanned the room looking at each person. Frustrated she sighed.

Aware of the surreptitious looks, she crossed her arms.

If someone wanted to fight, she was more than ready.

Chapter 56

The morning light was all wrong. Internal alarm bells began to ring. The flashing red light blinking on the nearby phone indicated at least one missed call. Miranda pushed the bed covers off, her skin goose-bumped at the sudden onslaught of cool air.

Shit, no, damn, she muttered looking at the alarm clock. Why hadn't it gone off? The clocks readout caused another flurry of muttered profanities. Ten o'clock. She was dead for sure, or at least fired. The phone's flashing red light caught her attention again and she pushed the button.

John's terse voice greeted her. Miranda cringed and pulled the covers back up. "Mandy you're late!" he exclaimed. "You had better have a damn fine excuse young lady. Get in here as quick as you can. I'm backed up to my eyeballs." He sputtered, hanging up abruptly.

Well at least she wasn't fired. With nothing more than a few swipes from a washcloth she was ready. No time to eat breakfast, Miranda settled for an old yogurt in the back of the fridge. She'd have to think up something good to soothe John's ego and still keep her job. It shouldn't be too difficult. She was actually getting pretty good at making stuff up.

Pedal to medal, she got there in no time. The line up inside the pharmacy was longer than she'd ever seen it before. A twinge of fear halted her steps as she saw John. He stood at the front counter with his face flushed, and a nervous smile fixed firmly in place. She'd forgotten it was social aide day, the busiest day of the month.

Disgruntled customers were waiting and Miranda heard their murmured complaints. Tina the cashier shot her a dirty look and said, "Finally."

Miranda ignored her and stepped behind the counter joining John. His eyebrows rose with a promise of *later.* Miranda knew the look and wasn't looking forward to the lecture. The counter was strewn with receipts. The merchandise on display was crooked, with one rack lying sideways. Someone had opened a package of breath mints helping themselves and then left the opened package to spill. Little white mints dotted the countertop. An elderly gentleman, she couldn't remember his name, picked one up and popped it into his mouth.

With a practised eye she calculated the most urgent matter, deciding to put the counter back in order before joining John and dispensing medication. She couldn't work in this mess. Not wanting to upset John further she picked up around him, trying not to get in his way. John's face changed shades, going from red to purple. Miranda wondered if the customers could feel his anger. He rang in a purchase and the till tape jammed. His smile remained firmly in place, adding an eerie look to his bulging eyes.

The crowd around them quieted suddenly queuing in. Miranda smiled and picked up where John left off. With hand motions, he indicated she was to meet him in the back room. Expertly she fixed the till tape, ripping off the wrinkled unusable part and reinserting the undamaged paper through the threads.

John turned and strode off. Miranda assured the customers she'd be right back and followed his retreating back. John walked stiffly. Miranda stifled a nervous impulse to laugh. With the door barely closed John, the smile no longer in place, began. "Where in the hell have you been?"

"I got a flat tire on the way in. My phone was dead and no one would stop for me. I tried waving down passing motorists and finally one guy stopped, but he said he was in a hurry. So I walked to the nearest garage and got help."

John stared at her. His nostrils flared. "Are you telling me the garage didn't have a phone?"

Miranda shrugged. "I wanted to get here as quickly as possible. I didn't ask if they had a phone. I'm sure they did, but I

Jagged Little Lies

was focused on getting here. I was worried and not thinking clearly."

The look on his face said he wasn't buying her story, but didn't have time to get to the truth. "I need to fill the new prescriptions. I want you to work the front counter."

Relieved she'd gotten off so easily she agreed. "Sure, John."

"And Mandy."

"Yes, John?"

"We'll talk about this later."

"Okay." The relief she'd been feeling dissipated. Worry set in once more. She might still lose her job if she was reading his face right.

They worked efficiently together, her and John. She knew what he needed before he did. She worked the front counter, answering phones and organizing medication orders. John dispensed the medications and Miranda supported the elderly and sick. As the line thinned, she even had time for a kind word or two.

She was dusting the shelf holding the allergy medicine when John's voice rang out. "Mandy!"

Yes master. Irritation flared. When John called, he expected you to come running. With the shelf half dusted she entered the back room worried *later* had arrived.

John was buttoning up his coat. He handed her a fist full of prescriptions saying, "These still need to be made up. I've got a meeting. I'll be back in a few hours." Without another word he left.

Miranda eyed the scribbles. A name caught her attention and she looked closely. Holy shit! She was making up medication for Susan. Something about the writing looked funny too. Miranda peered at it. The paper was crinkled. *Was that it?* She set the paper down aware of the unfilled scripts and scanned the next. Listening for the tinkle of the bell she got down to business.

With no time to waste, she gathered up the ingredients. It was a little like baking, she thought, carefully measuring and pouring. When she first started working with John, he'd explained everything to her. It wasn't long before she was doing just as much as he was.

Once the little bottles were filled, she checked and re-checked, before adding the labels. She'd even managed to scoop the odd pill for Declan, but he wouldn't be getting much. Miranda noticed a small white bag already made up and peeked inside. The prescription was made out to Cindy. The bottle held the heavy narcotic medications she required to ease the pain of her cancer.

There were one hundred pills. Cindy certainly wouldn't be counting them. She didn't think her grandmother would be either. Miranda swallowed. It was good John left. She'd been wondering how she could make something up for Declan with John around. Now was the perfect opportunity.

No Miranda. Don't do it!

Torn, wanting to please Declan, but feeling like a monster, she hesitated. Guilt tugged her heartstrings and she pushed the bag to the side. She couldn't. She just couldn't. The image of Cindy's sweet little face caused her too much pain. The poor little thing was already going through enough.

Miranda filled the bottle for Susan. No way would she pinch one off of her. At twenty she was sure to know. Anyways, that was way too weird. Susan already didn't like her, not that she'd ever know, should she catch on. John would never admit he'd let her fill the scripts. But still, she couldn't, the last time she'd seen the poor woman she'd looked terrible. Deranged even. She must really need every one of the little tablets. Although personally, Miranda thought anti-psychotics might be more useful. She shuddered hoping she didn't have to see Susan today.

The little bell out front tinkled. Miranda went to greet her next customer. Cindy's grandmother waited at the front counter

350

looking older. On the bench across from the counter sat Cindy. Her face was swollen, round, like the balloon she listlessly held to. Her eyes appeared glazed at she stared straight ahead.

"Hi Cindy." Miranda greeted, coming out from behind the counter.

Cindy nodded.

Grandma piped in with, "It's not a good day."

Miranda's heart broke all over again at the suffering Cindy faced. A lump wedged in her throat before she managed, "Oh?"

Cindy's grandmother nodded at the little figure sitting upright on the bench and whispered. "She's in a lot of pain. Doctor upped her medication. I don't know how the wee thing stands it, but she does. She sure won't put up with me fussing over her. Says we all have our cross to bear and hers is no different than anyone else."

Miranda looked at Cindy thinking her cross was an unbearable load for anyone to be carrying, let alone a child.

"I'll tell you this," Grandma said. "She inspires me. I'll not be complaining so easily about my achy knees, or sore back. Or even my thinning hair, or wrinkled face." The woman laughed tiredly.

Miranda laughed too, but it sounded weak and forced.

Cindy looked up at the two women and said quietly, "I can hear you grandma."

With another forced smile, Miranda found she needed to be closer to Cindy. Carefully, so as not to disturb Cindy, she sat next to her on the bench. She grasped the child's small hand noticing at once the black and blue marks from past IV's and how soft Cindy's hand was.

Moisture sprung from her eyes, as she wondered if this were to be the last time she might see the child.

Cindy smiled, patting Miranda's hand assuring her, "It's gonna be okay."

Miranda's lip wobbled.

Cindy's big, blue eyes lost their glazed expression and lit from within. "Sometimes I don't feel very good." She said looking at Miranda sincerely. "But I'm still all right. I'm very lucky you see. God gave me a wonderful grandma and he gave me cancer. Not everybody can handle it, but he chose me. I don't want to let him down by complaining about it. Cancer comes with a gift you know." She ran out of breath and stopped.

Cindy's grandmother crossed her heart and wiped the corner of her eye.

Miranda couldn't possibly think of any gift cancer might come with, but didn't want to argue with the child.

Cindy took a deep breath and continued. "Not everybody understands just how precious life is you know. But when you get cancer, it's like God whispers in your ear and tells you the most important secrets of all."

Miranda wondered if the medication might be too strong for the child. The poor little thing was hallucinating.

Cindy beamed her face alive with *the secret*. "It's so simple really, and it's funny too, because we already have it."

More to humour her than anything, else Miranda replied, "Have what Cindy?"

"Why, each other of course. Nothing's more important than *right now*, this second, and our love for each other. So you see I know how lucky I am. I have the best grandma in the world. I'm so glad I understand this. I don't want to waste my precious time wishing for something else. So many do you know." Cindy stopped, her piercing blue eyes looking far, far, older than any child's possibly could.

Miranda shivered. It felt like something *bigger* than Cindy was sitting next to her.

"Even if I don't have as much time as others, it doesn't feel bad. No, what's really sad is being *alive* but not really *living*. That's the real secret you know. It's not about how much time

Jagged Little Lies

here on earth God gives you, it's about what you *do* with the time."

Miranda's mouth opened then closed. She wanted to say something, anything, but nothing would come.

Cindy's grandmother knelt down to hug Cindy and Miranda felt it. The closeness and love they had for each other needed no words. Miranda was humbled and rocked to her very core.

The bravery of the little girl sitting next to her left her speechless and somehow *less* than. She wished there was something more she could do, but everything that could be done, had been. Not even words of encouragement, or false hope, would help. All they'd do is make Miranda feel better. They certainly wouldn't help Cindy.

And Cindy knew. She'd accepted it, whatever *it* may be. It was Miranda who was having the difficulties.

The balloon Cindy held to broke free floating above them. Miranda sprang from the bench glad she was able to help in this small manner. With the balloon once more in the hand of its rightful owner she said, "I'll get your medications."

The lump in her throat stopped her from saying more as she stepped into the back room. Cindy's bag was ready and waiting. She picked it up giving the label a final glance. There was so much medication and Cindy could always get more...

Miranda's faltered, bag in hand, torn, with Cindy's words ringing in her ears.

Chapter 57

Twitch scratched his head like a dog with fleas. His eyes wide as he attempted to stare Declan down, but it didn't work. Instead he blinked and mumbled, "Shit man, I can't do that."

"Yes you can." Declan argued.

"No man, I can't. You got a death wish bro?"

"I'm just trying to bypass the middle man. We can make ourselves some money. You'll be my partner." Declan promised.

Twitch twitched and then snorted. "Yeah, your *dead* partner."

"Look, you've already got the connections. We're just changing the merchandise up slightly." Declan persisted.

"Yeah? Where in the hell ya gonna get that kind of money from? Huh bro?" Twitch's attention shifted away from Declan for a moment as he picked an old scab on his forearm.

Declan shrugged. "I've got my resources. Let me worry about it. You just get me the pills and I'll do the rest."

"I don't know..." Twitch lost his train of thought, scratching furiously at his head.

"Come on man, no one will ever know you got them for me. It'll be our little secret. I'll give you more money than you're making."

"I don't know." Twitch replied, inspecting his arm for a new scab and spotting one, dug in.

Declan put on his most convincing face. "What are they paying you now?"

Twitch stopped picking, his face becoming shrewd. "Enough."

Yeah right. By the looks of Twitch he was getting paid in Meth. And plenty of it. Asking Twitch to be a part of this was risky business, but he didn't know who else to ask. Plus he didn't think Twitch had much going for credibility, which was a good thing. If it came right down to it, Declan was pretty sure he could out-bullshit him any day of the week.

Twitch stared at him, looking suspicious. The common area was starting to fill. The noise increased Twitch's nervousness. His cheek jumped, developing its own twitch. He fidgeted with his jumpsuit and eyed the nearest inmates. "This isn't good," he mumbled.

Declan looked around the room. Twitch was right, it wasn't good. They were attracting attention and he didn't want to be seen with Twitch just yet. Pretty much anywhere you went here, was going to be the same though. They were all under a microscope. Just like insects, all of them. With nothing else to do, your business was everybody's entertainment.

His bruised face was getting attention too, especially from Jesus, an older inmate who quoted from the Bible. Jesus had long stringy grey hair and a beard that hung to his waist. He seemed to get a lot of respect and Declan couldn't figure out why. The old guy was crazy, but maybe that's what it took.

The common area quieted as Jesus stood and pointed at Declan. "And Cain said unto the Lord, My punishment is greater than I can bear."

With a neutral nod, Declan glanced away from Jesus not knowing what else to do. Twitch's leg bounced beside him and Declan stilled the impulse to swat him. Whatever it was Jesus just said it seemed to have soothed the other inmates, bringing noise back into the room. Jesus pushed off the table sauntering in his direction. Declan watched through lowered lids as he drew closer, hoping to appear nonchalant.

"What happened to your face?" Jesus questioned his voice low.

"Fell out of bed."

Jesus peered at him closely. Declan tried not to squirm. Jesus sure did have some crazy ass eyes. They were, well, disturbing. He placed his finger on Declan's cheek and said, "Then be afraid of the sword for yourselves. For wrath brings the punishment of the sword. So that you may know there is judgment."

Declan flinched trying not to shiver as the icy finger trailed his cheek.

"Anger will never disappear so long as thoughts of resentment are cherished in the mind." Jesus whispered.

Holy shit!

Jesus poked his finger into Declan's eye. Declan felt a reptilian-like iciness enter his soul. "But pride makes us blind." He whispered again.

Jesus removed his finger and trailed it to Declan's other cheek. Tears spilled from his injured eye leaving a warm trail running down his cheek. Jesus stood rooted, apparently finding Declan's tears fascinating. He retraced the warm spill looking awed. "For the Lamb which is in the midst of the throne shall feed them, and shall lead them unto living fountains of waters: and God shall wipe away all tears from their eyes."

Horrified, Declan did nothing, as Jesus licked his fingers consuming his newly shed tears. For a moment Jesus smiled. A big, crooked-mouthed smile and then he hugged him. Declan could feel the frailty of the man through the embrace.

Jesus spoke again, this time in a louder voice. "Rejoice with them that rejoice, and weep with them that weep."

Twitch mumbled, "Aw shit," catching Jesus attention.

Jesus turned to Twitch. His eyes filled to the brim with tears. He smiled before turning away and shuffling back to the table.

Declan watched not sure what'd just happened. "What the hell was that all about?"

"Not sure.' Twitch answered. "For a minute there I thought the old guy was gonna make me eat his tears."

"Jesus." Declan whispered in a shaky voice.

"Yeah." Twitch murmured, squirming.

Whatever had just taken place was over. The men went back to joking and wrestling. Pods of inmates at different tables relaxed, as they one-upped each other on old war stories. Declan relaxed too. He'd been clenching his injured jaw and it throbbed.

Twitch looked around the room. "I think that was your initiation."

"My what?"

"Your initiation," Twitch explained. "The guys needed to know you're not a rat. By the looks of them," he nodded at a group of guys goofing off nearby, "I'd say you passed with flying colors."

"Yeah well..." Declan still felt the icy aftermath of the psychopath's finger. "What about our earlier discussion?" He reminded Twitch.

"I'll think about it. You sure you got the money?"

"Yeah, I'm sure." Declan replied thinking he better phone his mom.

"I'll get back to you." Twitch punched his arm before leaving.

Declan left the common area deep in thought. If he could get his mom to give him another five hundred bucks and Miranda to start bringing in the pills, he was pretty sure he could swing it. With Twitch's help, it shouldn't be long at all.

He might even give the other guys a run for their money. Hell, there was nothing wrong with trying to earn a buck while he was inside. He could just imagine Miranda's surprise when he got out with a fistful of cash. Maybe they could even take off somewhere for a while. That'd be nice. They'd go somewhere hot. They'd probably spend their first few days in bed, but after that...

"Pretty Boy!" Falsetto cooed.

Declan stopped in his tracks looking at the little freak. You never really knew who might come in handy in this place. Deciding he'd need more than his fair share of friends he winked.

Falsetto oohhhed and blushed.

Jagged Little Lies

Declan waved and continued on his way.

*No, it wouldn't be long now. Soon he'd get his revenge and then...*Rooster crowed interrupting his train of thought.

"What in the hell happened to you boy!"

"Fell outta bed."

Rooster smiled, poking him in the chest advising, "You'd best be paying attention boy! You don't want to make it a habit of falling out of bed now, do ya?"

Hot garbage breath bathed him in stink. He was winded, like the stench had sucked out his oxygen. He tried not to breathe. He didn't want any part of the old goat's garbage breath inside of him. Not wanting to talk he nodded and climbed up the ladder to his bed.

His face throbbed, but hatred was a great painkiller. It was all coming together. As Jesus might put it, "Vengeance is mine."

Better watch your back Rooster. It won't be long now you.

Chapter 58

It was a good thing she'd gotten comfortable in tense silences. Her question, "How are you feeling?" hung above them like a great grey cloud.

Shawna was crying. It was pretty much all she did. Eric looked like he was ready to explode and cast accusing daggers her way. Charlie whispered loudly to Rick. He had much to say, but no courage to say it. Russell and Sandra stared at the floor flinching with each *whack* of Irene's cane.

A final *whack,* this one louder than the last and Eric jumped from his chair. "Stop it!" He yelled pointing at Irene.

Irene's face flushed as she looked at him questioningly. "Why are you yelling at me?" She asked.

"Your cane is driving everyone nuts! We can't stand it anymore!" He turned and glared at Lyndsey. "Why aren't you doing something about this?"

Russell and Sandra looked up from the floor nodding. The group quieted as they waited for her answer.

On a roll now Eric continued. "I mean, you can see Irene's cane is upsetting to this group and yet you continue to ignore it."

Lyndsey eyed Eric. "Eric, please speak for yourself, not for the group."

Eric shot her a murderous glance and rolled his eyes.

Lyndsey looked questioningly at the rest of the group and asked. "How many of you are bothered by Irene's cane?"

Eleven hands rose, one very shaky, and Lyndsey eyed Susan closer. She sat next to Irene whose face changed from red to white, as she grasped her cane tightly looking offended. Susan didn't look well either. She looked like hell and that was putting it nicely. Making a mental note to get back to her Lyndsey said, "Other than Irene, the cane bothered all of you and yet you chose not to say anything about it."

361

Charlie nudged Rick and mumbled something.

Lyndsey sat up straighter. "Charlie it looks like you have something to say. I'd like you to share it with the group please."

Charlie shot her an angry glare, his lips thinning into pencil lines. Rick shifted in his chair uncomfortable with the attention.

"Charlie?" Lyndsey encouraged.

Charlie mumbled something Lyndsey couldn't quite catch and laughed.

Eric, obviously catching on, once again became spokes person for the group. "He said..."

Lyndsey interrupted him. "Thank you Eric but I'm asking Charlie to speak up. He's got something to say and I'd like him to share it with the group."

Charlie scowled and said, "Okay but you asked for it."

Lyndsey nodded.

Charlie cleared his throat. "I was saying to Rick this place is a joke. Why don't you do your job and fix this. It was obvious Irene's cane was a problem! It's been bothering me from the first *whack!* And she's not the only problem around here." He said nodding his head in Susan's direction.

"Why didn't you speak up?"

Charlie looked outraged at the suggestion. "It's not my place!" He sputtered.

"Whose place is it?" Lyndsey offered back.

Charlie nudged Rick as if to say *get a load of her.* The group gawked, all eyes. Charlie stuttered, "Why it's yours of course!"

Lyndsey smiled, "Why is it my job?"

Shawna finally finding her voice asked, "But isn't that what you're here for?"

Lyndsey smiled again shaking her head. "No, it's not. That's what *you're* here for." She said waving her arm to indicate the entire group.

Eric stomped his foot with impatience. "That doesn't even make sense!"

362

Jagged Little Lies

Susan rubbed her forehead and moaned.

"But it does make sense. That's why you're all here. To find your voice and speak your truth, to ask for what you need, instead of waiting for someone to give it to you."

Charlie looked at her suspiciously. "That's a cop out." He insisted.

"No Charlie it's not. I'm not responsible for your well being. You are. And if I jump in and look after you, then you never develop the ability to look after yourself. Without this ability you'll feel cheated and resentful, blaming others for not getting what you want. You remain a victim. One who is more comfortable in feeling sorry for themselves than doing anything about it. For most of us it's just easier to sit on the sidelines and complain. We make it somebody else's fault for the way things turn out for us."

Irene spoke up. "I'm sorry." She said, wiping a tear from her eye.

Charlie looked sheepish. "Aww...it's okay."

Lyndsey took in the group. Irene's tears once again shifted the mood. Their guilt was palpable.

Charlie looked at Lyndsey, his face angry. "Now look what you've done!"

"I haven't *done* anything Charlie." Lyndsey insisted.

"You made her cry."

"No Charlie, I didn't."

"Okay, I made her cry." He corrected.

"No Charlie, you didn't either. Really, you're just not that powerful and besides, you're not responsible for Irene's feelings. Irene's responsible for Irene's feelings." *She was going to sound like a broken record by the end of this week.*

Kim sat quietly on the other side of Irene patting her shoulder. Lyndsey took a breath, *here we go.* "Kim can you please stop patting Irene and tell us what you're feeling?"

Kim blinked. "What?"

"Your body language is telling me you have feelings. Can you name them?"

Kim's hand stilled. "I'm trying to make Irene feel better. Isn't it obvious?"

"I think you might actually be trying to make yourself feel better. What do Irene's tears bring up for you?"

"What?" Kim sputtered.

Deep breath Linds... "I asked what Irene's tears bring up for you. How do you feel when you see Irene crying?"

Chairs scraped as bodies fidgeted. The whispered comments, nervous twitters and body language spoke volumes in a room with few words.

Kim wrinkled her forehead and replied, "Why I suppose I feel sorry for her. Guilty maybe, I'm not sure what I did wrong."

"So you assume Irene's tears mean you did something wrong?"

Kim paled. "Well don't they?"

Lyndsey shook her head. "No they don't. They just mean Irene is experiencing her feelings."

Kim's free hand plucked at her skirt nervously. "Irene reminds me of my grandma. I feel so bad. I never spent much time with her. I was always so busy looking after my husband." Kim removed her arm from Irene's shoulder returning it to her lap. The free hand sat awkwardly, palm side up, in her lap before being joined by her other hand.

Irene pushed her cane underneath her chair and tried smiling at the group. The grin trembled on her lips for an instant and slid off.

Kim continued with a shaky breath. "My grandma died and I feel so awful about it. I was furious with my husband. We'd been up all night arguing when the hospital called. They said she wasn't doing well. I thought..." Kim stopped to dab her eyes before continuing. "I thought I would go and see her after I'd

Jagged Little Lies

gotten some sleep, but she..." Kim trailed off, the missing word hung in the air.

Irene stifled the impulse to pat Kim's arm. Without the cane to distract her she fidgeted and then settled back into her chair.

"I know it's not my fault, but I don't believe it. I keep thinking if only I'd been there, she might not have died. And I wonder what she thought when I wasn't there, if she knew. I couldn't bear it if she died thinking I didn't love her." Kim stopped. The weight of her words affecting all who listened. Emotion caught in her throat giving off a strangled hiccup sound. It was raw and profound.

Lyndsey shuddered, something deep within her responding.

Kim trembled, crying, as years of pent up guilt let loose.

Susan slumped in her chair, pale and wan. Her body shook, her leg bounced, her finger rat tat tatted the arm of the chair.

A rush of breath, and then, "You're right, I was trying to make myself feel better. Ever since I first saw Irene I felt awful. Well before that really, I never told anyone this before. I've just lived with it and wondered..." Kim stopped again. Tears trickled down her cheek, but she made no move to wipe them away as she whispered, "Grandma, please forgive me."

Irene's voice was strong and gentle. "She already has my dear. A grandmother's love holds no expectations and wants only happiness for her grandchild. She wouldn't want to see you tormented in this fashion. It isn't your grandmother's forgiveness you're after."

Kim raised her head locking eyes with Irene and whispered. "It's not? Whose is it then?"

With a solemn look Irene whispered back. "Why sweetheart, it's yours, of course."

Eric's mouth hung open like a newly caught cod. You could see his wheels turning. He was trying to intellectualize the experience, but hadn't quite managed to do it. Before he was able to formulate his thoughts, Susan bolted up from her chair.

Her legs trembled as she grabbed for the chair arm, almost landing in Rick's lap.

Rick's face paled. "Whoa." He said getting up to steady her.

Susan glared at him ordering, "Let me go."

The group looked on in shock, as Susan ran from the room on shaky legs.

Lyndsey watched her leave, torn as to whether to stay and debrief with the group, or go after Susan. Intuition directed her to Susan, and giving the group a five minute break she headed out the door.

Anger and worry hastened her steps.

The elephant in the room was about to be addressed.

Chapter 59

Susan looked on in disbelief as Irene whispered the words of a woman, long departed. Something really strange was happening here and she didn't want any part of it. The room quieted. Each person was transfixed. A quick glance at her watch told her it was almost time. The minutes dragged out, unbearable. Her skin sizzled when it didn't ache. Like an electrical wire had been placed underneath the top layer, sending volts of electricity shooting up and down her limbs. Her back ached and bubbles of anxiety crawled inside her flesh, like red ants stinging. She fought the urge to scratch, pretty sure if she started, she'd never be able to stop.

Lyndsey was jabbering on about feelings. The woman was a real prize. Seriously, she just never shut up about it. Susan felt like jumping up from her chair and screaming, "Enough already!" She shuddered, resting her elbows on her knees. The vibrations from her bouncing legs sent pains shooting up her forearm and into her jaw. The chair was unbearably uncomfortable as she shifted in it, trying to ease her discomfort. Worried, she placed a hand over her chest feeling the trapped little bird beneath. Just when she didn't think it could get any worse, her stomach made a disgusting noise. A long, wet, rumble and the room went silent.

How embarrassing! Heads turned in her direction and she scowled. They were idiots, all of them. *Had they ever heard a stomach gurgle?* And they seemed to be buying into this whole *group* thing. If they really thought being here was going to change anything, they were bigger fools than she first thought. At least she didn't buy into it, nor did she have much longer to wait. The guest speaker was coming after lunch and then, she was out of here.

It was a little strange though. She wasn't exactly sure why she needed to hear this speaker, she just knew she did. It was like that with her sometimes. Another glance at her watch told her it was time to go. Pushing her binder underneath the chair she stood up. Her knee popped with a loud snap, startling her. Once again she was aware all eyes were on her backside. She better get the hell out of this room, or she was going to lose it. The few steps to the door seemed to take forever. It was worse than being in kindergarten. Like a little kid she'd been worried she was going to be stopped, reprimanded, for not having put her hand up and asked to be excused.

The quiet hallways beyond the group room, was a breath of fresh air. Her shoulders relaxed, her jaw unclenched. The shroud of vigilance she wore departed. Her pills must be ready. Just knowing they waited for her seemed to soothe her aches, and her steps quickened. She rounded a corner and bedlam broke loose. The quiet hallways became loud and chaotic as doors opened dislodging the room's occupants.

She froze. Sweat broke out on her forehead. Muffled screams caught in her throat and she wondered if this were it. *The big one.*

A young man of Declan's age stood next to her offering his arm. His voice flattened as if coming from a long ways off. "Hi, you must be new here. Don't worry, it gets better. Detox sure is a bitch though."

Susan couldn't speak. Dark grey clouds thickened her vision and she felt like she was going to faint. She peered up at him squinting.

The young man spoke again, this time his voice tinged with concern as she leaned heavily upon him. "Are you all right? Are they giving you anything?"

His fingers grasped her forearm and she was thankful. His young face swam before her eyes. Grey glossy clouds swirled, allowing her pockets of sight. She noticed he even looked a little

Jagged Little Lies

like Declan. The last wisp of grey unfurled, rising above the young man's head and her vision cleared.

Her throat loosened and she croaked, "Anything?"

The young man sighed impatiently. "Yeah, you know, for detox."

Susan grasped his arm tightly, exhaling a sour shaky breath. It took her a moment to realize what the young man meant. Poor thing, he had her confused with one of the patients. "No, no." She murmured.

"You don't look so hot," he continued. "I think I need to get you to the nurse's station."

"Nurse's station?" she croaked, trying to make sense of his words.

"Yeah," he said with a tinge of impatience. "You're probably late for your detox meds."

The word meds caught her attention. "Detox meds?" She questioned.

The young man loosened her grip on his arm staring at her. He really did look like Declan, well maybe a little older. His hair wasn't as dark, his eyes a different shade of blue, but still...

"Yeah, you know, the Ativan they've been giving you, to help with withdrawal."

"What? They have Ativan here? And I can just go and get it?" she questioned, sure she was hearing wrong.

The young man released her arm, a sly look entering his eye. "Some people don't like it much, the detox meds. They say it makes them feel funny. You probably don't like them either. Let's say I help you out and take them off your hands."

"What?" Susan questioned still not following. She stared back at him noticing the change in his eyes. *Why he didn't look anything like Declan at all. What was she thinking?*

He grasped her by the arm once more, this time his fingers pinched. His tone turned smooth. "That's what we'll do. I'll walk you to the nurse's station and you can get your meds. They check your mouth, so you'll have to be careful." He warned.

Confusion blanketed her as she tried following the conversation. Her mind still stuck on the one word *Ativan*. Not sure if she'd heard him right she repeated her question. "Did you say they have Ativan here?"

His eyes darkened a deep, cobalt blue. They were shrewd and calculating. Susan looked away. He patted her on the shoulder, his tone upbeat and friendly. "Don't worry about it. I'll take it off your hands. Just use your tongue to move the pill between your back molar and cheek."

Susan hesitated. She didn't feel like driving. She was shaking so badly she probably wouldn't make it out of the parking lot anyways. Maybe she'd...

"Well? You coming or not?" the young man snarled. The corner of his lip lifted to bare a fang.

Susan tried pulling her arm free. "Excuse me?" She stammered.

The snarl slipped from the young man's face so quickly Susan blinked, not sure, if she'd seen it in the first place. "I said - "

"Frank!" A sharp voice spoke from behind. Frank let go of Susan's arm, his face flushed and turned.

His face morphed from one of wolf predator into boyish like charm. "Oh hi Lyndsey, you look nice today. I was just trying to help er...?" He broke off realizing he didn't know the name of the woman standing next to him.

Susan drew a breath not sure what to say.

Lyndsey stared at Frank and said, "Get to group."

"I was just trying to help." He whined.

Lyndsey laughed. "Yeah sure you were Frank. I want you to get honest in group."

"What do you mean?" He questioned.

Jagged Little Lies

"Frank, quit manipulating and get to group. I'll follow up with you later."Lyndsey's tone booked no argument.

Frank eyed Susan once more. Maybe he was just trying to remember her face, but whatever he was doing, she didn't like it.

"Jeesh!" He complained. "That's what you get for trying to help someone out." His shoulders drooped as he turned away shuffling off down the hallway.

Susan watched him go, wondering now what?

Lyndsey eyed her shrewdly. Her tone was soft and firm. "We need to talk."

"Um, I need to use the bathroom."

Lyndsey stood her ground. "I'll wait." She replied.

Susan nodded heading in the direction of the ladies washroom. Lyndsey's eyes burned on her back. She tried not to quiver as she walked.

Maybe if she sat on the toilet long enough Lyndsey would give up and go away.

The door to the washroom was heavy in her hand, taking her two tries to finally get it open. Both stalls were filled. Susan stood in line waiting for the bathroom she did not need. Someone was wearing perfume and its scent was thick and cloying. She almost gagged.

A woman was at the sink crying. Her eyes were swollen, her nose red. She grasped a soggy piece of tissue between her fingers and anxiously dabbed at her face. Susan tried not to stare. She hated it when people stared at her, but there was something *familiar* about the woman.

The woman stood alone in the midst of people. She was there - but not there. The pain consumed her, taking her someplace else.

A wave swelled deep inside her chest. Tears filled her eyes, her heart expanded and plumped. Susan moved toward the strange woman, drawn in a way she couldn't explain.

The woman stared woodenly in the mirror, not seeming to notice Susan's approach. Susan stopped just short of reaching her, horrified.

A toilet flushed and the door opened. She eyed the vacant stall wanting nothing more than the little piece of privacy it offered. Torn, she stole another glance at the woman.

The woman's lips moved noiselessly, mouthing words of pain and sorrow. Susan glanced at the free stall.

"I'm sorry." She whispered, patting the strange woman on the back.

Her words seemed to pull the woman back from wherever she'd been. The crying woman's eyes lost their vacant stare and met Susan's in the mirror. Susan's life mirrored back at her in the reflection of a stranger. Their eyes joined locking on one another, no words needed. Sorrow spoke louder than words ever could. The woman patted her eyes a final time with her soggy tissue and turned facing Susan with open arms.

One shaky step took her into the embrace. Thin arms circled her and she relaxed against them. The strange woman rested her head on Susan's shoulder and whispered back. "I'm so sorry too."

Pain, sharp and bittersweet, strangled her throat. *Somebody cares.* A sob rose from somewhere deep inside. It was primal. Susan wanted to howl from the force of it.

The door opened behind them.

In the entrance was Lyndsey.

Chapter 60

Miranda gave the countertops a final swipe, wishing she could just as easily clean away her disturbing thoughts. Cindy's words rang inside her head for the thousandth time that day. *It's not about the time you have left, but what you do with the time.*

Where in the hell did a little kid get such wisdom from? Cindy thought it was a secret from God and for a moment Miranda believed her. She'd not been able to bring herself to take even one pill from Cindy's medications. It wasn't that she thought she'd be caught. She was positive she wouldn't. It was just... well, like stealing from God.

She knew it sounded crazy. It wasn't something she'd tell to anyone else. She could just imagine it. *Hey guess what? I was thinking of stealing some pain medication for my boyfriend in jail, but this little girl with cancer sat beside me and God spoke.*

Jeez, get it together Miranda.

John should be back soon. She wasn't out of the woods yet. If she was lucky he'd forget about her being late, but she wouldn't bet on it.

The phone rang from the back room and Miranda hurried to grab it. Maybe it was John saying he wouldn't be back for the rest of the day. Wouldn't that be great! Sometimes he played hooky, especially when he thought she owed him. As if his absence was a form of punishment for her or something. A smile cracked her lips as she thought about it.

"Miranda speaking." She chirped.

"Meeraandaa." The words were spoken in a deep, throaty growl.

"Declan?"

"Listen babe, I haven't got very long." Declan purred.

Miranda's smile widened. Her pulse quickened. His voice was better than a double shot of espresso any day.

"Hey baby I mithh you."

"Declan? Why does your voice sound so weird? Are you lisping?"

A pause. "Declan?"

"Listen baby I didn't want to tell you this, but my cellmate beat me up pretty good."

The smile faltered and Miranda stammered, "Whaaat?"

"My roommate, Rooster. Remember I told you about him."

Confused Miranda tried to think back to her visits. Had he said anything about a roommate? "Are you Ok? What do you mean he beat you up? How badly?"

Declan sighed. She could just picture him as he stood at the phone, running a hand through his thick wavy hair.

"I'm alright babe. Well... sort of. I mean I hurt. My jaw feels like its broken and I think he might have busted a rib or two. I've got a black eye and my front tooth is busted."

"What!" Miranda screeched.

"Calm down. Please Mandy."

"Calm down! Are you kidding me? Declan you need to hang up this phone this instant and report this. Do you hear me?"

"I can't do that Miranda."

"What do you mean *you can't do that*? Of course you can do that. Declan if you don't do something, this Rooster, might do it again."

"Mandy listen to me!" His tone was sharp.

She bristled. "Don't you dare talk to me in that tone Declan!"

"Please Mandy. Honey, please. Listen to me. I don't have long and I didn't phone to argue with you. I miss you baby. You're the only thing that gets me through all this. If I didn't have you in my life, well, I don't know where I'd be. Life just wouldn't be worth living."

Jagged Little Lies

The bristles smoothed out into something far silkier. Her nipples hardened. Tingles awoke in her pelvic region. Her body responded with an eternal primitive need.

"I've got a favor to ask you honey."

His words were like ice, cutting through her brief, euphoric fog. Dread replaced the tingles. She'd heard that tone before.

"Honey?"

"I'm here." She whispered, praying she was wrong.

"I'm hurting real bad. Could you bring me in a little something on your next visit? I wouldn't have asked you but..." He stopped probably wanting to gauge her reaction.

A pain, deep inside her chest cavity blossomed. It was familiar. Despair weighed heavily on her. "Oh Declan, Jesus. You know I can't do that." She wouldn't tell him she'd been in the midst of making up just such a package for him. At the time it seemed like a good idea. But it was only a good idea if *she* thought of it. The fact that he was asking her to do this again...

"Miranda?"

"Do you know the shit I'll get in, if I'm caught? How can you even ask me this Declan? Don't you care about me?"

"Of course I do. You're my world. My entire world. I've never loved anyone the way I love you. You know that. I'd do anything for you Miranda. And I thought you felt the same about me."

Not thinking she blurted out, "I do feel the same way about you Declan. And I can't believe you're putting me at such risk. It's like you don't even care about me." Miranda heard the whine in her voice and grimaced.

"OK, OK. Forget I asked. I gotta go."

Panic coursed through her body. He couldn't hang up. Not like this! "Declan wait!"

"Miranda my time's up." His words were flat, and deadened, without a hint of their previous warmth.

The joy she'd been feeling when he first called fled with the tone of his words. Despair and anxiety cloaked her in its old familiar embrace. "Maybe I can," she stalled.

"Yeah, like how?" He questioned, his tone warming up.

"Well... Maybe I can...bring you in just a little something, *something*, she replied. Actually I was making up a goodie bag when you called." Miranda giggled nervously.

"Jesus Miranda, why didn't you just say so in the first place?" Declan complained in a friendly voice.

"I wanted it to be a surprise."

"Baby, you confuse the hell out of me!" Declan laughed.

Her body responded, heating up. She laughed with him.

"And just one other thing?" Declan wheedled.

"Hmm?" She replied.

"I'm a little short on cash. Could you bring me a few bucks? I'll pay you back tenfold when I get out of here. I promise babe."

Miranda pondered on that briefly before replying. "I can probably scrape up a few bucks. How much do you need?"

"A couple hundred would do it. That way I wouldn't have to bug you again."

A couple hundred! She didn't have that kind of cash! Not wanting to risk upsetting him further she said, "I'll see what I can do."

"You're the best Mandy. I can't wait to get you alone. I'd like to run my fingers up and down your body and – A loud angry voice broke into the conversation.

Miranda heard a muffled "Just a second," and then, "Miranda? Listen baby I've gotta go. A guy's standing here waiting for his call. I can't wait to see you honey. And don't forget what we talked about OK? Just like the last time baby. It will all work out. You'll see. Love ya. See you soon."

A soft click echoed in her ear. Miranda clenched the phone tightly unable to let go. Seconds passed and the dial tone bleeped. A vision of Cindy's bloated face surfaced before her.

Jagged Little Lies

Her fist unclenched and she dropped the phone as if she'd just been scalded. The phone crashed into its cradle and rolled off. The dial tone shrieked a shrill noise. The noise fought with Cindy's words, as they swirled inside her mind.

Her head felt like it was going to explode. She hung up the phone and the dial tone stopped instantly.

Only the soft whisper of Cindy's words echoed in the silence. Miranda tried to picture Declan's newly beaten face.

It didn't work.

With a grim determination, she picked up the newly disinfected cloth and began once again polishing the shiny countertops.

Chapter 61

The meat was supposed to be chicken. But he doubted it. Maybe it'd ran past one, once. The greasy, grey, lump of meat before him looked more like rat than than chicken. Declan winced as he tried another bite. The broken tooth was driving him nuts. He ran his tongue around the jagged edge for the thousandth time, wincing again. *It fucking hurt.* His tongue was like a heat seeking missile, drawn to the broken tooth as if not quite able to believe it really was broken. With each flick of his tongue, the pain renewed his hatred for Rooster.

Declan thought back on his conversation with Miranda. *Sorry baby, but a guy's gotta do what a guy's gotta do.* This brief moment of conscience fled with his next thought. Damn it. He should have asked her to bring a syringe. He was going to need one. Maybe Twitch? He might know where to get his hands on one.

A stringy piece of chicken caught on his broken tooth, interrupting his thoughts. He spat it out. Disgust overrode hunger and he pushed his tray away. A piece of white bread sitting on the dinner tray got his attention. The bread was still fresh and spongy. It might work. Declan pulled a large piece from the middle, leaving the slice with a gaping hole in it. He fit it over his tooth, hoping to ease the sting of the sharp edges meeting the inside of his mouth. The blob didn't fit right. He removed it working it like a stick of putty. With a little saliva and kneading, it even felt like putty. He tried it again making a few minor adjustments. *Better.* At least the wad kept his tooth from shredding the inside of his mouth. The relief was instantaneous, or maybe the pills finally kicked in. Either way, he was a hell of a lot more comfortable.

His eyes roamed the dining area, landing on Twitch. Tray in hand, he was making his way across the room. The inmates ate as if he weren't even there. Whatever had taken place between Jesus and him, he was one of them now. And when you were one of them, the tension lessoned.

Twitch didn't look so hot today. The color of his skin resembled the chicken on Declan's tray. "Hey buddy," he greeted, sliding into the vacant chair beside him.

Twitch raised his head frowning as he stared at Declan. "What's on your tooth?"

Declan grinned puffing out his chest. "I'm a fuckin' genius. Who knows, maybe when I get outta here I'll go into dental school. Huh? Whatta you think?"

Not able to focus long on anything, Twitch's attention caught on the chicken still on Declan's plate. "You finished with that?" He mumbled.

"Yeah, it tastes like shit." Declan complained.

Twitch leaned over Declan forking the grey lump of meat into his mouth, chewing with his mouth open. Declan's eyes were drawn to the grotesque massacre happening inside those open lips. Yellowed teeth, grey bits of stringy meat and his oddly shaped tongue, worked together grinding the meat into a viscous paste.

Worried he'd be sick, he forced his eyes elsewhere. "I'm gonna need a favor."

"Hmm?"

"I need a syringe. Can you get me one bro?"

Twitch swallowed his massive mouthful and looked at him. "I didn't think you were into banging?"

"I'm not." He stopped before saying more, realizing his words could get him killed. Backtracking he said, "At least I wasn't, but the pills aren't doing it for me. I want to try something stronger."

Twitch snorted. "Yeah, well, you can't just go shooting needles into your arm without a little practise. Do you even know how? You need to make sure all the air is out man, or you'll give yourself an air bubble. They say it kills you, but I've done it before and I'm not dead. Hurts like hell though."

Not a bad idea, Twitch master. But he needed the pills too. "Were you able to score anything for me?"

"A couple." Twitch replied, bending to scratch his leg.

"How much?"

Twitch's face grew sly. "Seeing how they're a rare commodity, I'm gonna need to up the price a little. Gotta make it worth my while you know. He grinned, his long, yellowed fangs giving him a wolfish appearance.

"No problem, my girl's bringing in the cash tomorrow."

"Kay, you can wait til then."

"No. I need them *now*."

"If I front, I charge double." Twitch was all business, his face serious and still. Not a twitch to be seen.

"I'm still gonna need the syringe."

"I can get it for you. I'll meet you in the common area tonight with it."

Declan thought for a moment. Patience was never his strong suit. He'd have to call his mom tonight. Between she and Mandy he'd have whatever he needed. He glanced around the room. As far as he could see nobody was paying any attention to them. He spotted Roosters back and smiled. It was all gonna come together.

"Well?" Twitch asked.

"Deal." Declan replied.

Twitch smiled, all twitchy again. His head bobbing as he rose from his chair. He staggered for a moment, his hand landing hard on Declan's dinner tray before he steadied himself.

"Tomorrow," He warned, stepping away from the table. He hadn't gone more than a few steps when the tray slipped from his hands crashing to the ground. The noise in the room grew instantly silent, all eyes on Twitch.

Declan smiled, Twitch, was a god damned genius! He pulled the little plastic package Twitch dropped beneath his plate, giving it a brief glance before bending to scratch his leg. Six, green little smarties, peeped out at him. Six! That should do it. Declan pushed the little package deep into his sock.

The silence broke followed by jeers from the inmates, as they settled back into their dinners. "Hey Twitch you trying out your new arms?"

Twitch twitched and his face grew redder. He hastily cleaned up the mess and stuttered, "Sssoorreee boys."

Declan eyed Rooster again. The guy was huge. He would need all of them, probably more. Hatred and need coiled inside of him. Not sure which one would win, Declan hurried back to his cell.

The cell was vacant. Praying he wasn't being watched he lifted Rooster's pillow. Nothing hiding there. He felt along the bed grossed out by the intimate exploration of Rooster's nest.Still nothing.

Declan got down on his hands and knees. A sharp stab accompanied his movements and he wondered again if he'd broken a rib. Hatred cooled his panic as he methodically felt the underside of the cot. His fingers encountered a bulge and he leaned in trying to see it.

The bulge was too far under the bed, he'd have to crawl under. This was going to be tricky. If he were caught under here he'd be dead. The hallways were still silent, but any minute now they wouldn't be.

Fear halted his movements. Hatred restored them. Declan pushed half his body under the bed. It was dark, and tight. The bulge crinkled as he touched it and he jumped, hitting the top of his head on the underside of the bed.

Stars and panic blossomed as he snatched at the bulge. The scream of the tape peeling away from its temporary home had him sucking in his breath. His throat tightened, the air whistling

382

Jagged Little Lies

loudly in the little room. Shakily, he backed out from beneath the bed. Any second now, he expected to feel a foot on his backside stopping him dead in his tracks. But it didn't happen.

His eyes widened at the haul he grasped. Holy mother of God! A plastic Ziploc baggie held more party than a guy could ever hope for. Miniature envelops made up the quantity of the baggie, but it held a few of his special goodies too.

Aware time was running out he opened his monkey suit and stuffed the plastic baggie inside. The elastic of his briefs held tightly to their newly found treasure. *Now what?*

He couldn't stay in his cell. If Rooster found the dope missing he'd be the first person he went looking for. If he kept it, he'd have to go through with it.

Could he really do this? Indecision and fear warred within him. If he left this cell there'd be no turning back. If he stayed, he'd be dead.

A shaky step, on rubbery legs, seemed to make up his mind. Another step and he lurched past the bed. A plan - inky at best - swam inside his head.

One step, two.

Declan left the bittersweet comfort of his cell, on wobbly legs, a walking pharmacy, and a possible dead man.

Chapter 62

Lyndsey burst through the washroom doors, not at all prepared for what she saw. A small lineup of woman flinched at her abrupt intrusion. The washroom was small, amplifying the woman's sobs as they echoed off the tiled flooring and bounced off the walls. Susan's head was buried deep into the shoulder of the woman who stood holding her. Pain etched sharp lines on the woman's face. Lyndsey recognized the woman from a past group.

The women waiting in line tried not to stare, but it was a little like trying not to look at a car crash. You didn't want to look - but you couldn't look away.

Raw emotion seemed amplified by the washroom's acoustics. It was stunning. It reminded Lyndsey of a documentary she'd once seen of a survivor in a war-torn country, keening at the death of a loved one. Susan cried, drawing in great gasping shuddery breaths. The hurt was palpable and honest. This wasn't the type of grief that said poor me, or save me. This was the real deal. The message loud and clear, *Heal me.* Although Susan didn't know it yet, she'd just taken the first step. She was on her way to getting back her life.

A moment passed and then another. The wails lessened and tears dried. Awkwardness hung in the air with the full return of logic. Susan sniffled, lifting her head and moving stiffly away from the woman's bosom. Discomfort and embarrassment filled the small washroom as the woman stared awkwardly at the floor. One woman looked to Lyndsey hoping she would say something to ease their discomfort.

Lyndsey remained silent.

The woman who had been holding Susan washed her hands and then spoke, breaking the silence. With her eyes on Susan's she said, "I'm Grace, and I'd know you anywhere."

Susan's face was covered in little strawberry sized blotches. Her were eyes swollen. She blinked looking confused and said, "Excuse me?"

Grace smiled knowing she made no sense at all, but Lyndsey understood.

"You're me," Grace continued, "just a little *before*."

The confusion slipped from Susan's face to be replaced by its usual mask of impatience. "I beg your pardon?" She snapped, leaning over the sink to splash cold water on her face.

The woman in line stared openmouthed until Susan gave them *the look*. Lyndsey opened her arm indicating the empty stall and the next woman in line quickly stepped into it.

Grace waited for Susan to finish washing her face before replying. "I mean you remind me of me. As a matter of fact, you are me. At least the pain part of you is me. Before I started attending these groups my life was falling apart. My marriage was in serious trouble and my son was in here. And if that wasn't enough we were almost bankrupt. It was a living hell and I..." Grace trailed off.

Susan gripped the porcelain sink. Her hands trembled. She looked sick. Lyndsey moved in closer to her.

Grace paused for a moment as she caught sight of Susan shaking and closed the distance between them before continuing, "I was on the verge of a nervous breakdown and I think you might be too."

Lyndsey took a deep breath. She waited for the blow up. Expected it. Prepared for it.

But it never came.

Instead Susan replied. "I don't think I'm having a nervous breakdown. I think I'm having a heart attack." She swayed standing at the sink plucking at her chest. The red blotches faded to leave behind a ghostly white countenance.

Not sure if Susan was being dramatic, Lyndsey wanted to avoid the chaos sure to erupt at any moment. The bathroom really wasn't the place to get into it. "Susan I think we need to find a quieter place to talk." Lyndsey glanced at Grace making a hasty decision. "Grace I'd like you to come with us."

Grace nodded, but it was too late, Susan crumpled to the floor.

One woman in line screamed.

Lyndsey crouched down feeling for a pulse. Susan's breath came in small, shallow gasps as her eyes fluttered open. Lyndsey looked at her hard, trying desperately to remember what she'd been taught in her first aide course. To the screaming woman she asked, "Please go and get the nurse. To the others in the room, if you don't need to be here, please leave. We need the space."

Grace turned to exist with the others and Lyndsey said. "Not you."

With Grace's help Lyndsey got Susan into a sitting position. Susan's body trembled and her legs shook. Lyndsey thought of their newly admitted patients in the detox and wondered again if Susan might not be in the wrong program.

Darlene, the head nurse, quietly entered the room. Her expertise and calm saying, nothing can shock me, I've seen it all before.

Lyndsey filled her in and Darlene spoke softly to Susan. "Susan, can you hear me?"

Susan moaned nodding.

"Does anything hurt?" Darlene asked while holding her wrist.

Susan's eyes blinked wide and then remained opened, "What happened?"

"I think you fainted." Darlene said. "Are you on any medications?"

Susan shook her head. "No not really." Her voice cracked, weak and shaky.

"What do you mean by *not really*?" Darlene inquired.

Susan tried to stand, her legs wobbly. Lyndsey thought she looked like a fawn just born, trying to stand for the first time. Darlene held tightly to her arm making sure she was steady.

Grace stood by wringing her hands, not sure what to do with them.

"Susan?" Darlene tried again. "What do you mean by not really?"

Lyndsey held firmly to Susan's other arm, mindful of the hard tiles below. Susan pulled her arm free and then relaxed.

"I mean," Susan paused licking her lips, the corner of which bore traces of white frothy foam, "*Not really.* I take a little something to help me sleep."

"Do you remember the name of this *little something?*' Lyndsey and Darlene spoke at the same time.

Susan's face grew shrewd before asking, "Why?"

"We need to know the medication you're using Susan, so I can tell the doctor."

Susan shook her head. "I already have a doctor."

"I know, but you've just fainted and I want you to see ours. Have you fainted before?"

Lyndsey watched Susan closely. The woman was lying. She was definitely trying to hide something.

Susan shook her head again. "It was nothing. I forgot to eat breakfast this morning is all."

Lyndsey nodded an unspoken *take her* to Darlene, as Darlene led Susan from the washroom to be checked over by the clinic's doctor. Grace went with them, following along with Susan's complaints. Lyndsey walked behind them.

Where was Drake? Was his day ever as crazy as hers? She wished he were here with her now. Sadness and longing rode her steps, adding weight to her worries. Here she was helping others get their lives back in order, but what about hers? The thought of going home to another night without Drake was tortuous. The thought of giving up Billy was impossible. What did one do in

388

these situations? No matter how she chose, someone would lose. And it was going to hurt either way.

Letting Darlene know she'd be right back Lyndsey headed for her office. The need to speak with Drake was urgent. It was an impulsive move on her part. It wouldn't change the outcome, but the urge to resist was just too strong.

Her foot tap tapped nervously as she wound a strand of hair around her finger. The phone rang once, twice. *Come on, come on, pickup Drake, please pick up!*

Drake's smooth deep sexy voice echoed in her ear. *Hi you have reached the voicemail of Drake. If you'd like to leave me your name and number and the time of your call, I'll get back to you as soon as I can.*

Lyndsey cradled the receiver against her breast. Loneliness grasped her in its cruel talons. Her eyes wandered the walls of her office. Cards from the various people she'd helped over the years, with colorful splashes of *thank you* dotting the walls. There was a picture of the two of them on a holiday together. Drake grinning and holding up the big fish he'd just caught.

A faded, dog-eared picture hung crookedly on the wall next to it. It was only recently hung, having been moved from home to here. She'd never been good at hanging pictures. For some reason she could never get them to hang straight. But the message was still clear. And it was one she desperately needed today.

Just three little words, but they still spoke volumes.

Git wel son.

Chapter 63

The med counter was a very busy place. Harassed nurses worked with an intense precision. Susan eyed the clientele. They were a fidgety lot. She noticed an elderly gentleman as he clutched at his heart, swooning and moaning. He tottered dangerously close to where she sat while waiting for the doctor. Alarmed she wondered if he was having a heart attack. Not sure what to do, she waited for the outcry. But it came in a different form than she would have imagined.

Darlene looked up from the cuff she was placing around a thin, young woman's arm and said, "Knock it off George! It's not time for your next dose. You're no more having a heart attack than I am."

George's arm fell from his chest as his posture changed from stooped over, to standing tall. The sick, elderly gentleman, morphed before her very eyes. The slackjawed countenance smoothed into one of a sneer. He kept growing, becoming stronger, darker, and younger.

Susan watched fascinated.

George took two sure, short steps to the counter and demanded. "I want my medications now!"

The young woman with the inflated cuff wrapped around her arm started to shake.

Darlene patted the young woman's arm and said to George, "If you don't knock it off this second I'll phone your daughter and she can come and get you."

George stepped away from the med counter, his face pinched. "No! Don't do that. Please, she'll put me back in the home."

He stumbled past Susan no longer a sick elderly gentleman, or a dark presence, but a chastened little boy. His shoulders slumped as he sat down obediently waiting.

The drama over, at least for the moment, Susan remembered her own aches and pains. An idea had begun to take shape and she didn't like it. Her hands shook and she was embarrassed. She was *not* like these people. She was not. And yet nasty little thoughts crowded her mind as she watched those around her. Darlene removed the cuff from the young woman instructing her to "hold out her hands." The young woman complied and reached her hands out in front of her as Darlene looked on. Darlene wrote something on a piece of paper nodding as the young woman lowered her arms.

The trembles in Susan's hands were far worse than the young woman's. What did it mean? She sure as hell hoped they didn't ask her to hold her hands out. Her heart rate increased, panicking at the possibility.

Darlene reached across the counter with a small Dixie cup of water and a pill in her gloved hand. Susan squinted trying to get a better look, but she was pretty sure the medication the young woman was receiving was the same as medication she took. For a moment she had the wildest urge to grab the medication out of the young woman's mouth. Her muscles tensed as she fought to stay seated. Susan observed Darlene looking inside the young woman's mouth before sending her on her way.

Her mouth watered. Her body ached. She was cold and clammy. Her stomach rolled with nausea. She felt anxious and on the verge of hysteria. One little pill. That was all she needed and she could make this go away.

A knowing of sorts, whispered words she tried to ignore. *You're just like them. You're hooked. You're a pill popper. Admit it.*

Grace tapped her on the arm interrupting her thoughts. "How are you doing?"

For a moment she'd forgotten about Grace. Susan shrugged at this strangely familiar new friend of hers.

392

Jagged Little Lies

Grace stood and stretched. She glanced over at Darlene and said, "I wonder how they do it?"

Irritation and spitefulness prickled. She wondered how she could politely ask Grace to get lost. Whatever it was that'd overcome her in the washroom was gone. Mortified, she felt ashamed she'd been so weak, weeping like a big baby in this strange woman's arms. Still, the woman had shown her more kindness than she'd seen in a long while. "Do what?" She mumbled, more out of guilt than interest.

Grace pointed at the line up of misfits waiting in line. "That."

Jesus she hoped her new friend wasn't a chatty Cathy. "I think it's their job." Susan replied, biting her tongue before the *duh* escaped.

Grace sat back down again glancing at Susan. If she'd heard Susan's sarcasm, her facial expression bore no traces of it. Grace smiled and shook her head speaking softly. "I know it's their job, but it's more than that. I think it must be their calling. I mean why would you ever put yourself through it, day after day, if you didn't have to? Nurses are always in demand. It's not like she couldn't get a job elsewhere.

Damn it, she was. A bloody chatty Cathy, just what she needed.

"It wasn't very long ago it was me sitting there, you know." Grace said.

Susan couldn't hide her surprise. "You mean as a *patient?*"

Grace smiled. "Yes, as a patient."

"Oh wow. I didn't think you were like them. I mean ah..."

Grace interrupted before she finished putting her foot in her mouth. "It's all right. I know what you mean. But *them* is us. You see, nobody starts out looking that way. They start out looking like everyone else. Life is going along and then all of a sudden - it isn't. Something happens, we all have different stories and none of us see it coming. For me it started when my marriage

393

broke up. The pain was unbelievable. I couldn't eat. I couldn't sleep. I couldn't function. And when I went to my doctor he gave me medications to help me through it."

Susan blinked, still shocked to think the kind, calm, loving woman in front of her, had once been one of *them*.

"I never saw it coming. Neither did these folks. It's subtle. It sneaks up on you. And before you know it, you're hooked. But that's not the worst part."

"It's not?"

Grace shook her head. "No, it's not. Not even close."

Susan willed herself to look away. To disengage and not ask the obvious question, but she wasn't able to. Instead she did the one thing she didn't want to do. "Well?" She asked, "What's the worst part?"

Grace thought for a second before replying. Her eyes turned a darker shade of blue before answering. "The worst part? Honestly? It steals *you*. Addiction takes away your hope and joy to replace it with despair and misery. It takes your integrity and respect and replaces it with dishonesty and self-loathing. It turns love into hatred. It erodes your intelligence, replacing it with delusion. You walk around thinking you've got them all fooled and you're only fooling yourself. You become the very thing you've always loathed, and then, you blame it all on someone else."

Grace's words resonated with her. She could relate. *Oh God she could relate.*

The intense blue of Grace's eyes changed color yet again. The startling blue faded to grey, perhaps mirroring the impact of Grace's next words. "Then, it gets really bad. You quit going outside. You don't want to see people." Grace laughed a sharp bark of bitterness. "You don't like people anymore. You can't stand them. I hated seeing married couples. I'd go out and it seemed like they were everywhere. Couples, couples and more couples. I'd watch them smiling, laughing, and holding hands. I felt like screaming and throwing things. I stopped trusting myself and hid in my home. The only thing I ever got to ever relief from were the little pills the doctor prescribed. But he wouldn't prescribe them to me for long and I found myself out there buying them off the streets. Then... well, it got really ugly. That's how I ended up here."

"You were here?" Susan said, wondering if she'd heard Grace right. *You could buy pills off the street. Where on the street?*

Grace smiled. It was beatific. "I was. And it's the best decision I ever made. Now I have the life I've always wanted, honey. Before, it was my children, or my husband, who I lived for. Now it's me. I'm a better mother and a far happier me."

Susan was still thinking about the fact you could buy pills off of the street. *Would Grace show her where? Or maybe she'd just go to the pharmacy. She wasn't shaking quite as badly now as she had been. But then what if they'd found out she forged the script? Would the police be waiting there for her?* Chaotic thoughts swirled around her brain causing confusion and a massive headache. She winced.

"You okay?" Grace looked at her with concern.

"I think so," Susan faltered. "Not really. I feel sick. I have a headache. I really need one of my-" she stopped, clapping a hand over her mouth horrified at what she almost said...

Grace placed a comforting arm on her shoulder and whispered. "Aw honey, you stand at a crossroads. The decision is yours. One road leads to an existence of endless suffering, hopelessness and death, *if* you're lucky. The other road, who knows? You haven't tried it yet. But it can't be any worse than the road you're on now. All you have to do is tell the truth."

God she was going to throw up. Nausea competed with Grace's words. She'd like to tell Grace to go to hell, or to stop talking, but it seemed, at least temporarily, she was out of words.

Together they sat together in a weirdly bound silence. It was like nothing Susan experienced before.

"Susan. Susan?" Darlene's voice interrupted her strange, trance-like state. "Doctor Stephenson will see you now."

It wasn't until she stood up that she remembered once again, why it was she needed the pills so damned much. Her legs creaked. Her feet wobbled. Her hands shook. Her vision swam. Darlene held tightly to her arm steering her. Susan turned to Grace needing to say something, anything, but nothing came.

Grace smiled. "You'll be fine honey. I'll be right here."

As Darlene led her from the room there was only one thing Susan was sure of. She'd fallen so far down the rabbit hole - she'd never find her way back up again.

Chapter 64

"Mandy I've decided to place you on probationary period starting now. If you're late one more time, consider yourself fired."

Miranda stared at John biting back a retort. There was so much she wanted to say. And he being a pompous ass was just the beginning. She lowered her head not trusting the anger simmering below the surface, not to show. Instead of saying what she wanted, she adopted a meek attitude and replied, "Yes, John."

"Now finish cleaning up the front. I want you in early tomorrow. You can make up for the time you lost today."

"Yes, John," She replied woodenly.

With his back turned to his newly chastened employee, John donned his coat and hat, jiggling his hands in his pockets. He whistled an old tune slightly off key. He left Miranda to close up shop, with a slight bounce to his step. Where ever he was going, he was looking forward to getting there. Or maybe he just found chastising a turn on. Who knew?

She, on the hand, found the experience completely demoralizing.

With a long, weary, drawn out sigh, she scanned the room trying to figure out how much longer it would be before she could leave. The pharmacy counter was scrubbed and tidied. The floor still needed sweeping. Miranda pushed John's chair in straighter. For some reason he'd never been taught to push in his chair. It was a pet peeve with her. Each time John got up from his desk, his chair remained pushed back. Miranda had bumped into it more than once. And so had John. Of course when this happened it was her fault for not putting *his* chair away. After all, that's why he'd hired her. Silly her, she thought she'd been hired for her pharmacy technician capabilities, but apparently maid was the more accurate description.

Little bottles lined the table with labels affixed and ready for their owners to come and claim them tomorrow. One bottle stood readied from today. Miranda picked up the bottle wondering why Susan hadn't come in for it. The original prescription waited next to the computer ready to be entered then archived.

Curious she retrieved it. Something about it had bothered her earlier. With a keen eye she took in the RX number, the address, and the billing number. Miranda stopped. Her eyes locked on the discrepancy and widened. The signature was wrong, it was flowery and to shaky. It looked like someone with Parkinson's disease had attempted this signature.

What the hell?

Miranda bent opening the lower cupboards where the archives were stored. The baskets were filed alphabetically and she found what she was looking for quickly. With the last script Susan brought in she compared the two.

Interesting!

The signatures most definitely did not match. *Wow.*

Miranda eyed the bottle. What did it mean? Was Declan's mother forging scripts?

Holy shit!

No, it couldn't be. But it was. The proof was right in front of her. Miranda shook her head not able to comprehend what she was seeing. Maybe the physician was distracted, or coughed, or something...

No way could she believe Declan's mother was a prescription-forging drug addict. It just wasn't possible. Was it? But just in case... She couldn't leave the bottle here to be found. John must have been blind not to notice the signatures. There was no way he'd miss it tomorrow though. When he entered and archived this little piece of paper, the gig would be up for sure. *And then what?* What if it really was forged? Miranda glanced again at the bottle. Her eyes saw what her brain couldn't grasp. What did this mean? Would Susan go to jail too? Wouldn't that be great, mother and son in jail, a real family affair.

What to do? What to do?

Really, there was only one thing to do. As much as she disliked Susan, she wouldn't hang her out to dry. Miranda replaced the original prescription and pocketed the forgery and the bottle of little white pills. She wondered what Susan would do when she returned for them and they weren't there. Maybe she'd complain, but Miranda doubted it. She'd want to play this on the down low for sure. She wondered why she hadn't returned earlier for them. Maybe she'd just chickened out?

With a final look around she turned off the lights, still baffled by this new turn of events. The fluorescents overhead made a clicking noise and flickered off. The darkness swallowed her instantly, leaving her momentarily blind, with nothing but a trace flicker of white behind her eyelids. Her imagination ran wild. She'd always been afraid of the dark. When she was little her mother made a game of looking underneath her bed for bogeymen and monsters. Miranda had been on the lookout ever since.

Her mouth dry, her pulse racing, she heard the strange clicking noises she made when she was afraid. It was an old habit. She wasn't sure why she'd started doing it. And it wasn't as if clicking would scare off monsters and bogeymen anyhow, but the clicks distracted her. And maybe that was the whole point.

Miranda punched in the code to set the alarm. The little green light flickered to red. Good, she was ready. She positioned her car keys between each finger - a self defense show she'd seen on TV recommended this for women on their own – and she crossed the parking lot to her car.

As she waited at the stoplight, she noticed an old church. She must have passed it a hundred times before without ever really looking at it. People stood around the entrance in little groups. Mostly women, but a few men as well and they varied in ages. A sign above them read, *"Are you tired of waiting for someone else to change?"*

The massive ornate doors swung open just then, giving her a glimpse inside. Miranda was curious. She'd never been inside a church before. She didn't believe in God and was never interested in attending church. She'd always imagined the people going there would look a little like, well... saints. They'd be freshly groomed, wearing suits and ties, dresses and aprons and big, beatific smiles.

These people were nothing like what she'd imagined.

A car behind her honked and she gave the driver her one-fingered salute. It seemed if you hesitated, even by a split second, you could always count on someone honking. Just to piss him off, she crawled through the intersection hoping he'd miss the light.

He didn't. Instead he stayed on her ass, honking like mad and flashing his bright lights before roaring off beside her, waving back with his own personal one-fingered salute. Miranda glanced at the church folk again.

Are you tired of waiting for someone else to change?

What exactly did that mean? Intrigued, she u-turned and drove into the parking lot. From the privacy of her car she watched the others. The massive doors remained open and she caught a whiff of coffee. Laughter floated on the air. A longing to be a part of it caught her off guard.

The car door eased open and she stepped out. Who were these people? Why were they so happy? Terror gripped her chest. *Stop!* Curiosity warred with the terror she felt, as her steps drew nearer to the door.

What are you doing Miranda? Stop right now!

Jagged Little Lies

The gravel below her crunched as she walked, announcing her presence. A woman about her mother's age noticed her and smiled.

"Welcome." She greeted, the one word laced in warmth.

"Uh, Hi." Miranda greeted back, feeling incredibly awkward.

"Is this your first meeting?" The woman queried.

"Um, meeting?"

"Don't worry honey. We all remember our firsts!" The woman smiled again adding, "I'm Maggie."

Maggie encircled her arm steering her inside and introduced her to some of the others. "That's Peter and Sarah." She said, smiling and waving at each person.

Miranda followed Maggie suddenly shy. The church was magnificent, and she was at a loss for words.

The interior was lit, showcasing the statue of the Virgin Mary and baby Jesus. The statue was beautiful and life-like. Miranda stared at the Virgin Mary. Her smile was one of wisdom and patience, and her eyes... Dear God, her eyes. Miranda felt as if the Virgin Mary could see right into her. For some reason she felt compelled to touch her and was surprised to find the statue hard and unyielding to touch. The rest of the church was just as beautiful with its magnificent stained glass windows. The pews were oiled and shiny, giving off a lemony scent. They remained empty with the people inside opting to sit in a small circle of chairs. The atmosphere was calming and *what*? The building spoke of something eternal, and for a moment Miranda wished she could bring Cindy here.

The smell of coffee was intoxicating. Its rich heady brew drawing others like her to pour a cup. Miranda sipped from the cup hoping to be invisible and trying not to stare

What did one do at church?

It wasn't long before she had her answer. Maggie sipped from her cup and then placed it on the table turning to Miranda.

LORELIE ROZZANO

"Ready?" She questioned, before once again grasping Miranda's arm and steering her towards the circle. Miranda sat down noticing the room had quieted, the mood shifting from one of gaiety to somber.

Chairs squeaked as others settled in. Alarm bells rang loudly in her head. She clutched the warm coffee cup wondering what in the hell she'd been thinking? For a moment she fought the urge to bolt. It would draw to much attention and she didn't want to make a spectacle of herself.

Calm down Miranda. Don't worry. As soon as this is over, just say thank you and then politely get the hell out of here.

Maggie reached for her hand as the group said a prayer. It wasn't the Lord's Prayer, But a new one she'd never heard before, something about serenity.

Miranda closed her eyes wishing she could just disappear as she listened.

Her eyes weren't closed long before blinking open wide.

She almost fell out of her chair at what she heard.

Chapter 65

Declan's knee bounced as he waited for his mom to pick up. *Come on. Come on. Answer would ya?* The phone rang again, a long, plaintive wail. He ran a shaky hand through his tousled hair. He'd never been any good with patience before and he wasn't now.

Where in the hell could she be?

It wasn't like she had a life. She wouldn't be visiting friends, she didn't have any. He couldn't remember the last time she'd gone anywhere, or done anything. And she'd never - not answered his call before.

The robotic voice of the answering machine clicked on asking him to leave a message. He paused not sure if he wanted to. A second ticked by and then, "Mom, it's me, Declan." *Oh that was stupid. She knows your name idiot.* "I ahh... I um, miss you. I was hoping to say hello. I need to ask a little favor. The money you sent me, um, is gone. Someone stole it and I really need a few bucks. Well more than a few. Another five hundred would be good. I've borrowed money off a guy in here just to get by. Mom, if I don't pay the money back, he's gonna break my legs," Declan muffled this last sentence with a little sob, *might as well make it believable.*

Declan hesitated changing his tone yet again and lowered his voice. "Mom you really gotta help me out here. Can you give the money to Miranda? I don't want you to bring it here. Trust me. You don't want to see me like this. I... I don't want to put you through it. Please Mom, I'll pay you back. I gotta run now. Mom...? I love you."

For once no one stood waiting in line behind him. Declan glanced around just to be sure. He didn't want anyone overhearing his words. He'd never hear the end of it if they did. He patted his waistline. *Yup it was still there.*

403

He'd heard you could dissolve the oxy in Pepsi. It was supposed to break the time release thing. He'd need a good spoon too. Not the crappy little plastic forks and knives they gave you to eat with. There was an old tin spoon that just might work in the laundry area.

The bag chafed his belly as he wandered past the common area and stopped. Better find Twitch first. Declan glanced around. Inmates were everywhere just hanging out. Some bent over small round tables fiercely concentrating on the cards fisted tightly in their hands. Cards, it was a big thing here. Even if you didn't have money, there was always something, somebody wanted off you. Anything from sex acts to servant and everything imaginable in between.

Declan spotted Twitch off in the corner holding up a wall. He sidled over. Twitch, Declan was beginning to notice, was not always what he first appeared to be. It was easy to write him off as just another methed out mess. And most of the time he still believed it. But there were moments, glimpses, of a shrewd brain hiding behind his spaced out appearance. It was one of those moments Declan hoped to avoid now.

"Hey," he tried for nonchalance, as if it were no big deal, him, trying to get the syringe.

Twitch grunted, nodding back. Well, it wasn't quite a nod, more a wobble, like the bobble heads you see on car dashboards. His face wore its usual, slack-jawed expression. His eyes drooped, hanging at half mass.

"So did you -" A sharp jab in the ribs shut Declan up. He looked down in disbelief.

Twitch, faster than he'd ever seen him move before, jabbed him again. The sleepy, doped-out expression was gone. For a second Twitch stilled standing tall. His words were clear and precise. "Shut the fuck up. They're watching."

Jagged Little Lies

It all happened so fast Declan wasn't sure he'd seen it. He noticed his mouth hanging open and closed it. *What the hell was that all about?*

Once again Twitch twitched beside him. His thin body vibrating as he leaned up against the wall.

Who was watching?

Terrified it might be Rooster, Declan surreptitiously looked about. A guard stood in the middle of the room looking bored. It wasn't the old guy, but a younger version of him. The television was on in one corner. An old movie he'd seen once when he was a kid with his dad. He watched for a second as the Volkswagen fought off the bad guy who tried to steer from inside. Laughter followed the antics from a couple of the inmates watching, as the VW careened into a curb. The doors of the bug opened and the bad guy flew through the air landing on the ground beside the triumphant Volkswagen.

One table looked a little tenser than the rest, but Declan put it down to the card game and the stakes being higher. Whatever it was Twitch was seeing, he wasn't. And he didn't have all day. Aware with each passing minute Rooster could return to their cell finding out he'd been robbed, Declan tried not to panic.

Fuck it.

"Twitch I need -" Once again he stopped, this time to help Twitch stand up as he fell against him nearly knocking him over. "Jesus! Would you watch it?" He snarled.

"Give me a minute and then follow." Twitch whispered, before once again leaning back against the wall.

Christ he was acting weird. Or should he say weirder?

Twitch mumbled something incoherent and stumbled away.

Declan watched him go trying to see if anyone else was watching. As far as he could tell no one was. Twitch's stumbles and stoned out state, was a way of life. What'd be surprising, were if he weren't.

A minute passed and then another. With a deep breath he sauntered back the way he'd come. He hadn't gone more than a few steps when Jesus waved him over. *Dammit, not now.*

If he ignored him he was sure to gain unwanted attention. If he didn't, he'd lose Twitch. A trickle of sweat dripped into his eye stinging. Declan blinked hoping no one noticed.

Jesus stopped waving and ordered, "Come here my son."

With no other choice, Declan changed directions. He stopped within a foot of Jesus, hoping to look respectful and interested he stared a little to the right of Jesus. You really wanted to avoid eye contact in prison. That is if you valued your eyes, or your life.

Jesus rose from the chair and gripped him by the arm. Crazy, intense eyes, met his. Declan blinked, trying not to stare. Posters of the damned could be made from Jesus' eyes. "My son," he whispered.

Not sure what was expected of him, Declan did what he always did in situations like these. Nothing.

Jesus took a deep shuddery breath and began. "I will make you into a great nation and bless you." Jesus stroked Declan's arm the way Miranda might have.

Declan fought the urge to pull away, knowing it would only make matters worse.

Jesus spoke again, this time the words rattled deep inside his chest. "I will make your name great and your blessings many." His fingers stilled and then trailed up Declan's arm.

Cold, shivery bumps, rode the skin where ever Jesus touched. Declan tried not to flinch.

"I will bless those who bless you," Jesus' fingers touched his neck, tracing a small circle. "Whoever curses you, I shall curse." He whispered, smiling and licking his lips.

Declan's gut twisted. His scrotum shrank. His ass puckered.

"And all people on earth will be blessed by you." Jesus removed his hand, looking at it in wonder, before kissing him on the forehead. His face radiated a malady of madness and beauty. It was a darkly fascinating combination.

The kiss seared Declan's forehead as if he'd been branded. He hung his head in humility. Not sure if this were the right thing to do, he raised it again.

Jesus smiled at him. His smile was a twisted slash of a crooked mess. With a final caress to Declan's cheek, Jesus turned his back on him, returning to his table.

The guard harrumphed, breaking the spell and Declan moved away.

He passed by the card players thinking.

You didn't have to be here long to realize what you first thought scary, was really nothing. The truth of prison was far more disturbing than that. It played with your mind, unraveling the little sanity you still held onto.

Prison didn't come with a textbook or even *how to*. It came with no instructions at all. Besides, he was pretty sure, you couldn't put rules to it anyhow. For how did one take into consideration the madness, the psychopaths, the murders? To have a *how to* book you'd need a capable audience. One that was predictable and teachable. One who wouldn't slash your throat the very first chance they got.

Nope, he wasn't going to find any type of manual 101 for better prison living inside these walls. That was damned sure.

But what he was going to find - was Twitch.

Chapter 66

Lyndsey heard their complaints before she entered the room.An unattended lot, left missing a group member and facilitator. She didn't blame them either. Most people, when it came right down to it, liked to be entertained. Idle chitchat seemed to be a way of the past.

One person's voice was louder than the rest. Lyndsey listened from the other side of the wall. Eric seemed to be the ringleader again. It was his voice she picked out over the others.

"Jeez you sure pay a lot of money to sit here doing nothing." He groused.

This was one thing that'd always been her pet peeve. The walls were too thin. She knew if she could hear them, they could hear her. To bad she didn't always remember it.

Lyndsey frowned. What she needed was time.

Eric's voice rose in level. "If I was running this place -"

Lyndsey missed the rest of Eric's sentence. But she'd heard enough. *Be careful what you wish for!* With a grin, she went in search of him.

The group members sat in their circle looking at Eric. His face was a mottled red. His chest puffed out. No one noticed her approach until she was right in front of them. She stepped closer to Eric's chair laying a gentle hand on his back.

"I mean what does a guy gotta," he stopped, startled by her touch.

"Eric," Lyndsey kept her tone neutral.

Eric's face turned a deeper shade of crimson. *Busted.* Lyndsey turned to the group. Awkwardness and dis-ease etched the features of the faces before her.

She took in each individual, once again profoundly touched at how people would go to any lengths to avoid emotion. Even when it turned them into blamers and victims, it was just easier to point the finger elsewhere.

It was her job to teach them.And for today's lesson? Humility.

"Eric," Lyndsey repeated gently. What she really wanted to promote, above all else, was trust. The folks attending these groups were bereft not only emotionally. They'd all been hurt somewhere along the road. And they'd developed crusty scar tissue from their wounds. It was something they'd come to expect.

So she did the unexpected.

Tense muscles bunched beneath her fingertips. Lyndsey removed her hand making eye contact. "I'd like you to facilitate group please."

Eric's face changed from crimson, to a softer pink. "What?"

"I'm going to be in a meeting. I'd like some help."

Eric scratched at his chin looking sheepish. The puffed out chest deflated, revealing the scared little kid hiding just below. "Ah... I don't know?"

Lyndsey smiled. "Please ask the group to start check-in. You can lead by example. If you can go around the room and each describe a feeling you're having in the moment. I'll be back shortly to check on your progress."

Irene sputtered.

Lyndsey walked away.

It was time for Irene to start taking more responsibility for her own needs. It would be easy for her to do it, but she wouldn't be helping Irene.

Irene harrumphed.

Lyndsey wondered if she'd pick up the cane.

Two steps form the door Irene spoke. "Where's Susan?"

Lyndsey stopped replying. "She'll be joining us shortly."

Irene's nostrils flared as she asked. "Do you really think it's a good idea to have Eric run this group?"

Jagged Little Lies

Shawna nodded, her eyes downcast.

Encouraged by Shawna, Irene continued. "I mean, what credentials does he have?"

Lyndsey paused. Sometimes she felt like crying. She was tired and out-numbered. She loved the group members in front of her, in a way they'd never be able to conceive. Yes, she loved them, but they drove her crazy. Hoping it was the love, not exhaustion, they'd pick up in her tone she replied. "Irene, it doesn't take a Ph.D. to talk about feelings. It only takes courage. The very worst thing you might encounter is embarrassment. Embarrassment doesn't last and it won't kill you."

"Well, Irene stammered. I'm not sure..." She trailed off looking confused.

Eric spoke, stepping into his new role. "Irene? Would you care to start us off? How are you feeling?"

Lyndsey smiled and turned away. *That's it. Now you're getting the hang of this.*

Too bad the smile didn't last. Her steps dragged in a way she'd come to despise. Still no closer to a solution for her own life, she stepped into her office again. It'd been a long time since she'd experienced the deep desire to hide. But she experienced it now.

Lyndsey felt an urgent need to go and see Billy. At least with him held tightly in her arms she'd know this suffering had purpose. Pain and turmoil were merely part of the human experience. She didn't like it, but she wouldn't try and avoid it either. Sometimes, she really thought she felt things *too much.* Years ago, before she'd sobered up, it felt like her feelings would kill her. They'd been so enormous and overwhelming. Since then, she'd come to know you couldn't really die from emotions, although on days like today, it was more difficult believing it.

Determination squared her jaw. Shoulders back, head up, she took a breath. A silent prayer, whispered in the quiet of her office. *Please God without you I can't do this. Give me the courage and strength, to follow your direction. Remove my need for constant assurance. Help restore my faith. Renew my energy. Above all else, be it your will, not mine, be done. Amen.*

Whether it was through prayer, deep breaths, or quiet, her anxiety dissipated. Just like deep pockets of pointy daggers, breaking loose and lifting. Not quite all the way gone, but...

Better.

Sobriety wasn't rocket science that's for sure. Then again, neither was life. Still there were a few small things one could do to make the journey more enjoyable. Sometimes, it was as simple as doing the next right thing.

The next right thing. The next right thing.

The words resonated.

It took her a moment to realize, she'd just found her answer.

Chapter 67

The room spun. Susan felt faint and twitchy. *Was she developing symptoms of epilepsy? What was happening to her?* She used to be so healthy. She remembered when Declan and Dick would get sick. Every year, just like clockwork, you could count on it happening. First Declan, his would start with a sore throat, then congestion and coughing. It was the fevers that scared her though. Then it would be Dicks turn.

A brief flash of sadness pierced her heart. The room was bringing back to many memories. Memories of when they'd all been a happy family. The times they'd sat together in rooms just like this. Dick had been so strong in those days. He would hold her hand, assuring her everything would be fine. The sight of Declan sick always caused her to panic. He knew it too and he really tried to help.

Why didn't she listen to him? Why was it, everything he ever did, or said, just wasn't good enough? Why did she always want more from him?

Thinking back, she couldn't remember a single time when she'd told him how important he'd truly been. All she'd ever been able to see were his faults, especially when it came to fathering Declan. In her mind, she really truly thought *she* was the capable one and the one who *always* knew best, when it came to Declan.

And the secrets she'd kept from Dick. It started when Declan was just little. They would whisper and giggle, always ending with *don't tell daddy*! It was her and Declan against the world. They'd been such a team, at least for a little while. It was funny back then. Kind of like a game. An exclusive game and one only they knew how to play.

She'd never said no to Declan. Not ever. She said maybe and we'll see, but all those words ended up being were a slow yes.

The lies she told to Dick hadn't bothered her either. She'd always been able to justify them in her own mind. In a way, she'd almost been forced to lie. I mean what else was she supposed to do, when she wanted something for Declan and Dick said no?

Still... She never dreamed it would end up like this. Too bad you couldn't go back in time. Maybe there was a magic wand you could wave. She'd pick it up in a heartbeat, but then what?

How can you ever undo a lifetime of injuries?

A sob shuddered up from her diaphragm and lodged in her throat, startling her with its intensity. Her shakes increased. *Was she dying?*

An open cupboard door caught her attention. She scrubbed a shaky hand over her eyes as she studied it. The cupboard was long, tapering towards the bottom. The door stood ajar and she could just make out the various bottles inside. The paper sheet beneath her crinkled as she moved, shifting, trying to get a better look.

The medical bed she sat on was high off the ground. Darlene had marched her into this little office demanding that she "wait right here."

Well waiting was what she'd do. Just not on the bed.

On trembling legs Susan backed off the bed keeping a cautious eye on the door. If the doctor, or Darlene for that matter, came in she'd just say she needed to stretch her legs.

It was only a few short steps to the cupboard. Susan squinted peering inside, this time close enough to read the labels. Tylenol, Gravol, Advil, Tums.

Damn. Not what she was looking for.

With a quick glance at the door she reached inside the cupboard. In the back were smaller bottles. On tiptoes she tried getting a closer look. Her heart pounded wildly in her chest. Little black dots floated before her eyes making it difficult to see.

Jagged Little Lies

When had she last eaten anything? Maybe she was trying to kill herself and she didn't know it? Was that even possible?

Every cell of her being screamed with hurt. Nasty, viscous thoughts warred within her mind. Her hand reached deeper into the cupboard.

Stop!

No, get the pills.

Don't do it?

Do it!

What has happened to you?

Who cares?

At war, she stood on the brink, teetering, reasoning blending with insanity.

Unfortunately, her need was just too great. Not able to stop herself she grasped one of the small bottles and pulled it free. The label was small but she could make it out. It read, *Clonazepam. Take one as needed for anxiety.*

Clonazepam, wasn't anything ending in pam similar to what she'd been taking? The small bottle was half full. Susan's mouth watered in anticipation.

Should she take the whole bottle with her? Would they miss it? Could she?

Why not?

But first she needed to take one. There was no way she could wait any longer.

With shaky hands she twisted the cap. It wouldn't budge seemingly stuck. *Shit.* She tried again, this time biting her tongue in her efforts. Her bitten tongue brought tears to her eyes and she stopped to wipe them away.

The pills inside the bottle rattled against the plastic cylinder in sync to her shaking hand. Gritting her teeth she bore down with all her weight twisting. The cap still stuck, not budging.

What the hell?

Footsteps just outside the doorway alerted her to the fact someone would soon be joining her any second.

Shit!

Quickly she closed the cupboard door and jumped back up on the bed.

The door to the medical room office opened, giving Susan her first look at the doctor. The pills were firmly entrenched in her sweaty hand, as she hastily pushed them into her bra hoping he didn't notice.

Time slowed. The bottle stuck on her shirt button preventing it from fully submerging into her bra. Gravity worked against her as she pushed harder and the bottle slipped free of her sweaty grasp with a *plop*.

Susan watched in horror as the bottle rolled across her stomach, bounced off the bed and landed on the floor below.

The impact knocked the lid off and the tiny white pills inside, spilled out.

Not able to stop herself, she jumped down after them.

She was on the ground, bent over on hands and knees. Her hands trembled fiercely. "Come on, come on," she mumbled unaware.

For some reason her fingers wouldn't work. Panic strangled her throat, turning her breath into a wheezy, asthmatic sound.

A well-manicured, tanned hand appeared in her peripheral vision.

Oh God, he's going to stop me!

A white coat joined the hand and the darkly clad legs.

Susan whimpered. Adrenaline raced throughout her body. She heaved a dry wracking noise.

A gentle hand caressed the top of her head. A disembodied voice, calmly announcing, "It gets better you know."

Using both hands she managed to trap one of the pills on the shiny linoleum. It was strange, what you were aware of, at times

416

Jagged Little Lies

like these. The lemon scented floor wax filled her nostrils. Her saliva tasted like bitter acid and the salty tang of sweat.

The caress stopped for a moment before starting again. "This too shall pass. Why don't you let me help you?"

Susan's palms were sweaty and it worked in her favor. With her fingers to twitchy to pick anything up, the little pill stuck to the palm of her hand. Her sweaty palm acted like a bonding agent. Carefully, she slowly raised her palm to her mouth.

The little white pill was her sole focus. Nothing else mattered. The room disappeared with everything in it. As carefully as one would hold their newborn child, Susan cradled the pill bringing it to her lips.

Twelve inches, then ten, it seemed to take forever, with her hand traveling at a snail's pace.

From far above, "Why don't you sit up on the bed? We can talk."

Six inches, then five, Susan licked her lips.

"Here, let me help you up."

The tanned hand grasped her upper arm firmly, halting it. The pill stopped just inches from her mouth.

Susan shrieked, jerking her arm free, only realizing her mistake to late, as she watched in stunned disbelief.

The little pill flew across the room and rolled under the examination bed.

The thread of sanity she'd been clinging to snapped.

Chapter 68

The girl introduced herself as Laura. Miranda thought she might be a year or two younger than she was. Laura's face was alive and animated. Her blue eyes sparkled and her blond curls bounced, emphasising each word. She could be a poster girl for health magazines with her clear skin and bright white teeth. The vibrancy of her tone was rich with passion and her cheeks flushed as she spoke about her brother.

"I think he's killing my mom. I really do. I mean, he doesn't care. It's like all he ever thinks about is drugs. It's really hard -" Laura broke off overcome by emotion.

Miranda realized she was staring at Laura and lowered her head.

Laura squared her jaw and began again. "You know, it's like I've lost both of them. My brother to drugs, and my mom to my brother, I mean -" She stopped swiping at a tear.

Maggie nodded, encouraging Laura.

Laura stared off in the distance frowning. "My mom hardly ever sleeps. She barely eats and all she ever talks about is Shawn. Shawn this and Shawn that. Shawn, Shawn, Shawn. It's like the rest of us have disappeared. He's taken over her mind. I think she might be more addicted to Shawn than he is to his drugs. At least it seems that way to me. I mean why else would a person, who used to be a loving mother turn into a raving lunatic? Oh -" Laura keened, curling into a little ball.

Maggie reached over patting Laura's shoulder. "Laura you're okay and you're right. We tend to think it's the person using the alcohol or drugs who's the sick one, but the truth is, we get sick too. Sometimes..." Maggie trailed off gazing up at the ceiling. As if to clear away cobwebs she shook her head before continuing. "Sometimes," she repeated, "I think we might be the sicker of the bunch."

Laura nodded. "Yeah, well, Shawn seems to have a whole team of people on his side. I mean you wouldn't believe how many are helping him out. He's got everybody, doing everything, for him. He doesn't have to do anything. Well, except for getting high, that is."

Maggie's face paled. "I was like that. When my husband would come home drunk, I'd make excuses for him. If his boss wasn't such a jerk, he wouldn't have to drink. Or, he worked so hard he deserved it. Besides, for a little while it made him happy, and if he was happy, so was I. As a matter of fact it sort of became my purpose to keep him happy. It seemed it was the only way I felt good. On the days he felt terrible, so did I."

Miranda's heart raced. She bit the inside of her cheek. *Wow! Could she ever relate to Laura and Maggie? Is this what happened at church? Weird, it wasn't anything like she thought it would be.*

"The terrible days were the worst." Maggie continued. "Of course by the end, it seemed like that's all there ever were, just awful, terrible, days. By then I thought *everything* was my fault. I was always making excuses for him. He wasn't feeling well. He had a headache. Or maybe it was me? If I'd just tried harder -"

"You're just like my mom!" Laura interrupted Maggie. Her blue eyes, opened wide.

Maggie glanced around the room, her smile a terrible parody of pain, regret and perhaps something else, something wise.

Miranda couldn't help herself. She stared at Maggie. The woman looked worn. Worn and what? She couldn't quite put her finger on it. Miranda wondered if she was still looking after her husband this way. Maggie reminded her of someone, not in the way she looked, or spoke. More in what she said. Miranda gasped.

Oh God please no!

Jagged Little Lies

Maggie glanced at Miranda, a look of concern reflecting in the deep dark pools of her eyes. "Miranda, would you like to share?"

Share? "Ah... no, um... Thanks." She finished the sentence awkwardly and cringed.

Maggie's face was like an open book, almost too painful to look at. It was like she wore no shield, her thoughts and feeling were easily readable. She stared at Miranda as if debating something, before she spoke.

"Of course it never started out this way. It started out like nothing I'd ever experienced before. He swept me off my feet. Alan, that's my husband, said things to me nobody had ever said before. Things like how beautiful I was, and how he'd never be able to live without me. When he smiled, the sun turned on. It warmed my heart and..." Maggie's cheeks reddened, as she finished off with, "well, other parts."

"Well..." Laura sputtered. "Your story doesn't explain why my Mom is acting so crazy!"

"Sometimes Laura, we just see what we want to see. What we wish were happening, versus what really is happening. I remember when Alan used to want me to spend every moment with him, even when he wasn't at home, or at work. He never liked my friends or family, he said he felt judged in their presence. In order for me to stay with him, I had to give up everyone else. Now here's where it gets really crazy. I actually liked that he didn't want me spending time with anyone else."

Miranda's head bopped up and down nodding, before she stopped, mortified.

Laura's cheeks bore two large red spots and her eyes narrowed. "Why would you like that?"

"Because..." Maggie's shoulders slumped as she settled back into her chair. "Because," she started again, "I was in love. At least I thought I was. I let him speak for me. I began to think like him. I adopted his beliefs and attitudes. Soon, I was less me and more *him*. That's when things started getting really bad. I needed him by now and he knew it. I was hooked."

The words were out before Miranda could stop them. "You can't actually get hooked on someone can you? I mean, it's not like they're a drug or anything -" She stopped abruptly, clapping a hand over her mouth.

"I don't know." Maggie argued. "I think you can. I sure did. The more I needed him, the nastier it got. I started doing things I'd never done before. Things I'm not proud of."

Miranda thought of Cindy and the little white bags.

"Things," Maggie continued, "I'd never do in my right mind."

Dread thickened in her chest as she listened to Maggie's words. *Things like smuggling cigarettes and pills into a prison, you fool.*

"Things," Maggie stated solemnly, "which were illegal and deadly."

Things, Miranda thought, like stealing pain medication off a child.

"If I don't have the courage to talk about it," Maggie smiled her horrible smile, "I will live like this again. It's easy for me to make excuses for other people. It's even easier for me to *love* the idea of being in love. The truth is so much harder to take. If I don't come to these meetings, it won't be long till I'm right back at it. See I'm the same as your mom Laura. We kid ourselves we're helping, but the truth is; we're not. Real help doesn't involve secrecy and isolation. It involves honesty. Alan was giving me something I needed, purpose. It felt good, euphoric even. And I'd like to tell you that all of this was his fault, but it wasn't. I was just as much to blame, maybe more. At least he had the excuse of being a drunk! But what was my excuse? I mean I acted crazy, cold stone sober! Don't kid yourself; there was a payoff in it for me, just like there's a payoff in it for your mother."

422

Jagged Little Lies

"I'm not sure Maggie? I mean, what could possibly be the payoff for my Mom?" Laura queried.

"Well... for one thing," Maggie said, "she never has to upset him. That way she doesn't have to feel upset either. She's probably fooled herself into thinking she's helping somehow. At least that's how I justified it. But you *know*. You really do. I mean how's it helpful to another's addiction, when you enable them? All you're doing is helping the person you love stay sick. But you would rather help them stay sick than lose them altogether. Let's be honest here, what you're really trying to avoid is confrontation, so you give in. In the end, you just keep making excuses, and *you* get sicker."

"Oh." Laura whispered, her cheeks losing their twin red spots.

Oh my God. Is this what was happening to her? She wasn't like these people, was she? No, at least she didn't think so.

Miranda studied the room. The people sitting here didn't look crazy. Not at all. They looked like everyone else. Nice, ordinary, everyday people. *If you were sick, wouldn't you look it?*

The room quieted. Maggie sat next to her dabbing her eyes.

A minute passed and then another. Chairs groaned their occupants shifting in them.

Why was it always so awkward in silence?

Peter cleared his throat and asked, "Anyone else like to share?"

Maggie spoke up. "I just want to say thank you for listening and welcome to our newcomer." She turned beaming at Miranda.

Miranda squirmed wondering what a newcomer was.

Peter cleared his throat, the sound thick with phlegm. Clearly, he was a lifetime smoker.

Miranda shuddered. She *hated* that sound.

"Okay then, if that's all, we'll close." Peter cleared his throat again, sending another ripple of disgust through her.

Miranda froze, panic gluing her to the chair. *She should have said something! She shouldn't just leave like this. Should she?*

Chairs scraped pushing back as people stood up.

Maggie remained seated. She leaned over to Miranda whispering, "Go for it."

Peter looked at her uncertainly, asking again, "Miranda? Would you like to share?"

Now in the spotlight, with nowhere to hide, she opened her mouth to say *no*. She'd get out of here as quickly as possible. She'd never see these people again. Feeling relieved it would soon all be over she sat up.

Her mind formed the word no.

But her lips said "yes."

Maybe it was Cindy, or God. Maybe it was timing. Maybe it was simply the things she'd heard here tonight. Whatever it was, it came from a place she hadn't known existed. Shaking her head no, she said yes and before she knew it...

It was out.

Chapter 69

The prison's laundry room was eerily quiet. The enormous room was a cavernous maw, jammed with commercial sized washers and dryers. The steel industrial ducting above him pinged. Declan jumped. Laundry hampers on rollers, stood emptied, lined up like soldiers waiting for the next day's linen.

Alive with shadows, the room seemed threatening. Declan sidled up next to one of the monstrous machines. The dryer doors were open and he looked inside. You could easily fit a couple of grown men in there. He needed a place to hide, but he didn't think this was it. Next to the washer was a small, narrow space. Declan eyed the narrow space closely. An idea began to take shape. It was a tight fit and it wouldn't leave him much room to move around in, but it might work. The plastic bag irritated his belly, as he squished in between the wall and the machine.

Where in the hell was Twitch?

Declan tried not to fidget. *Come on. Let's get this show on the road.* If he waited much longer he might not be able to resist. He'd need enough to do the job. His stock was dwindling, speaking of which...

He fingered the plastic bag wistfully. Maybe he could take another one? Just one more, it should still be enough. If this whole thing went sideways he wanted a backup plan. And if Rooster found out about it, he'd be dead, or at the very least, badly beaten. He'd have more than a few broken limbs *if* he was lucky.

Nah...

He'd be dead.

Fear dried his saliva to a thick leathery paste. He swallowed his tongue dry.

Fuck it.

There was no way he could do this without a little help, just a little something to get him through the next few minutes, and if he was caught? He sure as shit didn't want to feel it.

Declan opened the makeshift plastic bag removing one of Roosters pills. Satisfaction was sweet as he swallowed the bitter pill. It was ironic. Rooster's own pills would be his undoing. The old goat was so cocky, so sure. This would be his undoing too.

As far as he could tell, Rooster wouldn't check his stash tonight. He could pretty much predict what the old goat might do by now. He'd come back to the cell after a game of cards. He'd settle into his bed with a book. Then the orders would begin. "Scrub the toilet boy. Clean the sink. Get my Cheetos would ya?"

Once it'd been made clear Declan was Rooster's subordinate, the tension would ease. By then Rooster would just be... well, Rooster. Other than picking his teeth and farting, you'd hear him smacking his lips as he chewed his Cheetos, thumbing through his book.

Declan closed his eyes imagining it.

After he injected the dope into Rooster he planned on watching him. He wanted to be the last thing Rooster saw. He'd look into his eyes watching, as the dope drowned him from the inside out. Then he'd spit on him. He'd send him to hell, waving, with a big, shit-eating grin, on his face...

If Twitch got here that was.

Christ it was freezing. He shivered, clamping his lips tightly together. By tomorrow this would all be over. Miranda would visit him bringing with her more of what he needed, along with a nice fat envelope filled with cash. She wouldn't be very happy about seeing his Mom. But he'd deal with that one later on.

His hyper-vigilant senses picked up sound. Declan listened keenly, ready to bolt if necessary.

Steps, definitely steps, and they were getting closer.

Twitch?

Jagged Little Lies

He wasn't sure. Declan strained his ears, squinting into the hallway.

A figure emerged, tall and lean, as the footsteps stumbled closer.

It was Twitch. Relieved, Declan stepped forward.

Twitch stumbled into the laundry area, his gait uneven and on the verge of collapse. *Christ he was in bad shape.* Pity and rage warred within Declan. He needed the guy at least semi-coherent.

Declan left the crevice he'd been sandwiched into, afraid that Twitch might stumble into one of the hampers giving them away. "Twitch, he whispered, over here."

"Huh?" Twitch mumbled.

The arm Declan grabbed was surprisingly muscular for a skinny freak. "Sshh for Chrissakes man, you're gonna get us busted."

"Whaaa?"

"Jeez Twitch. You're a mess. Did you bring the syringe?"

"Ya sure?" Twitch questioned. A small droplet of drool escaped Twitch's mouth, running from the corner of his lip before he sucked it back up.

Declan's disgust evident, he shuddered. Man this guy was pathetic. What a mess. He'd get the syringe and go. Hanging out with Twitch was a crap shoot. The guy was a walking loser, and he was going to be caught, soon.

"Yeah, I'm sure." Declan stated.

Twitch stood taller, his words were more pronounced. "So you want to go ahead with this? You really want to kill Rooster?"

"Jesus Twitch." *What the hell was this guy on? Whatever it was, it sure seemed to wear off fast.* "For Chrissakes, lower your voice."

"Well? Do you?" Twitch looked at him shrewdly.

"Just give me the syringe."

"Not until you tell me why."

"What the hell, you a cop or something? Jesus Twitch, you know why."

"I want to hear you say it." Twitch stared at him intently.

Declan stared back. Twitch must be crazier than he'd first thought. He wasn't just a messed up junkie. He was a sick fuck too. But he might as well play along. "OK. I'm going to kill Rooster. Ya happy now?"

Twitch nodded. "It's enough." He said shaking his head sadly.

Declan smiled. "Now give it to me would ya?" His hand reached out expecting to find a syringe. The smile quickly slid from his face as his wrist was encircled by metal. The snapping of the handcuff correlated with the overhead fluorescents blinking on.

The room was bathed in harsh white light. Declan watched stunned, as guards stepped into the laundry room.

He turned to Twitch. "What the fuck!"

Twitch shook his head sadly. His face wore a sober, solemn, expression. His tone was crisp and precise. "Declan, you are under arrest for attempted homicide. You have the right to remain silent. Anything you say can and will be used against you in a court of law." Twitch stopped removing the key from the cuffs. Declan's wrists were now joined tightly in front of him.

Frozen with disbelief Declan craned his neck. A total of three guards were in the room with them. Twitch finished with the cuffs, giving them a final pat before turning back to Declan.

Gone was anything resembling a junkie. Instead, a new man took his place. One who spoke with authority. "You have the right to speak with an attorney. If you cannot afford an attorney, one will be provided for you."

Declan gawked at Twitch still not able to grasp the facts. "Is this a fuckin' joke?"

428

Jagged Little Lies

Two of the guards stepped forward. Each took an arm. Twitch moved from his side to stand in front of him.

Dark, steel grey eyes, met his. "No joke."

Declan's world turned upside down. The suddenness of events staggered him and he bumped into the guard. His bowels quivered and for a second, he thought he might shit himself.

Reality blurred with shock. His mind grappled with horror and confusion. "You're a fuckin' cop?" He whispered, finally figuring it out.

Twitch nodded.

The guards moved forward dragging Declan with them.

His mind raced with the news. His lips whispered what he was just now beginning to comprehend. "He's a fuckin' cop." "He's a fuckin' cop... But how?"

Declan's legs dragged behind him as the guards' pulled him down the hallway in a direction he'd never before been.

Even the pills didn't help, as the bag rubbed up against his belly. The truth was he was caught red handed. Trapped. Not even his Mom or Miranda could get him out of this one.

A large steel door loomed in front of him.A guard produced a pass key and opened the door. He shoved Declan roughly inside. Declan staggered, nearly falling, not able to get his hands out.

A harsh "Sit" was spoken, before the doors closed.

The room was small, holding only a steel desk and a single chair on either side. Declan moved the chair to sit, but it was bolted to the ground. He sat sideways on the chair waiting for what, he didn't know.

Nausea churned in his guts. Acid crawled up his throat. He swallowed the bitter brew wishing he could spit it out. Little white dots shone behind his eye lids predicting a migraine. His legs shook. His teeth chattered as he fought off another wave of nausea.

Time passed. Seconds, minutes and then, he wasn't sure. Declan wondered if he was being watched and looked around for a camera.

The walls were dirty and bare. A glob of something green and disgusting just above his head caught his eye. He looked away quickly. You didn't want to think about a glob like that for long. Not when you were already on the verge of puking. Declan checked every inch of the small office, but couldn't find anything resembling a camera.

A wave of self pity washed over him. It wasn't fair. He'd been trapped. Entrapment, wasn't it against the law?

The deep ache of his bones distracted him. He tried to think of something else.

Anything, but the facts were just too damn dismal to dismiss.

He moaned like a girl. Scared, lonely and confused he pushed it down. It bubbled back up. Declan lowered his head cradling it within his arms. Without anyone watching, he cried like a little baby.

For the truth was, he was so very, very, screwed.

Chapter 70

The door closed with a soft *snick* behind her. Hope lifted her spirits and she took a few deep breaths. Lyndsey paused, keys in hand, savouring the moment. Too often she ran from one place to another, never really stopping to appreciate the view.

Free at last. She loved her job, but the feeling she got from leaving the building after a day's work was *freedom*. It'd been a particularly difficult day too. She'd tried calling Drake a few more times but his phone was off, or he was avoiding her calls. Whatever, she knew to give him his space.

Faith was something you couldn't see, taste, touch or smell. But you could feel it. It wavered in her uncertainty with Billy. It wasn't fair she needed to choose between Billy and Drake. Then again, faith wasn't about fairness. Sometimes, she didn't think it fair she was sober, when so many others weren't. Why spare her and not the others?

The only answer she'd ever been able to come up with was faith and choices.

Choices involved the decisions you made. You could take the easier softer road. The one leading to what you *want*. This road required little effort and was satisfactory momentarily. However the satisfaction never lasted and it wasn't long before you were left looking for your next fix.

The beat of her heart was a steady thump. She was alive and grateful. Fear had no place in faith. You couldn't be in both places at once. The evening air was crisp as it filled her lungs. *Two more*, she thought drawing two deep breaths. You'd never notice, if you happened to be walking by. The little deals she made within herself. Deals like stop, look, listen. Little deals which kept her heart and spirit full. It was all the little things she'd been blind to for so long, that filled her well these days. It was like taking a drink from where ever you stood. Just being a part of something slaked her thirst. Without the ability to connect wherever she planted her feet, she ran dry.

Tears filled her eyes. The hum was back. Energized, she went in search of Billy.

The drive to the hospital was short. Lyndsey turned down the stereo, needing the quiet. She pulled into the parking lot and circled. It was visiting hours and the parking lot was full. She continued circling, hoping to find someone leaving. She passed a familiar looking truck and stopped, staring.

Drake? What was he doing here? Was he hurt? Was he visiting Billy? Oh God, is this why he wasn't answering his phone? Was there an emergency? That must be it!

Worry blossomed in her chest dislodging the hum. Lyndsey panicked. *What if he was in surgery this very moment? Where the fuck is a parking spot!*

She pulled into a handicapped spot, debating. *Oh shit, I can't!*

Reversing directions she pulled out to quickly, almost rear-ending the car behind her. *Calm down Lyndsey, think!*

Not able to find a parking spot she drove to the front of the hospital, the car hugging its curb. The main doors were electronic, made out of clear glass, and she could clearly see the people coming and going through them. The sign in front of her car read No Parking.

Screw it. Purse in hand she left the car willing to risk the ticket.

The hallways were crowded with patients and their visitors. Lyndsey made her way to the admitting desk and stood in line. It seemed to take forever. It was all she could do not to scream or shriek. The lady behind the desk looked on with disinterest, as the woman in front of her tearfully asked for the room number of her mother.

With a wave and a pointing finger, the woman behind the desk wearily said "Next" pointing at Lyndsey.

Jagged Little Lies

"I'm looking for Drake."

The woman smirked saying "Aren't we all honey."

Confused, Lyndsey said, "Pardon?"

The smirk disappeared. "Last name?"

"Oh! It's Ryerson, Drake Ryerson."

"When was he admitted?"

"I'm um, I'm not sure."

One stenciled eyebrow arched up, "You family?"

"Yes, I'm his wife... please, what floor is he on."

With a curious look at Lyndsey, the woman tapped a few keys on her computer screen. A furrow emerged, competing with the eyebrow, and her tapping increased. Finally she looked up. "Are you sure he's here? We don't seem to have anyone here with this name."

"Oh! I..." Lyndsey halted, no longer sure. "I thought he was. Sorry."

She backed away from the counter embarrassed.

Clearly the woman had seen it all. Lyndsey heard her disembodied "Next" as she fled down the hallway.

Lyndsey ran all the way to Billy's room. The door to his room stood open. She could see Billy in his crib, with a big grin on his face, standing on his tiptoes. His arms reached "Up" to the figure standing with his back to her.

Lyndsey stopped in the doorway. Relief washed over, her mingling with a fresh wave of tears. *She knew that back. She'd run her fingers tips over every square inch of it.*

Drake picked Billy up, hoisting him high into the air.

Billy squealed with joy waving his arms.

Drake laughed and tossed him back up again.

Billy giggled. His mouth, open showing his teeth. His giggle was infectious and Lyndsey responded with one of her own.

Billy turned from Drake, his smile getting even bigger. His eyes lit up with excitement. He wriggled his arms, while his

433

body bounced, and his legs kicked. Illegible words tumbled from his lips, noises really, erupting in the sweetest of fashion.

Drake looked up seeing Lyndsey standing in the open doorway. He moved Billy to his hip and asked, "You coming in?"

She crossed the threshold uncertain. *Why was he here?*

His eyes looked weary. His face exhausted. He scratched his head, while looking at her. There was stubble, tinged with grey, on his cheeks. He looked older than when she'd last seen him. There time apart hadn't been easy on him either.

"Drake?"

He shook his head.

She didn't need to ask what he meant. She knew. He wanted her to listen, to really listen and not interrupt. So he could tell it his way.

She nodded.

"I've been thinking," he said, looking down at Billy running a hand through his soft clean hair. He paused and looked back up at her.

Her heart stopped, and then started again.

"I've been thinking," he repeated, "about what I would do, with all my free time."

Lyndsey heart fluttered. She bit her cuticle listening.

"I can go fishing with the guys. They've been bugging me for awhile now." Drake scrubbed his chin, leaving a raspy sound in its wake.

No don't! She wanted to shout - but didn't.

"I can rent a cabin and sit on the beach, or work around the clock." His eyes grew serious locking onto hers.

Intimacy still scared the shit out of her. It was awkward to look, but she did. The enormity of his love was hard to miss. His eyes devoured her, stealing her breath.

"But," he continued, "What I'd really be doing is running from you. Thing is," he stopped, his voice cracking a little.

Jagged Little Lies

It was everything she could do not to run into his arms. But she didn't. She knew Drake would need this time.

"Thing is Linds," his voice lowered to the deep, sexy timbre she'd come to love, "I can't outrun you. See you've gotten to me in a way nobody else ever has. You're in my thoughts, and my dreams. I can't stop thinking about you. The things we've accomplished together are bigger than I ever dreamed possible. I think about us and our future and where we'll be in ten years. When I go to work, you know what I love more than anything else? What makes all of the endless, backbreaking, work I do - doable? *You.* It's coming home to you. I imagined myself fishing, or on the beach. Without you beside me, it's empty and pointless."

"Oh Drake," she whispered nodding. She did know.

"I can't even work right." He said, holding up his thumb with its newly purpled nail.

Billy caught sight of Drakes thumb and latched onto it.

Drake smiled looking at the sweet little boy holding his thumb and said, "Sometimes I'm such an asshole.'

"Drake!"

His cocky grin was back, his tone no longer solemn as he admonished. "Relax, Linds. This boy needs a father, one who might cuss from time to time."

Billy cooed sweet baby noises, bringing Drake's thumb to his mouth and suckled.

"Whoa!"Drake exclaimed, grinning. "See Linds, he's a little confused, he needs me."

"You're right," she replied, grinning back. "He does need you." She agreed, crossing the room to stand next to him.

Lyndsey stood on tiptoe kissing Billy's cheek before turning to Drake.

He opened his arms and she moved into them, closing the circle. Time stopped as she made the deal. *Just two.*

One deep breath, then another, *stop watch and listen.* The arms circling her were strong. She leaned against them knowing they'd keep her safe.

It wasn't just Billy who needed Drake.

Lyndsey reached up bringing Drake's ear to her mouth. She'd never liked needing anything before. She didn't like it now. But it was true.

With her lips fused firmly to his ear, she finally said it out loud.

"I need you too."

Drake smiled and shifted Billy. He pulled her tighter as she put an arm around Billy's little shoulder while still holding onto to Drake. Maybe families were more than just genetics. Maybe they were simply about learning how to work through difficult situations together. Whatever defined family, Lyndsey felt it in the safety of Drake's arms.

Together the three of them huddled closer.

Chapter 71

With her arms wrapped around herself, Susan rocked back and forth. The floor was hard and she was vaguely aware of this. Shame and misery rooted her to the ground. The fine thread she'd been holding to for all these years, gone. Exhaustion washed over her in waves. The fight was over. She just couldn't do it anymore.

Her head felt like it weighed a thousand pounds. Her eyes felt gritty. From between her arms she noticed the doctor's hand. It reached out to her, palm up and outstretched.

"Please, won't you let me help you up?" He repeated.

Susan sighed, and reached her thin arm out to him.

His hand was warm and dry. It encircle hers with a strong, sure grip.

"That's it," he encouraged, helping her to stand.

The room tilted as she stood, and she swayed. Doctor Stephenson wrapped a reassuring arm around her shoulder, guiding her back to the makeshift bed. He helped her get settled as she sprawled half sitting, and half lying down. She watched in helplessness as her hands shook wildly in front of her. Worried, she met his eyes. "Do I have epilepsy?" She questioned.

Soft green eyes met her own. He shook his head indicating no and said, "I don't think so, but why don't I ask you a few questions, just to make sure."

Susan glanced away, her fingers clenching the paper sheet beneath her. A longing to lie down and sleep overcame her.

"Susan?"

She looked up wondering if it would be all right to lie down. Instead, she shifted around until her back rested up against the wall and propped one arm on her knee, resting her chin on it.

"Susan?" He repeated.

437

"I'm listening," she said, once again meeting his nice green eyes.

"Have you or anyone in your family ever experienced epilepsy before?"

"No." She shook her head.

"Can I be frank with you?" he asked, his green eyes growing more serious.

Worried now she nodded, sure she was about to hear she was dying, she waited.

"When was the last time you used?"

"Used?" Not sure she heard him right; she stared up at him in confusion.

"You know, taken anything?"

"I'm not sure..." *Did he know about the pharmacy? How?* She glanced around the room thinking. Her eyes spotted the bottle still lying on the floor.

The doctor bent down scooping up the bottle of medication and spilled pills. Then he got down on his hands and knees, retrieving the one from under the bed. He wiped at his leg, removing a bit of fluff he'd picked up. Then he held the bottle up for her inspection. His eyes shifted from hers as he screwed the lid back on. "How long have you been taking these?"

Embarrassed she stuttered. "Not long." She stopped and looked at her trembling hands. She was too tired to lie any more. "For quite awhile," she admitted.

"Okay," he said, as if this were just an ordinary conversation. "What medication are you on?"

"Valium or Ativan and sleeping medication," She replied, far too tired to try and explain why. Briefly she wondered why he didn't ask.

"Do you have kidney or liver problems? How much are you using? What is the dosage? When was the last time you took the medication?"

438

Jagged Little Lies

Susan thought back. It was pretty blurry. "My liver and kidneys are fine... At least I think they are. I was taking two milligrams, usually two to four times a day. Less lately, my doctor wanted me to cut down."

Dr. Stephenson's cool dry fingers encircled her wrist. Her pulse raced below his fingers tips and she blurted out, "Am I dying?"

"No, but you are detoxing."

"What!" Susan screeched.

"Susan, the medication you're on is highly addictive. For a short time this medication is helpful, but it's only temporary. It was never intended to be used long term, at least not for most things." He stopped. His gaze questioning as he asked. "Why was it prescribed to you?"

Susan blinked. She thought back over the years. Such hollow, wasted, empty years. "I'm not really sure," she murmured. "I couldn't sleep. Dick and I had just separated. My world was crumbling and I... I felt like I couldn't breathe." The feeling came back strangling her by the throat and she panicked.

"You're fine," Dr. Stephenson reassured her. "You're okay."

Her throat relaxed somewhat at his assurance and she continued. "The pills just made it all easier. They made the pain go away. Pretty soon I... I... needed them." Tears thickened her words, slurring them ever so slightly.

"Did you ever talk to anyone about it?"

Susan shook her head. "I was too embarrassed. I couldn't. Then I started to hate Dick and everyone. It... It changed me."

The doctor wrote something on a piece of paper before asking her to hold her hands out.

Susan held her hands straight out, the way she'd seen the young girl do at the front desk. Her wrists and hands trembled wildly.

Doctor Stephenson made a grunting noise indicating she could lower her arms. His pen scratched rapidly over the paper.

She looked up at him worriedly.

Taking the stethoscope from his neck, he listened to her heart and said. "Resentment will do that to you."

"Am I going to be okay?"

"You will be," he replied.

"Can you help me?"

"I can," he said. "However," he warned, "you may not like my help."

"Oh?"

"First, I'm going to give you a small dose of Valium. I don't want you having a seizure."

"A seizure?" She squeaked. "Why would I have a seizure?" Alarm slammed its heavy fist through her once more.

The doctor poured some water into a Dixie cup before opening the cupboard. The bottle he'd picked up from the ground went into his pocket. "These will need to be disposed of. They're contaminated now." His eyes swept the ground and she blushed.

"Here." He said, giving her the cup.

Susan grasped it carefully, trying not to spill the liquid inside. Water sloshed out anyway.

Not seemingly the least concerned she was spilling her water, Dr. Stephenson removed a small bottle from the shelf. With practised ease he unscrewed the lid and shook one small pill into it.

"There, this should help. But before I give it to you, I need to know you'll follow my orders." His green eyes bored into hers.

Susan's gaze remained fixed on the pill, as she shook her head indicating yes.

"You haven't heard what I've said yet." He cautioned.

She glanced up at him questioning.

"I want you to go back to your group and talk about this. All of it, including what you were doing in my office."

Jagged Little Lies

God she was tired. So tired. Susan nodded opening her mouth. The pill stuck on her tongue before being washed down. With the last few drops of water remaining, she rinsed away the bitter aftertaste.

Dr. Stephenson walked her back to group, his steps confident and assured, hers dragging and heavy.

He turned to her at the door. "I'm going in with you, just in case you need a little extra support."

Anger flared briefly. "You don't trust me!" she accused.

The door opened, her words floating in the air before her.

Heads rose turning in her direction. The room quieted.

"What!" She accused, awkward with the attention.

Lyndsey and Eric got up, each taking a chair from the pile stacked up against the wall. Chairs scraped, pushing back to make room for two more.

Susan and the doctor sat down joining the group. Doctor Stephenson spoke first. "Susan has something she'd like to share with you," he said simply.

She shook her head. "I can't," she whispered.

Lyndsey spoke up from across her. "Yes, you can."

Susan risked a glance at the others from the corner of her eye, expecting to see anger or impatience. But all she saw was concern reflected in their gaze.

Her eyes found Irene. She stared at her defeated, as Irene attempted a smile while rubbing away a tear.

With no other choice, Susan voiced what she'd been choking back for years. "I'm hurting, and I need help." She admitted.

The group gathered around her, all ears.

Chapter 72

Peter, Maggie, and Laura stayed behind. Miranda held onto her coffee cup, its warmth comforting in her cold hands. She was still dazed. "I don't think I've ever talked this much in my whole life!"

Laura twirled a strand of hair around one finger. "I know. It's weird isn't it? I say stuff in here I'd never say out there," she said pointing at the doors.

Miranda agreed. "You know, I never really knew what happened in church before. I sure didn't think it'd be like this."

Peter, Laura, and Maggie looked at her in surprise and then Maggie laughed. "Oh Miranda, this isn't church honey," she said, making a sweeping motion with her arm then stopped. "I mean it is. We're sitting in church, but this is an Al-Anon meeting."

Miranda wondered what an Al-Anon meeting was and asked. "Al-Anon?"

Peter spoke up. "Al-Anon is a group of people who have been affected by a family member drinking. They come together to share their experience strength and hope."

"What?" Miranda queried.

Laura jumped in. "We come here to talk about our lives. And the thing we all have in common is we love someone who's an alcoholic or an addict."

Peter spoke again, this time his tone firm. "Actually, Al-Anon is for families who are impacted by *alcohol*. Nar-Anon is for the families of addicts," he clarified. Then he confessed. "I'm cheating."

Maggie shook her head. "Let's not get into the politics of it Peter, please. Personally to me, it doesn't matter if you love someone who's an alcoholic, or an addict. It's the same pain and unmanageability. It still ends the same."

443

Laura agreed. "Yeah, and you still get sick either way."

"It's hard to think of myself as *sick*," Miranda said, not quite following. "It seems kind of a stretch, don't you think? I mean, I see sick people every day at work and I'm not like them. I don't really think it's fair to say we're sick. It's like giving us an excuse or something. And it's not fair to the really sick people, either."

"It's a difficult word to get your head around for sure," Maggie said. "However, there's no doubt in my mind, sick is what we are. If you look up the definition of illness, you'll see. The definition describes *a disease or period of sickness affecting the body or mind.*"

"Oh?" Miranda replied, still not sure.

"How else would you explain what I did?" Peter asked.

Miranda not knowing what he was referring to stared at him blankly.

Laura gave Peter a playful jab reminding him, "She doesn't know your story Peter."

"Oh yeah," Peter grinned. "I've told it so many times, sometimes I forget."

Curious, Miranda asked, "What happened?"

"Well," Peter said, all playfulness gone. "Before my son cleaned up..." His voice choked. "I ah, he um," Peter cleared his throat and Miranda winced. "He used to say to me, 'Dad, you just don't understand.' I'd been on him for years to clean up his act. He started out smoking pot. At first I thought it was just a phase. You know, a kid thing and it'd pass. But it didn't, it got worse. Don't let anyone ever tell you pot is harmless. It isn't and it frustrates me to no end when I hear people saying it." Fire burned in Peter's eyes as he stared into a place only he could see.

"Peter," Maggie warned.

Peter scrubbed a shaky hand across his face. "Sorry, I get off track sometimes. Where was I now? Oh yeah. So my son says, 'Dad, you just don't understand.' He'd been fired again and he was trying to get money off me. You know what? He was right. I

444

didn't understand. I thought he should smarten up. The truth be told, I was ashamed of him, and he knew it. If I'm honest I was just as worried about what people would think of me. Maybe they'd think I was a bad father. I don't know." Peter stopped to take a breath. Tears slid down his cheek.

Miranda gawked. Peter was older than her Dad. She'd never seen a man cry before, but she was seeing one now. It moved her and her own eyes welled up.

"Anyhow," Peter started again. "Maybe it was guilt. Maybe it was curiosity. I don't know, but I sure as hell wasn't in my right mind. Your description there Maggie, fits me to a tee."

"What did you do?" Miranda asked.

"The stupidest thing in my life, ever," Peter replied, "Although it made perfect sense at the time."

"Well?" Miranda really wanted to know. She couldn't imagine this sweet old guy doing anything wrong. At least nothing like she'd done.

Peter looked at Miranda and swallowed. "I almost killed myself," he gulped. "I'm lucky to be alive and I don't always appreciate it."

"Did you try and commit suicide?" Miranda gasped. "I'm sorry. I shouldn't have asked you that."

Maggie reached over giving her arm a gentle squeeze and smiled. "It's okay Miranda. You can ask all the questions you want here."

"Hmmm," Peter said, apparently taking her question into consideration. "Did I try to commit suicide? I suppose now that you mention it, yes. Of course at the time it wasn't my intention. See my son always said I didn't love him enough. Somehow his troubles were my doing. He said if I was in his shoes I'd understand. Well... one day I decided to try his shoes on."

"What?" Miranda looked at Maggie to see if she was following Peter's story.

Maggie stared at the ground. Miranda couldn't see her face, but she got the sense she was crying.

Peter shook his head. "I don't know what came over me. It was a bad, bad, decision. I think I must have gone mad. My son was living with me, *again*. I tried everything I could think of. Begging, bargaining, and threatening. You name it, I tried it, but nothing I tried seemed to work. No matter what I did, I couldn't get him to stop using. Finally I asked him, *what do I have to do?"* Peter took a shaky breath. "You know what he said to me?" He asked looking at Miranda.

Miranda shook her head no.

"He said," Peter lowered his voice, "the only way I could help him was to know how he felt. So that's what I did."

"You" – Miranda broke off her question hanging.

Peter nodded. "I did. I used heroin with my boy and it almost killed me. He warned me. I wouldn't listen. I told him if I was going to do this, it was a one shot deal. He just wanted me to try a little bit. I was hoping to scare him, you know? When I woke up in the hospital I realized. My boy wasn't the only one sick. Somehow his illness had gotten to me. My thinking, the way I felt, the way I act, everything about me had changed. I needed to change it back. That's why I came here in the first place. I hoped once I'd gotten better, I could help my boy."

Miranda couldn't believe it. She looked closely at Peter as he sat tapping a hand on his jeans. She was pretty sure he wasn't kidding. *Wow! Using heroin with your son? What were you thinking?* Then again, what was she thinking, stealing medication from a sweet little girl with cancer? Peter was no different from her.

"Well? Did you help your boy?" She questioned.

Peter's chin went up and down in quick short jabs. "I did, but not in the way you'd think. Everything I did for him back then only helped him to stay sick. So I ah, well, I got out of the way. These meetings helped me to understand I didn't cause my son's disease, I can't cure him and I can't control him either. I let the consequences of *his* actions fall on *his* shoulders, not mine. It took awhile and it sure wasn't easy. I couldn't have done it without this place."

"Where's your son now?" Miranda asked.

"He's gone back to school and he's working. He wants to be a probation officer. He spent some time in jail. It was the best thing that could have happened to him. It was the time he spent in jail that changed him. Got him thinking and he wasn't able to get his hands on any heroin. I thank God the prison he was in didn't prescribe to the methadone program." His cheeks flushed as Maggie stopped him.

"Peter," She warned.

He gave her a crooked grin then looked at Miranda. "Anyways, he's got over two years clean now." Peter's sat up straighter in his chair, his chest puffing out as he spoke.

"Wow, can you imagine what would have happened if I hadn't come into this room tonight?" Miranda spoke directing her words to all three of them. "I still can't figure out how I got here. I never even knew you existed. If I hadn't wanted ice cream and taken a different route," she stopped shaking her head, overcome with relief.

"You might not have known about us, but *something* knew about you." Laura whispered, waving at the statue.

"I would have taken the pills to Declan. What if I'd gotten caught? I can't seem to think straight when I'm around him. Everyone tried to warn me, but I wouldn't listen. Does this mean I can never speak to him again?" Miranda sat up ramrod straight in her chair, horrified at the notion.

Maggie reached for her hand. "Honey we can't really answer those questions for you. You will need to do that, but what I can say is you shouldn't speak to him without at least speaking to us first. What do you think Miranda? Be honest. What feels right for you?"

She closed her eyes. The room disappeared and she could see Declan's face. A face she'd come to love *and* hate. Sadness filled her at the thought of never seeing him again. Fear surfaced shortly after. If she did see him she knew she'd fall under his spell again. It was like he held a strange power over her. One she couldn't resist.

Wet warmth landed on her cheeks and she realized she had her answer. Miranda opened her eyes.

Maggie nudged her. "Well?"

"I guess... for right now, I ah, can't. I really can't. I mean, no offense Peter, but I don't want to end up like you," Miranda stopped. She hoped she hadn't offended Peter. She looked over at him expecting an angry glare, but instead he grinned at her.

Peter slapped his knee with excitement. "That a girl. I don't want you to end up like me, either!"

"Or me," Maggie interjected.

"Or me," Laura quipped. "Living in resentment isn't exactly what I'd call *good times*." She laughed, no longer living there.

Miranda stood up. Her legs felt weird, like the rest of her. Changed in some way she was only beginning to understand.

Each of them embraced before departing. A new family, their bonds forged from their shared experiences, their futures dependent upon their unity.

As Miranda drove away, she glanced in the rear view mirror. The lights were off, the doors closed, the parking lot empty. Yet she wasn't alone. Something had happened to her inside of that building and she carried it with her now.

It gave her a sense of hope. She still didn't know what would happen with Declan, but she didn't need to know. For the moment, she was okay with not knowing.

Miranda thought about her parents and all the secrets she'd kept from them. No more secrets. No more lies, she vowed. She missed them badly and needed them right now. It was late. Miranda hesitated. If she didn't go now, she might not go at all.

Jagged Little Lies

It was late, but what the hell? Wasn't that what family was all about?

For the second time that evening she made a u-turn.

This time, she was going home.

Epilogue

Declan clenched the phone, his knuckles white. *Rehab? Who the fuck wanted to go to rehab?* Still, it was better than being here. Here, he was a dead man. It was just a matter of time before Rooster got to him. He knew there must be a hit out on him by now. Twitch, or should he say 'John,' could only protect him for so long and then... He wished he could stop thinking about it. Just for one lousy minute, he'd like to make it all go away.

He punched in the numbers Twitch had written down for him. Maybe it wasn't such a bad idea after all.

The phone rang as Declan sat wondering what in the hell he was supposed to say. *Yeah I just ratted a guy out, but before that I'd really meant to kill him and this meth-head freak turned out to be a cop. I was framed and... Uh, I was wondering if I could come to rehab?*

Jesus. He shivered, listening to the ringing of the phone. The methadone was wearing off and it was too soon for another dose. The miserly bastards in the prisons infirmary doled it out like it was liquid gold.

As he sat listening to the phone it occurred to him this might just be the ticket. Rehab must be loaded with goodies. No way was any self-respecting junkie gonna walk through those doors empty handed.

The phone rang again and his shoulders slumped. *Why wasn't anyone picking up?*

The guard poked his nose into the room and harrumphed. "Time," he warned giving him a sideways look.

Declan nodded at the guard and mumbled "Just a sec."

The guard moved in closer. "I said time." He growled his voice low and threatening. Declan looked at him more closely.

451

The guard was new. Declan didn't recognize him. He was well over six feet and bore a nasty scar on one side of his face. He looked like a guy you wouldn't want to mess with. Declan's mouth dropped open as he noticed his arms. Thick, rope-like muscles, bulged from his forearms, but that's not what caught his attention. His eyes locked on the guards tattoos.

Prison tattoos.

Shit, this guy wasn't a guard!

The phone in his hand took on a whole new meaning. Declan stared at it, silently praying someone would answer.

The guard drew another step closer. They were almost touching now.

Declan clenched the phone so hard his fist ached, as it continued to ring in the tiny room.

****

Lyndsey adjusted the picture on the wall. Git wel son. Her mantra. She smiled, gathering up the rest of her files. The phone in her office beeped once, announcing the call was coming from the front desk.

"Hey," she answered.

"Hi Linds," Sandy said. "John the police officer dude is on the phone again, can I put him through?"

Lyndsey glanced down at her watch. She hadn't been able to return his last call and she really didn't have the time to talk now either. "Ya put him through. I'll have to make it quick though."

"Okay hon, I'm putting him through," Sandy twittered, with a loud snap of gum.

The messages stacked on her desk were sitting in a nice neat pile. Lyndsey rifled through them trying to remember what he'd called about earlier, something about a kid in jail?

The phone rang indicating he was waiting on the other line. Lyndsey picked it up, "Lyndsey speaking."

"Hi Lyndsey, my name is John. I'm a police officer who works with the DEA and I'm trying to place a young man in treatment. Can I ask you a couple of questions about your place?"

Lyndsey glanced down at her watch again. Her group was waiting on the other side of these walls. It was their last day together. They'd worked really hard this week and their efforts were paying off, especially Susan's.

"Hi John, listen, you caught me at a bad time. Can I call you back?"

"Sure, when's a good time?"

Lyndsey laughed. "Good question, what's this about?"

"Well there's a young man, who I've kind of taken under my wing. He's in prison, but what he really needs is treatment. Can you guys take him in?"

Lyndsey hesitated. "I don't know John. I'll need to take down some information about him, before I can answer your question. I'm not even sure if we have an available bed." *And this kid sure as hell wasn't going to get Susan's.*

Susan had finally agreed to stay for treatment. After an exhausting go around, she'd finally admitted defeat. Surrender to win, as the saying goes.

"Yeah, well, the young fellow will be calling you himself. That's part of the deal. As a matter a fact, he should be calling any minute now."

Lyndsey set down the files and picked up a pen. "Listen John, I'm going to have to cut this short. I've got people waiting for me. What's the best number to call you back?"

"Jeez, I'm just heading out of the office. How about I give you my cell?"

"Sure, that'll work," Lyndsey jotted down the number before hanging up.

Huh, a prisoner. She'd bet her bottom dollar all prisoners had some kind of troubles with alcohol and drugs. Too bad they had such a screwy system. It should be mandated. Anyone going to prison for alcohol or drug related crimes should be sent to treatment. Not jail.

It was just too bad she didn't have the time to talk with John's young man right now.

Lyndsey gathered up the files again, heading for the door.

After the group said goodbye and she had Susan situated, she was looking forward to a couple of days off. Rest and relaxation and of course, family time. Billy was finally home and she couldn't wait to introduce him to her friends and family.

Lyndsey smiled again thinking about Drake. She'd left him this morning, preparing his special sauce for the ribs he'd be serving tonight.

Yup, if you can't find him handsome, you can always find him handy.

Lucky for her, she found him both.

The door clicked shut behind her. The pile of messages lay scattered on her desk.

The phone in her office rang just as she was sitting down to join her group. *Damn. It was probably the kid.*

Ring. Ring.

Eric looked at her questioningly and she shrugged. It had become somewhat of a joke, the paper thin walls.

The phone rang a third time and Eric asked playfully, "Want me to answer it?"

Lyndsey grinned and shook her head. "How about you facilitate check in, while I answer the phone." With a final glance over her shoulder she assured them, "I'll be right back."

The End

Don't miss Lorelie's first story in the Jagged Series...

Jagged Little Edges

Jagged Little Edges. That's how it had felt for her as long as she could remember. Like cuts, coming first in words as they tore little pieces of her innocence, trust and self worth, evolving into the physical form with a smack to the head, a cuff to the ear and at times, welts and bruises on her back side. By far the greatest damage of all was what couldn't be seen. A soul torn asunder, left with an open wound, a vast emptiness and a hunger that screamed to be fed.

Lyndsey wanted nothing more than to be on her own. Problem was that's what she'd been doing her entire life. She didn't trust others and always held a piece of herself back. Lyndsey knew something was missing and she was determined to find it. Not comfortable in her own skin and trying to fill the vast emptiness, she stood on the edge.

Needing to belong to somebody, Lyndsey discovers love, the kind of love that's sick and leaves her needing more. She'll do anything for him and does. Lyndsey learns that love hurts, but still, she searches for her happy ending. Not able to find what she's looking for in people, places or things, Lyndsey descends into a spiral of hopelessness.

This story follows a ten-year journey on the need for love and leads readers through the depths of despair and addiction. It will move and inspire. It will leave readers on the edge of their seat wanting more...

About the Author

Lorelie Rozzano is an author, mother, grandmother and family counselor for Edgewood Treatment Centre in Nanaimo, BC. She works a program of recovery herself, and really understands, first-hand, the benefits of healthy families. She began working at Edgewood in 1998 and has had the privilege of working with both patients and their families. In the past few of years, Lorelie has written two fiction books: Gracie's Secret and Jagged Little Edges. She is currently writing her new book, Jagged Little Lies. Lorelie hopes the honesty found in her books will help those dealing with addictions - the individual, families, co-workers and anyone who cares about the well-being of other humans. Please check out her books at www.jaggedlittleedges.com